SPECIAL MESSAGE TO READERS

THE ULVERSCROFT FOUNDATION
(registered UK charity number 264873)
was established in 1972 to provide funds for research, diagnosis and treatment of eye diseases. Examples of major projects funded by the Ulverscroft Foundation are:-

- The Children's Eye Unit at Moorfields Eye Hospital, London
- The Ulverscroft Children's Eye Unit at Great Ormond Street Hospital for Sick Children
- Funding research into eye diseases and treatment at the Department of Ophthalmology, University of Leicester
- The Ulverscroft Vision Research Group, Institute of Child Health
- Twin operating theatres at the Western Ophthalmic Hospital, London
- The Chair of Ophthalmology at the Royal Australian College of Ophthalmologists

You can help further the work of the Foundation by making a donation or leaving a legacy. Every contribution is gratefully received. If you would like to help support the Foundation or require further information, please contact:

THE ULVERSCROFT FOUNDATION
The Green, Bradgate Road, Anstey
Leicester LE7 7FU, England
Tel: (0116) 236 4325

website: www.foundation.ulverscroft.com

Annie Darling lives in London in a tiny flat, which is bursting at the seams with teetering piles of books. Her two greatest passions in life are romance novels and Mr Mackenzie, her British Shorthair cat.

TRUE LOVE AT THE LONELY HEARTS BOOKSHOP

It's a truth universally acknowledged that a single woman in possession of a good job, four bossy sisters and a needy cat must also have want of her one true love. Isn't it? Not for Verity Love. Jane Austen fangirl and an introvert in a world of extroverts, she is perfectly happy on her own, and her fictional boyfriend Peter is very useful for getting her out of blind dates. But when a case of mistaken identity forces her to introduce a stranger as her real boyfriend, Verity's life suddenly becomes much more complicated. Johnny could use a fictional girlfriend too. Against Verity's better judgement, he persuades her to partner up for a summer season of weddings, big-number birthdays and garden parties with one promise — not to fall in love with each other . . .

Books by Annie Darling
Published by Ulverscroft:

THE LITTLE BOOKSHOP
OF LONELY HEARTS

ANNIE DARLING

TRUE LOVE AT THE LONELY HEARTS BOOKSHOP

Complete and Unabridged

CHARNWOOD
Leicester

First published in Great Britain in 2017 by
HarperCollins*Publishers*
London

First Charnwood Edition
published 2018
by arrangement with
HarperCollins*Publishers*
London

A catalogue record for this book is available
from the British Library.

ISBN 978–1–4448–3738–4

Published by
F. A. Thorpe (Publishing)
Anstey, Leicestershire

Set by Words & Graphics Ltd.
Anstey, Leicestershire
Printed and bound in Great Britain by
T. J. International Ltd., Padstow, Cornwall

This book is printed on acid-free paper

Dedicated to my beloved Mr Mackenzie.
He would like you to know that he's
appalled at any similarities between
himself and Strumpet and
he intends to sue.

1

'It is a truth universally acknowledged that a single man in possession of a good fortune must be in want of a wife.'

Peter Hardy, oceanographer, was the god of boyfriends.

He was good-looking: blond and tanned from all that time spent diving into oceans in exotic locations, his eyes as blue as those deep seas he mapped, but not ridiculously, intimidatingly good-looking.

He was also clever. After all, you couldn't be an oceanographer without a clutch of A-levels and at least a couple of degrees. He had a great sense of humour too — a little bit dry, a little bit goofy, and was particularly skilled at sourcing hilarious cat videos on YouTube.

But don't think Peter Hardy's perfect boyfriend credentials ended there. He always remembered to call his mother on Wednesday evenings and Sunday mornings, was punctual to a fault and if he was going to be more than five minutes late, not that he ever was, he sent an apologetic text. He was also both attentive and enthusiastic in bed, but not into anything too weird. Peter Hardy would never ask a girl to dress up in a pink rubber catsuit or slap him around the face with a wet sock.

Whichever way you looked at it, Peter Hardy

was a prime catch, a paragon of boyfriendly virtue, and Verity Love, though she was a vicar's daughter and meant to lead by example, was going to have to kill him off at the first opportunity.

No time like the present, Verity thought as she clutched a glass of vinegary Pinot Noir and smiled weakly at her friends, who were still fangirling Peter Hardy, boyfriend extraordinaire.

'He sounds so lovely. Sweet but manly,' Posy said enthusiastically. 'Now, when are we actually going to meet him?'

'Well, you know how it is. He's so busy with his job. I mean, he's hardly ever around. That's starting to become a problem when . . . '

'We get it. You want to keep him all to yourself.' Nina nodded. 'We've all been there, but Very, it's been months and months. You can't keep your hot oceanographer boyfriend locked away indefinitely.'

'Has it really been that long?' Of course it had. It was now the end of June and Peter had conveniently come along at the end of the previous November to save Verity from flying solo for the Christmas party season. In fact, she'd been a no-show for most of the festivities but who could blame her for bailing when she was feasting on prime oceanographer goodness after a three-year dry spell? 'Gosh, it's been over six months! Wow!'

'Don't be so coy. I bet you're still in the first throes of mad shagging, what with him being away so much,' Nina said. She tucked her currently platinum-blonde hair behind her ears

2

then sighed a little. 'Oh God, I miss being in the first throes of mad shagging, before you start arguing about whose turn it is to take the bins out or why he's physically incapable of putting the loo seat down.'

Verity took another fortifying gulp of wine. They were sitting in the pub just around the corner from the Bloomsbury bookshop formerly known as Bookends where they all worked, and now known as Happy Ever After since Posy had inherited it a few months before and transformed it into a 'one stop shop for all your romantic fiction needs'.

Many an evening after a hard day's bookselling, the staff retreated to The Midnight Bell. It was a tiny pub, which still had its 1930s Arts & Crafts wood panelling intact and art deco tiles in the loos. You could also get a bottle of wine and two grab bags of crisps for under a tenner before eight so who cared that it reeked of chlorine from the swimming pool of the health club a couple of doors down and they could never put their bags on the floor because they'd get slobbered on by Tess, the pub dog? Tess could sniff out half a bag of Bombay mix or an apple lurking at the bottom of a bag at fifty paces.

'Actually, talking of Peter, I don't think we're going to last much longer,' Verity said hurriedly then drained the last sour dribble left in her glass and forced herself to look at Posy and Nina, who had both assumed matching expressions of goggle-eyed dismay.

'No!'

'You said he was perfect!'

'I didn't say he was perfect,' Verity protested. '*You* said he was perfect. I just said that he was quite nice.'

'He is perfect.' Posy was absolutely not to be swayed. Even though Posy was a newlywed, there were times when Verity thought that Posy was more into Peter Hardy than she was. Though considering that Posy had plighted her troth with the rudest man in London, maybe her preference for Peter Hardy wasn't that surprising. 'Why would you not hang on to a man like that with every last ounce of strength in your body?'

'Because he'll never love me as much as he loves, um, oceans and the sea can be a very cruel mistress.' Verity was pretty sure she'd stolen that line from *Moby Dick*. Or possibly *Titanic*. Something featuring a lot of sea. 'He's away all the time and if things did get serious, if we had children, what kind of security would we have, knowing that he could be eaten by a shark or that his diving suit might spring a leak at any minute?'

'I didn't know that oceanographers worked in shark-infested waters,' Nina said with a frown. 'Aren't there health and safety rules about that kind of thing?'

'They make them sign a waiver.' Enough was enough. This had gone on too long. Verity stood up on wobbly legs that weren't as strong as her resolve. 'I really have to go.'

'But we haven't even finished the first bottle!' Nina held up the offending bottle to show Verity the trickle of wine that was left in it. 'And it's not

4

even half-past seven. Are you sickening for something?'

'Something like Peter Hardy, oceanographer?' Posy asked with a sly smile.

Verity shook her head as she picked up her bag. 'I don't know why you say his name like that. Like oceanographer is the second bit of his surname. Anyway, I'm sorry to bail but I did say I could only stay for a bit. You know I don't like to go straight from work to a social situation.'

'Oh my God, you're meeting Peter Hardy right now, aren't you? Are you going to break up with him?' Nina looked like Marilyn Monroe's tattooed and pierced younger sister, but she'd once told Verity that she'd been an awkward teenager ('buck teeth, braces and bee-stings for boobs') and had made up for it by being animated. She'd long grown into her spectacular, fifties pin-up girl prettiness but still had an exaggerated expression for every situation. Now she widened her big blue eyes, wrinkled her nose and let her mouth hang open.

'I haven't decided. Maybe.' Verity inched herself out from where she was trapped in the corner and almost fell over Tess, a stout Staffordshire bull terrier, who'd barrelled over to see if there might be some crisps going spare.

'But you can't break up with him before we've had a chance to meet him,' Posy lamented. 'Can we come too? Just long enough to say hello . . . '

'You don't need to say hello to him, you're married,' Verity pointed out.

Posy gave a start. 'Oh God, so I am! I keep forgetting.' She gathered herself. 'Anyway, it's

5

not Victorian times. Married women are allowed to say hello to men who are not their husbands.' She shook her head and let out a breath. 'I still can't believe I have a husband. Ugh! Sebastian Thorndyke is my husband. How the hell did that even happen?'

It had happened during a whirlwind few weeks in which Posy had relaunched the bookshop and through some strange and bizarre series of events that Verity still couldn't begin to process had fallen in love with Sebastian, her arch nemesis, and married him a couple of weeks ago at Camden Town Hall. There'd barely been time to chuck confetti at the allegedly happy couple before they'd hurried over the road to St Pancras station to catch the Eurostar so they could celebrate their wedding in Paris before the ink had dried on their marriage certificate. No wonder that when Posy wasn't walking about with a blissed-out smile on her face, she looked rather dazed.

Now Verity took advantage of Posy's dazedness to back away from their corner table. 'You should probably go home to Sebastian now. I mean, technically you are on your honeymoon, aren't you?'

'Don't go. Don't be one of those women who forgets her friends just because she got married,' Nina pouted and as Posy turned to her, Verity took the opportunity to hurry for the door even though Nina shouted after her, 'But why isn't Peter Hardy on Facebook? That's just weird!'

It was weird but then as Verity had explained to them, and her sister, Merry, had backed her up, being an oceanographer meant that Peter was in the employ of several governments and knew lots of confidential information about climate change so he wasn't allowed to use social media.

Something like that anyway.

It had rained while she'd sat in the pub. Verity could smell the heavenly scent of petrichor rising up from the damp, hot summer pavements as she walked along the slick cobblestones of Rochester Street, past the shops she knew so well: the Swedish deli, the old fashioned sweet shop, the boutiques. Verity did think briefly of going home but the flat above Happy Ever After, which Posy had offered to Verity and Nina rent-free, didn't feel like home yet. Besides, it was Friday evening, the start of the weekend, and Verity had Friday evening rituals and routines that were set in stone.

Verity rounded the corner into Theobald's Road, hurrying past shops and offices and the estate agent with the brightly coloured Eames chairs, then turned left onto Southampton Row, which was bustling and brightly lit, full of people hurrying to meet friends or standing outside pubs in happy, chattery clumps. Verity ducked down a tiny road on her right, past a pub even more charming and olde worlde than The Midnight Bell, and stopped when she came to a small Italian restaurant. Its paintwork was red, its windows were steamed with condensation and when Verity pulled open the door she was greeted by the sound of people laughing and talking, glasses clinking, and a nose-twitching aroma of garlic and herbs.

Verity had discovered Il Fornello one Friday night several years ago when she'd been walking the streets (not like that — she was a vicar's daughter) to delay going back home. Home had been a double room she shared with her sister Merry in a house in Islington owned by the daughter of one of her father's parishioners. The family had five children, a Spanish au pair, two bichon frises, one rabbit, a couple of guinea pigs and a goldfish. The noise and the smell were often overpowering. And to compound matters, Verity was also newly single after three years with Adam, her ex-boyfriend. It hadn't been a good break-up, far from it, and it was very hard to brood in a noisy, smelly house where she didn't even have her own room.

So, that long-ago evening, footsore and heartsore, and even though the thought of dining on her own in a restaurant made Verity break out in a cold sweat, she'd been lured into Il Fornello by Luigi, the owner, who then, like now, was coming forward to greet her.

'Ah! Miss Very! You're late tonight. We'd almost given up on you. Your usual table?'

'Had to make a quick stop on the way.' As she made her way to her usual table (tucked away in the corner so she wouldn't be bothered by any lone wolves hoping to strike up a conversation) Verity looked back to check that she'd closed the door only to see Posy and Nina peering in at the window.

Oh, they hadn't!

They bloody well had!

8

Their curiosity about Peter Hardy, oceanographer, had triumphed over common sense and they'd followed her. Now they were sure to burst in once they spotted Verity rooted to the spot amid the rustic tables and benches. Her heart quickened even as time seemed to slow down until it came to a grinding halt, much like Verity had. She let out a shaky breath. It would be all right. She could handle this; brazen it out. Except brazen was never a word that could be applied to Verity Love.

She had only two options. Fight or flight, and Verity chose flight every time. She could race up the stairs to the ladies, lock herself in and refuse to come out.

Except, that wasn't a plan. It was ridiculous. She was a fully functioning adult and would simply have to stand her ground and come up with an excuse. Say that Peter Hardy, oceanographer, had stood her up and actually, she had tried to tell them that he'd been rather distant of late, oceans between them, etc. This could be the perfect opportunity to kill him off . . . but Verity was well aware of her own limitations and winging it was one of them.

Think! Think! For the love of God, think!

Verity looked wildly around the room, dimly aware of Luigi still at her side. 'You've gone bright red, Miss Very. Are you all right? It's very humid tonight, isn't it? I hope you're not going down with something.'

Down with this ship, Verity thought helplessly and then she saw him.

He was sitting at a table for two at the back of

9

the room, an empty chair just waiting for her to skid over to it and sit down, which she did, hoping against hope that his date wasn't in the loo.

The man frowned and looked up from his phone. He was young enough. Thirties anyway. No noticeable neck tattoos, wasn't wearing anything horrible, just a plain white shirt under a jumper that almost matched the colour of his startled blue-green eyes. He'll do, Verity decided. At a pinch, he'll do.

'Hello?' He said it coldly, like a question. Like, who the hell are you and why are you sitting down at my table?

Verity risked a glance back at the room to see that her worst fears had been realised. Nina and Posy had come in and were looking round for her. Then Posy caught sight of Verity and nudged Nina who waved at her. Verity turned back to the solo diner. Oh God, he didn't look very happy.

'I'm so sorry about this. Are you on your own?'

He looked down at his phone and frowned again. Though really he hadn't stopped frowning, it was more that his frown had deepened. 'Apparently so.' The frown evened out and he smiled at her tightly, perfunctorily. 'I know the restaurant's busy but I'd rather eat on my own, if you don't m — '

'Very! Don't pretend that you can't see us!'

Verity closed her eyes and wished that not being able to see Nina and Posy would mean that they couldn't see her either. Sadly, life was never that kind. 'Please,' she whimpered. 'I beg of you. Just go along with this. Please.'

'Go along with what?' he asked, but it was too late. Verity felt hands land heavily on her shoulders and smelt the heavy rose fragrance that Nina favoured.

'Very! Aren't you going to introduce us?'

2

*'I certainly have not the talent which some
people possess, of conversing easily with those
I have never seen before.'*

Verity kept her eyes shut and sat there frozen in
an agony of mortification. Her shame lasted for
aeons or maybe only a few seconds, until she felt
a slight displacement of air, then something that
felt like cashmere brushed against her cheek and
a voice said, 'I'm Johnny.'

She reluctantly opened her eyes. He, the man,
Johnny, had stood up to shake hands with Posy
and Nina, who pulled her confused face.

'Johnny? You're not Peter Hardy, oceanographer, then?' Nina's voice was breathy with
gleeful horror. At some later date, Verity was
going to kill her. After they'd had words,
post-watershed words. There were rules about
this sort of thing. You didn't catch a friend
allegedly cheating on her alleged boyfriend, then
rat her out to the man she was cheating on him
with. You just didn't. It was against the basic
rules of feminism.

Johnny looked down at Verity, who shut her
eyes again because his expression was the
absolute opposite of encouraging.

'No, not Peter,' she managed to say, even
though it was hard to squeeze the words out past
the lump in her throat and the dead weight that

12

was her tongue. 'I didn't actually say I was going to meet Peter. You just assumed.' At least now the worst was over and Verity could just lie. Lie through her teeth. Say that Johnny was the son of one of her father's parishioners (her father's parishioners had, conveniently, a lot of children between them) and they'd arranged to meet here because he needed some spiritual guidance. Even though spiritual guidance was really more her father's department. 'Anyway, Johnny is — '

'I know this is still quite a new thing but I didn't realise that you were seeing other people too. Just who is Peter Hardy, oceanographer? Is he someone I should be worried about?' Verity could feel the heat sweep across her chest, up her neck, along her cheeks so that even her earlobes felt as if they'd been plunged into boiling-hot water. She'd been hoisted by her own petard, 'h-ed by her own p,' as her family was fond of saying, and this had now gone from bad to worse to verging on absolutely bloody catastrophic.

'Verity Love, you bad, bad girl!' Posy gasped in delight. 'You never said anything about juggling two men. And you a vicar's daughter, too!'

It was their go-to line whenever Verity did anything even a little bit not good. From swearing, to saying uncharitable things about reality TV contestants, to apparently playing two men off against each other.

'Oh, well, the thing is . . . Gosh . . . I don't really know . . . ' Whole sentences would be great. Would be peachy, in fact. Verity felt hands on her shoulders once more, squeezing her gently, then Nina rested her chin on top of Verity's head.

'Please don't get the wrong idea about Very,' she said and Verity steeled herself for Nina to overshare on her behalf. Knowing Nina, she'd probably tell this unimpressed-looking stranger that Peter Hardy left Verity on her own far too much when he was away on ocean-related business and that Verity had needs and so she wasn't to be blamed for letting her attentions wander. It was something that Nina had often pondered aloud, usually when the shop was full of customers, because Nina had no respect for other people's boundaries. 'Let me tell you about this woman. This woman once borrowed her landlord's car and drove through a rainstorm on a school night to pick me up from a campsite in Derbyshire where I'd been abandoned by my bastard ex-boyfriend. She's got the kindest heart of anyone I know.'

The man, Johnny, was still standing up. He was lean and tall, tall enough that Verity had to tip her head back to catch the considered look he gave her as if there might be something more to her than a presumptuous, gatecrashing liar.

'Look, we haven't had the talk about whether we were exclusive or not yet. I mean, we haven't even been on one date.' Verity had managed to spit out two complete sentences and she'd managed not to lie. Well, hardly lie. And it was all going to be fine because Johnny sat back down and smiled, not tightly this time but lazily, as if this was all an amusing distraction from whatever he'd been frowning about before.

'No time like the present for that talk, I think.

Ladies, it was a pleasure, I'm sure we'll see each other again soon.'

They only backed away when Verity turned and gave them a look that said very plainly, 'I can think of at least ten ways to kill the pair of you and make it look like an accident.' She could have quite happily stayed like that forever, but Posy and Nina were at the door, giving her double thumbs up and mouthing things like 'Get in there!' and 'You go girl!' until Johnny pointedly cleared his throat and Verity had to turn around.

'I'm so sorry. I panicked and I couldn't think what else to do,' Verity confessed, as she stared down at her white-knuckled hands clenched around the lip of the table. She had a splodge of black ink on her thumb.

'Probably not as sorry as Peter Hardy, the oceanographer.'

'There is no Peter Hardy. Look, I really am sorry and I've taken up enough of your time — '

'What exactly do you mean when you say there's no Peter Hardy?'

Johnny's voice was cultured and precise, which was just a fancy way of saying posh, but also warm, like he was smiling, though Verity could neither confirm nor deny this as she was still gazing at the ink splodge on her thumb.

Verity looked up. There hadn't been time before to do anything other than check that he was in full working order, but now she could see why Posy and Nina had been practically shoving each other out of the way to get a better look at him.

But who could blame Posy and Nina when this Johnny was actually very handsome in a *Brideshead Revisited*, oh-yes-in-my-spare-time-I-do-a-spot-of-modelling-for-Burberry way? He was high of cheekbone and if he weren't smiling then his full lips, lush and pillow-y, would look positively sulky. He had thick, glossy brown hair cropped close at the back and sides, then left free to roam on top so he could keep pushing it back, all the better to display his ridiculous cheekbones and eyes which were bluey green or maybe even greeny blue and it would probably be a good idea to stop gazing into them like a small woodland animal trapped in the crosshairs. He was a grown-up version of the pale, sneering boys doing Foundation Art at the local college that Verity had yearned after when she was a teenager. Sadly, those boys had always sneered at her yearning because she was one of the vicar's five odd daughters and she wasn't beautiful enough for the oddness not to be an issue.

She wasn't hideous either, not by any stretch of the imagination, but still Verity had never once managed to get their attention. Not like this stranger who was waiting a little impatiently, if the drumming of his fingers on the table was anything to go by, for her to start speaking.

Peter Hardy, oceanographer. Where to begin?

Well, she could always start with the truth.

'So, um, Peter Hardy started from a silly conversation with my sister Merry about what my perfect boyfriend would be like. Eventually we had a whole back story for him but he was only ever an imaginary boyfriend, until my friends . . . they mean well . . . but you see, they kept trying to set me up with any random man going spare or signing me up for dating sites and, oh God, do you know about that dating app, HookUpp?'

He shuddered. 'Everyone in my office under thirty is obsessed with it.'

'I was forced to install it on my phone because it was easier than explaining for the hundredth time why I wasn't interested in a relationship, then one night I left my phone on the table in the pub while I went to the loo and when I came back, they'd been up-swiping some absolute horrors and I suddenly heard myself saying that I already had a boyfriend and his name was Peter Hardy.'

'The oceanographer.' Johnny nodded again. 'Do you want a drink, Very Love?'

Hearing her name said in that dark-grey velvet voice made her name sound less like a cheesy Valentine's card translated from English to Japanese and back to English again. She suppressed a shiver. 'It's Verity, really. My name. But everyone calls me Very. Sorry.'

Verity really should have made her excuses and tucked herself away in her usual corner, but she agreed that a drink would be nice and then Luigi hurried over so they could order a glass of Malbec each.

It was easy to pick up the thread again that stitched together all of Verity's dating woes. She'd been single for three years, after her first, last and only relationship had imploded spec-tacularly and messily and painfully. After the

17

fallout of fallouts with Adam, Verity was happy to be single, but the world wasn't happy that she was happy.

'They're not being mean, my friends. They're really not. It's just most of them are coupled up or obsessed with being coupled up and they expect me to want to be one half of a couple too. Also, they have very low standards when it comes to picking out dates for me.' Verity winced at the memory of an awkward blind date with a man Nina had met at a party who turned out to be what he called a 'full-time dominant' and wanted to know if Verity 'needed a man in her life who could wield some affectionate but firm control?' Verity hadn't known what to say but luckily her most glacial look had said it all for her.

'I get set up by my friends too. It hasn't been a great success,' Johnny said as their drinks arrived. He lifted up his glass so Verity could clink hers against it. 'Cheers. And judging from the women they try to pair me with, it seems like my friends think very little of me. Usually it's girls who are so young that I feel like I need to ask them to provide photo ID, or bitter divorcees. The last one wanted to take out a hit on her ex-husband. Of course when I complain, my friends accuse me of being picky. Say that I should settle.'

'That's why I went with the fake boyfriend. It's also very convenient that his job means that he's not around much.' Verity couldn't believe that she was talking about her imaginary boyfriend with a complete stranger. 'I'm

18

absolutely one hundred per cent happy being single but I'm having a hard time getting my friends on board with that.'

Johnny pursed his lips thoughtfully, which did delightful things to his mouth. 'Maybe you just haven't met the right person.'

'I don't want to meet the right person. I have a busy job, great friends, an extremely needy cat. I don't need anyone else in my life.' Verity clutched her glass tighter. 'So, what's your story, then? Surely you can't have any trouble meeting women?'

Johnny ducked his head. Verity was sure it was to hide his pleased but bashful smile. He must have mirrors in his house so he could see that he was very pleasing aesthetically. 'No, no trouble meeting women.'

Of course! It was obvious. Now that she was no longer crucified on the altar of her own embarrassment, Verity could process the raw data sitting opposite her. No man could look like that and . . . 'Oh, right. You're gay. OK. And you haven't told your friends? Really? Well, it's none of my business, I suppose.'

'I'm flattered that you seem to think that,' Johnny said, his voice all barbed wire now, instead of velvet vowels. 'You didn't even make it a question, just an unequivocal statement, but no, not gay.'

Verity put her hands to her crimson cheeks. 'Sorry. I don't usually run around outing people . . . One of my best friends from uni is gay. And two cousins. I'm all about the LGBT rights. I love the gays!'

'Well, I'm glad to hear that but I'm still not gay.'

Johnny's eyes were a very definite blue now. Like the sea in winter; frost-tipped and cold. Verity suspected that he was a Darcy. It was very rare to meet a Darcy.

It probably came from having read *Pride and Prejudice* so many times that she knew it off by heart, but on meeting new people, Verity always found herself assigning them roles in *Pride and Prejudice*. She'd met a lot of Jane Bennets and Charles Bingleys, far too many Mr Collinses, an occasional Wickham, but a Darcy was rarer than a single man in possession of a good fortune who was in actual want of a wife. And actually meeting a Darcy wasn't that much fun.

In fact, it was unbelievably awkward for a count of ten, then Johnny's phone beeped. As he picked it up Verity realised that there was no good reason to stay and suffer.

She said goodbye, quickly got up, though Johnny was riveted to his phone and gave no acknowledgement of her hasty departure. 'Stick both glasses on my tab,' she yelped at Luigi who still couldn't hide his disbelief that Verity had broken with her usual Friday night routine for the first time in three years. Not only that, she'd also been seen in the company of a man.

3

'*This is an evening of wonders, indeed!*'

Her plans for dinner thwarted, Verity retraced her steps back to Rochester Street and There's No Plaice Like Home for a small cod and chips and a tub of mushy peas to go.

'And can you take your cat with you?' asked Liz from behind the counter. 'Been out the back for hours making an awful sound.'

'I'm so sorry,' Verity muttered. She'd only moved into the flat above Happy Ever After the week before and had been determined to keep Strumpet indoors for at least a month so he could acclimatise to his new home and not make tracks back to Islington. But as soon as Strumpet had realised that his new home was less than one hundred metres from a chippy and a Swedish deli with a smokehouse in its backyard for curing salmon, he'd become determined in his efforts to make an escape. Usually the laziest and most languid of moggies, lately Strumpet had taken to racing through any open door so he could taste freedom . . . And fish.

Verity had been reduced to putting posters up all along Rochester Street featuring a photo of Strumpet in all his fully fleshed glory and begging her neighbours 'Please do not feed this cat. He's on a strict calorie-controlled diet.'

Strumpet hadn't got the memo about the diet.

21

He was at the back door of the chippy, up on his hind legs (Verity was amazed that they could support the rest of him) as he demanded entrance.

'What are you doing?' Verity demanded but Strumpet pretended that he couldn't hear her. He did that a lot. Somehow he managed to remain deaf to Verity's pleas to leave her alone and stop using her face as a pillow but could hear a sliver of cheese being munched from several rooms away in the middle of a thunderstorm.

In the end, Strumpet would only let himself be lured away from the chippy by Verity breaking off a tailpiece from her own fish supper. Then she scooped him up and carried him, furiously squirming, along the street and into the cobbled mews where Happy Ever After née Bookends had stood for over a hundred years.

Rochester Mews had really smartened up its act in the last few weeks. True, there was still a row of empty, dilapidated shops along one side of it, but Happy Ever After was resplendent with its new smudgy-grey and clover-pink makeover. Verity hadn't quite got used to the burst of pride in her chest (though some of that burst was currently Strumpet's claws) when she caught sight of her place of employment and her new home.

She wasn't the only local resident pleased about Happy Ever After's change in fortune. Since Posy had spruced up the wooden benches and pruned the trees in the mews, it had become the preferred hangout of a gang of hoodies from the nearby estate who now congregated at the benches most evenings to smoke weed.

Nina had asked them if they'd mind smoking weed somewhere else, but apparently all their usual haunts ran the risk of them being spotted by a parent or teacher. They had agreed that they'd only assemble after closing hours and Nina and Verity had decided it was best to stay friendly and establish an emotional rapport with them.

'All right, Very? You be looking fine, girl,' the smallest hoodie said and Verity smiled in a way that she hoped was polite but not the least bit encouraging and hurried over to Happy Ever After, keys clutched in her hand so they could double up as a weapon if need be.

Strumpet still unhappily wriggling under her arm, Verity unlocked the door and stepped inside the shop. She took one moment for another burst of pride as she surveyed the shelves, some of which she'd painstakingly painted herself, and inhaled the whiff of new books and the lingering scent of the Happy Ever After candle they'd had specially commissioned.

The large main room of the shop where Verity stood had space for three sofas in various stages of sagging decay arranged around a display table, which doubled up as a lovely shrine for Lavinia, their late and erstwhile boss, featuring her favourite books (from Nancy Mitford's *The Pursuit of Love* to Jilly Cooper's *Riders*) and a vase of her trademark pink roses.

One of the walls was completely lined with books, the other taken up with vintage display cabinets full of romance-novel-related giftware from mugs and the aforementioned scented candles to stationery, jewellery, T-shirts, greeting cards and wrapping paper. And tote bags. Posy was obsessed with tote bags.

Then on the left and the right of the main room were arches that led to a series of anterooms, each section — Classics, Historical, Regency, YA, Poems and Plays, even Erotica — signposted in clover pink on the grey woodwork. And finally, at the furthest reaches of the anterooms on the left, were a set of glass double doors, which led to the tearoom.

Or it would open as a tearoom in approximately two weeks but currently it was a work in progress and the bane of Verity's existence but not quite as much of a bane as Strumpet who had now reached peak-squirm. Verity quickly locked the shop door behind her then gratefully relinquished her grip on nine kilograms of wriggling blue British short-hair cat.

'You are a pain in the arse,' Verity told Strumpet who stalked over to the counter, then stood by the door that separated the shop from the stairs to the flat, swishing his tail and meowing impatiently. 'You can meow all you want, I'm not sharing my dinner with you,' Verity told him, as she followed him up the stairs. 'I'm going into the living room and shutting the door so I can't hear another peep out of you. It's been a long day and I need quiet.'

The meowing increased in fury and decibels. Other people had cats who were silent and judgemental; Verity longed to have a cat like that.

24

She resigned herself to the fact that when she put her fish and chips and mushy peas on a plate and poured herself a glass of red wine, she'd have Strumpet in her lap, face all up in her dinner.

But if Strumpet was eating, then at least he'd be quiet.

Quiet.

Verity stood at the top of the stairs and took one deep breath. Her shoulders dropped, her limbs slackened as she let that breath out. She closed her eyes, allowed herself another deep breath, in through the nose, out through the mouth, and already she could feel the strains of the week and, in particular, the traumatic events of the last two hours, ebbing away to be replaced by a lovely sense of calm and tranquil —

'HIYA!!! I let myself in, hope you don't mind.' The living room door crashed back on its hinges. 'Oh! Are you doing your mindfulness meditation bollocks? Why are you doing it at the top of the stairs? Do you need me to shut up? It's all right. You won't even know I'm here.'

Verity opened her eyes all the better to glare at her sister. As ever, it was like looking at herself through an extremely flattering Instagram filter. Our Vicar and Our Vicar's wife, as Verity's parents were usually known, had the good fortune to be blessed with five daughters. Con, the eldest, Merry, then Verity and, bringing up the rear, were twins, Immy and Chatty. Unlike their sisters who had inherited the lean athleticism of their father's side of the family, Merry and Verity both favoured their mother.

They were decidedly shorter but 'slender' as Merry would have it, though Verity thought 'scrawny' was more accurate. Though their Great Aunt Helen never failed to remind them that the women on their mother's side all ran to fat in later years.

They also both had indeterminate hair that was neither straight nor curly but any point in between depending on the weather, and which tended towards mousy in winter and not quite so mousy in summer. They had wide-set brown eyes under delicately arched brows, but Merry looked softer and sweeter while Verity already had frown lines on her forehead. Certainly, Merry had sucked every last drop of confidence and self-belief out of the gene pool, leaving none for Verity, though the gene pool had replenished itself in time for the arrival of Immy and Chatty. Still, that didn't mean that Verity was going to go down without a fight.

'I gave you a key, against my better judgement, to be used only in an emergency.'

Merry glared back at her. 'Dougie's pulled the evening shift this weekend and I was bored.'

As far as Verity's sisters were concerned, being bored *was* a state of emergency. Verity shook her head and sighed.

'Don't sigh at me, Very!' Merry dogged Verity's heels at the same time as Strumpet almost tripped her over as she headed for the kitchen. 'You have the most passive aggressive sighs of anyone I've ever heard,' she added as Verity unloaded her fish, chips and mushy peas onto a plate, grabbed knife, fork and glass then tucked a

26

bottle of red wine under her arm. 'That's an awfully big portion. Can I have some?'

'No! I'm going into the living room. I'm shutting the door and you're not to bother me for thirty whole minutes. Let's synchronise watches.'

Merry looked at her watch and muttered the time out loud but with bad grace and a pout that Verity ignored. She was immune to pouts. 'What am I meant to do while you're eating dinner and refusing to give me any even though I haven't eaten yet?'

'You can draw on your reserves of inner strength,' Verity said without any sympathy. 'You must have some.'

Then she shut the lounge door in Merry's sulky face and Strumpet's outraged one, deposited her plate on the coffee table and collapsed on the sofa. It was a very comfortable sofa, in a rather garish floral print. Verity stretched out and even though her fish and chips would soon be cold, she shut her eyes and tuned out everything, even the sound of Strumpet yowling from the other side of the door.

The door which suddenly swung open and, a second later, Strumpet landed on Verity's chest, knocking the wind out of her. Merry stuck her head in.

'Can I have some of the cheese in the fridge?' she asked plaintively.

'Yes!' Verity replied through gritted teeth. 'Take this cat with you.'

The next interruption came after Verity had managed twenty deep breaths. 'Sorry, it's just you took the whole bottle with you and I wondered if I could have some wine.'

The door closed behind Merry and Verity's bottle of wine, only to be opened again immediately.

'Sorry! It's just I have cheese and wine and now I need crackers. Do you have crackers?'

Verity kicked her legs out in pure exasperation. ' "Have a little compassion on my nerves. You tear them to pieces." ' She swung herself into an upright position. 'You might as well come in. That was your plan all along.'

' "I have the highest respect for your nerves, they are my old friends," ' Merry said, quoting *Pride and Prejudice* right back at Verity. 'Can I nick some of your chips?'

Verity gave in to the inevitable. 'Knock yourself out. Also, I have some sad news.'

Merry turned to her sister with a mouth full of lukewarm chips. 'Oh?'

'I've had to kill off Peter Hardy. Or rather Posy and Nina caught me cheating on him.'

Verity would have preferred to mull on her predicament in silence but that wasn't going to be an option so she quickly hit the highlights for her sister.

'Really, it's all their fault,' Verity mused unhappily after she'd finished blaming Posy and Nina for forcing her into the path of another man.

'But, Very, your fake boyfriend was only meant to stick around long enough to get you through the Christmas party season,' Merry reminded her.

It was Verity's turn to pout. 'Shouldn't a fake boyfriend be for life, not just for Christmas?'

'How would that even work? Would you have had fake children too at some point? Maybe even a fake dog?'

'Not a fake dog. Strumpet prefers to be an only child,' Verity said as they heard the shop door suddenly slam shut, then the sound of footsteps growing louder as someone thundered up the stairs until Nina appeared in the living room doorway.

'Oh. My. God!' she announced by way of greeting. 'Have you met him, Merry? Have you met the gorgeous piece of posh totty that your sister has been seeing when she was meant to be in love with Peter Hardy, oceanographer?'

'I haven't!' Merry said gleefully. She waved a dismissive hand. 'Anyway, Peter Hardy's been on the outs for ages. So, this other guy — Very's kept him all to herself. Is he fit?'

'Not just fit, but foxy too. And he's got one of those voices, like Benedict Cumberbatch or Tom Hiddleston. You know? Knicker-dropping voices,' Nina said, pulling out her phone. 'I managed to get a picture of him. It's a bit blurry though.'

'Lemme see!' Merry practically climbed over her sister to get to Nina's phone. 'Such a pity that the back of your head is in the way, Very. You might have thought to shift to one side.'

'I'll be sure to remember that next time,' Verity said. She munched ruminatively on a now cold chip.

'So, tell me everything,' Nina demanded, plonking herself down on the sofa so Verity was now sandwiched between her flatmate and her sister. 'How did you meet? He must have approached you. I mean, you're not the approaching type. Did you give him your dead-eyed stare when he first came up to you?'

'I might start using that dead-eyed stare myself,' Merry piped up, nudging Verity and grinning like this was actual fun. 'It's ensnared Peter Hardy, oceanographer, and now this other guy. What's his name again?'

'Johnny,' Nina replied. 'I don't normally go for posh boys but for him, I'd make an exception.'

'I love a posh boy,' Merry said. 'Dougie's actually quite posh though he tries to pretend that he isn't. Just cause he drops his aitches doesn't cancel out the fact that he went to St Paul's and belonged to the army cadet corps.'

'I went out with a squaddie once,' Nina said as Verity levered herself up off the sofa: her presence wasn't needed any longer. Especially as Nina was now over-sharing about her former squaddie beau and a trick he used to perform involving his erect penis and half a pint of lager and Merry was squealing in horrified delight.

She squeezed past the boxes and bags in the hall, still waiting to be unpacked, to get to her room. It had been Posy's old room, although when it had been Posy's room every surface had been covered in piles of clothes and books. Verity loved Posy dearly but, as Sebastian had once rightly pointed out, she was a total slattern. Now with Posy's goods and chattels mostly off the premises (though Verity had discovered half a dozen single socks, several dog-eared romance novels and a half-eaten Bounty bar so ancient that it had calcified under the bed), and with most of Verity's belongings yet to be unpacked, the room was empty but still welcoming.

There was a large bay window that looked out onto the courtyard, and shelves set into the alcoves on either side of the beautiful Edwardian tiled fireplace, just waiting for Verity to arrange her books and keepsakes on them. Verity had a huge armchair that she and Merry had found in a skip on the Essex Road and Verity had spent money that she didn't have getting it reupholstered in inky blue velvet. It was her reading chair. Her sanctuary chair. Her snuggle-up-under-a-blanket-and-let-the-world-forget-her chair.

Verity retrieved the patchwork blanket that had been knitted by her great grandmother and curled up in her chair. Despite all that had happened that evening, unbelievably it was still only nine thirty. It was late June, the days at their haziest, their longest, and the sky outside her windows was still light. If she strained her ears, Verity could hear squeals and giggles coming from the living room and the sound of voices raised in argument in the courtyard down below.

So Verity chose not to strain her ears. Tuned out the noise, the static. Hugged her knees to her chest and all was silent. Finally, Verity could hear herself think, but she chose not to think too, because when she did, all she could think about was a handsome man with greeny blue eyes seated across from her, looking at her, maybe even laughing at her.

Nothing good could ever come from a man
like that.

32

4

*'And what am I to do on the occasion? —
It seems an hopeless business.'*

Even without having to tend to a fake boyfriend
any more, Verity found that she hardly had a
moment to spare the next few days.

In the three short weeks since Bookends had
become Happy Ever After, the shop had gone
from deserted to heaving with customers
hellbent on buying books. Some of it was the
usual summer upturn and some of it was
because their romantic rebranding had been
featured in the *Guardian, The Bookseller,*
countless book blogs, and Posy had even
appeared on *BBC News South East.*

The constant sound of the till opening with
the triumphant ping it always gave was music to
Verity's ears. Cashing up every night was no
longer a tedious chore but a source of joy and
wonder. The only thing that Verity didn't like
about becoming a destination bookshop was the
endless chatter of the romance-novel-buying
public and their frequent cries of 'Do you work
here?' whenever Verity ventured onto the shop
floor. It was a fair question when Verity was
wearing the now obligatory staff uniform of grey
T-shirt with the pink Happy Ever After logo on
it.

'I'm admin,' Verity would mutter, stiffening in

case any customer dared to touch her. There had been the time that an old lady with a grip of steel had yanked Verity over to the counter and demanded that she phone E.L. James to tell her to get a move on with her next book.

And Verity *was* admin, though Lavinia had appointed her shop manager a year ago as Verity was the only member of staff responsible enough to be trusted with the petty cash. Behind a door marked 'private', she ordered stock. Inputted stock. Chased up stock. Dealt with the orders that came in through the shop's new and improved website, orders which had increased in the last few weeks and needed to be fulfilled before noon and five p.m. each day to catch the post.

But even from the seclusion of her office and with several anterooms full of books supposedly muffling the noise, Verity could still hear the constant banging and drilling coming from the tearoom, which was being restored back to its former glory. She also had to deal with Greg, and occasionally Dave, the two workmen, continually popping in to ask for money so they could nip down to the builder's yard or to hand her receipts from the builders' yard or to complain about Mattie, who had taken over the tearoom.

Verity took a while to warm to strangers but even though their acquaintance had been a short one, she already liked Mattie a lot. Especially as Mattie was busy testing recipes and using the Happy Ever After staff as human guinea pigs for a mouth-watering, never-ending supply of cakes, tarts, biscuits, cookies, breads, shortbreads, sweet rolls, savoury rolls and something Mattie called a Muffnut, which was a muffin/doughnut hybrid. Despite its appalling name, it was slathered in butterscotch icing and was so delicious that Verity had almost cried when Nina had pinched the last one.

But it wasn't her way with a mixing bowl and a handful of ingredients that had won Verity's respect but the fact that Mattie was a woman of few words. Unlike certain people Verity knew, who took silence as a personal affront, Mattie only spoke when she had something to say, which was why Verity had offered Mattie a desk in the back office for when she was working on tearoom admin: a privilege that very few of the staff had earned. Only Posy and that was because technically she was the boss, and not so technically, she paid Verity's wages.

But not even Posy could make Verity willingly deal with the book-buying public, either in person or on the phone. 'Emailing. I'm great at emailing,' Verity would remind Posy countless times a day. 'There is nothing in my job description that says I should answer the phone or make phone calls.'

Lavinia had never given any of the staff job descriptions; she believed they'd naturally gravitate toward the tasks that suited them best. But from the mutinous look on Posy's face whenever Verity shied away from the ringing shop phone or a customer desperate for help, she was thinking of issuing job descriptions for all the staff.

There was no hiding though when Emma, sister of Merry's boyfriend, Dougie, hunted her down to demand that Verity respond to the invitation to Emma's thirtieth-birthday-slash-housewarming party that she'd mailed out in May. Emma insisted that she was there to support Happy Ever After but it felt a lot like being hunted down.

'Yes or no, Very?' Emma shouted over the counter as she paid for the new Mhairi McFarlane novel and a *Reader, I Married Him* T-shirt, which she said she was considering wearing as a hint so that her boyfriend Sean might propose. 'And you are bringing Peter Hardy, oceanographer, aren't you? Although Merry said you'd dumped him for being a marine-life bore.'

'I did no such thing!' Verity gasped indignantly. Then she realised that she no longer had to come up with excuses as to why Peter Hardy was absent yet again. 'Although we did agree to split up. It was very amicable.'

'So, I'll put you down as a single, then.' Emma smiled brightly. 'No need to look so glum. There'll be loads of spare men. I'll make sure to send over a steady supply of them.'

'Oh my God,' Verity said aghast. 'It's like you don't even know me. Promise me you won't do that.'

Emma closed her purse with a triumphant snap. 'Good! So you are coming, then. And if things change and you get back with the mysterious Peter, then you're welcome to bring him along. Such a shame about you two.'

'Well, these things happen,' Verity said with a heartfelt sigh. She gestured at the office behind her. 'Work. I must do some work now.' Then she remembered her manners. 'But I'm super excited about your party.'

'Let's not exaggerate, Very,' Emma said. 'I've known you five years and I've never seen you super excited about anything.'

'Moderately excited,' Verity amended.

'You should be,' Emma told her with a glint in her eye. 'We're hiring a karaoke machine. Participation is mandatory.'

Then she left, her words having struck fear in Verity's heart so she was rooted to the spot, an anguished expression on her face. 'Such a pity that you dumped Peter Hardy, oceanographer,' Nina commented as she bagged up the next customer's books. 'You'll have to go on your own.'

'Though Peter Hardy, oceanographer, was so often away sailing the world's oceans that he probably wouldn't have been around to plus one you anyway,' said Tom, part-time Happy Ever After employee and part-time PhD student, with the faintest of derisory snorts. Verity had always had a suspicion that Tom didn't believe in her fake boyfriend.

'I don't see why I should have to go to all these things. Engagement parties and birthdays and housewarming dos,' Verity grumbled, folding her arms and letting her chin rest on her chest.

'Yes, how horrible of your friends to want to share their significant life moments with you,' Posy said, coming in from the little kitchen off

37

the office with a tray of tea. 'I'm so sorry that I insisted that you come to my wedding and the small but intimate party for close friends and family that we had the evening before.'

'I didn't mean it like that. I love my friends. I try to be a good friend.' Verity frowned as she contemplated how she performed in the friend stakes. She wasn't very good at hugs or effusive advice or anything that involved her friends in one big, shrieking, drunken shouting-over-the-top-of-each-other pile but one-on-one she was great. Golden. A good listener, there with practical help for any pal recently broken up, sacked or evicted, and though she would never come close to Mattie's baking prowess (she'd just wandered into the shop with a plate of chilli cheese straws), Verity had a bread machine and many a friend in crisis had been comforted by her banana chocolate chip bread. 'I just find it hard to socialise en masse. That doesn't make me a bad person, does it?'

'Of course it doesn't,' Nina assured her. 'Anyway, can't you take your new bloke, Johnny, along?'

'No! It's too soon,' Verity said quickly. Then she realised that she was doing it again — lying about having a boyfriend and she'd sworn that she wasn't going to do that any more. 'Anyway, he's not my new bloke. He's not my anything.'

Tom smiled, though his smile was second cousin to a smirk. 'Johnny? Who's Johnny? I can't keep track of all of Very's boyfriends. Is this one an oceanographer too?'

It was one of those rare moments when there

was no one left waiting to pay and none of the shoppers browsing the shelves had any enquiries or books that needed to be looked up on the system. Damn them! Nina, Posy and Mattie, who was still there with her delicious cheese straws, all turned to Verity with expressions that could be described as extremely curious. 'Yeah, Very, what does he do?'

Verity couldn't bear it any longer. 'He works very hard at his job,' she said sternly. 'Like you should all be doing instead of standing about gossiping. And much like I should be doing because I have lots of orders to fulfil before the last post.'

And as she had so often done in the past, usually when Posy was trying to persuade her to man the till for ten minutes, Verity fled for the safety of her office sanctuary.

★ ★ ★

Verity was still in flight mode at six when Posy flipped the shop sign to closed. Nina had finished cashing up, Tom was tutting as he reshelved a pile of books that had been left piled up on the sofas and Verity was sweeping the floor.

'Pub,' Nina said, as she so often did when bookselling was done for the day. 'Who's in?'

There were general sounds of agreement but Verity shook her head and there was only a token effort to talk her round because everyone knew that Verity rarely did the pub on a Friday evening. Not without half an hour to decompress in a dark room first.

But once the others left, Verity realised that sitting in her chair with the curtains closed wasn't really going to cut it. Living over the shop was wonderful in so many ways. Rent, nil. Commute, ten seconds and down one flight of stairs. Central London location. Able to go to the big Sainsbury's in Holborn twenty minutes before it closed and make out like a bandit on heavily reduced perishables. But living above the shop also meant that there was very little work/life balance when you spent most of your time in one building.

Luckily, Verity found that walking was almost as good as sitting in a dark room. She stuck to the side streets, the little cobbled mews of Bloomsbury, occasionally venturing into one of the big garden squares. It was still light enough that she felt perfectly safe, but she crossed over the road numerous times to avoid the huge crowds of people standing outside the area's many pubs. All demob happy, jackets discarded and slung over railings and shoulders, clutching drinks and bags of crisps.

Verity saw a different side to the city when she walked. A city full of hanging baskets and window boxes full of bright flowers: geraniums, lobelias, petunias and trailing begonias. There were blue plaques to the great and good. The house where Charles Dickens had lived, now the Foundling Museum, just a few doors down from where E.M. Delafield had taken a flat when she was in town and written *The Provincial Lady Goes Further*.

As her stomach made its presence known and reminded Verity it had been a while since those chilli cheese straws, she pushed open the door of Il Fornello, to find Luigi waiting for her.

'Miss Very! Usual table?' he asked. 'You're not going to be joining any random strangers tonight?'

Verity shook her head. 'I am not,' she confirmed and she followed Luigi through the packed restaurant, nodding and smiling at each waiter she passed until they came to the little corner with room only for a small table set for one, where Verity could slide into the chair that Luigi pulled out for her.

It had taken quite a few weeks at the start of Verity's patronage of Il Fornello for Luigi to understand that she would always be dining alone. That she wasn't waiting for anyone. And she certainly didn't want to be fussed over or have her wine or water glass constantly refilled and to be asked if everything was all right with her meal.

All Verity wanted was to sit and read a book with a glass, or two at most, of red wine, a side salad and a cast-iron dish full of lasagne, the cheese crunchy on top, and so hot she couldn't eat it for five minutes. It wasn't so much to ask. It wasn't as if she were a hermit — that was what so many people didn't understand; she quite enjoyed being in a crowded restaurant, listening to the hum of conversation around her, she just didn't want to participate in it.

So, Verity opened her current book, an epic sweeping romance set in the heady months leading up to World War Two, took a sip of her wine and speared a green olive from the complimentary bowl Luigi always slipped her. If there was a finer way to spend a Friday evening after a long, hard week, then Verity couldn't imagine it.

And it *was* perfect — until a tall man suddenly swung through the room, grabbed hold of an empty chair and plonked it down on the other side of Verity's table. She looked up with an indignant gasp that died before it left her mouth, eyes widening in horror and disbelief.

Oh God, it was Johnny.

5

'It was necessary to laugh, when she would rather have cried.'

'Hello again,' Johnny said easily, as he loomed over her table. Seven days had been long enough to dim his beauty so that when Verity had thought about their awkward encounter, though she'd tried really hard not to, his eyes had become a bog-standard blue. His cheekbones dulled. His hair had lost its lustre. His body wasn't lean and lithe but gangly and gawky. But now he was back in full gorgeous HD definition, which was neither here nor there when his presence was as unwelcome as a meter reader at the door before eight a.m.

'Hello,' Verity said, politely but perfunctorily. Experience had taught her that sometimes, though not as frequently as she'd like, men slunk off in the face of zero encouragement. She turned back to her book and made a big performance of finding her place. Really, it was Oscarworthy. She even traced a sentence with her fingertip, though the black type on white paper might just as well have been written in Martian for all the sense it made.

Was Il Fornello Johnny's new Friday night haunt? Had he just moved to the area and didn't know anyone so had decided that Verity would do until he found some new friends? Was he going to talk and talk at her when she just wanted to be left alone?

'Please, I beg of you, just go along with this,' Johnny said as he sat down opposite Verity and she could hear his smile as he echoed her own words back at her. Now he had her full, stony-faced attention. 'I didn't know how else to find you. I did try googling Verity Love but all I came up with were several very poorly designed goddess websites . . . anyway, I digress. I hoped you might be here so we could talk in person. It's the kind of thing that would probably be better if we just chatted it out.'

Verity closed her book and willed her face to become even more stone-like. 'Chatted what out? Is this about me thinking you were gay? Because, I get it, you're absolutely not gay.' Though he was protesting far too much for someone who was allegedly straight.

'Oh, no, it's nothing to do with that! When you maintain a certain standard of grooming, people always think you're gay.' Johnny waved away the idea with an airy gesture. 'It's about Peter Hardy, oceanographer.'

Verity inched her chair back. 'What about him?' she asked tightly.

'Genius idea, an imaginary fake boyfriend, but why does he have to be imaginary? Why not have a real fake boyfriend? It kills so many birds with one almighty stone.'

Verity looked at Johnny briefly from under her lashes, just in time to see him smile at her. He was lovely to look at, even lovelier when he smiled, and Verity still had all kinds of feelings

44

that kicked in when a lovely-looking man smiled at her. That didn't mean that she had to act on them.

Luckily Luigi arrived with her food: lasagne still bubbling in its dish, side salad and a beaker full of garlic breadsticks. 'Just yell if you need anything,' Luigi told her pointedly with a sideways look at Johnny. Then he made a big fuss of shaking out Verity's napkin and placing it reverently on her lap, before he brandished the big pepper grinder, not at her lasagne, but in the direction of Johnny, in what could be taken as a threatening manner. 'Anything at all.'

Verity took her time selecting a breadstick then held it aloft. 'I'm fine,' she said, because much as she was alarmed that Johnny had hunted her down and was talking about fake boyfriends, both imaginary and real, she would expire from sheer embarrassment if Luigi and a couple of his burlier kitchen staff escorted Johnny off the premises. 'We're fine. Are you going to order something?' she asked Johnny who turned his lovely smile on Luigi and soon they were chatting happily about Luigi's wood-fired oven (his pride and joy) and the provenance of his mozzarella.

As soon as Luigi left to prepare Johnny's pancetta and mushroom pizza with his own hands, Johnny's gaze was back on Verity. She wanted to squirm and fidget, but despite the panic rising up in her, there was something calm and measured about him. Something still. Like he was a fixed point in a chaotic world. 'I'm not gay,' he said yet again. 'That's not why I'm

45

single. If you really must know it's because I'm in love with a woman that I can't be with. Not right now, no matter how much we both desperately want to be together.'

'How very romantic and *Wuthering Heights*-y,' Verity said dryly. She had spent a lot of her impressionable teen years dressed in black and pretending that Weelsby Woods in Grimsby was rough moorland and not a splendid municipal park. She was far less impressionable now. 'Surely if you want to be together, you should well, just be together. Oh, I didn't mean to upset you,' she added as Johnny's face fell. 'Here, have a garlic breadstick. They're really good.'

Johnny took a breadstick, but it wasn't the cure-all that Verity had hoped it would be. His light glowed a little less now. 'We can't be together,' he said again. 'It's very complicated.'

It sounded like the simplest thing in the world to Verity. If two people loved each other, really and truly loved each other, then they moved oceans and landmasses, spurned the ties of blood, laughed in the face of every obstacle that stood in their way. She might not want love herself but Verity was emphatically pro-love for other people. But it probably wasn't the best time to go down that particular road.

'I'm sorry to hear that,' was what she did murmur, then she was just about to ask what Johnny's complicated romantic status had to do with her when his pizza arrived and there was a flurry of cutlery and more pepper grinding and *did they want extra Parmesan* until they were left alone to eat.

Eating together, or rather eating in front of a stranger, wasn't quite the ordeal that Verity expected it to be. In fact, it almost felt companionable until Johnny was halfway through his pizza and started talking again.

'So, what I was thinking was that we're both alone, for our own reasons, but that doesn't mean we can't join forces,' he said as he cut the crust off a slice of pizza. 'Just as a stopgap. A short-term solution to fend off our friends.'

'What do you mean when you say 'join forces' and 'stopgap' and 'short-term solution'?' Verity asked, even though she was quite familiar with all of these phrases and their meanings. It was just that she couldn't quite get her brain to process what they meant in connection to Johnny and herself.

'Well, you see, they're not just setting me up with unsuitable women any more, my friends, now they've started sending passive-aggressive emails with links to dating sites and then there are the invites to weddings and . . . ' He stopped as his phone beeped. 'Ah, talk of the devil.' He looked at the screen then smiled. And suddenly the smiles Verity had seen up to this point were whispers, grainy photocopies, nothing like this smile for the unknown, unseen person who'd just texted him. It was a smile of pure joy, instant happiness. What would it be like to have Johnny, anyone, smile at her like that? She couldn't even begin to imagine.

Johnny texted a reply, thumbs moving as fast as humming-bird wings over his touchscreen, then he looked up. 'I'm sorry. How rude. Where was I?'

Verity picked up his thread. 'You were proposing we joined forces in a short-term kind of way. Something about wedding invites and passive-aggressive emails.'

'Right, right.' Johnny nodded. 'Well, you see, I've been inspired by your tales of Peter Hardy, oceanographer,' he said as if Verity had spent *hours* regaling him with all sorts of imaginary exploits that her imaginary boyfriend had got up to. 'It got me thinking. If I, *we*, turned up to a couple of things together, in the company of a real live human being of the opposite sex, then it would get our friends to stop with the endless matchmaking.'

'But my friends *have* stopped with the endless match-making since Peter Hardy,' Verity pointed out quickly because it was best to shut this down immediately.

Johnny narrowed his eyes. 'Hmmm, but I bet then they started pestering you with so many questions and queries about Peter Hardy — '

'It's natural that they'd be curious!' Verity blustered.

' — because they never once met him and how could they? He wasn't real. He was just a figment of your imagination.' Johnny was relentless. And ruthless. So ruthless.

'Not just my imagination. It was my sister who said he should be an oceanographer,' Verity muttered. She put down her fork, which she'd been using to stab at her lasagne instead of eating it. 'All right, I'll admit that my plan was

48

flawed but it did get my friends off my back for a little bit. God, it was great while it lasted.' She ended on a wistful sigh. 'My friends just want me to be happy but they think being single must make me unhappy so I get their work colleagues and second cousins and dodgy flatmates all shoved in my direction. 'This is Verity. I'm sure you two have got so much in common.' ' She clapped her hand over her mouth. She'd said far too much and Johnny was smiling smugly.

Verity was pleased to note that his smug smile didn't do anything for him. Not a thing. It edged him into Wickham territory.

'Well, there you are then,' Johnny said as if it really could be that easy. 'What I'm proposing is simple. You come and meet my friends and I'll meet yours and it will buy you some time from introductions to second cousins and dodgy flatmates and you can save me from any more advances from divorcees with fake breasts . . . '

'My breasts could be fake for all you know,' Verity said and regretted it immediately. She hadn't meant to sound flirty and she certainly hadn't meant to draw attention to her breasts. Johnny probably wasn't gay because as soon as she'd mentioned them, his eyes were immediately drawn to her chest.

'I think not,' he said playfully, teasingly, as if they were really flirting. 'I'm an architect. I know about false structures.'

He was still looking thoughtfully at Verity's breasts and when she folded her arms, his gaze skittered from them back to her face, which she hoped looked stern and disapproving.

Verity was wearing a black and white striped top, dark jeans and a pair of purple Saltwater sandals that she'd got for half price in last year's sale because not many people wanted purple sandals. Her hair, lightened by the sun so it wasn't quite as mousy as usual, was pulled back in a ponytail — not one of those perky ponytails that bounced from side to side as she walked either. She dressed exactly as you'd expect from a twenty-seven-year-old woman who'd studied English Literature at university and was now manager of a bookshop that sold only romantic fiction, had embraced spinsterdom and owned a cat who regarded legs as nothing more than the things you climbed up so you could jump into your owner's arms and cling. And Johnny was sitting across from her with his perfect smile and his perfect face and his perfect hair and his perfectly cut suit and perfect white shirt on his perfect body.

They were chalk and cheese. Oil and water. Spots and stripes. No one who had eyes in their head would ever believe that they were boyfriend and girlfriend.

While this had all been fun — the commiserating about being single — it was time to get real. Verity pushed away the second helping of breadsticks that Luigi had discreetly placed in front of her, because the waistband of her jeans was starting to dig in.

'The thing is you think that pretending you're in a relationship is simply one harmless little lie to get your friends to back off. But that one harmless little lie quickly turns into so many lies

50

that pretty soon you need a spreadsheet to keep track of them all.' Verity scooped up a breadstick, but only so she could admonish Johnny with it. He sat there very calmly, waiting until she was done, which she wasn't. 'Also, it's very wrong to lie to people but at least Peter Hardy, oceanographer, was a fake lie. What you're proposing is a real lie with acting and a back story.'

'OK, all right.' Johnny held up his hands. They did look like the hands of an architect. Verity could imagine those hands unfurling blueprints and making notes with monogrammed Staedtler pencils. Or even gently cupping the face of the woman he loved desperately but couldn't be with right now. 'But we don't have to act like we're madly in love. If we met each other's friends as a one-off, then all we'd have to say is that we were seeing each other. And technically we are seeing each other right now, aren't we?'

Johnny was starting to sound a little desperate and the whole thing was crazy. What was even crazier was that Verity was considering it. Not seriously and only for a second but she did wonder what it would be like to walk into a party with Johnny with his perfect everything so all her friends would say, 'Who *is* that with Verity? Is it that Peter Hardy bloke?'

That was as far as Verity got though, because then everything in her baulked, like a rookie filly getting to Becher's Brook during the Grand National and deciding that they wouldn't jump, because actually they preferred all their fetlocks intact, thank you very much. Walking in

51

anywhere with Johnny looking the way he did and Verity's friends not having seen her with a man in years would mean that Verity would be the centre of attention. Quite frankly, she'd rather die.

'I can't,' she said firmly and with what she hoped was an air of finality that would shut this thing down once and for all. 'I just couldn't do it. No way. Sorry.' She proffered the discarded breadsticks as a consolation prize. 'You can have these if you want. Luigi always gives me an extra portion.'

'That's very kind but I'd hate to have to get my tailor to let out the fat straps on my suit,' Johnny said gravely, even though his charcoal suit was so slim-cut that Verity doubted it had room for fat straps. 'I suppose it was a pretty left-field idea. I hope I didn't offend you.'

'No! Not at all,' Verity assured him, because Johnny was sitting there, with his chin resting on one hand and looking rather disconsolate like he had an urgent social gathering first thing tomorrow morning and had been expecting Verity to jump at the chance to be his plus one. 'Anyway, I'm sure there must be women queuing up to be your fake real girlfriend.'

'Maybe I should put an ad on Craigslist.' Johnny sighed. 'Or perhaps I should call the last bitter divorcee I got set up with though she's bound to be even more bitter now because I promised I'd call her and I never did. I'm probably on her hit list along with her ex-husband and all the other men who have done her wrong. Maybe she'll forgive me though. And maybe she'll have changed her perfume too. It was very cloying. Really caught at the back of my throat and made my eyes water so . . . '

'Just stop! Please stop!' Verity covered her face. It was best not to look at Johnny. He was beautiful in his suffering and she was a notorious soft touch. She'd bought Strumpet for fifty quid from a bloke in a pub after he'd told her that Strumpet was a she and the runt of the litter and that her mother had rejected her. The vet later told Verity that Strumpet was most definitely a he and the fattest runt he'd ever seen in all his thirty years of vetting.

'Of course once I've been on a second date with her, she's sure to think that we should have a third date,' Johnny said with a sniff. 'And it would be rude to refuse. It would hurt her feelings, which have already been brutalised by her ex-husband.'

'I'll think about it!' Verity yelped. 'Oh God, I'll think about it. I'm not promising anything more than that, but enough already with this emotional blackmail!' It was as if Johnny had been taking lessons from her sisters.

Johnny straightened up and rewarded Verity with a smile that was more devastating than any of his previous smiles. It made her feel quite light-headed. 'I was hoping you'd say that,' he said and Verity suspected that she'd been totally played. It was a very Wickham move and she'd be on her guard from now on.

★ ★ ★

53

As soon as Verity left the restaurant with Johnny's number in her phone, his business card in her purse, her cheek still tingling from the brush of his lips when he'd said goodbye and a good half of her gargantuan lasagne in a takeaway carton, she texted Merry.

I bumped into that Johnny again. Where are you?

The reply came back so quickly that Verity hadn't even tucked her phone away.

OMG! 😂 😂 Am in your flat, eating your snacks. Hurry home!

Merry had left the flat and Verity's snacks and was waiting for her sister on one of the benches in the courtyard, which was free of hoodies for once. 'I showed them a picture I had on my phone of what smoking weed does to the human brain and they made their excuses and left,' Merry informed her when Verity asked what had happened to them.

Merry was a medical researcher at University College Hospital and had all manner of disgusting yet strangely fascinating photos of dissections and diseased body parts on her phone, which she liked to whip out at inappropriate moments.

'So, Johnny then . . . ' Merry prompted as they walked into the shop. 'Tell me everything and don't skimp on the details.'

So, Verity told her everything, though the one part she left out was the realisation she'd had after Johnny had insisted on paying the whole bill and not going Dutch, that they'd been sitting there together, talking, for well over an hour and she hadn't minded at all (not after she'd got over her initial shock) or felt in any way antsy. No point in giving Merry false hope that Verity was just waiting for the right man to come along.

Besides, Johnny had made it perfectly clear where Verity stood, just in case she was getting ideas. 'Just so we're on the same page,' he'd said as he held the door open for her as they left the restaurant. 'If you do agree to appear in public with me as a fake one-off girlfriend, and I really hope you do, please don't start thinking that this might lead to anything more serious.'

For one second, Verity had thought he was joking because it was such an arrogant thing to say. Yes, Johnny might be ridiculously easy on the eye but Verity resented the assumption that she was likely to swoon at his feet without too much encouragement.

'I don't think there's any danger of that,' she had said, her tone both hurt and offended, though both hurt and offence were lost on Johnny.

'I'm sure you're a wonderful woman, but I'm not going to fall in love with you,' he added as if Verity was harbouring fantasies that he might just do that exact thing. 'I'm already in love. I don't need the added complication.'

'In love with this unknown woman that he can't be with although he really wants to,' she told Merry. 'Which now that I think about it, seems odd. Shady, even. What, in this day and age, can possibly be keeping them apart? Has she taken a restraining order out against him? Is he some kind of grade A stalker?'

'Hardly. His unknown woman is dying,' Merry stated matter of factly. 'She has a tragic terminal illness and she's determined to do the decent thing and keep Johnny at bay so he can have some semblance of a normal life after she's snuffed it. I mean, obviously.'

'Obviously,' Verity echoed with heavy sarcasm. Though she pretended that she only read literary fiction, Verity knew very well that Merry had a secret weakness for the sort of florid, overblown romances that even Posy would declare too saccharine for her tastes. 'Anyway, whatever the story is with his unknown woman, it doesn't really matter. I'm not his type. Believe me, that was perfectly clear.'

They were sitting on the sofa, taking it in turns to dip their spoons into a tub of peanut butter ice cream, though Verity's heart or stomach wasn't really in it. As it was she felt as if she was minutes away from giving birth to the food baby that had rounded out her belly and was making her feel winded. Now, Merry swivelled round so she could stare at her sister.

'Why are you not his type? Did he actually say that? That's kind of harsh.'

'No, but he didn't have to.' Verity put down her spoon. 'He's gorgeous, Merry. Even if I did want a boyfriend, which I don't, I so don't, he is way out of my league and . . . '

She couldn't say any more than that because Merry clapped her hand over Verity's mouth.

'Wrong!' Merry shouted. 'Everyone thinks we're twins and I'm generally considered a knockout so that makes you a knockout too. We could have anyone we wanted. Anyone!'

'Did you forget to check your ego at the door?' Verity snapped, pushing Merry's hand down. Though it was true that Merry and Verity's resemblance to each other went beyond a sisterly similarity. It hadn't helped that they'd been in the same year at school as there was only eleven months between them. Apparently Mrs Love had got quite tipsy at a church social and, as she cheerfully confessed to her horrified daughters sixteen years later, 'I didn't think I could get pregnant if I was breastfeeding.'

Still, it didn't really matter where Verity stood on some arbitrary scale of attractiveness. 'Like I said, I'm not on the market. I'm too busy officially mourning the end of my short but intense relationship with Peter Hardy. And I only agreed to consider this thing with Johnny because he put me on the spot. I'm not actually going to go through with it. I am done with fake boyfriends. They're almost as much work as having a real boyfriend. There's a reason why lying is included in the ten commandments,' she added rather piously. 'Because it's wrong.'

'Thou shalt not lie isn't one of the ten commandments,' Merry said loftily. 'Any fool knows that.'

'It might not say 'Thou shalt not lie' but it does say 'Thou shalt not bear false witness against thy neighbour', which is pretty much the same thing, which you would know if you

57

weren't an absolutely rubbish vicar's daughter.' Verity tilted her head and gave Merry a smarmy smile, which she knew drove her sister teeth-grittingly, fist-clenchingly mad. It was the way of sisters the world over.

And maybe that was why, to get her revenge, when Verity popped to the loo, she came back into the living room to find that Merry was wearing an equally smarmy smile and holding Verity's phone. 'I decided that one shouldn't waste a perfectly decent fake boyfriend so I texted Johnny and invited him to the opening of the tearooms next Saturday. He's already texted back to say yes. Seems very keen. It's all right, Very, no need to thank me.'

6

'She was in no humour for conversation with anyone but himself; and to him she had hardly courage to speak.'

Verity was going to wait seventy-two hours, then text Johnny to say that she'd changed her mind.

Everyone knew that there was a standard three-day cooling-off period after agreeing to a date. Even Nina said so.

But just as the seventy-two-hour window was approaching and Verity was spending a lot of her time mentally composing the apologetic text she'd send Johnny ('I have been diagnosed with a rare tropical disease and am quarantined until further notice') he rang her.

What normal person would actually ring someone they'd arranged a date with? There was a reason why text messages had been invented.

Besides, it was common knowledge that Verity only answered the phone to her immediate family. Except Johnny didn't know her well enough to be aware of that fact and, hopeful that perhaps he was having second thoughts, Verity really felt she had no choice but to answer the phone.

'Hello?'

'Hi Verity. How are you?'

'Um fine. What do you . . . I mean, how are you?'

59

'I'm very well. Just checking we're still good for Saturday. Is there anything I should be aware of?'

Briefly, Verity wondered if her father knew of any nunneries with vacancies. 'Like what?'

'Your text message wasn't big with specifics. This tearoom; is it being opened by friends of yours?'

Verity shut her eyes as she realised the enormity of what Merry's text message had wrought. That Johnny would be coming to her place of work. Her home. Meeting her colleagues, her boss, her friends. If Merry turned up, which she was sure to do, because free cake, then he'd even meet her family — or one very annoying member of it.

She found herself launching into a garbled explanation that took in a potted history of Happy Ever After, formerly Bookends. At one point, she even referenced Lady Agatha Drysdale, former Suffragette, who'd founded the shop.

The whole time Verity was willing herself to say the words 'Look, shall we just call the whole thing off?' but the words never came because each time she tried to reach for them, Johnny would ask her a question about whether it was all right to turn up in jeans and if he needed to bring a gift and 'Look, we'll just keep it really casual. Say we're friends. What's the harm in that?'

Oh, where to begin. Verity shut her eyes again. It seemed as if she'd had her eyes closed for the majority of their conversation. 'Why don't you come around at about seven, in time for the speeches? You don't have to stay for very long.'

It was a phrase that Verity often had occasion to utter. Her sister Chatty had once even cross-stitched 'I'M NOT GOING TO STAY FOR VERY LONG' on a cushion for Verity's last birthday. Her twin, Immy, had cross-stitched another of Verity's favourite sayings, 'I CAN'T HEAR MYSELF THINK', on a contrasting cushion.

But now Johnny was agreeing that he didn't have to stay for very long. 'So I'll see you Saturday then. I'm looking forward to it.'

I'm not, Verity thought as she ended the call and she still wasn't looking forward to it on Saturday, which was the kind of beautiful English summer's day that made you want to take tea on the lawn and watch a cricket match. It was perfect weather to open the tearooms with some fanfare, though secretly Verity had been hoping that it might rain so they couldn't have guests milling about in the courtyard and the whole thing would be over quite soon. But no such luck and actually wishing for storm clouds and a torrential downpour was very mean-spirited and uncharitable when all the staff, but especially Mattie, had worked so hard in anticipation of this day.

On Saturdays Verity would usually do any tedious bits of paperwork she never got round to during the week, but this Saturday after the website orders were done, Verity presented herself in the tearoom ready to do Mattie's bidding.

Normally Mattie seemed a little sad (she'd arrived back in London from Paris under a cloud; 'I bet it was a man-shaped cloud too,' Nina had said) and unflappable, but this morning she was extremely flappable.

'I made a list,' Mattie told Verity, her poker-straight black fringe sticking up at all angles. She held up a batter-splodged piece of paper. 'There are too many items on it. We'll never get everything done.'

'We will,' Verity promised. 'I guarantee that in a few hours, the tearoom will be ready to reopen its doors.'

Posy's mother used to run the tearoom, but by the time Verity had joined the staff five years ago, Posy's mother and her father, who'd managed the shop, were no longer there and the tearoom had become a junk room, a shadow of what it had been.

Now, the sun streamed in through the windows, shadows all banished, and the tearoom was restored to all its former, mismatched glory. The wooden floor and half-panelled walls gleaming, the primrose yellow Formica counter, which had been put in in the 1950s, was groaning under the weight of a shiny new coffee maker that was the sole domain of Paloma, who Mattie had taken on because she was a trained barista and didn't leap a foot in the air and shriek whenever it started hissing and huffing.

There was also an old-fashioned urn for tea and soon Verity would put out all the tempting treats that Mattie had been working on for weeks. Moist layer cakes stood proudly on the vintage cake stands they'd found stashed in a cupboard. Buns and scones, biscuits and brownies displayed on plates also found in the cupboard, none of them matching but all beautiful whether they were adorned with birds or flowers or polka dots.

Verity set herself to washing and drying the equally mismatched cups and saucers Posy had bought from eBay. She also made a mental note to tell Posy to stop buying stuff off eBay.

Then, Verity folded napkins. Put Prosecco to chill in the little fridge in the office kitchen, told Mattie countless times to calm down because everything would be fine and told shop customers, distracted by the tantalising smells coming from the tearoom, that they weren't open yet even more times.

Eventually, it was six o'clock. Time to close the shop. Verity, Nina and Mattie slipped upstairs to change. Mattie was done in five minutes. Shrugging out of her jeans and top to shrug into a little black dress then an insouciant flick of eyeliner and a slick of red lipstick and she was done. 'I must check on my buns,' she said and slipped back downstairs.

Meanwhile Nina had already commandeered the bathroom — it took her a good hour to upgrade her daytime make-up to an evening make-up — so Verity sat cross-legged in her big velvet chair to wait. Would anyone notice if she skulked up here until everyone had gone home?

Of course they would. And they'd be cross, rightly so. And Johnny would turn up and ask after her and that wouldn't be good, especially if

63

Merry got to him first. The thought was enough to have Verity springing out of her chair to demand that Nina let her have the bathroom for a measly five minutes so she could have a quick shower. Then Verity pulled on a short-sleeved, knee-length navy-blue dress in a crisp cotton, which was practically identical to most of the dresses hanging up in her wardrobe, though in winter she preferred long sleeves and a cosy jersey cotton.

Because it was a special occasion and because Johnny, so Sunday supplement perfect, was about to turn up and act as if he and Verity were good friends, Verity knew that she needed to make a little more effort than securing her hair in its usual non-perky ponytail. Actually, a *lot* more effort. She braided a front section of hair and pinned it back, then dug out her make-up bag and was just dabbing helplessly at her face with tinted moisturiser when she became aware of Nina standing in her bedroom doorway, gawping.

'Make-up?' Nina queried. 'Verity Love is putting on make-up? You must be serious about this Johnny dude. You never put on make-up for Peter Hardy, oceanographer.'

'I'm sure I did,' Verity said, as she decided she'd done enough dabbing and rooted around for the mascara that she'd had since 2007, giving it a good shake as it tended to go clumpy.

'Oh God, I can hardly bear to look!' Nina turned away as if Verity's inept make-up application was causing her untold agony. She was back a minute later with the three-tier IKEA trolley she used to stash her huge collection of cosmetics. 'Look, I have all these free samples of stuff,' Nina said, pulling out a couple of bulging make-up bags. 'I can never resist one of those 'Spend fifty quid, get a twee make-up bag full of stuff you're never going to use' deals. There's a couple of lipsticks in here that would look so much better on you, plus mascara that won't give you conjunctivitis.'

To Verity's shame, Nina achieved more in five minutes with six products than Verity had been able to do in fifteen years. She still looked like herself, there'd been no wild Kardashian contouring, but a more put-together, less frowny version of herself.

'I would never have thought of using brown mascara,' Verity said as she slowly blinked at herself in the mirror then pursed her lips, which were now faintly glossy with lip stain because lipstick was simply too much lip and too much stick for her. She looked all right. Really all right. Like she wouldn't look completely out of place if people saw her with Johnny. Now she understood why Nina called make-up 'her warpaint'. She did feel a little braver. 'And I never saw the point of blusher before. Thanks, Nina.'

'Another six months of living together and I'll have you pierced and tattooed,' Nina promised, as she spritzed herself with perfume, though it sounded more like a threat.

'Or else I'll have you attending bible study and joining me in a prayer circle. We can sing 'Kumbaya' at the end,' Verity offered. 'It will be fun.'

Nina's mouth fell open. 'Never! Not that I'm down on religion or your God but it's just . . . ' Her eyes narrowed as Verity smiled serenely at her. 'Hang on! I've never once seen you near a bible or heard you praying. You're joking! I hate it when you do that, Very. You might give a girl some warning first.'

'Me? Joke? I never joke,' Verity did indeed joke and, with a squawk of faked outrage, Nina turned on her heel and walked out of the room.

'Come on! We've got a party to attend,' she called over her shoulder. 'There's two glasses of cold Prosecco with our names all over them.'

Verity tugged at the skirt of her dress: would it do? Would *she* do? 'You go down,' she told Nina. 'I'm right behind you.'

★   ★   ★

It took another half hour and a text each from Posy, Nina, Mattie and Tom before Verity had psyched herself up enough to venture down the stairs and face her real-life fake boyfriend. Well, that and Posy's threat to fire her, though Verity knew full well it was an empty threat — she was the only person who knew how the stock system worked and even then it was a very vague kind of knowing.

Strumpet was at the bottom of the stairs, alternately hurling himself at the door that separated the flat from the shop and yowling furiously because food was being eaten and he wanted in.

It was an epic battle, woman versus cat, but

eventually Verity made it through the door, her dress covered in cat fur, Strumpet's angry and betrayed face seared into her memory.

They'd locked the doors that connected the shop to the tearoom so Verity had to step outside into the courtyard, which was positively teeming with people. Favourite customers, book bloggers, food bloggers, friends, friends of friends and yet Verity immediately spotted Johnny. Not just because he was taller than about ninety-eight per cent of the other guests (only Posy's husband Sebastian was taller) but because he was deep in conversation with Nina.

That couldn't be good.

Verity forgot her plan to skulk and hurried over in time to hear Nina ask: 'So, how did you two meet? Very plays her cards very close to her chest, she never tells us anything.'

'I tell you so many things,' Verity protested but now wasn't the time or the place. 'Do I need to make formal introductions or did you just launch straight into the interrogation?'

Nina put a hand to her heart as if she were mortally offended. 'I got Johnny a drink and a cheese straw *then* I launched into the interrogation. I wasn't raised by wolves, Very.'

'Great cheese straws,' Johnny said, so Verity had to acknowledge him, look at him, instead of focussing on Nina. 'Hello,' he added and he kissed Verity on the cheek so she got a lovely whiff of his aftershave, which made her think of expensive soap and warm, folded laundry. He smelt clean, fresh and ever so slightly lemony. It suited him, matched the clean, elegant set of his

67

face as he smiled down at her. He was wearing jeans and a T-shirt that might have started out life as black but was faded to grey, its white logo now indecipherable. And he had nice arms. Not ripped. Not 'sun's out, guns out' as they said to Tom when he slipped off his cardigan in deference to the fact that it was late June and the shop had no air con. But Johnny definitely had muscles, lean muscles, like he had a gym membership and wasn't afraid to use it.

She had to stop staring. 'Shall I get some more cheese straws?' she gulped, half-turning to hide what felt suspiciously like a blush in order to make for the kitchen.

Nina yanked her back. 'You'll do no such thing. Not until you guys tell me how you met.'

There was a moment of silence — Verity was absolutely certain that her cheeks must be scarlet by now. It seemed to last for several millennia as Johnny looked at Verity and she looked back at him and held her face very still so she didn't grimace. 'Er, it's quite a funny story really, isn't it? How we met.'

'Yeah, one to tell the grandchildren about,' Johnny said casually. 'I was waiting for someone in a restaurant but they stood me up and Verity was waiting for the legendary Peter Hardy, who'd stood her up too.'

'Not Peter Hardy, oceanographer?' Nina gasped indignantly. 'He sounded too nice to stand anyone up!'

'And there was a misunderstanding and the restaurant thought we were waiting for each other and so here we are!' Johnny put his arm

68

round Verity who tried not to stiffen.

'Yes, here we are,' she echoed with a pointed look at Nina. 'Nina, didn't Posy ask you to keep an eye on Sam and Pants? Because they're currently having a competition to see how many macarons they can cram into their mouths in one go.'

'Urgh, boys! I expected better from Pants!' Nina exclaimed and she tottered away to tell off Sam, Posy's fifteen-year-old brother, and his best friend Pants.

Which left Verity alone with Johnny. Technically they weren't alone, there had to be over a hundred people in the courtyard, but they were standing off to the side and it felt oddly intimate.

'You look very nice,' Johnny said after a small pause.

'Thank you,' Verity said stiffly. 'You too. I like your, erm, T-shirt.' She stared at the ground and stifled a heartfelt sigh. 'Erm, more cheese straws? And let me get you a Prosecco.' If they were eating and drinking they wouldn't have to talk to each other.

'Sounds like a plan,' Johnny agreed and he followed her through the crowd to the tearoom so they could load up on supplies.

Their progress was slow as a steady stream of people kept stopping Verity in her tracks, their eyes wide like they couldn't believe that she was with a man. Then they'd goggle at Johnny, who'd smile equably though Verity was sure that he was now regretting the whole imaginary boyfriend scheme. 'So, is this Peter Hardy, oceanographer?' Verity's waylayers would all ask.

'No, I'm Johnny, I'm an architect,' Johnny said every time until finally they were Prosecco-ed up and each had a plate laden high with delicious baked goods just as Posy swung a metal ladle at the new tea urn to get everyone's attention and perforate a few eardrums while she was at it. Then she nudged Mattie forward.

'You have to say a few words,' she hissed in a loud voice. 'Welcome people, your tearoom mission statement, introduce our special guests, blah blah.'

'Don't worry if it's not as good as Morland's speech of a few weeks ago,' Sebastian added kindly, from over Posy's shoulder. 'I mean, it won't be, but that's not your fault.'

Posy and Sebastian were still in the first flush of married love where they seemed to think the other one was the reason that the sun shone and flowers grew and life was generally beautiful. Somehow Sebastian managed to convey all this and still be rude to everyone who wasn't Posy.

Which was why Mattie rolled her eyes, even as she took off her apron. 'Thank you, everyone, for coming to our opening. I've dreamed of this moment, of standing in my own café, since as long as I can remember and even though it's happening right at this very moment, it still feels like a dream,' she said.

She didn't get any further than that because her French mother, who they'd all been introduced to earlier, an older but still equally chic version of Mattie, promptly burst into tears. 'It's just that I'm so proud of you,' she sobbed as Mattie's brother, Jacques, handed her a tissue.

He had a whole box with him as if he'd anticipated that they might be needed. Verity glanced sideways at Johnny but he was texting, eyes intent on his phone screen, and was missing all the drama.

Once Mattie's mother's sobs had quietened down to the occasional hiccup, Mattie continued. 'I went to Paris to learn patisserie and fall in love — though learning patisserie was a much happier experience than falling in love,' she said darkly as the assembled company stared down at their glasses. 'Anyway, here I am and here you are, at the grand opening of The Tearoom at Happy Ever After and now I'd just like to welcome our special guests to declare us officially open.'

'Who is the special guest?' Johnny suddenly whispered in Verity's ear. His breath tickled, not in an unpleasant way.

'It's actually two special guests,' Verity whispered back, shifting slightly so that he didn't have to lean in quite so closely. 'A woman who won *Great British Bake Off* a couple of years ago and her mother who happens to be a romantic novelist. Quite convenient really.'

'Why is it convenient that her mother's a romantic novelist?' Johnny wanted to know but Very's reply was drowned out by a polite round of applause as the guests cut a big red ribbon that had been hurriedly stretched over the tearoom doors. These then burst open to reveal Little Sophie, their Saturday girl, and Sam, carrying a massive croquembouche between them. Everyone 'ooh'ed and 'ah'ed as they caught sight of the high tower of profiteroles welded together with salted caramel and adorned with sparklers and the clapping got distinctly more enthusiastic.

Unfortunately the dramatic impact was rather lost on the staff of Happy Ever After. They'd been required to taste-test so many different flavoured crème patisseries (in the end Mattie had gone with a hazelnut praline) that Verity and Tom had vowed to each other that they would never eat another profiterole as long as they lived.

'Do you want some?' she asked Johnny as plates of profiteroles began to be passed around.

He shook his head. 'Actually, I haven't got that much of a sweet tooth. If it were a cheese tower, I'd be mowing down anyone who got in my way. What was that you were saying about romantic novels?'

'What?' Verity scrolled back to their conversation BC (before croquembouche). 'The bookshop. We specialise in romantic fiction.'

Johnny didn't pull an agonised face like he was scared of getting romantic fiction cooties, like Dougie, Merry's boyfriend did, every time Verity talked about work. He jerked his head in the direction of the glass doors through which shelves of books could be glimpsed. 'The whole shop? Really?'

'I'll give you the guided tour, if you like.' Verity wasn't just offering to be polite. More and more people were pouring into the tearoom on a hunt for profiteroles and it was inevitable that soon Verity's personal space bubble would become pierced in all directions. She and Johnny inched closer to the doors that led to the now-closed shop, which she unlocked so they could slip through undetected.

Verity took Johnny through the deserted rooms and explained how Happy Ever After had been transformed over the last couple of months.

They ended up sitting on opposite sofas in the main room as Johnny looked around with interest. 'I'm getting a very strong sense of déjà vu,' he said, as his eyes rested on the rolling ladder. 'What did the shop used to be called?'

'Bookends,' Verity said and Johnny's face lit up with a smile. Verity smiled back because there was something about this version of Johnny's smile, how welcoming it was, how it pulled you into its orbit, which automatically made her want to smile too. But then, like the sun slipping down behind the London rooftops, his smile faded.

'I've been here before,' he said. 'Lots of times before.'

'When it was Bookends?' Verity dared to ask because it seemed as if the subject suddenly had a Keep Out notice pinned on it and she liked to be as respectful of other people's boundaries as she hoped they would be of hers.

'We had a spelling test at school every Friday and if I got all my answers right, then my mother would bring me here to choose a book then we'd visit the tearoom for a cake. I had a much sweeter tooth back then,' he said, eyes faraway as if he wasn't seeing Happy Ever After but the shop as it had been, which in the day had had a huge children's section.

73

'I used to get a gold star if I got all my spellings right,' Verity offered because Johnny had shared something personal and she found that she wanted to do the same. 'Once I'd collected ten gold stars, I was given fifty pence to spend on penny sweets in the newsagent.'

'Fifty pence to spend on penny sweets was untold riches when we were kids, wasn't it?' Johnny asked with a grin, his mood lightening again, but Verity shook her head.

'It really wasn't. Not when you have sisters,' Verity remembered sadly. Her sisters, who never, ever got ten gold stars, would always want in on Verity's fifty pence mix up and would hang over the sweet display in the local newsagent and argue.

Johnny laughed when Verity told him that the newsagent got so fed up he'd stuck a sign on the door. 'Only two Love sisters allowed in the shop at any one time.'

This wasn't as bad as she remembered it being. Talking to a man. Dating. Not that they were dating. Or were even friends, but it wasn't as awful as she'd imagined it to be.

'What books did you like when you were a kid?' Verity asked Johnny and he admitted to an obsession with Biggles. 'There was this guy who used to work here who'd track down out-of-print Biggles novels for me. His wife used to run the café. She made the most amazing flapjacks.'

'I think you must mean my mum and dad.' Verity's heart jack-knifed in her chest when she heard Posy's voice from the doorway and then she thought she might burst into tears. 'My

74

parents used to run the bookshop and the café.'

'Really? Cause I'm going back nearly thirty years,' Johnny said doubtfully, twisting round to smile at Posy.

'Mum and Dad took over the shop twenty-five years ago and my mother made the best flapjacks in the world, so it had to be them,' Posy said.

'Well, they must be very proud of everything you've accomplished,' Johnny said, which was absolutely the right and kindest thing to say in the circumstances. Verity had been worried about him coming here — to her work, her home, to meet her friends — but he fitted in like he really was a new boyfriend on his best behaviour.

Except he'd just talked about Posy's parents in the present tense and Sebastian, who'd come up behind Posy because they couldn't bear to be a minute apart from each other, brushed his hand against Posy's cheek. It was a tiny, tender gesture that made Verity's heart jack-knife again. She also couldn't believe that Sebastian Thorndyke, of all people, was capable of such tenderness. 'You all right, Morland?' he asked.

Posy nodded. 'I'm fine, honestly.' She smiled bravely at Johnny. 'I hope that they would be proud of me but, you see, they died nearly eight years ago.'

Johnny's intake of breath was swift. 'I'm sorry . . . ' he tailed off, took another deep breath. 'My mother died ten years ago, when I was twenty-five . . . I would hope that she's proud of me too. You know, she loved this shop. It was one of her favourite places.'

'Thank you,' Posy said and then nobody knew

what to say; even Sebastian felt moved enough to keep quiet. Johnny glanced over at their new-releases shelves long enough for Posy to give Verity a thumbs up and mouth, 'I love him!' Then Johnny turned his attention back to them and Posy smiled brightly. 'No lurking in here. This is meant to be a party. So, let's get back to partying.'

Of course, the first person Verity saw as they stepped out into the courtyard was Merry, who'd just arrived with Dougie. Like a heat-seeking missile, she immediately homed in on where Verity was now trying to hide Johnny behind a tree, dragging Dougie over with her.

'There you are!' she called out, but she had eyes only for Johnny. Or one eye because she stood there violently winking at Johnny so one side of her face was completely contorted.

'This is my sister, Merry,' Verity said. 'Please ignore her weird, disfiguring facial tic. And this is Dougie, her boyfriend.' Verity waggled her fingers at Dougie, who waggled his fingers back. He'd known Verity long enough now to understand that a finger waggle was far more acceptable than a hug. 'This is Johnny.'

'I know who he is!' Merry pointed at her eye. 'I don't have a weird facial tic. I was winking! To let Johnny know that I'm in on the scam, but don't worry, your secret is safe with me. Very, I need cake, I'm incredibly hungover. Dougie, alcohol, go and find some. Johnny, you come with me.'

Then Merry yanked a bemused-looking Johnny over to one of the benches that had just become vacant and there was nothing that Verity could do but break the land speed record to get cake and bring it back to her sister who by then was happily regaling Johnny with tales of Love family life.

'There was no room to move when all of us were at home at the same time and Our Vicar and Our Vicar's wife said that TV would rot our young minds, which is ironic because now they're both completely addicted to *Cash in the Attic*, and so we had to make our own fun. Mostly we pretended to be the Mitford sisters, though we all used to fight to get to be Unity. Not because we were Nazis but if it was your turn to be Unity, you got to shoot yourself in the head, then lumber about like a lunatic. We also used to play *Pride and Prejudice*. Did you know that Very has the entire book memorised? She has a quote good to go for every occasion. So, what about you, then? Do you have any siblings? Where do you live? It's so weird that you're single. I mean, you're ridiculously good-looking. There's plenty of women who wouldn't kick you out of bed for eating a cracker, not that you want to be getting ideas about my sister, because hmmmppffff — '

The only effective way to silence Merry was to shove a large piece of cake at her mouth. Verity couldn't even bring herself to say anything. There were no words. It was left to Dougie to remonstrate because sometimes — admittedly not very often — Merry did listen to Dougie.

'Merry, stop sticking your nose into other people's business.'

Merry managed to swallow the piece of raspberry meringue layer cake. 'Very isn't other people!'

'I am people,' Verity pointed out. 'And I'm your family, so you should be more respectful of my — '

'Family shamily!'

Dougie rolled his eyes. 'That doesn't even make sense, Merry.'

Johnny didn't need to be witness to this familiar old squabble. Verity gingerly tugged at his T-shirt, both of them tensing as her knuckles made contact with what felt like quite taut musculature under the soft brushed cotton, and led him away.

'Isn't this a little rude?' he said. 'I've barely said two words to your sister.'

'Merry is genetically predisposed not to respond to hints or gentle coaxing.' Verity sighed. 'Sometimes rudeness is the only way to go.' They were leaving the courtyard now, turning into Rochester Street where Verity stopped. 'I'm sorry about your mother,' she said. 'She sounds lovely.'

Johnny got that hazy look that he'd had before when they were sitting in the silent shop and he was remembering. 'Being back in the shop where I spent so many happy Friday afternoons with her was strange, sad, but also rather wonderful. Thank you for giving that back to me.' His smile became sharper, more in focus. 'You know as first dates go, this one wasn't so bad, was it?'

It wasn't really a first date. Technically, it was more like a third date. Actually it wasn't any kind of date at all. And Verity couldn't do this again.

Her heart couldn't take the strain.

'Shall we just call it quits?' she asked a little desperately. 'This was only meant to be a one-off and I only agreed to it under duress!'

Johnny gave a little start, as if she'd shocked him. 'Oh no, you don't wriggle out of it that easily.' He wagged a finger at her. 'You showed me yours, now I get to show you mine. It's only fair. My friends have a rotating open-house brunch kind of thing on Sundays and I know they'd love to meet you. What time shall I pick you up tomorrow?'

Verity resisted the urge to stamp her foot. 'OK, fine. One thing each, then we're even and I am done. Agreed?'

Johnny smiled patiently as if he were humouring her. 'So, is ten o'clock good for you?'

7

'She hardly knew how to suppose that she could be an object of admiration to so great a man.'

Sunday dawned bright and early. Too bright. Too early. Verity could hear Nina snoring as she tried to do some yoga in the living room to calm her inner chi. Mostly she contemplated brunch. It was a very vague, woolly concept, brunch. Neither breakfast, nor lunch but occupying some neither here nor there place in between and was never the brunch that Verity had seen when she was watching repeats of *Sex and the City*. All perfect egg-white omelettes, avocado on sourdough toast and mimosas. Whenever Verity met Merry and their friends for brunch, it always meant a glorified fry-up with alcohol.

Verity was ravenously hungry at the thought of bacon but couldn't eat anything more substantial than rice cakes, for fear of offending her unknown hosts at this open-house brunch thingy. It would probably be buffet-style, which would be awkward. Having to hold a drink in one hand and plate in the other and not knowing what to do when she was introduced to one of Johnny's friends and needed a hand free for shaking. Unless they did air kisses. Or worse, proper kisses.

Then again, it could be a sit-down brunch and

even if Johnny was on one side of her, Verity barely knew him and the person on her other side would be a complete stranger.

Each possible scenario was more nightmarish than the last. As Verity pulled on a loose, drapey, bird-print top (a genuine designer item found in the Oxfam on Drury Lane, which always had rich pickings), and her favourite skinny jeans, she was surprised she didn't have hives popping out all over her body. She accessorised with the silver leather hi-top, zipped sneakers that Merry had bought in an internet flash sale then realised they were a size too small.

Verity hoped that the overall effect would be a little fashion forward but not too fashion forward. Then she tried to replicate her make-up of the night before with so-so results.

It was still only nine o'clock. There was another hour before she'd grudgingly agreed to meet Johnny on the corner of Rochester Street and so, munching on another rice cake, this time smeared with peanut butter for energy, Verity googled him.

Googling Johnny was fair game because he'd already admitted to googling her first and their relationship origin story yesterday had sucked and she didn't want to walk into brunch unprepared and all right, she was curious. There was no crime in being curious.

After she typed in his full name, right at the top of her search page was a link to Johnny's company WCJ Architects, because apparently, he owned his own company. The second item was an article in the *Guardian* about his four-storey

Canonbury townhouse, which he'd bought as a derelict shell and painstakingly brought back to life.

While he was studying for his architecture degree at Cambridge, Johnny would spend his holidays working on building sites, instead of at the family firm, which he took over when his father retired five years ago. 'I'm actually a certified plasterer, but I've learned a bit of everything over the years from bricklaying and carpentry to plumbing and rewiring.'

These skills were all put to good use in 2007 when, on qualifying as an architect, Johnny moved to New Orleans to work with Habitat for Humanity to provide new homes for families affected by Hurricane Katrina.

Now settled back in London, WCJ Architects, under his guidance, has grown from strength to strength and specialises in lovingly restoring nineteenth and early to mid twentieth century buildings while updating them for the rigours of twenty-first century living.

Nowhere was this more apparent than in the pictures of Johnny's Canonbury house. It was full of natural light and period details mixed with modern minimalism in shades of white and blue.

Much too big for one man to live in all by himself, Verity thought, though it must be idyllic; all that space, all those empty rooms. Even with a couple of flatmates, you could still have all the peace and quiet you needed.

Verity stared intently at a picture of Johnny that had been taken in his airy, light kitchen so the glint of the sun turned his hair almost blond. He was wearing jeans and a white shirt and perched on his burnished steel kitchen table, fingers clasped round a black and white graphic mug that Verity had lusted after in Liberty then hastily put back on the shelf because it cost over forty pounds. Of course, Johnny photographed extremely well; his eyes looked especially blue . . .

Verity shook herself out of her stupor and glanced up at the clock. She only had ten minutes before she was due to meet Johnny and she needed to do something about the thick rice cake and peanut butter paste that was coating every inch of her mouth.

★   ★   ★

Verity was two minutes early, but Johnny was already waiting at their allotted meeting place. He was wearing jeans again and another faded T-shirt, which thankfully meant that Verity hadn't got the dress code horribly wrong, and carrying a large bouquet of flowers, wrapped in brown paper, because the fanciest, most expensive bouquets of flowers were always presented in humble brown paper.

'Oh dear,' Verity said by way of greeting, taking a step back when Johnny tried to lean down to kiss her so he had to give it up as a bad job. 'Am I meant to bring something too? I should, shouldn't I? It's so rude to turn up at someone's house empty-handed when you're expecting them to feed you.'

'It's fine. The flowers can be from both of us,' Johnny said. 'We should probably get going or we'll get there for lunch instead of brunch,' he added as if he instinctively knew that Verity hated being late for anything.

The brunch was being held in Primrose Hill. As they stepped onto Theobald's Road, Johnny was already hailing a taxi. 'Shall we get out at Great Portland Street and walk through Regent's Park?' he suggested and Verity nodded, even though walking through the park would mean walking and talking.

Verity needn't have worried. As they settled into their seats, Johnny's phone beeped. Text message incoming. Then, like the day before, he was glued to his phone. As soon as Johnny sent a message out into the ether, he got a message back within seconds.

Maybe it was an architect emergency. Something to do with subsidence or dry rot, Verity thought as she sat and stared out of the window at the familiar London streets thronged with Sunday shoppers, sightseers, tourists with backpacks and comfortable shoes.

Even when they got out of the cab at Park Square Gardens, Johnny batting Verity's hand away as she tried to give him a fiver towards the fare, and began the long stroll through Regent's Park down the Broad Walk towards London Zoo, Johnny was still riveted to his phone.

It was actually quite bad manners to invite someone to a brunch to meet all your friends, and ignore her for the entire journey. Peter Hardy, oceanographer, would never have behaved in such a rude fashion.

'I'm so sorry about that,' Johnny murmured as if he could read Verity's mind. He slipped his phone into a pocket. 'You now have my undivided attention.'

Then again, Verity wasn't sure that she wanted his undivided attention. 'Oh, it's fine,' she mumbled and every step she took felt as if it were taking her nearer to her execution. That sounded very melodramatic. Not execution but maybe a little light torture. 'So . . . um, whose house are we going to exactly?'

'Now that I think about it, we should be better prepared than we were yesterday.' Johnny gave a rueful chuckle. 'Shall we stick to the story that we met when we were both stood up?'

'Yes, let's,' Verity agreed as she had no better ideas. Merry had come up with the meet cute for Verity and Peter Hardy. He'd dropped a scuba mask at the top of the escalators at Angel tube station and Verity had managed to catch it before it brained someone.

'So, this brunch . . . it's being hosted by my friends Wallis and Graham. Wallis is American, a barrister, grew up on something called a dude ranch, and I was at school with Graham. In fact, I was at school with most of the people at the brunch. They're all good sorts. Not at all scary, I promise.'

Johnny went on to explain how he and his old

school friends met for brunch on the third Sunday of every month and took turns to host. 'Though when it's my turn, I get it catered and I can't cook eggs to order. I feel like I let the side down.'

'I'm sure you don't,' Verity said. 'I could never cook eggs to order either. Far too much pressure.'

'I've been meaning to ask, just how many sisters do you have?' Johnny asked before Verity could think of a tactful way to grill him on how long exactly they were expected to stay at the brunch.

'Four of them, though it feels like more.'

'Four?' Johnny whistled. 'Older or younger?'

'Both. I'm the middle child.' Verity was a classic middle child, if ever there was one. The quiet one, the peacemaker, the odd one out. 'Which is why they always tried to stick me with being Mary Bennet when we were playing *Pride and Prejudice*.'

'Merry mentioned something about that.' Johnny shot Verity a sideways look as they walked by London Zoo, past the huge netted aviary. 'What's wrong with Mary Bennet?'

'Have you never read *Pride and Prejudice*?' Verity asked him in scandalised tones. If Johnny had been a proper boyfriend then not reading *Pride and Prejudice* would be a total deal breaker.

'Can't say I have. Not really my kind of thing. Too many bonnets.' Johnny held up his hands in protest. 'Please stop looking at me like that. Like I've just admitted to kicking kittens and punching puppies.'

'It's almost that bad,' Verity said and she tried to briefly précis the plot of *Pride and Prejudice* and the role of Mary Bennet, which was hard when it was her favourite book. 'So, to get my revenge on years of having to be Mary, whenever my sisters are arguing, which they do, all the time, I quote her being particularly priggish. 'But we must stem the tide of malice, and pour into each other's wounded bosoms the balm of sisterly consolation.' It winds them up like nothing else,' Verity admitted at the end of her pitch. 'So, no siblings, then?'

'I was a lonely only,' Johnny said. They left Regent's Park through the Gloucester Gate, crossed over at the traffic lights and began to walk along Gloucester Avenue. 'It wasn't so bad. I had lots of friends and my parents were the fun kind of parents. They were both architects and for my sixth birthday, they built me a treehouse in the back garden in the style of a pirate ship so I was very popular at school.'

'I really am sorry about your mother. I know she passed away a while ago, but she sounds like such a wonderful, warm person,' Verity said and Johnny dipped his head in acknowledgement, and though he was in profile, he suddenly looked so sad that Verity felt sad too. Sad by proxy. 'Sorry, I'll shut up if you don't want to talk about her.'

'Actually, I never mind talking about her because I don't ever want to forget how beautiful and kind she was. And last night when I was thinking about her, about being back in

Bookends, I remembered that each time we went, she'd buy a romance novel.' Johnny frowned at the memory. 'Said it was a special treat for getting all *her* spellings right too. My father would tease her; complain that she already had enough romance in her life. I'd forgotten all about that until yesterday.'

Verity knew then, that if Johnny's mother were still alive, she would have liked to have met her. Also, that she'd approve of her favourite bookshop's transformation. 'I'm pretty sure your mother must have read *Pride and Prejudice* then, despite its high bonnet count,' she said and Johnny smiled at her gratefully as if he needed a little bit of light relief because memories of lost loved ones, even good memories, were always painful.

'I'm pretty sure you're right,' he agreed. 'I must ask my father.' Johnny sighed. 'However much I miss her, my father misses her more. They really were soulmates.' Their pace slowed as Johnny told her about how his father, William, and his mother, Lucinda, had met as students at Cambridge and had never spent a day apart until Lucinda died. William, still heartbroken from the sound of it, now lived in the basement flat of Johnny's house. 'He's not quite so heartbroken any more but my mother was his one and only love and so I suppose his heart will never completely heal.'

'He even takes care of his ageing Papa, could he be any more perfect?' asked a voice in Verity's head that sounded like a composite of all her sisters, her mother, Mrs Bennet and also

88

Chandler Bing and was so loud she barely heard Johnny thank her.

'Huh? Thank me? For what?'

'For asking me about my mother. For not ignoring it because it was awkward. That was very kind of you,' he said gently.

'Just because something's difficult to talk about doesn't mean it should be swept under the carpet. My family doesn't believe in sweeping anything under the carpet. I mean, you met Merry . . .'

'Is she the bossy sister?'

Verity couldn't help but laugh. 'Not the bossiest. She's about a seven on the bossy scale. Five and a half if I stuff enough cake in her first.' Johnny looked incredulous. 'Con, she's the eldest, is the bossiest sister. Hands down, then Chatty and Immy, the youngest, they're twins, share joint second on the leader board.'

'Four bossy sisters. I can't even imagine what that must be like.'

'Very, very noisy for one thing,' Verity told him.

There had been many times that Verity had longed to be an only child. Especially stuck in a three-bedroom prefab house (the original vicarage had been destroyed by bombs during World War Two and the diocese had yet to rebuild it) so there had been nowhere to get away from four sisters and the unholy racket that accompanied them. Our Vicar wasn't much better. He had a booming voice all the better for sermonising with, but even when he wasn't in the pulpit he was still booming away, usually singing from a selection of classic musicals accompanied by his wife. You couldn't even have a wee in peace, without someone hammering on the door and demanding to know how long you were going to be.

'You're not at all noisy,' Johnny noted.

'I do ramble sometimes,' Verity said, 'but that's just nerves.'

'There's nothing to be nervous about.' Johnny had come to a halt, which meant Verity had to stop too. They were standing outside a huge stucco-covered house, wisteria clinging lovingly to its walls, a perfect match for the front door, which was painted the same shade of lilac. 'Anyway, we're here.' He unlatched the front gate. 'After you.'

8

'Where she feared most to fail, she was most sure of success, for those to whom she endeavoured to give pleasure were prepossessed in her favour.'

Though she longed to turn tail and run, Verity squared her shoulders and followed Johnny down the path to the lilac front door.

Johnny rang the bell and she even managed to return the encouraging smile that he gave her, though it was as limp as a week-old lettuce.

Verity could hear people chatting, laughing, children shrieking and footsteps that got louder and louder until the door opened and a tall, elegant blonde woman stood there. Her face lit up. 'Johnny! You're late!' She had a soft, lazy American accent. Her gaze rested on Verity and she gave a little start, blinked, regained her composure and smiled again. 'And you've brought someone?'

It was definitely a question. Not a statement of fact. Like Johnny hadn't bothered to tell his friends, his matchmaking-him-with-fake-breasted-divorcees friends, that he was bringing a woman to their open-house, rotating brunch thingy.

'This is Verity,' Johnny said breezily. 'You're always telling me that I'm welcome to bring a guest.'

'You are and Verity, I am *so* pleased to meet

you. I'm Wallis. Please, come in!'

No sooner had Verity taken one step over the threshold than she was gathered up in Wallis's arms for an enthusiastic hug.

Nobody had said anything about hugging. Verity tried not to stiffen but she didn't do a very good job of it and was Wallis stroking her hair?

She was, then Wallis took Verity's hand and pulled her down the hall, Verity shooting a pained glance back at Johnny who smiled encouragingly again, and into a huge country-style kitchen absolutely full of people all milling about and helping themselves to a selection of fruit, juices and pastries set up on the kitchen island. There were also savoury items keeping warm on a hot plate, the sight and scent of crisp bacon making Verity's dry mouth suddenly water, and a tall man with a harried air was manning a frying pan and asking loudly if anyone wanted chopped chives in their omelettes. Yet more people were pouring themselves coffee then spilling out of the open patio doors into a large garden.

The whole scene was like something from an advert. *This isn't just any brunch. This is an M&S brunch.*

At least no one seemed to be paying them any attention, Verity thought just as Wallis pulled her forward. 'Guys! Guys!' she called out, her voice now doing a good impersonation of a foghorn. 'Guys! Johnny's here and he's BROUGHT A FRIEND! Everyone, this is Verity!'

Verity looked down at that point just to make sure that she wasn't naked because she'd had an anxiety dream very similar to this although that had also involved being thrust on stage to sing 'Agadoo' with the appropriate hand gestures. No, definitely not a dream, no amount of pinching herself awake was going to rescue her from this living hell.

She'd hoped that Johnny's friends wouldn't be too intimidating, that they'd be polite if a little reserved about the interloper in their midst. But never in her wildest imaginings had Verity expected that they'd fall on her with effusive and enthusiastic greetings.

'Look at you!' one woman cried as she clasped Verity to her bosom. 'What a lovely girl.'

'And isn't Johnny lovely too? We're so pleased that he's finally met someone nice. Is it serious?'

'Well, it must be serious if he's bringing her to brunch.'

Verity was surrounded on all sides by women in their mid to late thirties, all wearing brunch casual; jeans and Breton tops, glossy hair pulled back from faces all fixed intently on her.

'It's not serious,' she bleated. 'We're just friends, aren't we? Aren't we?'

She turned to find Johnny, to plead for back-up, but he was in the middle of a group of men, dressed as if they all had shares in Boden, who were slapping him on the shoulders and saying things like 'You sly, old dog!' and 'About bloody time!' until Johnny's phone rang and he excused himself to take the call, leaving Verity on her own.

Except, Johnny's friends didn't leave her on her own. She was supplied with a glass of

Prosecco topped up with orange juice, a bagel with scrambled eggs cooked to order ('not too runny, please') with a side of bacon, then led out into the garden to be given the seat of honour on the decking while the women arranged their chairs in a fan pattern around her.

'So, Verity, where did you and Johnny meet?'

She stumbled through their prearranged answer and had barely tasted her first forkful of scrambled eggs, when someone else piped up.

'And do you live near here?'

'Bloomsbury.'

'Bloomsbury! You lucky thing!'

There were coos of approval. Verity glanced around the half circle of affluent North-London-dwelling women. It wasn't even that they were older than Verity; they also came from a very different place to her. It was apparent in the confident way they carried themselves, the ease and assurance that prep and private school and redbrick university had given them. Verity would have been surprised if any of them had gone to a run-down comprehensive or grown up in a leaky prefab on the edge of a sink estate because the old bishop had had it in for Mr Love after he'd refused to denounce single mothers and homosexuals from the pulpit.

But being a vicar's daughter also taught a girl some valuable life skills. For all her awkwardness, for all her shyness, Verity had spent her formative years mixing with all sorts of people. Whenever there'd been a knock at the vicarage door, Mr and Mrs Love expected all their daughters to be considerate of whoever was standing on the doorstep, whether it was a grieving widow or proud new father or even Billy from the greengrocers who was convinced that the devil had taken up residence in his potting shed and called around weekly to ask Mr Love to perform an exorcism.

So, in this moment Verity knew that she'd be fine as long as she tamped down her nerves and made a concerted effort to remember to breathe.

'I work in a bookshop and I live above the shop.' She pulled her lips back in something close to a smile. 'I couldn't afford to live in Bloomsbury otherwise.'

'A bookshop! I love bookshops!' Wallis said and as Verity answered their questions about where she'd gone to university, where her family lived (Mr and Mrs Love were now settled in an archetypal rambling vicarage in a charming village in the East Lincolnshire Wold since the bishop who'd been her father's nemesis had retired), what her plans for the summer were (undecided), each reply was greeted with big smiles and cries of rapturous delight as if Verity had entertained them all by balancing her plate on her nose like a performing seal or broken into a pitch-perfect rendition of 'My Heart Will Go On'. She had done neither of those things. She was just a girl sitting in front of a group of comparative strangers insisting that she and Johnny were just good friends.

And where was Johnny while Verity was being gently interrogated? He was pacing up and down at the bottom of the long, lushly green garden, phone clamped to his ear.

'Johnny is such a wonderful man,' one of the women, Lisa, said when she saw where Verity's attention had wandered. 'We've all been hoping that he'd meet an equally wonderful woman. He's been single for *years*.'

'We'd practically given up hope, hadn't we?' chirped one of the blonder women there. 'We've tried so many times to set Johnny up with so many wonderful women, but none of them stuck. And now, here you are!'

'It's early days. Very early days,' Verity insisted with a fixed smile. 'We're just taking it slowly. So slowly. I'd say we were more friends than anything else.'

'Of course you are, but he really is a great guy,' Lisa insisted and the other women agreed that Johnny was hewn from greatness as the man himself glanced over at Verity. She gave him a feeble finger waggle and wished that he were close enough that she could glare at him so he'd get the message that it was not cool to abandon your fake girlfriend within thirty seconds of introducing her to your friends. Not cool at all. 'He really deserves to be happy.'

'Oh, I think he's happy enough,' Verity mumbled and finally Johnny was finished with his call, phone back in his pocket and striding up the garden.

'Sorry. Sorry,' he called out, a rueful smile on his face. 'Didn't mean to abandon you.' He reached the group of women and stood behind Verity's chair so he could put a hand on her shoulder. Verity wanted to wriggle away but forced herself to stay still. 'I hope you haven't

96

been telling Verity all sorts of embarrassing stories about me and scaring her off.'

'They've been telling me how lovely you are.' If Verity were Nina, this would be where she'd bat her eyelashes, or if she were Posy, she'd blush prettily, but she was Verity so she just sat there with her agonised smile and wondered how she'd got herself into this mess.

'I'd be lovelier if I hadn't left you to face the Spanish Inquisition all by yourself.' Johnny smiled at the assembled company who were staring at the pair of them and making no attempt to hide their avid interest. 'Shall I take you away from all this?'

Verity didn't bother to hide her relief. 'Yes, please.' She hauled herself up from her chair then remembered her manners. 'It was so nice to meet you all.'

Verity had thought they were going. They'd already been there for what felt like hours, but as Johnny walked her through the kitchen, person after person wanted an introduction, until finally they were greeted by their host, Johnny's friend, Graham, who'd cooked Verity's scrambled eggs to non-runny perfection.

He was as tall as Johnny, his light-brown hair streaked with grey, his kind, open face half obscured by a pair of black-framed glasses. 'Johnny,' he said urgently. 'I've been hearing some crazy talk that you've only gone and got yourself a gorgeous new girlfriend. It can't be true, can it?'

Johnny sighed in a good-natured way then gently pushed Verity forward. 'This is Verity.

We're just friends. Please don't scare her off.'

'Hello, we kind of met before. Or rather you made me some scrambled eggs. They were very nice,' Verity said with as much genuine feeling as she could muster but if she was scooped up into another hug or subjected to another interrogation, she might possibly cry. Thankfully, Graham did neither, but gravely shook her hand and said that it was very nice to be formally introduced.

Maybe Johnny was as great as all his friends claimed he was, because he caught the pleading expression on Verity's face and said, 'I'm afraid we're leaving now. We've got another thing to go to.'

'The other thing,' Verity echoed vaguely as they headed down the hall.

'Don't you want to say goodbye to everyone?' Graham asked. He smiled slyly. 'I'm sure Wallis has thought of at least another fifty questions to ask Verity.'

'I expect you can make excuses for us,' Johnny said firmly.

Another three steps and they were at the door, which Graham opened for them. More farewells were exchanged — 'Yes, it was really lovely to meet you too. And you don't mind saying goodbye to everyone? Yes, I'm sure we'll see each other again' — and then freedom. Freedom! Verity practically skipped down the steps and ran up the garden path until she was back on the street and taking huge gulps of air as if she'd been trapped down a mineshaft for days.

'See? That wasn't so bad, was it?' Johnny asked as he caught up with her.

Verity was all set to tell him just how bad it was. How it had been agony for her. Absolute, untold agony. But actually had it really been *that* bad? To insist that it had been bad would mean that she was being unkind about his friends, who'd been unfailingly welcoming, even if they had asked a lot of questions.

One thing was bugging her though. 'When was the last time that you brought a woman to meet your friends?'

They were walking in the direction of Chalk Farm but Verity's question stopped Johnny in his tracks. His lips were moving, as if he were doing sums. He frowned. 'About five years. Give or take a few months. God. How can it have been that long?'

Verity stared at him discreetly from under her lashes. Checking that yes, he was still as handsome as he'd been the last time she'd looked. And the time before that and all the other times because he was so handsome, so pleasing to the eye, that she wanted to look at him rather a lot. He had good manners, good conversation, he could build houses with his bare hands and yet, he was single.

It made absolutely no sense. But then he wasn't single by choice.

Usually Verity avoided personal questions, both the asking and answering of them, but she had to know. Otherwise, there was a possibility that she might become the first person to ever die of curiosity. 'This woman . . . the woman you're in love with but you can't be together — '

'Please, Verity. Can we just not?' Johnny

99

interrupted, an awkward smile on his face to soften the blow.

But she had to. 'Has she met your friends?' Another thought grabbed hold of her. 'Is she the one you're always talking to on . . . Oh! What on earth are you doing?'

Johnny had dropped to his knees the better to seize hold of one of Verity's hands. For one awful, world-spinning moment she thought he was about to ask for her hand in marriage. 'Verity. Verity. We've come this far, met each other's friends . . . '

Immediately, Verity knew where he was going with this but this was where she jumped off the fake girlfriend train back at singleton station. 'We have and it's been fine. But we agreed that this was just a temporary measure to get said friends off our case. A one-off kind of deal — '

'But it worked so well, why stop at one weekend? I like you, I hope you like me too.' His voice seemed to falter and he looked up at Verity with eyes as greeny blue as any ocean that Peter Hardy had ever graphed.

What would Elizabeth Bennet do? Verity asked herself as she had done on many an occasion. Elizabeth Bennet would stay strong. Resolute. And possibly have something sassy to say on the subject. 'I do like you,' Verity said hurriedly because that really wasn't the point. 'But no good can come of this.'

'You're wrong. Only good could come of this. A whole summer of good,' Johnny insisted. 'I've taken it right down to the wire in RSVP-ing to all the invites I've had to weddings and fortieth

100

birthday parties because I've been dreading having to turn up on my own. Yet again. But if you agreed to be my plus one for the season, it wouldn't have to be such an ordeal. In fact, it would be the perfect solution.'

It was ridiculous. Johnny was being ridiculous, except . . . 'Do you know . . . under my bed, stuffed in a box, I have seven invites that I haven't replied to. Leaving parties and house-warmings. Engagements and thirtieth birthday parties. I never even RSVP-ed to Con's Save the Date for her wedding.' Verity sighed.

'So, let's make this a summer thing. We'll get dressed up, go to some parties, dance to some naff eighties tunes,' Johnny said cajolingly, and his reasoning might have worked on some people but Verity wasn't some people.

'Those are easily three of my least favourite activities,' Verity said with great feeling so Johnny would know what a party pooper she was. 'Look, this has been . . . I don't even know what this has been . . . Like I said yesterday, let's just quit while we're ahead.'

For someone who hated lying, Verity was already planning how she'd tell Nina and Posy that she and Johnny were over; that it was too soon after Peter Hardy to jump straight into another thing with another man. She was racking up fake relationships like they were in a closing-down sale.

'But we *are* ahead.' Johnny stood up and reached down to brush the London dirt off his jeans. The muscles in his arms rippled pleasingly and Verity was glad of the distraction. 'We've met, what is it now? Four times. So we're on the road to becoming friends. Friends who are seeing each other. Friends who are helping each other out of a tight spot. Please, Verity! We were made for each other. We're both happy to be single *and* you work in what was my mother's favourite shop, which now sells her favourite kind of novel. It's a sign.'

He obviously had Verity down as a soft touch when actually she was made of very stern stuff indeed. Now, she crossed her arms and fixed Johnny with a reproachful look. 'Did you really just play the dead mother card? Really?'

At least he had the good grace to break eye contact and shift uncomfortably where he stood. 'Oh well, I suppose I just have to resign myself to being on the singles' table with a bunch of people I have absolutely nothing in common with and nothing to do but drink away my despair. Though probably a buffet would be worse because then you have to mingle.' He shuddered and Verity shuddered too.

'I hate mingling,' she said.

'I think small talk is worse than mingling though, isn't it?' Johnny mused. 'I hate small talk even more than I hate chutney.'

Verity was quite partial to chutney herself but her feelings on small talk weren't quite so positive. 'I hate small talk more than I hate having to navigate the Hangar Lane gyratory system or people who say 'pacific' when they mean specific.'

'Although those people are deplorable,' Johnny agreed. He reached a hand towards Verity as if he were thinking about touching her in anti-small-talk solidarity. Then he glanced at her face, which was still in stern mode, and withdrew his hand. 'It's just that, we could save each other from the small talk. From people asking in concerned voices, 'So, are you seeing anyone?' From the bitter divorcees and the dodgy flatmates. From the pitying glances and the 'I just can't understand why you're still single when you've got so much going for you.' '

Verity knew exactly what Johnny was talking about. Knew and loathed it herself in equal measure. Peter Hardy had been useful for a while but only in the off-screen sense, though Merry had been desperate for Verity to hire an out-of-work actor at least once to play the part of a love-struck oceanographer. She'd even promised to pay half his fee.

But if Verity had a real imaginary boyfriend, one made of flesh and blood and very nice suits and bluey green eyes and a killer smile, she wouldn't have to go to every party on her own. She also wouldn't have to spend a considerable amount of time being introduced to spare men and making stilted conversation with them while she wished for sudden death.

'I keep forgetting about the horrors of the singles' table,' Verity muttered and as if he could tell that she was wavering, Johnny took hold of Verity's hand again, stern look be-damned.

'I have a fortieth birthday party to go to next weekend,' he said mournfully, his brow furrowed as if he'd just said he had six months to live. 'Come on, Verity! Have a heart!'

Verity did have a heart and she also had an older sister who'd threatened to seat her next to their father's curate at her own wedding. Jane Austen's Mr Collins had nothing on George, a mansplaining, manspreading menace who had already declared his intentions to make an honest woman out of one of the Love sisters. But if Verity turned up with Johnny . . .

She and Johnny would never be something, but they could be friends. Verity was absolutely fine with having friends and once you'd delegated a man to the friendzone, then nothing could ever come of it, according to Nina.

'Well . . . I suppose, a fortieth birthday party is a special occasion,' Verity remarked tremulously.

'It is.' Johnny nodded in agreement. 'Very special. Big do in the country. Marquee. Overnight stay. I'll book us separate rooms, I promise. Please, say you'll come. And then I'll return the favour. I haven't met all your friends yet, have I?'

He hadn't. He'd only met her Happy Ever After friends and her Happy Ever After adjacent friends like lovely Stefan who ran the Swedish deli in Rochester Street with his girlfriend, lovely Annika. Verity had a lot more friends than that and they were all making the transition from hooking up to coupling up and couldn't understand why Verity wasn't doing the same.

'No, you've hardly met anyone,' Verity said slowly. 'But . . . an overnight stay?' That hadn't been in the contract.

'I can get down on my knees again, if it will make any difference,' Johnny said and he was

104

already lowering himself. Verity grabbed at his arm, fingers touching warm skin and she had to ride out an unexpected and tiny quiver of delight.

'No, don't do that,' Verity said and it wasn't that small frisson of flesh on flesh that had done it, or even the horror of the singles' table, but the sudden thought that spending more time with Johnny wouldn't be horrible. In fact, it would be quite pleasant. 'Let's see how we feel after one more fake-date each, right?'

'Right,' Johnny agreed. 'Let's shake on it.'

He held out his hand and Verity had no choice but to let him wrap his fingers around hers and there was that tiny quiver again, like she was dying for the touch of a man.

Which she wasn't. She absolutely wasn't.

9

'It is very often nothing but our own vanity that deceives us.'

The next day the staff of Happy Ever After were rendered speechless at the news that Verity was going out of town in the company of a man. Though once they'd recovered from the shock, they were very supportive. Perhaps a little too supportive because Posy insisted that Verity could have the Saturday off, when Verity had hoped that Posy might refuse to release Verity from the shackles of paid employment. No such luck.

'In fact, take as many Saturdays off as you need,' Posy declared wildly, though as soon as she said it, she looked around to make sure that Nina and Tom weren't around to hear her being so generous about Verity's holiday allowance. 'Don't worry about the website orders. Me and Little Sophie can muddle through.'

'That doesn't inspire any confidence,' Verity told her. 'At least let me make you a flowchart guide on how to fulfil orders.'

'No need for that,' Posy said blithely. 'How hard can it be?'

Coming back to chaos on Monday morning would be just reward for all the lies. How Verity longed to tell Posy and Nina the awful truth but then she'd have to confess to making up Peter

Hardy. So, Verity had no choice but to continue to lie, though she did feel really guilty about it, especially as Posy and Nina were so encouraging about Verity's budding 'romance'. Although not as encouraging as her sisters had been.

'Very's going away with A Man. On a minibreak,' Merry announced to Con, Immy and Chatty, the other three Love sisters, as the five of them had assembled on Tuesday evening in front of assorted screens for a live wedding prep chat.

Verity gave Merry, who was sharing her sofa and her laptop screen, a shove. 'It's not a minibreak and I'm not going away with a man. And this is not what we're here to talk about!'

'She is,' Merry confirmed, shoving Verity back in order to hog the screen.

'You are!' Con squealed and peered closely at her phone screen so they all had a good view of the headdress and veil she'd fashioned out of kitchen roll.

'Our little girl's finally become a woman,' Immy added very condescendingly for someone who was two years younger than Verity. 'Good on you, Very!'

'So, is this the third official date? Do you think you'll sleep with him? You're meant to on a third date, aren't you?' Chatty wanted to know as Verity put her head in her hands and groaned.

'Dear God, can we please talk about centrepieces?' she pleaded.

At least Nina's support was of a practical nature.

'I'll lend you my weekend case,' she offered as soon as she heard of Verity's plans. 'It's vintage.

Looks much more expensive than it was and remind me to show you how to do a smoky eye.'

It didn't take long though for Verity to feel less burdened by guilt. It was about the same time as Nina started to refer to Verity's brief jaunt to the country as 'your dirty weekend'.

'It's not a dirty weekend,' Verity kept repeating wearily. Oh so wearily. 'It's one night away from London.'

'It's a third date, isn't it? You have to sleep with him if it's a third date. It's industry standard,' Nina shouted, because she was on the till in the shop while Verity was in the back office so all their customers were able to hear Verity's personal business.

'You said fifth date if there were extenuating circumstances,' Posy reminded Nina. 'Verity's a vicar's daughter, surely that counts as an extenuating circumstance.'

'What number date did you sleep with Peter Hardy, oceanographer?' Tom called from across the shop floor where he was restocking the new-release shelves. 'Although I have to say that I never really got the sense that you and Peter Hardy, oceanographer, were that committed.'

'Shut up everybody and get on with your work,' was Verity's only comeback but Nina was still speculating about possible third-date sexual activity ('You don't have to go the whole hog, I suppose, but at least half the hog. Oral sex seems only polite, doesn't it?') and Tom was still theorising on the absence and indeed the existence of Peter Hardy ('Very convenient that he's out of the picture but I suppose that's the upside of dating then dumping an oceanographer') the day that Wallis swept into the shop.

It was an exceedingly rare occasion as Verity was on the till. Only under duress and only to cover Nina's lunch break and only because she continued to feel guilty that she was taking advantage of Posy's good nature.

'I've tracked you down!' Wallis announced triumphantly as she approached Verity, who waved feebly. Tom was the only other staff member in the shop and Verity was sure he was earwigging as Wallis leaned over the counter to clutch hold of Verity's hand. 'I'm so pleased you and Johnny are seeing each other. Isn't he lovely? We all think he's lovely.'

'He seems very nice,' Verity said gamely.

'And I'm so pleased that you're coming to Lawrence's fortieth this weekend: you can meet everybody,' Wallis continued as she gazed around the shop. She had to be on her own lunch hour because she was wearing a beautifully cut grey trouser suit, her streaked blonde hair pinned back. Johnny had said she was a barrister. 'You know, my chambers are just round the corner on the other side of High Holborn, but I had no idea this place existed. It's so charming.'

Verity didn't have time to extol the charms of Happy Ever After. 'So that wasn't everybody on Sunday?' she squeaked.

'Not even half of everybody. It's June and so many people leave London for the summer, don't they?' Wallis smiled. 'Lucky them. Not like us wage slaves. You know, now that I am here, I might as well browse. I still need to get a gift for

Rich and Carlotta's wedding. You'll be going to that too, won't you?'

'Oh, I don't know. It's very hard to get the time off. So busy. Summer. Tourists. Rushed off our feet.' Verity wasn't even capable of full sentences in her fear of having to meet *everybody*. At least she wouldn't have to attend the unknown Rich and Carlotta's wedding at some point in the future. One more date each, that was the deal and by God, she wasn't going to be persuaded otherwise.

'But didn't Posy say that you could take any Saturday off that you wanted?' Tom helpfully reminded Verity. Inevitably he and Nina had found out about that and were furious about it. 'Posy, she's the owner, she's very supportive of Verity's love life. We all are. I'm Tom, by the way. We have some beautiful pieces in our display cabinet over there, perfect for gifts, let me show you.'

Tom stepped towards them, a rare smile on his usually quite stern face. As he put his hand on Wallis's elbow to guide her across the room, she glanced back at Verity and fluttered her eyelashes. Verity couldn't see it herself but Tom was like bookseller catnip to any customer over the age of thirty.

That had been Thursday and now it was Saturday morning and Verity was being driven through the outskirts of North London in Johnny's car. Because he had a car that he could drive because he was a fully functioning, fully employed, fully paid grown-up. None of Verity's London friends had cars or could see the need for one. Except Sebastian and he was as rich as God. Probably richer.

'There's no need to look quite so anxious. We're getting out of London. The sun's shining. The champagne will be flowing. It's all good,' Johnny said, with a sidelong glance at the passenger seat where Verity was white-knuckling her seatbelt.

Merry had given her a similar pep talk the night before when she'd come round to drop off the posh frock that they both had a fifty per cent share in. She'd also drawn a diagram on a Post-it note and stuck it on the fridge.

There *was* something magical about how big and blue the sky was as the rows and rows of shops and streets full of houses gave way to open green fields with sheep and cows grazing or studded with the brilliant yellow of rape-seed, then the sudden stench of manure filled the car so they had to hastily roll up the windows.

Johnny had switched on the radio, a gentle panel show on Radio Four, so they didn't have to talk but still they guessed at answers to the quiz, arguing, even laughing.

Verity always felt she could breathe easier in the countryside. When Johnny drove them off the motorway, said he knew a place where they could stop for lunch, which turned out to be a village pub that looked as if it was often used as a location for a bucolic country inn in period dramas, Verity even suggested that they go for a walk first to stretch their legs.

Maybe she was just trying to delay having to meet *everybody*, but there was something about a country lane that sent Verity's soul soaring; the sound of birdsong and scent of wildflowers in the air. She didn't even mind having a companion on her walk, especially as Johnny was glued to his phone, though the constant beep of his message alerts made Verity grind her teeth.

Yet when they did talk over a ploughman's lunch, cheddar and pickles so sharp that they both winced then sighed in delight, it was much more stilted than their previous conversations.

'How are your four sisters?' Johnny asked and Verity, sure that Johnny didn't want to know about kitchen-roll wedding veils or Chatty and Immy's thoughts on the third-date rule, could only say that they were fine.

Then Verity enquired after Johnny's architecture practice and his father and both of them were fine too. Verity could feel her mouth go dry and her heart start to thud and flutter as she tried desperately to think of something to say.

Alas, the words proved elusive.

'Oh, I haven't told you anything about Lawrence, have I?' Johnny finally said, as easily as if the last fifteen minutes hadn't been at all hellish and awkward. 'He's the birthday boy. Well, I say boy but he's going to be forty, though in my head he's forever seventeen.'

Johnny went on to explain that Lawrence had been a few years above him at a smart London day school; captain of the cricket team while Johnny had been a plucky young midfielder. At Lawrence's eighteenth birthday party, Johnny had been dared to climb out on the roof, got stuck between two chimney pots and had to be rescued by the fire brigade.

'So, if anyone suggests a game of truth and dare tonight, don't let me pick dare,' he pleaded with Verity.

'Though maybe picking dare might be a safer option than choosing truth,' she pointed out. 'What with us being elbow deep in subterfuge and all.'

'Like agents on a secret mission.' Johnny frowned. 'Though I suppose all agents' missions are secret or what would be the point?'

When they got back in the car for the second leg of the journey, Johnny kept Verity entertained with tales of his misspent youth. Of teenage drinking and lusting after girls from the neighbouring school and congregating in Camden Town for house parties and picnics on Primrose Hill. It all sounded very exotic to Verity whose teenage years hadn't been at all misspent. Once Con had managed to persuade a boy called Tim to take

113

her to the cinema, but he hadn't made it past Our Vicar.

'Farv opened the door, took one look at Tim, who wasn't exactly blessed of face, and quoted Corinthians chapter one, verse thirteen at him: 'If I can speak in the tongues of men and even of angels, but have not love, I am only a noisy gong or a clanging cymbal.' Then Tim turned tail and ran and that was the very last time a boy ever came to the house, unless they were delivering stuff for the church jumble sale for their parents,' Verity told Johnny, who whistled under his breath.

They were cruising along B roads overhung with heavy branches, hedgerows and fields a pleasant green blur; through small villages, each one more picturesque than the last, until they arrived at their destination. Oakham Mount had everything one could want in a village. A village green, a general store and a church, which Verity dated as Medieval, though it had been badly renovated during the mid-Victorian age when they'd added some Gothicky bits and bobs, which really did it no favours. She and her sisters had spent a sizeable part of their school holidays being dragged round churches by Our Vicar and her head was stuffed full of knowledge about naves and fonts and lych gates that would never leave her.

The village also had an extremely well-appointed pub, The Kimpton Arms, gaily bedecked with hanging baskets as befitted an establishment that had come second runner-up in 'Britain's prettiest public house' for three

114

years running, according to the chalkboard outside. Johnny pulled into the car park.

'This is us,' he said casually, like it was no big deal. 'I thought you'd be more comfortable here than staying in Lawrence's house or in the grounds, apparently they've hired some yurts . . .'

'Here's fine,' Verity assured him, because yurts sounded a lot like camping and there'd been a lot of sleeping in tents during those childhood summers of being dragged round every church in the country. 'I'm not a big fan of waking up with a slug in my hair.'

'Good, good.' Johnny climbed out of the car and before Verity could even get her seatbelt undone, he was opening the passenger-side door for her. 'Let me get your bags for you.'

You couldn't fault his manners, Verity thought to herself as she followed Johnny and her bags into The Kimpton Arms. Or his shoulders. He had good shoulders.

There were greeted immediately by the man serving behind the bar. 'Call me Kenneth,' he said when Johnny explained who they were. 'Or mine host, whichever you prefer. Let me go and find my good lady wife.'

Linda, Kenneth's good lady wife, had a perm and a steely glint in her eyes that Verity recognised as belonging to a woman who was clearly a stalwart on every committee that Oakham Mount had to offer. She ushered them through a side door and up some stairs.

'Normally we don't like guests coming and going at all hours but as you're here for Mr

115

Lawrence's party, we can make an exception, though we would like you back at eleven thirty at the very latest,' she said in a resolute voice. Verity didn't doubt that she'd lock them out if they returned after curfew. 'I do need my beauty sleep, after all.'

'Oh, I'm sure that you'd still be just as beautiful without it,' Johnny said with just a hint of a drawl that made Verity look at him nervously and Linda simper as she opened a door.

'Our best room,' she said with a flourish. 'Comes with en suite. Though the shower is a law unto itself. Enjoy your stay!'

Then she was gone in a cloud of Rive Gauche. Verity turned to Johnny, her hands on her hips. 'Their nicest room. *Room*. You said . . .' She scrolled back to what Johnny had said when he'd begged her to come to this party with him against her better judgement. 'You said you'd book us separate rooms.'

'I did. I intended to but they only had one room left and it is a twin.' Johnny held out his hands to indicate the two single beds, both of them trussed up with all manner of floral encumbrances from pillows and valances to an alarming number of scatter cushions. 'I thought if I told you, then you wouldn't come.'

In romance novels, of which Verity had read more than her fair share, it was a common occurrence — you could almost call it a cliche — for the hero and heroine to find themselves booked into one room, with no other accommodation available. It didn't matter whether it were a Regency coaching inn or a modern five-star hotel; it happened all the time.

Then other things would happen too. Maybe a murderous intruder would be foiled so emotions would be running high. Or there might be a raging storm outside and the heroine would have a mortal fear of thunder and lightning and would need to snuggle against the hero in her terror instead of manning up. Alcohol would be consumed. A negligee or towel would slip down a few crucial centimetres revealing either a tantalising glimpse of cleavage or pert bottom.

To cut a long romance short, when a man and a woman were thrown together in one hotel room, passionate love-making was sure to follow.

But not here. Not today. No thank you.

'Too right I wouldn't have come,' Verity told Johnny crossly. 'We can't share a room. I hardly know you and even if I did, I still wouldn't share a room with you.'

'Honestly Verity, you don't have anything to worry about,' Johnny said coolly enough to douse any fevered fantasies Verity might or might not be having. 'I have absolutely no intention of making a pass at you and I really hope you're not going to make a pass at me.'

Verity was saved from having to snap, 'In your dreams!' by Johnny's phone ringing. It hadn't rung or beeped at all during the latter part of their journey, which had to be some kind of record for the short time that Verity had known him. Now Johnny glanced down at the screen and his features tightened.

'I have to get this,' he said, opening the door of the en suite. 'Darling, does this mean you're not still mad . . . ' Verity heard him say before he shut the door behind him.

It was his other woman. The woman he was desperately in love with to the exclusion of all other women. The woman he couldn't be with for some mysterious reason that he absolutely did *not* want to talk about. The woman whose existence meant that he could share a twin room that looked like an explosion in a Past Times closing-down sale, with a woman who wasn't The One, and no funny business would happen. Not even if Verity paraded around in her lingerie, not that she had any lingerie, just matching bras and pants from M&S.

Anyway, Verity didn't want any funny business to happen either, so it was just as well that she wasn't Johnny's sort, as he was at great pains to point out at every available opportunity. So, what harm would it do to sleep in the same room together? No harm. No harm at all.

Mind made up and only slightly regretful that life wasn't even a little bit like a romance novel, though being the sort of woman who drove men to giddy heights of passion would be quite annoying and very time-consuming, Verity unpacked her case.

By the time Johnny exited the bathroom, a hangdog expression on his face that Verity was getting to know very well, she was changed (hurriedly, behind the ajar door of the wardrobe) into her shared posh party outfit, a sixties-style black and white polka-dot shift dress.

'I'm so sorry,' Johnny murmured in a way that was also becoming very familiar. He caught

Verity's eye in the mirror where she was attempting to do her make-up as per Nina's instructions. 'I had to take that call. Now, look about the room . . . '

'I'm OK about sharing the room,' Verity said, her voice strained as she was trying to do a smoky eye and talk at the same time. 'You've made it perfectly clear, on more than one occasion, that you don't have designs on me.'

'I'm not saying you're unattractive because you are,' Johnny quickly assured her. 'Attractive that is, but even so I would never — '

'It's all immaterial because you're in love with another woman,' Verity said rather shriekily because she wanted to end this agonising conversation as quickly as humanly possible. 'And I've sworn off any kind of intimate relationship ever again.'

Johnny's eyebrows shot up. 'Really? Because I did wonder why you were so resolutely single.'

'There's no big mystery. Some people are happier on their own and I'm one of them.' Verity narrowly avoided jabbing herself in the eye with her mascara brush in her alarm. 'Are you ready? What time do we need to be there?'

10

*'The more I see of the world, the more am I
dissatisfied with it; and everyday confirms
my belief of the inconsistency of all human
characters.'*

It was a short stroll from The Kimpton Arms,
through the village then left to crunch up a
gravel drive.

Verity had been worried that Lawrence, the
birthday boy, and his wife Catriona, would live in
some huge stately pile not dissimilar to Downton
Abbey, but the pretty detached house was large
enough that it had probably once been home to
some local swell — a doctor or solicitor — but
certainly not one of the landed gentry.

Even so, they followed the sound of music and
a trail of balloons round the side of the house
and unlatched a gate to a garden that was less a
garden and more several acres of land.

'I guess we should head for the big tent,'
Johnny said. There was a huge white marquee in
the middle of the lawn, people milling about
outside its entrance, children in their best party
outfits chasing each other around its perimeter.
There were also grumpy-looking teenagers
pressed into waiter service bobbing about with
trays of drinks.

Verity looked longingly at the champagne on
offer, but she had to pace herself. It was only five

o'clock and with curfew at eleven thirty, they could be here for over six hours. She didn't want to be steaming drunk before it was even dark, not that she'd ever been steaming drunk but now really wasn't the time for that kind of voyage of personal discovery.

As they got nearer to the tent, Verity realised that all eyes were upon them. Even people who weren't actually looking at them were quickly nudged, words whispered in their ears, so they swivelled around too. It was a lot like the scene in every Western that Verity had ever seen (which admittedly wasn't that many) when the new sheriff walked into the saloon in a godless frontier town and everything went silent.

However, from inside the marquee a band murdering 'Music to Watch Girls By' played on and a short, jolly-looking man detached himself from the throng and waved. 'Johnny! Whoever let you in?'

'That's Lawrence,' Johnny muttered for Verity's benefit and then he tried to take her hand but she flexed her fingers away.

'I'm not a very touchy person,' she explained in a whisper.

'Oh, I am. Touchy. Tactile. Sorry,' he whispered back then he opened his arms wide as they reached Lawrence who also spread his arms and then they were hugging each other and slapping each other on the back in that hearty way that men did because they were just as uncomfortable with touching each other as Verity was with touching anyone.

'I've missed your ugly mug!' Lawrence said as

they detached themselves. 'In fact, I think you're even uglier than you were last time I saw you.'

'And you have even less hair than you did a few months ago.' Johnny grinned and ruffled Lawrence's luxuriant mop of thick dark hair. 'You're practically bald.'

'Can't understand how someone with a face like yours has managed to persuade such a pretty young lady to spend time in your company. Are you having to pay her?' Lawrence asked teasingly. He was ruddy cheeked and had a good-natured face, a ready smile, so Verity doubted there was malicious intent behind his words even as Johnny sucked in a shocked breath.

'I'm not a paid escort, I just quite like spending time in Johnny's company even though he isn't much to look at, is he?' It was one of only three times in her entire life that Verity had ever managed to say something vaguely witty at the right time. 'I'm Verity, by the way.'

'I'm Lawrence and I can immediately tell that you are far, far too good for the likes of him,' Lawrence said and he took Verity's hand and kissed it and now really wasn't the time to tell anyone else that she really wasn't a touchy-feely kind of person.

Over the course of the next hour, Verity was hugged and had her hands held and her cheeks kissed by what felt like every person in attendance. Her face ached from smiling as she was reintroduced to all the people that she'd met at the brunch the Sunday before and newly introduced to everybody else.

Verity knew that if she felt uncomfortable, then it was more to do with her lamentable social skills, and very little to do with the warm way she was welcomed into the fold of Johnny's friends. They were unfailingly polite and accommodating but also relentless in their curiosity. Verity couldn't count how many times she had to recite verbatim the account of how she and Johnny had both been stood up at the same restaurant. Every time she did, the reaction was the same. 'About time,' his friends would say or words to that effect. 'If ever a man deserved the love of a good woman, it's our Johnny.'

Verity and Johnny weren't in love and she certainly wasn't a good woman, not when she was currently defrauding all his friends, so it was a huge relief when he finally detached her from the crowd gathered around them.

'Come on, let's find a little quiet spot,' Johnny said, after they'd filled their plates from a groaning buffet table. Verity was sure that she was looking a little exhausted, a little wild around the eyes, at being the centre of attention for so long. 'It's been quite full-on.'

'There has been a lot of new people,' Verity admitted. 'I couldn't even tell you half their names.'

'Luckily for you, I know a secret path through the shrubbery,' Johnny said and he suddenly disappeared through a gap in the hedge. 'Come on!'

Verity followed Johnny down a little meandering trail bordered by manicured bushes that came out by a pond where fat, exotically coloured fish swam lazily about. Past the pond was a pretty summerhouse painted mint green and hung with bunting and on its porch (because it was a big enough summerhouse to merit a porch) was a wooden bench.

Verity couldn't help the huge sigh of relief as she sat down. Not only could she rest her feet, which were aching from being hoisted into a wedge sandal after months of flat shoes, but she could rest her mouth too. Just be quiet. Not say a word or have a word spoken to her.

'So, that was — ' Johnny began but Verity held up a hand in protest.

'Not another word!' she begged. 'Please . . . just for a few minutes.'

Johnny shot her a slightly offended look but stayed silent as they picked their way through the food on their plates, drank their champagne and listened to the faint sound of the band playing down the other end of the garden, accompanied by birds singing as they made the most of the evening sun.

It was lovely and Verity felt as if she could breathe again. All too soon though, Johnny clinked his empty glass against hers. 'Permission to speak?' he asked with a hint of amusement.

'Permission granted,' Verity decided reluctantly.

'We should probably go back into the fray,' he said. 'We've caused such a stir that they're bound to notice that we're missing. I expect there'll be lots of sly comments about getting up to no good in the rose bushes.'

As they retraced their steps back to the house,

it was Verity's phone that beeped first. How's it going? Merry wanted to know.

It wasn't going badly, not by any stretch of the imagination, but as everyone had turned to look at them again as they stepped through the patio doors into a large conservatory, Verity felt sure that the second part of the Inquisition was about to start.

She didn't really have the words so she settled for emoji instead.

'I think they're about to make speeches,' Johnny said and that was fine with Verity because if people were making speeches, then no one was going to try and speechify with her.

They stood at the back of the room as Lawrence's younger brother toasted the birthday boy with a lot of rugby club banter (the word 'scrotum' was mentioned several times) that had Verity wincing in a couple of places. She was saved from having to give the speech her full attention, by Merry texting her back.

Am perturbed by your uncharacteristic use of emojis. Is it really that bad? How much have you had to drink? Perhaps you should drink some more? Could borrow Dougie's mum's car if really that awful and come and rescue you.

It was a tempting thought but really it wasn't even halfway to being *that* awful, Verity decided. She didn't often take Merry's advice but as a waiter came into her orbit with a tray of drinks,

Verity grabbed another glass of champagne and one for Johnny too.

'For the toasts,' she said, because she was meant to be his girlfriend and she could absolutely do this and not be such a wet weekend about it.

The speeches went on forever. Long enough for Verity to drink another two glasses of champagne. Not enough to be drunk, just enough for the world to become soft focus and when Johnny left her side when his phone rang and he just had to 'take this very important call' she was quite happy to hang out with the North London contingent of Johnny's friends. Wallis had told them all about her visit to Happy Ever After and for a while Verity fielded enquiries about working in a shop that only sold romantic novels, which quickly segued into a quite thrilling conversation about which was the best adaptation of *Pride and Prejudice*, which was obviously the BBC version and not the awful sham that featured Keira Knightley simpering and Matthew Macfadyen in a truly terrible wig.

'Colin Firth emerging from a lake in a white shirt, which clings damply to his chest, I rest my case,' Verity said as she'd said many times before because this was a conversation she often had with her sisters and Posy and Nina, and Verity never failed to be surprised that there were women unmoved by the sight of a young Colin Firth in a damp shirt.

Verity had had worse Saturday nights than this. In fact, she realised, she was actively enjoying herself. Whoever would have thought it?

But as talk turned to a new TV series that everyone was watching, she was happy to murmur, 'Excuse me' and retreat to the loo.

She'd have liked to have stayed there for a few minutes just to gather and regroup, but mindful that there was a queue of women outside, Verity took thirty seconds to assure herself that she was OK, she still had some charge left in her batteries, and it was just gone nine now so they only had to stay another two hours, then they could go back to the pub.

Because it was past nine and the champagne had been flowing like fizzy pop, most people had passed pleasantly buzzed and were rapidly heading towards drunk. Back in the marquee, there was a lot of dad dancing going on. As Verity moved through the tent trying to find Johnny, she suddenly felt quite lost and alone, as if she didn't have as much charge left in her battery as she thought she had.

She wandered back out into the garden. The sun was sinking behind the trees, which were strewn with paper lanterns so Verity could see quite clearly that Johnny was nowhere to be found. She decided to retrace their footsteps; to find the gap in the hedge and from there, the pond and the summerhouse, but before she could, Verity heard unsteady footsteps behind her then an even unsteadier voice.

'Yoo hoo! Johnny's lady friend! Stop! I need to talk to you!'

Verity cast her eyes to the heavens then turned round. She'd been introduced to the woman earlier but back then the woman's blonde hair

127

hadn't been so tousled, her mint-green lace dress not quite so rumpled, her tasteful pinky nude lipstick not so smudged. 'I'm so sorry.' Verity winced. 'I can't remember your name. There's been so many new faces and . . . '

'Oh, never mind that!' Verity was suddenly yanked forward so she almost fell face first into the other woman's cleavage. As it was she was folded into a sticky, warm embrace. Verity barely had time to tense every muscle before she was thrust away, the other woman keeping hold of Verity's upper arms so she couldn't get away. 'I just wanted to say thank God for you. Johnny is such a lovely man, I tried to have a crack at him myself when we were younger, but he was already head over heels in love with *her*. Can you believe that he's wasted all that time being in love with *her*?'

'*Her*?' Verity ventured, though taking advantage of a very drunk woman to get some information on Johnny's mystery woman was wrong. Wrong but also impossible to resist.

'*Her!*' the woman confirmed. 'Actually, I probably shouldn't be mentioning this to you, of all people, but you know, right? Johnny and you have had the talk, haven't you? It must be pretty serious if he wants you to meet *everybody*. All this time and the pair of them thought that nobody knew but I knew and it was such a strain pretending that I didn't. You can't imagine what an ordeal it's been for me. That love triangle was old when we were at Cambridge. Now it's positively geriatric.'

So much information to take in; Verity could

128

feel something short-circuiting in her brain. 'Exactly what love triangle are you talking about?' she asked.

The woman gave a hollow laugh. 'It's such a cliché isn't it, when a woman comes between two good friends? But when Johnny went to the States after his mother died, we all thought it was over. I mean, it *was* over, she married Harry, forgodsakes. Then Johnny came back and it all started up again. I only know because I saw the two of them with my own eyes, these eyes . . . ' The woman pointed at her bloodshot eyes in case Verity was in any doubt over which eyes she was talking about. 'Johnny was going out with a wonderful woman at the time, an architect like him, but that didn't last and no wonder when I saw him and Madam holding hands in the bar of the Stafford Hotel in Mayfair. And since then? He hasn't dated anyone else and now he turns up with you. I really should hug you again. Everyone thinks you're a cracking girl.'

There was still so much to unpick. 'Really? They do?'

'Of course they do, because you are,' Johnny said from behind Verity and she froze, as if her insides had suddenly turned to ice.

11

'You may ask questions which I shall not choose to answer.'

Verity dared to turn and look at Johnny who simply raised his eyebrows at her and smiled a bland sort of smile so it was impossible to know what he was thinking — or how much he may have overheard.

He took a couple of steps forward so he was at Verity's side. 'Julia, I think Matthew is looking for you,' he said in a mild voice to match his smile.

Julia nodded. 'He probably is. Just as well he's driving us home.' She staggered uncertainly for a moment. 'It's the first time in seven years that I haven't been pregnant or breastfeeding and I think I've overdone it on the champagne.'

Verity and Johnny took an arm each so they could guide Julia back up the garden, through the house and to the entrance hall where a harried-looking fair-headed man stood jiggling his car keys.

'Oh Julia, I knew this was going to happen,' he said sorrowfully when he spotted Verity and Johnny's lurching cargo. 'You're going to feel absolutely rotten tomorrow and my mother's coming to lunch.'

'Bloody hell,' Julia exclaimed as she tottered towards her partner. 'Shall I phone her now and tell her not to bother?'

'Best not to. She still hasn't forgiven you for what you said last Christmas.'

'Well, she did provoke me and her stuffing *was* dry . . .'

Julia and what sounded like the long-suffering Matthew disappeared down the drive.

Johnny looked at his watch. 'It's gone ten. Do you want to go back to the pub? By the time we say our goodbyes, we should just be back before curfew.'

Verity nodded but didn't move. 'Instead of saying goodbye . . . can't we just ghost?'

Johnny frowned. 'Ghost?'

'You know, the French exit. The Irish goodbye. We just disappear without having to spend an hour telling everyone we're about to disappear.' Verity was done now. She was out of juice. Fading fast. No reserves left. Having to stay for another hour with a smile pinned on her face while Johnny's friends, all pissed now, made jokes about the two of them and what they'd do when they were alone, was more than she could handle.

As it was, if they did ghost, everyone would draw their own conclusions anyway and imagine that they'd sneaked off to have sex, which was hilarious given the circumstances.

'Isn't that a little rude?' Johnny asked and maybe it was, but it wasn't as rude as getting Verity to agree to a fake relationship without telling her exactly what she was getting herself into.

'I have a headache,' Verity said and it wasn't a

lie. She could feel the telltale throb at her temples that she always got when people were trying to make her have fun against her will. 'I need quiet time.'

'Oh well, I'd hate to deprive you of quiet time . . . '

As luck would have it they met Lawrence as they started down the drive so Johnny could tell him they were going and Verity could thank him for a fantastic party and they were back at The Kimpton Arms before Ken could call last orders. Verity left Johnny in the bar exchanging pleasantries as she escaped upstairs.

Someone had been in their room to turn down the beds and leave a Ferrero Rocher on each of their pillows, which was an unexpected treat.

Verity longed for a bath, but Johnny would be up soon and it would feel weird to be naked on the other side of the door from him. Though actually, everything felt weird, Verity decided as she had the quickest shower she'd had since she'd left home and not had four sisters demanding entry to the bathroom, or running the tap in the kitchen to make the water go cold and evict her that way.

By the time Johnny did knock on the door of their room, Verity was in stripy pyjamas, in bed, covers pulled up to her neck. She was hitting every romantic novel cliché out of the park this evening. Certainly she was as nervous as a virginal debutante marooned with a sardonic stranger at a remote country inn as she granted Johnny leave to enter in a breathy voice.

Johnny came into the room, gave her a wary

132

smile and headed straight for the bathroom.

Verity could hear him brush his teeth then gargle and spit mouthwash. Water running. Rummaging in his shower bag. Everyday sounds suddenly turned into an intrusion because they were coming from a stranger.

A man she'd met only a couple of weeks ago. Had seen him a handful of times since then, knew a handful of facts about him (Cambridge, architect) but really she knew nothing about him at all. And now there were so many things she wanted, *needed*, to know.

'So, exactly who was Julia talking about?' Verity asked as soon as Johnny came out of the bathroom. He was wearing boxer shorts and a T-shirt and Verity averted her eyes from the sight of his long, lean legs. How Verity wished that she could be blase and light-hearted and treat this situation as a series of amusing anecdotes to entertain her sisters with.

Johnny folded up the clothes he'd been wearing, placed them on a chair then got into bed. Had he not heard her or was he simply determined to ignore her?

'Light off?' he asked. She murmured her assent and the room was plunged into darkness.

Verity was never going to be able to sleep. Not now, when her tenseness had upgraded to locked muscles and a thumping headache. She was going to have to turn the light back on and get out of bed to take a couple of tablets and . . .

'Julia was talking about the love of my life.' Or maybe Verity would stay right where she was to hear Johnny's whispered confession. 'It's too bad that she married my best friend.'

'Your best friend?' Verity confirmed in a hoarse whisper.

'Yup.' Johnny popped the *p*. 'We had a fight, I went to the States and she married him on the rebound. *He* was the rebound guy. Anyway, that's why we can't be together.'

'She can't get a divorce then?' Verity believed in the sanctity of marriage — she was a vicar's daughter after all — but she also believed that if two people were unhappy being married to each other then there should be a get-out clause.

Johnny sighed so loudly that Verity expected Linda to suddenly bang on the door and ask them to keep it down. 'No,' he said. 'It's very complicated.'

'Why? Are they Catholic?'

'No.' The word was dragged out of him.

'So, they've had children? Right, yeah, that would make it complicated.'

'No, no children.'

Verity really didn't see what the problem was then. Unless Merry's crackpot theory had been on the money . . . 'Oh dear, has she got a terminal illness . . . ?'

'No!' It sounded like Johnny was about to snap.

Verity upgraded her headache from thumping to pounding. 'Haven't you ever thought that it might be easier to call it quits and find someone else? Someone who wasn't married?'

'Why would I want to date anyone else? My heart already belongs to her.' He didn't sound very happy about this ownership of his heart or

134

maybe he was annoyed with Verity for refusing to let the subject drop but she was finding it very hard to understand the specifics.

'So, are you two sleeping together then?' Verity decided it was best to get right to the nub of the matter. Because Johnny was using a lot of fancy words but it still meant he was having an affair with a married woman, no matter how much he tried to dress it up.

For a moment Verity was sure she could feel Johnny glaring at her in the darkness.

'No.' He packed an entire afternoon into the 'no', it was that drawn out. Also, a little exasperated. 'What we have . . . it's not about sex. If I wanted sex that badly, then it's easy enough to go out and pick up a woman who also wants to get laid with no promises, no strings attached. End up in bed together for a night of meaningless sex that satisfies you at the time, scratches the itch, but then leaves you feeling just as empty as you were before.'

His voice. It was a voice that would have Tom Hiddleston suing for copyright infringement, and it was talking about sex, no-strings sex, which always seemed like it would be more abandoned, more hanging-from-the-light-fittings than other kinds of sex, and it was making Verity feel all sorts of things. Things which made her squirm, her body becoming heavier, languid, as she pictured Johnny in some dive-bar giving sultry looks and a seductive half smile to a woman then taking her back home, both of them kissing and grinding against each other as soon as the front door shut behind them, tugging at

135

each other's clothes so they could be naked, free, Johnny's lean body on top . . .

That was quite enough of that! Verity snapped on the light, eyes screwed shut against its brightness, but also so she wouldn't have to look at Johnny. 'Headache,' she bit out. 'I need tablets.'

It was quite the feat to get from bed to bathroom with her eyes shut but Verity managed it, though she did get intimate with the Corby trouser press at one point. She lurked in the bathroom for a while after she'd taken a couple of ibuprofen, in the hope that Johnny might be asleep, but when she felt brave enough to sidle back into the bedroom, he was awake. Worse than awake; he was sitting up, arms folded, eyes fixed on Verity as she quickly shuffled back to her own bed.

'I didn't realise that this weekend arrangement meant that we had to bare our souls to each other. It's only fair that it's your turn now,' he said baldly. 'So, what's your story? Why have you sworn off dating?'

Verity had her back to him as she climbed into bed so she could grimace to her heart's content that suddenly it was her romantic lifestyle choices, or lack of them, that was up for debate.

'I told you, I'm too busy for dating.'

'I don't believe you,' Johnny said and Verity couldn't bear doing this any other way than under cover of darkness, so she turned off her bedside lamp again.

It was hard to put it into words. To explain it to someone who wasn't family, hadn't known or

136

worked with Verity long enough to understand her foibles, her funny little ways.

'Well,' she said. 'Well, the thing is that, it sounds so melodramatic when I say it out loud, but the best way to explain it is . . . I'm an introvert.'

There was a pause. 'When you say you're an introvert, what exactly do you mean?' Verity could hear the doubt and scepticism in Johnny's voice that she'd heard many times before, usually from people just before they said, 'God, you talk a hell of a lot for an introvert.'

'It's not that I'm shy, not really, or that I hate people, because I don't, it's more that I find the world noisy and exhausting. Like, when I'm put into a new situation or meet too many people, after a short time, I can feel myself shutting down. Like a computer that's got too many browser windows open.'

She sighed at the thought of browser windows. It was Verity's unhappy lot in life to exist in an age of technology. 'The world is such a noisy place. There are car alarms and shop alarms, sirens blaring, even the self-service tills in the supermarket get uppity and insist that there's an unexpected item in my bagging area when there absolutely isn't.'

From across the room Johnny chuckled. 'That's true enough.'

'And then there are people. So many people, every single one of them without filters or indoor voices.' Verity was on a roll now. 'Having to express every single last thought that comes to them. I can't even go for a restorative walk in a

137

park without someone having a loud conversation on their phone, or listening to music on their phone and assuming that the rest of the world wants to hear it too. There's only so much I can take!

'I have to work because I don't have a trust fund,' Verity continued as she neared the end of her long, rambling rant about how noisy modern life was. 'I have a very large, very loud family that I love, I have friends too but dating, a boyfriend, it's just too much.'

Johnny didn't say anything for a while as if he were having trouble processing all this information. 'Why is having a boyfriend too much?'

'Because if I'm dating then I will never have enough time for myself,' Verity said a little desperately. 'And the thing is, I don't miss dating or boyfriends. Holding hands and hugging is really not my jam but it's not even the touching, it's being intimate with someone emotionally, I can't do that. It's *exhausting*. I suppose I think of myself as an island, really.'

'And do your four sisters think you're an island too?'

'No, they think that when the right person comes along, everything will magically slot into place.'

'You never know, it might,' Johnny said as if he hadn't listened to a single word that she'd said. 'You must have had boyfriends in the past?'

'Of course I have!' Verity said indignantly, because her singledom was self-enforced, not because she was and always had been repulsive to the opposite sex. Even so, it wasn't as if she'd

138

been beating off prospective suitors. For most of her teen years, she'd been one of the local vicar's five odd daughters. Maybe even the oddest. Then when she'd left home, left her sisters, it was hard enough to make friends, let alone form any romantic attachments until . . . 'I was with this guy, Adam, that I met at university for three years so it's not as if I've given up on relationships without knowing what it is that I'm giving up.'

'So, you were in love with him?' Johnny gently probed.

'Yes, I loved him,' Verity said with heat, because she could never think about Adam without becoming emotional. 'I wouldn't have spent three years with him if I didn't love him, would I?'

Three years of trying to make things work, of trying to let Adam in, to lower her guard. All that Verity had succeeded in doing was making him unhappy, seeing the light dim in his eyes every time she pushed him away.

She didn't want to be responsible for someone else's happiness — it was far too much pressure. But it was much, much worse to be responsible for someone else's unhappiness.

'So, if you've been in love then I guess you're not a misanthrope?' Johnny queried and Verity thought she could hear just a hint of amusement in his voice as if he wasn't taking her coming out as an introvert or anything that she'd just said that seriously.

'Really not. That's not what being an introvert is about. I don't want to live in a cave like a hermit and shun all human contact. I like people. There are people I love dearly but . . . just in small doses,' Verity finished, because she *was* finished. Done with this conversation. 'For example, I'm all talked out now.'

'Me too.' Verity heard Johnny shift in his bed, the sound of the pillow being thumped back into shape. 'We should probably get some sleep.'

They both mumbled goodnight. Verity had barely got comfortable when she heard the beep of Johnny's phone then his sigh as he picked it up from his nightstand.

'So, is that who you're *always* on the phone to?' she asked.

'Yeah.' Johnny was distracted. Verity stuck her head out from under the covers to see his face lit up by the screen as he replied to the text. 'I suppose you're angry that I never told you she was married but, and I mean this in the nicest possible way, it's not really any of your business.'

Verity should have been angry with him, especially for that last dig, but she was too exhausted. Even so, she was definitely a little bit cross. 'You don't think that you've made it my business?'

'Not really,' he said in an off-hand voice as he stared at his phone. 'If you hadn't bumped into Julia and she hadn't been so steaming drunk, then you'd have been none the wiser.' He looked up with a weary expression. 'I'm going to switch my phone off now until morning. Can we please try and get some sleep?'

That was precisely what Verity had been attempting to do before his infernal phone had beeped for the gazillionth time with a message from the love of his life who just happened to be married to someone else — his best friend no less. So, even if he wasn't sleeping with her, he was doing something not-quite-right with his *best friend's wife*. And yes, it was a big deal and absolutely yes, Johnny should have told her right from the start exactly why he was so in need of a fake girlfriend.

It didn't matter about the many whys and wherefores of the situation; married people were out of bounds. That was one of the most fundamental rules of being a grown-up.

12

'One cannot know what a man really is by the end of a fortnight.'

The next morning, with both of them huffy and puffy-eyed from tiredness, they drove back to London in near silence. It was that precious silence that Verity normally craved, though this silence was so loud it was practically screaming.

Finally, and it couldn't have come soon enough, Johnny was pulling into the corner of Rochester Street.

Verity scrambled to disengage her seatbelt. 'No need for you to get out too,' she said quickly. 'As long as the boot's open, I can take it from here.'

She smiled weakly at Johnny; he smiled weakly back at her, both of them embarrassed by their late-night confessions. Verity seemed to recall that at one stage she'd referred to herself as an island. Who did that? She did that, apparently.

'Look, Verity . . . ' She was already halfway out the car when Johnny spoke for the first time since they'd left the motorway at Brent Cross and he'd asked if she still wanted the air con on. 'I should have been honest with you from the start. I understand if you want to break off our arrangement, but I really hope you don't. I still owe you a fake-date.'

'It's fine. I'm fine. Honestly, everything's fine,'

Verity assured him. She finished her inelegant scramble from the car. 'I promise I'll be in touch.'

She had her fingers crossed behind her back so it wasn't a lie. Verity had done too much lying recently, starting with Peter Hardy. Peter Hardy had come with many complications but he had nothing on Johnny and his decades-long love triangle.

'So, I've decided not to see Johnny any more,' Verity told Posy the next day during their mid-morning bun break. 'Neither of us — are in the right head space for a relationship right now.'

Since Mattie had opened the tearoom, they now had a mid-morning bun break and a mid-afternoon cake stop and the waistbands on all Verity's jeans were feeling a little snug.

'That's a shame,' Posy sighed. They were sitting in the office and meant to be going through the post-launch sales figures but everything stopped for buns. 'You're definitely going to call it quits, then?'

'I think so,' Verity said as if she were still pondering the matter when she'd already decided before she'd even shut the boot of Johnny's car that she was never going to see him again. If she carried on with this fake relationship sham, then Verity was condoning Johnny's sex-free, text-heavy affair with his best friend's wife. Then there was the sheer skin-flaying embarrassment that Verity experienced when she remembered what she'd confessed in the darkness of their twin room. It was painfully obvious that she and Johnny

143

needed to stop. Quit. Never see or speak to each other ever again. Even if Verity couldn't stop thinking about how nice his arms looked in a T-shirt. 'We're not really a good fit,' she said firmly.

Posy was getting that romantic, dreamy look on her face that she so often had these last few weeks. 'Maybe you shouldn't be so quick to end things with Johnny. On paper, me and Sebastian aren't a good fit but look at us now.' Just in case Verity couldn't take the hint, Posy waved her hand in front of Verity's face so she could see the platinum wedding band and beautiful sapphire engagement ring that Sebastian had placed on her third finger.

'Quite frankly, and please don't take this the wrong way, I'm still trying to process you and Sebastian,' Verity said.

'Oh God, me too.' Posy pulled a face at her orange-and-cardamom bun. 'But this isn't about me. I think you should give Johnny another chance. Men like him don't come along too often.'

'I know that he seems handsome and charming and . . . '

' . . . has a great sense of humour. He cracked a very funny joke about P.G. Wodehouse at the tearoom opening,' Posy reminded Verity. 'Compared to Nina's latest horror show of a boyfriend, Johnny is in a class of his own.'

'I can hear every word you're saying!' Nina shouted from behind the counter. They really had to start shutting the office door. 'Gervaise is not a horror show. He's just going through stuff.'

144

Gervaise was a performance artist who described himself as sexually fluid, though as far as Verity could tell being sexually fluid simply gave him free rein to cheat on Nina with other women *and* men. Nina had finally kicked him to the kerb while Verity had been away for the weekend, only for Gervaise to turn up in the courtyard very late on Sunday night and shout up at their windows that he was going to immolate himself unless Nina took him back.

'Do you think he could immolate himself quietly?' Verity had asked.

'Oh, Very, you wouldn't understand,' Nina had said sadly. 'A life without passion is a life half-lived.' Then she'd opened the window and told Gervaise to bugger off.

Posy was right. Compared to Gervaise, Johnny was a prince among men. But still, Johnny came with so much carry-on baggage.

'I keep asking myself 'What would Elizabeth Bennet do?' ' Verity told Posy. 'And Elizabeth Bennet would definitely be too smart to — '

'Say that again!' Posy demanded.

'I didn't even get to finish saying it once before you interrupted me!'

'Never mind that, Very. What did you say about Elizabeth Bennet?'

'You know what I say about Elizabeth Bennet,' Verity reminded Posy with a touch of exasperation because sometimes it felt as if no one listened to a word she said. 'Whenever I'm faced with a difficult problem I think, 'What would Elizabeth Bennet do?' It's surprisingly helpful.'

'Well, it would be.' Posy had a glint in her eye

that Verity had come to recognise only too well over the last few weeks. ' 'What would Elizabeth Bennet do?' Genius, Verity. It would look *amazing* on a tote bag.'

'I'm not letting you order any more tote bags until we've sold at least fifty per cent of the tote bags you've already ordered,' Verity reminded her. 'But yes, when we're ready to reorder, you may use my life philosophy.'

Later that day Verity had an email from Emma, Dougie's sister, about the housewarming party she was having on Saturday night. 'I know you, Very, and I bet you're thinking of an excuse to bail out of the party. If it's any consolation, I was joking when I said I was hiring a karaoke machine. It will be a karaoke-free zone so you HAVE to come and you're not to turn up and immediately say you can't stay very long. Also, bring this Johnny that Merry's told me about. I can't wait to meet him.'

Immediately and reflexively, Verity started to think of a bulletproof way to wriggle out of this Saturday night socialising. Then she stopped and forced herself to look deep within, to even seek counsel from Elizabeth Bennet. She was a grown woman and she really shouldn't need a fake boyfriend to get her through life — she could go by herself. Also, technically, it wasn't a housewarming but a boat-warming as Emma's boyfriend Sean had inherited a dilapidated houseboat complete with mooring and Verity was curious to see their new floating living space.

So, come Saturday, Verity was more or less content to head party-wards with Merry and

146

Dougie, who had a rare Saturday night off from commis chef-ing.

They caught the bus to Great Portland Street station and then, because it was a hot, sticky July night, decided to walk through Regent's Park to get to the Regent's Canal — almost the same route that Verity had taken with Johnny to get to the brunch in Primrose Hill.

Verity hadn't heard from him since she'd got out of his car on Sunday afternoon almost a week ago. True, Verity had said that she'd be in touch but if Johnny had really been that keen to see her, to carry on their arrangement, he could just as easily have contacted Verity. He hadn't.

And Verity was fine with that. Really fine and not even a passive aggressive 'I'm *fine*.'

Meanwhile Merry was not fine with Con who was now having second thoughts about the hog roast for her wedding reception. 'If the wind's blowing the wrong way all you'll be able to smell is roasting pig,' she'd complained via Skype the previous evening even though it had been the only item on a list of roughly two hundred items that she'd reached a decision on.

Dougie's solution was to hand out shower caps in Constance's signature wedding colours ('Yeah, when Madam has decided what those signature colours are') so that people's hair wouldn't reek of hog roast.

'We have to wear hair nets at work,' he mused. 'Though that's more of a health and safety thing.'

'I'm surprised they don't make you wear a beard net too. It can't be very hygienic when you work in food services,' Verity said. Over the last few months Dougie had cultivated a luxuriant, hipster-issue beard. It had turned out far more ginger than anyone had expected and though it wasn't really long enough, Dougie liked to tug on it when he was deep in thought. Also, Merry said it was very, very scratchy when they were kissing.

Now Merry piped up: 'Very, do you think Dougie should shave his beard off?'

Verity didn't even have to think about it. 'A thousand times yes.'

'You don't think it makes me look distinguished?' Dougie asked.

'No,' Merry said wearily, as if they'd had this conversation many times before. 'It makes you look like you're hiding a weak chin. And your chin isn't weak. From what I can remember, it's very strong and manly.'

'Don't you find that you get crumbs caught in it? What happens when you eat spaghetti?' Verity peered at Dougie's facial growth to see if the remains of his breakfast were still lodged in there somewhere. His hand shot up to cover it.

'Don't gang up on me!' he protested. 'Honestly, I expected better from you, Very. You're meant to be the sensitive one.'

'She's sensitive, not blind,' Merry spluttered. 'And any fool can see that your beard does nothing for you.'

Merry and Dougie continued to bicker about his beard all the way to the Regent's Park Canal. When they got to where the *Scarlett O'Hara* (Emma loved a romantic novel as much as Verity did) was moored, it was to discover that Emma had set up a rota system for touring the vessel because there was a distinct possibility that it might capsize if there were too many people on board all at once. It didn't inspire much faith in *Scarlett's* seaworthiness so Verity and Merry decided to stay on the firm ground of the canal path until the party retired en masse to the beer garden of a nearby pub.

Verity snagged a corner table with Merry and Dougie, who had finally stopped bickering about his beard and were now arguing about whose turn it was to go to the bar.

'Or Very could go?' Dougie asked hopefully.

Merry and Verity both gave him pitying looks. 'I never go to the bar,' Very said. 'Too many people in my personal space bubble.'

'But Very always gets her round in,' Merry said loyally and Verity had just taken a twenty-pound note out of her purse when Emma and Sean arrived from locking up the boat.

'Are you all right?' Verity asked Emma, because fierce patches of red adorned her friend's cheekbones and throat. 'You're not going down with something, are you?'

'I'm all right,' Emma said and she looked at Sean and he looked at her and then they both smiled. It was a smile that was solely for each other and not for the benefit of anybody else.

Then Sean sniffed. 'I thought *Scarlett* had sprung a leak but it turned out someone had spilt their lager.'

'But we've had worse Saturdays,' Emma said and thrust out her hand. 'Look!'

There was a gorgeous antique ring on the third finger of her left hand. It was a perfect match for the smile on Emma's face. She was lit up and glowing and it was obvious why, but Sean still said, 'I asked Emma to marry me.'

'And I said, God, yes!'

It was all a blur after that. Thirty-odd people surged over to offer their congratulations and a lot of hugging. Then Merry cried because she'd introduced Emma to Sean, the cute research assistant who worked in the lab next to hers, and Verity got all choked up because Merry was crying and the assembled company decided it was so soon after payday that they could all club together to buy a few bottles of something fizzy to toast the happy news.

The giddy mood slowed down a little after the toasts but most of the girls still gathered around Emma as Merry tried on her ring for size, held it up to the light and then, rather uncharitably, said, 'Will you have an engagement party? Do we have to buy engagement presents? God, I'm going to be bankrupt before summer is over.'

Verity was going to have to have another talk with Merry about the difference between thoughts it was OK to say out loud and thoughts that it was best to keep to oneself. Then Verity caught the look that Dougie gave Merry. It was a thoughtful though slightly wary look as if Dougie might not be immediately planning on proposing to Merry but he was thinking about it. A lot.

And all of a sudden, Verity felt a pang for something she'd never known but could see on the faces of her friends. Three years ago, after a

150

disastrous minibreak in Amsterdam with Adam, when Verity had searched her soul for answers, and decided that she wasn't the loving kind, it had all seemed very clear. Simple. Precise. But a lot had happened in those three years. Verity looked around the five tables that they'd annexed and confirmed her worst suspicions. Somehow, while she'd been busy needing alone time and inventing imaginary boyfriends, everyone else she knew had coupled up. Become units of two. Verity was the only singleton in attendance. Actually, the only singleton she knew. Even Posy, who'd rarely shown any interest in boyfriends, had skipped the whole dating thing and simply got married instead. Nina was never without a boyfriend, no matter how skeevy that boyfriend might be, and Tom? Who knew what Tom got up to? He played his cards so close to his chest that, for all the staff of Happy Ever After knew, he could have a wife and four children stashed away somewhere.

Then there was Verity. Happy to be single. And being alone wasn't the same as being lonely, but there were times, like right now on a Saturday night surrounded by her loved-up social circle, when one really did feel like the loneliest number.

Her phone was just sitting there on the table in front of her. It was a simple matter to pick it up and send a text message.

Am at houseboat warming party, which has relocated to Rutland Arms in Primrose Hill, if you fancy it? Very

151

Verity then knew sixty-five seconds of dread and turmoil and what-on-earth-had-possessed-her, before her phone beeped.

Be there in 30. Johnny

How lonely did Johnny have to be that he had nothing better to do at half-past eight on a Saturday night than immediately agree to meet up with a woman who'd cold-shouldered him for a whole week after he'd confessed, under duress, his deepest secrets to her?
Pretty bloody lonely.

* * *

Verity strived to appear casual as she waited. She didn't even tell Merry that Johnny was coming because Merry would seize on the news and grill Verity to within an inch of her life about this development. Instead, she clutched her glass and nodded and smiled brightly as Emma talked about a possible winter wedding until Merry gave a low whistle.
'Isn't that your fake fella, Very?' she hissed under her breath and Verity looked up to see Johnny, standing at the entrance to the beer garden. He was wearing jeans, a heathery blue T-shirt and a quizzical expression, which transformed into a smile when he caught sight of Verity. 'Why didn't you tell me he was coming? Sisters don't have secrets!'
'But are you really my sister? Con and I still reckon you were found on the church doorstep

152

and Farv and Muv didn't have the heart to tell you,' Very hissed back, because she and Con had been tormenting Merry with their changeling theory for years and it still remained one of the most effective ways to stop Merry in her tracks.

'That wasn't funny the first thousand times I heard it,' Merry grumbled as Johnny reached their far-flung corner and squeezed through to reach Verity's side. He leaned over as if he were going to kiss her cheek, thought better of it, then settled for the patented Verity Love finger waggle.

'Hello,' he said. 'I'd given up all hope of ever hearing from you again.'

'Sorry, I've been very busy,' Verity mumbled as Merry snorted derisively into her glass. 'Wasn't sure you'd be free at such short notice.'

'You had me at houseboat.' Johnny smiled and ran a hand through his thick hair which then fell back into its usual artfully tousled shape, so that quite a few of the girls present stopped what they were doing so they could have a good stare at him. 'I can't resist a houseboat.'

'It is quite an amazing houseboat,' Verity said as Merry coughed 'Get a room' into her glass and Emma turned round with a smile.

'That's so sweet, Very, when it's not even a little bit amazing. But it is mostly watertight so there's that.' Emma turned her attention and an even broader smile on to Johnny. 'You must be Verity's new boyfriend. Hello. I've heard absolutely nothing about you.'

Introductions were made and though Johnny was a little older than Verity's friends and he was better dressed than them even in jeans and a T-shirt, he seemed to fit in with ease. He also insisted on buying a couple of bottles of champagne when he heard about the engagement then taught Sean and Dougie a nineteenth-century drinking toast. 'Champagne for my real friends, real pain for my sham friends,' they kept hooting at regular intervals until Emma cuffed Sean and handed the keys to the houseboat to Verity.

'Why don't you give Johnny the guided tour?' she suggested then raised her eyebrows at Verity in a very unsubtle manner, which Verity chose to ignore.

Verity stuffed her hands into the pockets of her gingham smock dress as she and Johnny walked to the mooring. Why was it always so hard to find the right words to say?

It was Johnny who broke the silence first, but then he always did. 'I was convinced you hated me,' he said as they navigated the stone steps down to the water. 'I've replayed the conversation we had in the hotel room after the party again and again and I come across as either a callous marriage wrecker or a delusional lovesick fool.'

'Yes, well, I'm sure I came across as some kind of bitter recluse, which I'm not. Well, I am, but only for an hour after work while I decompress,' Verity said, because she didn't want to dredge up what had happened last weekend, though she did think that Johnny was a little callous, a little delusional to be in love with someone for so long with no hope of a reprieve. But then, she was

154

hardly in a position to judge him. 'We both have our own reasons for staying single and being in need of a fake other half.'

'That we do,' Johnny agreed and he sounded relieved that Verity didn't have anything further to say about their own respective shortcomings.

They'd reached the *Scarlett O'Hara*. Verity deigned to let Johnny take her hand as she was wearing her ancient Birkenstocks, which weren't designed for clambering on board. Then she unlocked the door and they went inside.

'I told you about my pirate ship treehouse, didn't I?' Johnny asked Verity as he looked around the cabin. 'Ever since then I've always wanted to live on a boat.'

'I don't mind the odd pleasure cruise but actually living on the water would not float my boat,' Verity said in the flat way she always delivered a joke but Johnny must have got it because he smiled.

Most of the space in the cabin was given over to a kitchen diner cum lounge with a small separate bedroom and shower room. It was liveable but decorated in a tired, seventies chic; mahogany and brass as far as the eye could see.

'Sean inherited the boat from his uncle, who lived on it for forty years or so. Apparently, there were pigeons roosting in the engine room,' Verity said as Johnny took out his phone. For once, there was no urgent text or phone call that he had to deal with; he wanted to take pictures of the fixtures and fittings.

'There's so much they could do in here,' he said and started talking about a simple design

155

scheme, clean but cosy, with all sorts of clever, space-saving features. 'I take on two post-graduate trainees every year who run their own project. This would be perfect. Also, their services would be free. Do you think Emma and Sean would be offended if I nominated *Scarlett O'Hara?*'

'Offended? I think they'd be delighted. Emma will probably make you sign a legally binding contract on the back of a beermat,' Verity said because ever since Emma had qualified as a solicitor, the power had gone to her head.

'Are you all right?' Johnny was on his knees investigating a cupboard built into the bottom of the corner seating, when he glanced up and saw that Verity was swaying slightly and grimacing. 'You look like you're about to keel over.'

It was a still night, not even the faintest breeze, but it felt to Verity as if the boat was pitching this way and that on storm-tossed water. No wonder she was so churny of stomach. 'I don't have . . . sea legs. I thought I'd be all right on a stationary barge but apparently not,' she said. 'I need to be on dry land . . . um, now!'

Verity sent up a silent prayer: 'Please Lord, don't let me throw up in the Regent's Canal or anywhere else for that matter,' as Johnny swiftly bundled her out of the cabin, across the deck, then all but lifted her back onto the bank.

She sank down on the stone steps, took a couple of deep shuddering breaths and waited for her tummy to stop roiling. 'Are you feeling better?' Johnny called out as he locked up the boat.

'I think so. We Loves generally don't travel well.' The twins, Chatty and Immy, got travelsick if they sat too near the front on a bus.

They headed back to the pub to return the keys and present Emma and Scan with Johnny's proposition, which was received, with unconfined joy. Verity thought they should stay for at least one more drink though she was beginning to flag — far too much social stimulation and almost puking would do that to a girl — but Johnny gestured to the gate, which led back to the street.

'If you've had enough, I'll see you home,' he said.

Verity had had enough. She'd also had enough of Merry smirking every time she looked at the two of them. They'd be having words about that later too. Verity made do with a retaliatory pinch when Merry said loudly, 'Don't do anything I wouldn't do,' as Verity and Johnny said their goodbyes.

'What's it to be?' Johnny asked once they left The Rutland Arms. 'Cab, bus or shall we walk for a bit?'

'Walking's always good,' Verity decided and because it was nearly ten and Regent's Park was now closed and Camden High Street was best avoided on a Saturday night, they skirted through the back streets.

There were things they should probably discuss but Verity hardly knew where to begin and Johnny wasn't inclined to talk either as they walked through Camden. The streets were a little rougher, less fragrant; more kebab shops and all-night convenience stores, and quite a few drunken hordes of youths lurching at them.

Though she didn't do tactile, Verity was relieved when Johnny offered her his arm. It was very gallant, like something out of one of Posy's regency romances.

'I love walking through London at night. You notice all sorts of details that pass you by when the streets are busy,' Johnny said and he pointed up at the building they were passing, a row of shops with flats above them. 'See the datestone up there? It tells you the year the building was erected and who the builder was.'

Johnny made the London of long ago come alive. He showed Verity a plaque on the wall of an anonymous block of council flats commemorating Mary Wollstonecraft, an eighteenth-century writer, feminist and mother of Mary Shelley, author of *Frankenstein*, who'd lived in a house on the site. When they crossed Euston Road, he told her about the Euston Arch, which had stood at the entrance to the old Euston station. It was long gone now but Johnny's parents, then newly qualified architects, and a group of their friends, had climbed the scaffolding surrounding the arch before it was demolished in the sixties and hung a huge 'Save The Arch' banner.

'There's a campaign to rebuild the Arch, especially now they've recovered a lot of the original stone,' Johnny explained. 'My father is quite beside himself.'

'If ever Our Vicar and Our Vicar's Wife come to visit, you'll have to give them a guided tour.

They love this kind of stuff,' Verity said and then she realised that she'd just invited Johnny to meet her parents. Like, they were actually dating. Even if they *were* actually dating, it was far, far too soon to talk about meeting parents. Like having sex, there was probably some industry-standard period of time before parents were met: three months of exclusive dating and one minibreak. 'Before you read anything into that perfectly innocent remark, FYI, I'm not getting notions.'

'Good to know,' Johnny said with an easy grin, then his phone, which miraculously had stayed silent for the last two hours, beeped imperiously. He took it out of the back pocket of his jeans, glanced at the screen and his face, which had been animated and very smiley, even when Verity was suggesting that he might like to meet her parents, became still, tense, as if he were fighting not to betray his emotions.

It really wasn't any of Verity's business, except if they were having this arrangement, which apparently they were, then it kind of was. 'Is that your, er, *friend?*' She tried to sound casual but her voice broke on the last syllable.

'What?' Johnny blinked and the spell was broken. 'Yes.'

'So, what does she think of you having a fake girlfriend?' Verity had obviously spent too much time Skyping her sisters lately because deeply personal questions were much more their style. 'Does she mind?'

'She's not really in a position to mind, is she? What with her being married,' Johnny said a

159

little sadly. 'Anyway, we both agreed at the start of the summer that it was best to give each other some space.'

Verity didn't think phoning and messaging someone all the time, especially when he was at social gatherings, really counted as giving Johnny some space but she refrained from mentioning it. After all her motto in life was 'What Would Elizabeth Bennet Do?' Not 'What Would One of My Incredibly Tactless Sisters Do?' So she just said, 'Oh, is that so?'

'That's the idea. I haven't seen her in weeks. We were actually meant to be meeting that night you gatecrashed my table in that Italian, but she stood me up. No, that's not fair. She said that we needed to take some time away from each other to decide what we both really wanted, though she could have told me that before I'd booked a table and waited for the best part of an hour.'

The impression Verity was gaining of this other woman wasn't entirely a favourable one.

'You being stood up worked out quite well for me, I suppose.' Verity shot Johnny a sideways look. 'Though you could have just played along and pretended to be Peter Hardy and made life a lot easier for the both of us.'

'I could have,' Johnny agreed. 'But then we'd never have become friends.'

Verity rarely made friends solely on her own merits. Yes, Posy and Nina and Tom were her friends, but that was a very lovely by-product of working together so they were forewarned of Verity's odd little ways. Then there were her sisters' friends who became Verity's friends by

160

default (befriend a Love sister, and you got another one as part of the deal, like a free gift with purchase). Again, by the time Verity had achieved friend status in her own right, they all knew what they were getting into.

They were skirting the edge of Russell Square now; Happy Ever After was a brisk five minutes' walk away. 'Are we friends though?' Verity wondered aloud. 'I'm not sure what we are but tonight was the first time I can remember that none of my other friends took me to one side and said that they knew this great guy they wanted to set me up with. So I guess our fake relationship scam did have its benefits.'

'And since you've managed not to get any notions, I think we can happily call it a success,' Johnny said and for the life of her Verity couldn't tell if he were joking or not. 'Unless you are secretly in love with me.'

'Nope, still not in love with you,' Verity confirmed. 'Sorry to disappoint.'

'I'm sure I'll recover,' Johnny said with the hint of a smile. 'So . . . would it really be that much of an ordeal if we spent the rest of the summer attending assorted functions simply as friends, because I do genuinely consider you a friend now, who our other friends think are dating?'

Verity thought for a moment. She had already been to an open-house brunch and a birthday, which had necessitated an overnight stay. She'd met *everybody*. She'd faced her fears, confronted her demons and the world was still turning. 'It's not our fault if they've got the wrong end of the stick,' she decided eventually. 'So it hardly counts as fibbing.'

'Oh good,' Johnny said smoothly. 'Because there's a wedding next weekend and when Carlotta heard I was seeing someone, she insisted that the seating arrangements weren't locked down yet and that I could bring you.' Johnny shot Verity another cool smile as if he were daring her to back out. 'I tried to tell her no, but she wouldn't hear of it.'

In truth, it did sting a little. Was that the reason Johnny had so readily agreed to meet her tonight? Because he wanted her on wedding duty next weekend? But then Verity couldn't have it both ways. She'd ghosted Johnny all week, then been happy that he'd had no other plans for a Saturday night so he could be a foil for her own singledom.

Anyway, friends did favours for their friends.

'A wedding?' Verity queried and she tried not to sound too Dowager Countess Grantham about it. 'Another overnight stay?'

'It's in Kensington so I was planning to get a taxi home but I'm sure we can find a hotel nearby if you really want to make a night out of it,' Johnny said dryly. 'You in, then?'

For the life of her, and she really did try, neither Verity, nor Elizabeth Bennet, could think of a good reason not to.

13

*'She is a selfish, hypocritical woman, and
I have no opinion of her.'*

As any couple might hope if they'd booked their
wedding for a Saturday in mid-July, the day
dawned golden, the sky a flawless blue, which
boded well for the obligatory photos outside the
church.

It didn't really bode that well that Con's
wedding was booked for the end of September
when the weather might be sunny or there could
be rain and gales. Con had asked Our Vicar to
put a special plea in with God, but Verity
doubted that would work. Not after all the times
that Con had forsaken God or taken his name in
vain, as Verity explained to Johnny as they
squeezed onto a Central Line tube train — there
was a citywide cycling event and getting across
London by cab in a timely fashion was never
going to happen. So they were armpit to armpit
with all the other strap-hanging tourists and
shoppers who gave them odd looks because
Johnny was in tailcoat and fancy waistcoat with a
yellow rose in his buttonhole.

It was a huge point in Johnny's favour that
when Verity had asked the dress code for the
wedding he hadn't said something vague and
mannish like, 'Oh, just wear something nice.' 'I'll
ask one of the ladies,' he'd said and true to his

word, he'd reported back an hour later that Verity needed to wear 'daytime formal and some kind of headgear. Not necessarily a hat.'

Verity had sought help from Con who'd read nothing but bridal magazines for the last six months, and Posy who gave Verity first dibs on all the dresses that their beloved late boss Lavinia had amassed over the last seventy years.

Verity was wearing her favourite pick: a fifties dress with boat neck, cap sleeves, nipped-in waist and full skirt, which had smudgy sprigs of red, orange and pink blooms on a black background. It was very comforting to wear a frock that Lavinia had worn, so it felt that in some small way Verity was carrying Lavinia with her, could hear her voice saying gently, 'Courage, my dear' as Lavinia always had when Verity was having a meltdown at work.

Also requisitioned from the depths of Lavinia's wardrobe was a fascinator — a wide black velvet band with a frivolous piece of black spot netting attached to it — and on her feet, half price in the Office sale, were black suede peep-toe shoes, which were going to kill Verity very slowly and very painfully for the rest of the day.

Nina had given a long, low whistle when Verity had walked through the shop that morning and even Tom had paused with his usual breakfast panini halfway to his mouth, which was practically an ogle as far as Tom was concerned. Then as Verity had been tottering up Rochester Street she'd bumped into Sebastian Thorndyke who hadn't bothered to hide his bug-eyed

164

surprise. 'Good God, who'd have thought that the vicar's daughter could scrub up all right?' he'd exclaimed. Verity had decided that it was best to take that as a compliment and it was actually quite . . . nice to get all dressed up and realise that for once she looked like a version of herself she'd only ever seen in her wildest, most optimistic dreams.

When they reached St Mary Abbots Church in Kensington, Verity didn't feel as if she was sticking out like a sore, socially awkward, shabbily dressed thumb. Anyone looking at her and Johnny, her arm in his, because that was appropriate touching now they were officially masquerading as a couple, wouldn't have thought that they looked out of place together.

Today was going to be a good day, Verity decided very uncharacteristically, as she caught Wallis's eye and waved. Then she turned to Johnny. 'Remember, I'm under pain of death to make sure I get one of everything: order of service, menu, placecards.'

Johnny stopped at a pew that was half the way down on the groom's side and ushered Verity in. 'I'm no expert in these matters but if your sister's getting married in September shouldn't she have already ordered her stationery?'

'You'd think, wouldn't you?'

Johnny gasped like he was shocked to the very core of his being. 'Are you saying she hasn't even sent out invitations?'

Where to even begin? Verity started by rolling her eyes. 'She's emailed out a Save the Date and then Chatty, she has an art degree, was meant to be designing the invitations but Con is a very infuriating mix of incredibly bossy and incredibly indecisive.'

'And her fiancé, what does he think about all this?'

Alex had already said, on more than one occasion, that he'd be quite happy to rock up to the church in his best trousers and nicest shirt then retire to the local pub. 'He thinks that the secret to having a long, happy life together with Con is to just stay out of it.' Verity looked around the church.

'I can't decide if that's good or bad advice,' Johnny said. Then he smiled, called out 'Hello' to a woman who was frantically waving at him from the other side of the aisle. 'I have absolutely no idea who that is. Oh! Look at that hat at your four o'clock. It looks like she's got a lilac jellyfish on her head.'

They spent a very productive ten minutes commenting on the hats on display and wondering whether the best man, who was red-faced and glistening, was going to pass out, until a triumphant chord suddenly rang out on the church organ and nearly gave Verity a heart attack. They stood up and turned as what civilians called 'Here Comes the Bride' (and what Verity called 'The Bridal Chorus' by Richard Wagner) soundtracked the bride walking down the aisle with her beaming papa.

The bride ('Carlotta, Spanish father, English mother, works for the Arts Council') was a vision in a strapless white lace, fit and flare dress and a lace-edged veil held in place with a small tiara.

The groom, Rich (had gone to Cambridge with Johnny, a wine merchant), glanced back at his bride to be, rocked back on his heels then actually wiped away a tear.

Verity was meant to be making notes on the hymns and the chosen readings (a poem by Pablo Neruda and a moving recital of 'We've Only Just Begun' by The Carpenters read by an actor friend of the couple that had quite a few people sobbing).

Although, as a vicar's daughter, Verity had attended more weddings than Elizabeth Taylor and Cheryl Cole put together, she was unexpectedly moved by the intimacy of the moment. Of both Carlotta and Rich, two strangers to Verity, choking back tears as they recited their vows, their hands clasped tightly together. Verity was struck anew by the solemnity, the promise, the commitment of the words, which she'd heard so many times before.

To have and to hold
From this day forward;
For better, for worse,
For richer, for poorer,
In sickness and in health,
To love and to cherish,
Till death us do part.

They meant something beautiful; something that had nothing to do with signature wedding colours or matching bridesmaid dresses.

Getting married meant pledging to spend the rest of your life with someone, to try to be the

167

best person you could be for that someone.

'Here, I came prepared,' Johnny whispered in her ear as he handed Verity a handkerchief. 'It's all right. It's quite clean. My father always told me to take a spare hankie to a wedding in case of tears.'

'I'm not crying,' Verity whispered. She blinked and that was enough to dislodge the one tear that had apparently been clinging to the bottom lashes of her left eye. She managed to catch it with Johnny's spare hankie before it did any damage to her make-up. 'Oh God, I can't believe I'm crying at two complete strangers' wedding.'

'If it's any consolation, I brought an extra spare hankie for myself.' Johnny leaned even closer so that Verity got a delicious whiff of the clean, crisp aftershave he wore. 'Don't tell anyone, I'm a bit of a weeper too.'

Verity gave him a look. Not what Posy called her patented dead-eyed stare, but a close cousin to it. Johnny winked at her and she softened.

'Your secret's safe with me,' she said and didn't even try to hide her smile.

He smiled too and their eyes met again so that now Verity felt as if she were experiencing another private, intimate moment, between her and this man that she was sort of friends with.

'I therefore proclaim that they are husband and wife,' the vicar proclaimed in a jubilant voice. 'Those whom God has joined together let no one put them asunder!'

Afterwards there were official photos taken outside the church. Johnny was called upon to herd people into position and Verity was quite happy to watch him herd, always with a ready smile and a joke. He even had a hug for the two smallest pageboys who had disgraced themselves while the register was being signed and a woman sang 'You Were Meant For Me' from *Singin' in the Rain*, by pummelling each other until the Maid Of Honour had hauled them apart.

Every now and again, Johnny would look round to check that Verity was where he'd left her, which was leaning against a handy wall to take the pressure off her already aching feet as she texted Con. Her oldest sister had sent her seven increasingly frantic messages while Verity's phone had been turned off during the service.

Signature colours are mint green and silver. Bouquet mostly pale green succulents with some white roses, tied with silver ribbon. Sending you pics. Stop bothering me. Vxxx

She'd just finished sending her text to Con with pictures attached of the ribbons swathing the end of each pew, the bridesmaids' dresses and the order of service, when Johnny returned to her side with two people, a man and woman, in tow.

'Verity! Sorry to neglect you,' he said and the herding must have been more strenuous than it had looked because he sounded breathless and had a hectic flush dotting his cheekbones. 'I want to introduce you to two very old friends of mine. This is Harry and Marissa.'

Verity immediately straightened up from her slouched position as if she'd just been called in

169

to see the headmaster.

'Not so much of the very old,' the man said, stepping forward. He was fair-haired, not as tall as Johnny, in fact very slight of build, but he had a way about him, a presence that drew the eye and Verity's attention. Or it could just be that there seemed to be a tension between the two men, which made the air crackle around them. Or so Verity imagined. 'Nice to meet you, Verity. What on earth are you doing with a rogue like Johnny?'

'I've never met anyone less like a rogue than Johnny,' Verity said stoutly, because she knew rogues — all of Nina's boyfriends past and present could be described thus — and Johnny, even though he was in love with another man's wife, didn't come close to roguedom. 'And we're just hanging out, aren't we?'

'We are,' Johnny agreed. 'And this is Marissa.' He gestured at the woman who'd been standing behind Harry. 'She's been dying to meet you.'

The air stopped crackling and disappeared altogether; suddenly sucked out of the day, like a huge storm was brewing, pressure mounting, everything in the atmosphere coming to boiling point.

Standing in front of Verity was a tiny ethereal blonde woman. She was as beautiful as any woman Verity had ever seen. In fact, she looked positively angelic with wide green eyes, a tiny snub nose and the perfect rosebud lips of a Disney cartoon princess. It wasn't a huge stretch to imagine that tiny woodland animals helped her dress each morning.

170

Verity, blinded by so much beauty, smiled shyly at Marissa. Her smile wasn't returned. Marissa's eyes swept over Verity in a swift assessment, ending at her feet where Verity's toes were curling nervously. 'Oh, you mustn't mind Johnny, he does exaggerate,' Marissa said crisply to Verity, who found she couldn't look the other woman in the eye. She glanced over at Johnny for some assurance but he and Harry were deep in conversation and paying the two women no attention. 'I just happened to remark that wherever I seemed to look, all I could see was your dress. Those flowers are very . . . *bright*, aren't they? Who's it by?'

Verity didn't have any dresses by anyone. She had dresses that she'd bought from well-known high street chains or charity shops, not from some fancy designer with a minimalist boutique in Mayfair. Except this dress. Once again, Lavinia came to the rescue.

'It's vintage,' Verity tried to say in an off-hand way like she was the sort of woman who found amazing vintage pieces in her local Oxfam. 'It belonged to a very dear friend of mine who — '

'Oh! It's second hand! Well, it's still very charming,' Marissa said in her lovely modulated voice and now instead of being pleased with her outfit, with how she looked, Verity was crushed to be wearing a garish, gaudy dress, which probably stank of mothballs. 'Anyway, it's very nice to meet you, Veronica.'

'It's Verity.' Verity knew that her handshake was as limp as a first-time marathon runner hobbling over the finishing line but that was how she felt. When the handshake was over, Marissa gave the faintest grimace and flexed her fingers, as if Verity's hand had been sweaty, which Verity was pretty sure it hadn't been. 'Nice to meet you too.'

'I'm sure it is.' Marissa's gaze rested beyond Verity as if she was desperate to find someone else to talk to. 'Oh! There's James and Emily. Harry, we really must go and say hello to them.'

And off she went in her pristine white dress, though anyone with even a modicum of good manners knew that you didn't wear white to a wedding unless you were the bride.

'Guess I'd better go after the old ball and chain,' Harry muttered and followed his wife so that only Johnny was left behind to smile apologetically at Verity.

'Sorry,' he said, though it wasn't his fault that his very old friend Marissa was so thoroughly unpleasant.

'Is she always like — '

'I didn't know it would take me ages to find the mother of the bride,' Johnny continued because his apology had nothing to do with Marissa. 'Were you on your own for ages?'

'It was fine. I had a lot of urgent texts from Con that I had to reply to. Honestly, it's all cool,' Verity assured him though emotionally she'd downgraded from limp marathon runner to deflated balloon because people being rude to her, and especially for no good reason, counted as a confrontation and Verity didn't deal with confrontations well. Also, her feet were officially killing her and she now hated what she was

172

wearing with a deep and fiery passion.

'Good. And by the way, I never said before but you look great. Your dress reminds me of those Dutch flower paintings,' Johnny said, because sometimes he knew exactly the right thing to say at the right moment.

Verity smiled and as the corners of her mouth lifted so did her mood. 'I thought that too!'

Her spirits remained buoyant during the fifteen-minute walk along Kensington High Street to the restaurant within the grounds of Holland Park, where the reception was being held. It was an odd but triumphant procession; the wedding party, including bride, groom and bridesmaids, mingling with shoppers and accompanied by much tooting of car horns and cheers as they tottered towards their destination.

With grave ceremony Verity was introduced to the two duelling pageboys, Rufus, Johnny's godson, and his younger brother Otto, and although she would have said she wasn't good with kids, she didn't need to do much but hold their hands each time they crossed a road and listen to them bang on in great detail about *Doctor Who* and say things like 'Oh, really?' and 'I didn't know you could do stuff like that with a sonic screwdriver' at regular intervals.

'You were a big hit,' Johnny told Verity once they'd finally reached the restaurant and were milling about in the garden as more photos were taken and, thankfully, waiters were circulating with laden drinks trays. 'And those two are a tough crowd.'

'I've faced worse,' Verity said and reflexively

173

she scanned the crowd for an elfin blonde in a white dress because she wanted to keep as much distance between her and Marissa as possible.

She even nervously peered around corners on her way to the loo but once she reached her destination, Verity was more focussed on easing her feet out of her peep-toed instruments of torture. She put on her ballet flats then came barrelling out of the washroom into the powder area only to find Marissa holding forth amid a small group of women.

'We left early in the end. It was full of the most *awful* people. It's official: the bridge and tunnel crowd have completely ruined Dubai,' Marissa was saying. 'Harry calls it Brentwood with a desert.'

Verity tried to make herself look as small and inconspicuous as possible as she squeezed past them but was stopped by a hand on her arm. The hand belonged to Elsa, who she'd met at Lawrence's fortieth birthday party.

'Hello, sweetie,' Elsa said warmly, pulling Verity into the circle. 'Love your dress. Do you know everyone?'

Verity didn't know any of the other women except . . . Marissa who stared blankly at Verity as if she'd never seen her before in her life.

Not everyone's good with names. Or faces, Verity told herself. 'We met earlier outside the church,' Verity reminded Marissa, whose beautiful features remained impassive. 'I'm Verity.'

'Oh, did we? I don't remember. But anyway, nice to meet you, Vera.' She turned back to the group with a skilful, elegant shrug of the

174

shoulder that somehow managed to completely cut Verity out of the circle. 'Now, where were we?'

As Verity left the restroom she wasn't channelling Elizabeth Bennet but her mother, Mrs Bennet, as she muttered furiously under her breath, 'She is a selfish, hypocritical woman and I have no opinion of her.'

Which was a lie because Verity had quite a few opinions about Marissa and none of them good ones.

Johnny was waiting for Verity with another glass of champagne and the news that they'd been asked to take their seats.

'Not on the singles' table either,' he said as he led her across the dancefloor. 'We're on the fun party table of couples who don't have kids.'

Verity wasn't a fun party table kind of girl but when they got to their table, there were only two other people seated so far, so she could ease herself into the fun gently. Jeremy and Martin were two beautifully chiselled men who were getting married themselves in a couple of weeks. After all those sessions with her sisters via Skype, Verity had become an expert in centrepieces, party favours and all other aspects of wedding planning.

'What is the deal with bunting?' Johnny asked as he tried to follow the conversation. 'Is it necessary?'

'It's mandatory if you're having a rustic country wedding,' Jeremy said. 'Is your sister doing mason jars?'

'Still undecided,' Verity said with a weary sigh.

'We've been collecting vintage teacups from charity shops in case she wants to go with that option instead.'

More of their tablemates arrived, the fun couples without kids, and it was a flurry of 'Pleased to meet you' and 'Bride or groom?' as people looked for their names on the place-cards. But it wasn't until the waiters had just begun to bring round the starters of pancetta-wrapped, pan-seared scallops on a pea puree that the last two guests slid into their seats next to Verity. Harry and Marissa.

'You've finally been upgraded from the singles' table, then, Johnny,' Harry said with a grin. 'Congratulations.'

'I owe it all to my lovely Verity,' Johnny said and he put his arm around Verity to pull her in and kiss her cheek. It was unexpected and decidedly unwelcome to be pressed against Johnny's side, so she could feel the heat and muscle of him, smell the crisp zing of his aftershave. Still, it would have been rude to squirm away, so Verity stayed exactly where she was, until Johnny freed her. 'I never asked before, how was Dubai?'

'Hot. Sandy. Marissa was pleased that we had good phone reception, as you know.' Harry's voice had become more challenging and Verity couldn't understand why, once again, there was a tension suddenly crackling between the two men, which made everyone else at the table stare down at their scallops.

'Oh Harry, don't be so tiresome,' Marissa said after a pause so long that Verity's nails had almost dug holes in her palms. 'I'm very cross with you, Johnny, by the way. You didn't even say hello before, just marched us over to meet your little friend.'

'I'm so sorry about my lapse of manners. Hello Marissa,' Johnny said evenly, looking up from his plate to glance across at Marissa who was wearing a soft smile on her face, which made her look winsome and vulnerable. 'You're well?'

'As well as can be expected,' Marissa agreed and Verity found herself paralysed by the strange atmosphere that had settled around them, though she'd promised Con that she'd take photos of the food.

With the arrival of Marissa and Harry, all the joy and good vibes of their fun, party-loving table were gone. In their place stilted small talk about how cute the little flower girls had looked and who'd ordered the salmon and who'd ordered the chicken.

Verity longed to get to her feet, mutter something about powdering her nose and then disappear into the July evening, never to be seen again. She even thought of surreptitiously texting Merry under cover of her napkin so Merry could give her a ring and Verity could pretend there was some dire emergency that required her immediate attention.

Instead she sat there stricken, playing with her food, until she felt a hand on her thigh. More specifically Verity felt Johnny's hand on her thigh. Not in an inappropriate, lecherous way but a comforting pat as he leaned in to whisper, 'I'm sorry. You look as if you aren't enjoying yourself. Is this hideous?'

'A little bit, everything feels very scratchy and I don't know why,' Verity admitted, leaning in even closer to Johnny so a waiter could take her plate. The feeling that she'd quite like him to pull her closer still so she could rest her head on his shoulder was unprecedented but very tempting.

Johnny brushed Verity's words away as if they were crumbs. 'Everything seems fine to me. I'm having a great time but I'm sorry that you're not.'

As soon as he said it, Verity realised how she sounded. Whiny and wet blanket-ish. She wriggled round in her chair so she and Johnny were facing each other and she had her back to Harry and Marissa. As she looked up at Johnny, his gaze was fixed on something or someone over her shoulder then his attention was back on Verity and he was frowning and she really needed to get her head back in the fun party-loving game.

'I'm sure I'll get my second wind soon because there's lots of good things going on here,' she insisted and picked up her glass. 'Free champagne, pudding to come, lots of wedding inspo . . . that reminds me, we need to take pictures of the top table.'

Johnny rewarded her with a smile. One of his really good smiles that always made Verity smile back. 'What's the camera like on your phone? Could you zoom in from here? Or shall we get up and casually walk in that direction?'

In the end they zoomed in with the camera on Johnny's phone, which had more pixels though

Verity was never sure exactly what a pixel did, then he sent the pictures to Verity. The whole time Verity couldn't help but be aware of Marissa's narrowed eyes and Harry's careful, considered gaze.

Then there was the tap of knife on glass and a cough into a microphone and the father of the bride was on his feet to make the first speech.

Everyone at the table gave a collective sigh of relief, and smiled at the first predictable joke about 'losing a daughter and gaining a son whose parents have a holiday home in Saint Lucia'.

Johnny angled his chair nearer to Verity so he could see the top table, which meant that he could share the occasional knowing look with Verity, even clutch his head to make her laugh when the best man's speech went on for a very dull twenty minutes. There were a couple of times when she felt his attention wander again, as if his mind was far, far away, his eyes not on the groom who was extolling the virtues of his radiant bride, but looking over Verity's shoulder. The room was full of his friends, his Cambridge buddies, so perhaps he was scanning the room for familiar faces. Perhaps one of the familiar faces belonged to his other woman, the love of his life? As soon as Verity thought it, she felt her heart quicken.

'You all right?' Johnny asked, because she must have given a start.

'Oh, look! They're bringing out pudding.'

They were — a selection of miniature tarts: lemon, strawberry and a salted caramel — then the newly-wedded couple took to the floor for

179

their first dance to 'Someone To Watch Over Me' by Cole Porter. Verity took a moment to message Con who'd just demanded a progress report.

It's a very stylish, very understated, very expensive wedding. Sorry to rain on your parade but none of us are stylish or understated. Besides can you imagine Great Aunt Helen's face if you served her scallops on minted pea puree? 😱

Verity had just clicked send and was trying to catch the eye of the waiter brandishing a coffee pot when Harry said, 'So, Johnny, are you going to monopolise the gorgeous Verity all evening?'

Johnny's jaw tightened. 'I have rather kept her to myself. Never even did proper introductions earlier. Very, Harry and I were at school together.'

'Really? Is there anyone that you *weren't* at school with?' Verity asked because by now the champagne had taken the edge off her nerves and it did seem as if Johnny had gone to school with pretty much every thirty-somethingish man in London.

'I was a scholarship boy from the wrong side of the tracks,' Harry explained with a grin. 'Johnny took me under his wing on my first day before anyone could flush my head down the loo for being a common oik and somehow, despite everything, we've been friends ever since.'

'They even went to Cambridge together, which is where I met them and broke up their little bromance, didn't I?' Marissa blinked her large blue eyes. 'I still feel guilty about it.'

180

Johnny smiled faintly. 'You know you're forgiven, Rissa. It's impossible to be angry with you for very long.'

Verity wasn't entirely sure she agreed but maybe Marissa improved on better acquaintance. Or perhaps she was simply one of those women who preferred the company of men. She certainly seemed to prefer the company of her husband for she batted her eyelashes at him, then nuzzled against him like a sleek, slinky pussy cat demanding attention. Harry kissed the top of Marissa's head then raised his glass at Verity. 'So, shall we swap life stories, Verity?'

Verity couldn't help but warm to Harry. He'd grown up on an estate in Islington, one of five kids, the first member of his family to get his A-levels, never mind a degree too. After Cambridge, he'd worked as a broker in the City and now had his own venture capital investment firm. Verity was always going to cheer for anyone who succeeded using their own drive and determination. And like Verity, Harry didn't quite fit into the chi-chi scene at a fancy Holland Park wedding reception either, but Harry made not fitting in feel like a virtue. If Marissa were a Caroline Bingley if ever there was one, then Harry as he asked Verity questions, then listened attentively to her answers, reminded her of the self-made Mr Gardiner, kindly uncle to the Bennet sisters.

Marissa, on the other hand, was hellbent on making Verity doubt all her lifestyle choices. From being one of five daughters of a vicar and growing up in Grimsby, to working in a bookshop that specialised in romantic fiction and owning a fat cat with boundary issues. Each new revelation that Harry winkled out of Verity was greeted with the arch of one of Marissa's perfectly groomed eyebrows and a smirk that made a mockery of her pretty mouth.

Johnny had his arm around the back of Verity's chair, his hand brushing her shoulder as if he were staking his claim. He even told Harry sharply to back off when Harry asked Verity with a theatrical wink what her views were on sex outside of marriage, 'you being a vicar's daughter and all?' But eventually, Johnny's hand stopped brushing against Verity until he removed his arm from the back of her chair altogether. Then, when the couple on Marissa's other side got up to greet some friends, Johnny unfolded himself from his chair so he could slip into the seat next to her.

Verity couldn't catch what they were saying, the band was going full throttle as they played Motown hit after Motown hit, but she could see Marissa's reaction to Johnny's words quite clearly. Gone was the blank-eyed, sneering creature of before, replaced by her doe-eyed twin who kept biting her lip and staring hungrily at Johnny as if all she wanted to do for the rest of her life was look at him.

And Johnny? He was staring right back at her. He swallowed once, like he had a lump in his throat. He looked away. Looked back at Marissa again and they shared a smile. A secret, sad smile and that was when it hit Verity with all the force of a ten-ton truck so she was amazed that she wasn't thrown across the room but stayed where she was, on her chair, her hands gripping the seat, unable to move.

14

*'There are few people whom I really love,
and still fewer of whom I think well.'*

It was Marissa. Marissa was the other woman.
The woman that Johnny loved. The woman he
couldn't be with for the very simple but very
complicated reason that she was married to his
old childhood friend.

And yet, Marissa was giving every appearance
of a woman madly in love too — and not with
her husband. No wonder Johnny couldn't quit
loving her when Marissa gazed at him like he
was a god.

' . . . and my gran, God bless her, reads a
romance novel a day, and still finds time to clean
her house from top to bottom,' Harry was saying
and Verity was forced to turn her attention back
to him. 'Particularly loves a saga, she does.'

'Oh, don't we all? You should bring her to the
shop,' Verity said vaguely. 'We have a tearoom
too. Very good cake. Talking of which, I really
need to take a picture of the cake for my sister.
Will you excuse me?'

It wasn't the most skilled of exits but Verity
didn't care. She did take a couple of shots of the
cake, a pristine white, three-tiered creation
adorned with some very tasteful, piped trailing
vines, and then scurried outside to the little
terrace where they'd had drinks before.

It was deserted now apart from a couple of defiant smokers. Verity sat down on a bench and took a couple of calming breaths. What would Elizabeth Bennet do? She would seek the advice of her sister, Jane. Obviously.

Oh, how Verity longed for the quiet counsel of a Jane Bennet but Merry would have to do.

Such was the severity of the situation that Merry listened mostly without comment as Verity hit her with the highlights. 'Can I leave, do you think?' she asked after she'd finished describing her epiphany about Johnny's love life. 'I took my bag out with me and I could just run through the park and be on the tube before anyone even noticed I was gone.'

'Very, you absolutely can't. You're at a fancy London wedding. Your bum on a chair probably cost the bride and groom a hundred quid.'

'I could PayPal them the money,' Verity said a little desperately. 'It's just this whole situation is unbearable. I'm with a man who wants to be with another woman . . . '

'Yeah, but you knew that was the deal with Johnny,' Merry pointed out. She was being very calm and reasonable about Verity's predicament, which wasn't the comfort that it should have been. 'Anyway, she sounds *vile*.'

'Ugh! She is,' Verity muttered. 'If I stay for much longer then I won't even like Johnny any more because how can I like someone who has such terrible taste when it comes to women?'

'I'm very much enjoying you having mean thoughts like the rest of us,' Merry said gleefully. Then she became more serious. 'Well, if you really want my advice . . . '

'I do!'

'You're just going to have to get drunk, Very.' Merry's tone was resolute. Also, it was her answer to everything. 'Nobody could be expected to go through what you're going through sober.'

So, Verity got drunk. Not drunk enough to lose her inhibitions because there wasn't enough alcohol in the world for that to happen, but drunk enough that she allowed herself to be pulled into the little group of women who were dancing around their clutch bags to 'Islands in the Stream'.

She tried to keep her back to the table where Marissa and Johnny were still deep in conversation. They were the last two left, everyone else having dispersed to dance or loiter purposefully near the cheese station that was being set up, seated close enough that their knees were almost touching, both of them leaning into each other.

Not that Verity was staring, but Wallis kept grabbing her hands and whirling her around so it was very hard not to see Johnny and Marissa's little tête-à-tête from every angle.

It was actually a relief when the music changed to something a little slower and Harry tapped Verity on the shoulder. 'Do you think Johnny will mind if I steal a dance?' he asked.

'I think I'm all danced out.' Dancing amid a gaggle of women was one thing, dancing with one other person, a man, whom she hardly knew was like asking her if she fancied walking barefoot over hot coals. Verity tried to smile, but couldn't quite pull it off. 'Actually, I was going to get a drink. Dancing to Beyoncé is quite thirsty work.'

'I know what you mean, I'm always parched after I've done the Single Ladies routine,' Harry said with a grin and Verity was grinning too as she let Harry lead her off the dancefloor and towards the bar.

It probably wasn't a good idea to keep guzzling champagne like it was fizzy pop, so Verity settled for a ginger ale with a lot of ice and she and Harry hoisted themselves up on a couple of stools, so they could survey the room.

All the usual suspects were in attendance. The dad dancers. The small children high on sugar, up way past their bedtime, running around and shrieking. Women easing off high heels as they caught up with old friends and then there was Johnny and Marissa.

It was just the two of them, deep in conversation, with eyes only for each other, as if there was no one else in the room.

What a mess it was. Verity sighed at the exact same time that Harry sighed too. She turned to him in surprise. Did he know? Oh God, should she tell him? Although it was obvious to anyone with a working pair of eyes what was going on.

'I wouldn't worry about it,' Harry suddenly said. He gestured at his wife and his best friend. 'This always happens.'

'Always?' Verity asked helplessly, because she was in way over her head.

'Yeah, 'fraid so. They both have a bit too much to drink and they moon over each other like

Romeo and Juliet. It's nothing. Honestly.'

What a lot of people seemed to forget was that Romeo and Juliet both ended up dead. Again, Verity was in an agony of indecision, not knowing how much Harry knew. For example, did he know about the phone calls, the endless text messages? 'Is it really nothing, do you think?'

'Nothing, but a lot of texting and hot air most of the time,' Harry said, which answered some of Verity's immediate concerns. 'Don't let this put you off Johnny. When he's not pining over my wife, he's a good guy. One of the best. So, if you two were getting serious . . . Is it serious?' He sounded hopeful.

Verity hated to be the bearer of bad tidings. 'We're only friends. Friends who see each other.' She pointed her index and middle fingers at her eyes and then at Johnny. She really had had quite a lot to drink. 'Just seeing. That's all.'

'That's a shame,' Harry said heavily, as if he'd half hoped that Verity might be the answer to all his marital woes. 'He really does deserve a woman who will make him happy.' Once more, they both glanced over to the table where Johnny now looked as if he were pleading with Marissa. His hands were spread wide in supplication, he was talking urgently while she shook her head at what he was saying. 'Whereas, those two wouldn't make each other happy. Not for one single day. They never did, not even when they were dating.'

Harry shifted around so he no longer had to look at the source of his frustration. Verity was only too happy to shift with him; she also could hardly bear to look at Johnny and Marissa's cosy huddle for a moment longer.

'Why do you put up with it?' she asked, because Harry didn't seem at all like the sort of man who would tolerate the texting, the mooning, another man infatuated with his wife.

'Because I love her,' Harry said immediately as if he didn't even have to think about it. 'And believe it or not, she loves me too. Look, are you sure that you and Johnny couldn't make a go of things?'

'I already told you . . .' Verity shook her head. 'It's not like that.'

'How could it be when he's so convinced that he's still in love with Marissa?' Harry shot a desperate look back at their table. 'Not without encouragement either, poor sod. She loves the attention, the drama, I'm not really a big one for drama, so Rissa has to find it where she can, but more than that she feels guilty. I feel guilty too. I hated myself for what we did to Johnny. It's why I haven't shut it down. Shut *him* down . . .'

Verity clamped her hands over her ears. 'I don't need to hear this,' she squeaked. 'It's none of my business.' Then again, it kind of was her business a little bit. 'When you say that you feel guilty . . . ' It was hard to think with so much champagne and emotion clouding her brain. What had Johnny said about his one true love's husband? That he was the rebound guy. 'Because you swooped in and . . . you . . . when they'd . . . '

'I'm the bastard who stole his best friend's

189

girl, right after his mother had died too just to really pile on the hurt,' Harry said. His lips twisted wryly. 'It always sounds so awful when I have to say it out loud but, in my defence, it wasn't *quite* like that.'

'Although it was a lot like that,' Johnny said from right behind Verity.

Verity jumped and she jumped again when Johnny's hands came to rest on her waist when there was no need for a boyfriendly gesture at this particular moment.

'You'd split up! And it wasn't like all the other times that you'd split up. You left the country,' Harry said without any heat but with a lot of weariness as if this was a well-trodden path that they'd both been down many times before.

'Yes, because, as you've just pointed out, my mother had just died,' Johnny said waspishly as if, unlike Harry, he still wasn't over all the whys and wherefores of his best friend and his girlfriend getting married behind his back, even though it had been ten years ago. 'I'm not going to apologise for daring to spend twenty minutes chatting with Rissa. We have a friendship, a relationship, that goes back years and is nothing to do with you, Harry. You don't own her.'

'That's right,' Harry agreed, but his weariness was gone and his temper was simmering now. Verity could see it in the flash of his eyes, the tightening of his jaw. 'She's a free woman. She can do what she likes and yet after all this time the one thing she doesn't want to do is *you*, mate. Funny that, isn't it?'

190

Verity felt like a pallid slice of luncheon meat trapped between two slices of dense bread.

'Trust you to reduce things down to their lowest common denominator.' Verity had never heard that sniping tone from Johnny before and she didn't much like it. 'Not everything is about se —'

'Enough!' she said sharply. 'That's quite enough from both of you. You,' she pointed at Harry. 'Go and find your wife and you,' she wriggled to get Johnny's hands off her, then wriggled again so she could swivel round on the stool to glare face-on at a flushed Johnny. 'You're staying here with me.'

Harry gave her a mock salute and strutted off and Johnny, at least, had the grace to look thoroughly discomfited.

'You can't even begin to understand the complexities of it all,' Johnny said dully. 'So there's no point in lecturing me about the errors of my ways. There's nothing you can say that I haven't already heard before, usually from the voice of my conscience.'

'No lectures,' Verity promised, because really? Where to even start? 'But I'd like to understand. Please.'

Johnny gave Verity a long, hard stare and she must have passed muster because then he nodded.

'All right then,' he said and sat down on the stool that Harry had just vacated. 'If you're sitting comfortably, then I'll begin.'

★   ★   ★

191

Once upon a time, some seventeen years ago, Johnny had met Marissa on his first day at Cambridge. Laden down with boxes, he'd been coming up a narrow twisty flight of stairs in one of the colleges as Marissa had run down them. They'd collided. Johnny's boxes and their contents had gone flying and, as they both bent to retrieve a copy of *A World History of Architecture*, they'd banged their heads and seen stars.

Fell in love at first sight, Johnny said, just like his father and mother had on their very first day at Cambridge, though to Verity it sounded a lot like Johnny and Marissa hadn't so much fallen in love as experienced a mild concussion.

The next three years at Cambridge had been a giddy, loved-up montage of punting on the Cam, riding bicycles everywhere together, a tiny flat that overlooked the river, weekends in London with Johnny's parents who had both adored Marissa, and also regular ferocious rows that led to them breaking up, realising that they couldn't live without each other and promptly getting back together.

'Because love isn't neat and tidy. It's messy, painful, real,' Johnny said and actually he and Nina had far more in common than Verity had imagined because she was also a big fan of china-smashing fights and subsequent declarations of love.

After they'd graduated from Cambridge, Johnny still had another four years of study before he qualified as an architect. He and Marissa moved into another tiny flat, this time in

192

Ladbroke Grove, and continued being giddy and loved-up, interspersed with the rowing and the parting and the getting back togethering.

In all this time, Harry was there too. Happy to be a third wheel or, if he was dating too, to make up a foursome. Not that any of his girlfriends lasted long and when Johnny and Marissa were on a break, he'd tell Johnny that he was being a bloody fool and that if he didn't come to his senses quickly some other man would come along and snap Marissa up.

And then in the final year of his postgraduate study Johnny's mother, Lucinda, had been diagnosed with stage three breast cancer, which had progressed to stage four faster than anyone thought possible. Johnny had been all ready to drop everything; his work, his exams, but his mother wouldn't hear of it. 'Marissa was an angel,' Johnny remembered, his voice hoarse like it still hurt to talk about it. 'She'd often sit with my mother as she had her chemotherapy and later, when she'd stopped treatment and was at home, Marissa would drop by of an evening. My mother, my father too, they liked that Marissa and I had fallen in love just like they had, in the same place too.'

'It *is* romantic, the similarities . . . ' Verity murmured, because it was.

'I asked her to marry me, you know,' Johnny said, his arms braced, his head back as if he was confessing to the fibre-optic stars twinkling above them on a black velvet background. 'She said yes so at least my mother knew before she died that she didn't have to worry on that score.

I'd found someone who I loved, who loved me. At least she had that.'

'I am sorry,' Verity whispered, reaching out to curl her fingers around Johnny's rigid wrist. It was a paltry attempt at comfort but she didn't know what else to do, what else to say.

'It's not your fault, Very.' Johnny glanced over at her with a small, sad smile. 'What happened next was entirely my fault. Marissa wanted to get married straight away, said that it was what my mother would have wanted, but it was too soon. My dad was devastated, in so much pain, and it didn't seem right to snatch at happiness and to skip over the sadness we all felt.

'We had a fight. It was what Marissa and I did. Fought. Made up. But the loss of her on top of everything and being in London . . . ' He shook his head. 'Memories of my mother everywhere and Dad and I needed to take some time out, some time away. It was a year or so after Hurricane Katrina and we decided to go to New Orleans, offer our services for people who really had lost everything. To build houses and make something good happen and while I was gone . . . ' He shook his head again. 'Well, you can fill in the blanks yourself.'

Verity really couldn't. Because Harry would have it that he and Marissa hadn't been able to help themselves when they'd fallen madly in love. Whereas Johnny believed that Marissa had married Harry in a fit of pique and that her love for Johnny hadn't changed, was still absolute. The truth was probably somewhere in the middle and might only be found by sitting down with the person right in the centre of it all, Marissa, and asking what her hot take on it was. Which was never going to happen, not in this lifetime. Besides, even though she'd only known Marissa a couple of hours, Verity felt sure the other woman was an unreliable witness.

Though perhaps she'd got Marissa wrong. Perhaps she really was a wonderful person and had no idea that Verity was a fake girlfriend. If the man who'd been in love with you for the last seventeen years suddenly rocked up with a new girl in tow, then that was bound to be a shock. Johnny had been in love with Marissa for so long that it had to be for a good reason and that reason couldn't be that Marissa was a humungous bitch.

'I'm sorry,' Verity said again. Those two words were all she could say.

'I have tried not to be in love with Marissa,' Johnny offered. 'I was seeing a woman a few years ago, another architect, I was even starting to think that we could be something but I was just fooling myself. When my father fell in love with my mother, that was it. His heart was taken. He hasn't looked at another woman in the ten years since she's been gone. Wouldn't want to because nobody could measure up. And I am my father's son; I fell in love with Marissa all those years ago and no other woman can take her place.'

There was so much Verity wanted to say but as a fake girlfriend, a casual observer, it wasn't her place. So she simply said, 'It looks like they're about to cut the cake.'

As she followed Johnny back to their table, his shoulders slumped, his head down, all Verity could think was what a terrible waste of such a good man.

15

*'There are very few who have heart enough
to be really in love without encouragement.'*

It was midway through July and the first week of
the school holidays. Verity had predicted that
both shop and tearoom would be heaving with
mothers and grandmothers and godmothers on a
hard-earned break from dragging youngsters
around the British Museum, but she'd been very
wrong.

Instead, the heavens had decided to open, the
rain poured down and, apart from the most
dedicated of romance readers, the shop stayed
largely empty.

'As long as it doesn't rain for ever and ever,
this is actually quite nice,' Posy admitted as she,
Verity, Nina and Tom stretched out on the three
sofas in the main room to have their
mid-morning tea break. 'Just like old times, isn't
it?'

'Ah yes, those old times when we had no
customers,' Tom said, hands behind his head,
legs stretched out in front of him. 'Now I'm
expected to work all day. Not that I mind,' he
added hastily.

'I like it when it's busy, the day goes so much
quicker,' Nina said, as she snagged another piece
of shortbread from the plate Mattie had brought
in with their tea and coffee. She'd forbidden

them from ever again opening a jar of instant coffee or box of teabags in her presence. 'Although we hardly ever get any men coming into the shop these days.'

'Except Sebastian,' Posy pointed out because she hadn't mentioned Sebastian for at least five minutes. 'Anyway, Nina, remember we had that rule about you not dating customers after Desperate Dan.'

Desperate Dan had been a loyal customer back when the shop had been called Bookends until Nina had gone on two dates with him, decided that he was too vanilla for her tastes and dumped him. He'd come in every day after that, not to buy anything, but to sit on a sofa gazing at Nina and offering to fight any man that dared approach the counter so she could ring up their purchases. Lavinia had had to ban him for life.

Verity sipped her tea and stared out of the rain-splattered window.

'That was a deep sigh, Very,' Posy noted. 'You've been awfully quiet these last few days. Quiet, even for you. I was beginning to think you'd taken a vow of silence until I heard you telling Merry to shut up on the phone.'

'I'm fine.' Verity left it there until Tom gave a pointed cough and she was forced to look up from deep contemplation of the knees of her jeans to see all eyes on her. 'Really I'm fine. I had to be very sociable at the wedding on Saturday and now I've used up my quota of words for the month.'

It also felt as if she'd used up all her reserves of energy too. Not just from all she'd witnessed;

the unpleasant encounters with Marissa, the heart-to-heart with Harry, Johnny's desperately sad confession, but from trying to make sense of it all too.

'Very, you don't look fine. You look like you're about to burst into tears,' Nina said gently. 'And last night you went to bed as soon as we came upstairs.'

'Though to be fair, you do often look like you're about to burst into tears,' Tom remarked. He leaned forward to peer at Verity sitting on the sofa opposite. 'Some girls have resting bitch face but you have resting mope face.'

'Hey! You're not allowed to call women bitches.' Nina took great delight in punching Tom on the arm.

'I didn't call anyone a bitch. It's a thing; resting bitch face. You know it's a thing.'

They argued about it for a while, Posy inevitably taking Nina's side because Tom was the only man on staff, and part-time too, so it was important that he knew his place in the pecking order.

It took a while for them to register the tinkle of the bell above the door that signalled that they might actually have a customer. Not Verity's problem, in fact, she should probably escape to the quiet of the office where there wasn't anyone to mind that she had a face like a wet weekend in Skegness.

Nina hoisted herself up from the depths of the sofa. 'Welcome to Happy Ever After. Are you looking for anything in particular?'

Verity had her back to the door so she couldn't

see their visitor but then she heard a pleasant, cultured, unfamiliar male voice say, 'I'm looking for a young lady by the name of Verity.'

Posy and Tom both widened their eyes dramatically and Verity swivelled round to see a tall man in a cream-coloured suit. He was in his sixties (but a very well-preserved sixties) and before Nina could gesture in Verity's direction, he looked at Verity and his eyes lit up as if he knew his search was over.

Despite her general ennui (or what any one of her sisters called her misery-guts-itis) Verity was intrigued and maybe a little unnerved. Did she owe someone money? Was she being sued? But she'd led such a blameless life. She got to her feet. 'Hello?' she enquired nervously.

'Hello!' The man strode over hand out-stretched so Verity found her own hand grasped in a firm but not crushing grip. 'I'm William. What a pleasure it is to meet you!'

'I'm Verity and er, it's nice to meet you too,' Verity replied. 'I'm sorry, have we met before?' The situation wasn't entirely unfamiliar. 'Are you one of my father's parishioners? Or perhaps you were at theological college with him?'

'I'm afraid I've never had a calling,' the man, William, said. He took Verity by the arm so he could gently pull her into the first side room as Verity's three colleagues craned their necks and strained their ears so they didn't miss a thing. 'I'm sorry to turn up like this. I'm Johnny's father. No! He doesn't know I'm here,' he added quickly as Verity felt her features rearranging into a horrified pattern.

'Um, er, why are you here?' Verity asked.

'I thought I'd rather take the two-birds-with-one-stone approach while I was in town. You see, I bumped into Wallis last week . . . Lovely girl. Was singing your praises and then I spoke with young Harry yesterday . . . '

Verity had to cling to the nearest bookshelf for support. 'You speak to Harry? Is that a regular thing?'

William nodded. She could see his resemblance to Johnny now. Not just in his height and ranginess, but in the jut of his cheekbones, the same oceanic bluey greenness of his eyes. 'Oh yes. Harry gives me lots of advice about where to invest my pension. And of course I've known him since he was eleven. He and Johnny were thick as thieves and would get up to all kinds of mischief. But yesterday when we chatted, well, you can imagine my surprise when he told me that my Johnny was seeing, and I quote, 'an absolute sort', when Johnny hadn't said a word to his dear, doting dad.'

Verity had never been described as 'an absolute sort' before. It was more the kind of compliment that Nina got from her gentleman callers. 'Was it a medium-sized surprise?'

'A huge surprise,' William clarified. 'Not once in five years have I heard of even the suggestion of a girlfriend. Not since he was seeing Katie. She was very nice, but alas, it was not to be.' He shook his head sorrowfully, then caught Verity's eye and visibly brightened. 'And now, here you are!'

'Oh, I wouldn't say I was a girlfriend exactly,'

Verity mumbled, her cheeks as red as the cover of a face-out copy of a collector's edition of *Madame Bovary* on the shelf she was leaning against. 'Johnny and I are just friends.'

'Friends with benefits?' William asked hopefully and Verity wondered if she might be having an attack of the vapours. 'Because who knows where that might lead? I'm not getting any younger and I would be very happy if there was even an outside chance that I might have grandchildren before I'm completely decrepit.'

Verity thought she might need smelling salts quite soon. 'Just friends,' she repeated maniacally. 'It's very early days. Very, very early.' She couldn't bear the look of disappointment on William's face and the subject needed changing immediately if not sooner. 'Was there another thing? You said two birds with one stone. Who's the other bird?'

'Just so you know, I'm not the sort of chap who ever refers to women as birds, but I was after a present for a 'friend' of mine.' William put quotes around the word with long fingers. He had a twinkle in his eye that was hard to resist.

'What kind of present?' Verity asked, hoping she could guide William back into the main room where they had vintage display cabinets full of gifts and she could offload him onto Nina, though Nina was hardly the soul of discretion. She'd pump William for information about Johnny and . . .

'A present for a very dear lady. A book, obviously. I'm not sure what she's read and what she hasn't. She has quite classic tastes but then again, she can also be quite eclectic.' William scratched his head. He had a rather magnificent mane of snowy white hair only beginning to recede ever so slightly, which boded well for Johnny, who would still probably be in love with Marissa when he was in his sixties.

Books. That was safer ground. And there was one book that could always be guaranteed to please the recipient. '*Pride and Prejudice*,' Verity said firmly.

'I'm sure she must have read it. Hasn't everyone read it?'

'Johnny hasn't,' Verity said, seeing her chance and grabbing hold of it with both hands. 'It's why we're only friends. I could never love a man who didn't love *Pride and Prejudice*.'

The twinkle in William's eye burned a little brighter. 'I shall make him read it immediately.'

Verity turned away to hide her smile because she was sure it would only encourage him. 'We have some gorgeous gift editions,' she persisted, pulling a couple from the shelf. 'This one has a cloth cover in a textile design from the year it was first published. Beautiful end papers too.'

'Oh, that is rather splendid.' William took the book from Verity. 'And you really think it wouldn't matter if she already had it?'

'I currently have seven copies of *Pride and Prejudice*,' Verity confessed because there was something about William with his twinkling and his ready smile that made you want to confide in him. He would have made a wonderful vicar if he had ever had the calling. 'The one that I've had since I was twelve, a spare for when that one

203

finally falls apart, one collector's edition and four to foist on people I meet who haven't read it yet. I'm sure that if your friend has read *Pride and Prejudice*, she loved it and if she did love it, then she wouldn't mind having another copy.'

William pondered her words as Verity heard Posy say loudly from the main room: 'I don't believe it! Verity is hand-selling books in there. It must be the End of Days.'

'I'll take it,' William decided.

'Great.' They were done here. Verity took a step towards the arch that led back into the main shop, keen that William should follow her, but he placed a hand on her arm.

'Oh dear, this is rather awkward,' he said, which were six words that never led to anything good.

With a silent prayer, Verity halted. 'What's awkward?' she asked even as she cringed at the thought of what William's answer might be.

'My friend, Elspeth . . . She really is much more than a friend. Possibly a friend in the way you and Johnny are friends . . . '

'No, but we really are just friends,' Verity said a little desperately. William patted her arm like he didn't believe a word of it.

'Your secret's safe with me,' he said conspiratorially. 'And I hope my secret will be safe with you because, goodness . . . I hardly know where to begin.'

'You really don't need to explain anything to me,' Verity said, but she was very confused. This Elspeth, William's dear friend, didn't fit in with what Johnny had told her at the wedding. That

William was so devoted to his wife, had been so devastated after her death, he'd vowed never to look at another woman. Not that Verity blamed William for breaking his vow but it did mean that . . . 'You haven't told Johnny.' It wasn't a question but a gentle statement of fact. 'He doesn't know about Elspeth.'

'I'm afraid not.' William's twinkle had gone and he suddenly looked so dejected that all Verity wanted to do was make him feel better. 'I was so sad after Johnny's mother, Lucinda, died. Sad doesn't even come close, really. I was broken-hearted, a broken man, and for such a long time afterwards I was adamant that I'd never love again. That I wouldn't want to. And I still believe that I'll never love anyone as I loved Lucinda but there are different sorts of love, aren't there?'

'I think so,' Verity decided. 'It would be pretty unfair if you only had one chance at love. My mother always says 'Broken hearts make the best vessels.' ' She frowned. 'Usually when one of my sisters has split up with a boyfriend. You are allowed to find love again. Life would be very lonely if you weren't.'

Verity's words had obviously moved William because he took her hand and squeezed it gently. And Verity was moved by her own words even though they went against everything she believed: that one could live a perfectly content sort of life without any kind of romantic attachment.

'I hope the fact that you're in Johnny's life means that he's changing his way of thinking on the subject of love,' William said rather alarmingly. 'It's probably my fault that Johnny's set so much store on this idea of one true love, of a perfect soulmate, like swans who mate for life.'

'Is it swans?' Verity said, playing for time. 'I thought it was penguins.'

'Maybe lobsters too. Lucinda and I always told Johnny how lucky we were that we found each other. That we were meant to be.' William was not to be dissuaded from discussing his son's theories on love. 'So he set his cap at Marissa, I take it you met her at the wedding . . . ?'

'I did,' Verity said and she couldn't help the way her top lip curled, but it was no match for the way that William's nostrils flared at the mention of Marissa's name.

'She's a nice enough girl, a little petulant for my liking, but Johnny always persisted with this idea that she was the only woman for him, when she quite patently wasn't. Thank goodness she saw sense and married Harry instead. They're far better suited, but I did wonder if Johnny was still holding a torch for her.' William shuddered at the notion and the fact that he wasn't a fully paid-up member of the Marissa fan club made Verity like him even more. 'She's not and never has been what my boy needs.'

'Your boy would be mortified if he knew we were discussing him like this,' Verity pointed out softly because this conversation had to end right the hell now. Short of talking about sex (dear God, no) Verity didn't see how it could get any more uncomfortable. 'You barely know me. And I barely know him. Honestly, we've been seeing each other, *only as friends*, for a few weeks.'

'But you've met all his chums and you're such a lovely girl,' William protested.

And Verity did want to grill him further, poke and pry and ask what Lucinda had really thought about Marissa because, according to Johnny, his mother had considered Marissa to be perfect daughter-in-law material, but it would be an absolute violation of . . . something. Johnny's privacy. Lucinda's memory. Husband/wife confidentiality. She held the cloth-covered edition of *Pride and Prejudice* in front of her like the protective talisman it usually was. 'Now, would you like the book gift-wrapped? We have some beautiful hand-painted cards that you might want to have a look at too.'

With that, and her hand firmly at the small of his back, Verity guided William back into the main shop where Posy, Nina and Tom suddenly became very animated, pulling books from the shelves, then shoving them back willy nilly so Verity knew that they'd spent the last ten minutes shamelessly eavesdropping on her conversation.

16

'A report of a most alarming nature reached
me two days ago.'

William's visit, followed by the sun deciding to
put in an appearance the next day, shook Verity
out of her funk.

But if she was still walking about with her
resting mope face on, it was because her heart
was still hurting on Johnny's behalf. He was so
unhappy even though he had so many people
focussed on his happiness; William, most of his
friends, even Harry, though obviously Harry had
an ulterior motive. He'd much rather Johnny was
happy with a woman who wasn't Harry's wife.

To show that there were no hard feelings after
all the hideousness at the wedding reception,
Verity texted Johnny to let him know that she
was out of town for the weekend, not that they'd
made any plans.

At my parents' for wedding prep bootcamp. With
all four sisters. Pray for me! Will be in touch next
week.

Then, she decided, next week, though the
thought of it pained her and even though they
weren't having a relationship, they were still
going to have to have A Serious Talk about where
this was headed and about other people's

208

expectations. As it was, Verity was pretty sure that Johnny regretted blurting out the deepest secrets of his heart to an almost stranger. She wouldn't be at all surprised if he never contacted her again. Which made her poor heart carry on aching and . . .

'Hey! Vicar's daughter!' Verity stopped her pondering when someone rudely snapped their fingers in her face. It was Sebastian, who knew perfectly well what Verity's name was, and he also knew, because Posy told him repeatedly, not to snap his fingers in people's faces. 'You don't get paid to daydream!'

'I wasn't daydreaming, I was thinking,' Verity hissed and she made a big show of staring at her computer monitor, which thankfully showed a spreadsheet and not Con's wedding Pinterest board. She even bashed away at her keyboard a whole lot of word salad that she then had to delete.

' . . . and I had to get a locksmith round because Morland was right, no one could find the keys, and even that wasn't enough to satisfy her . . . '

Sebastian was yammering on about who knew what? How could Posy stand it? Posy was a chatterer too but at least it was interesting chat about books and amusing things that Sam had done and . . .

'You haven't been listening to a single word I'm saying, have you?' Sebastian suddenly demanded. 'I wonder why I bother sometimes.'

'I'm very busy,' Verity explained, hammering at her keyboard again. 'Was there something

209

specific you wanted from me?' She heard Sebastian's annoyed growl and perhaps she should be more helpful. After all Sebastian was married to Posy and Posy rather seemed to like him and Posy did pay Verity's wages. 'Sorry, it's just these are very important spreadsheets.'

She looked up to see Sebastian pinching the bridge of his nose. 'I already said, your bloke's outside. You need to go and distract him, take him a cup of tea or something, because he's giving Morland ideas and I live in terror of Morland's ideas and . . . where are you going?'

Verity was already on her feet and at the door of the office. 'Johnny's *outside*? And anyway, he's not my bloke and why didn't you say something?'

She didn't wait to find out his answer, but she did hear a small explosion as if Sebastian had spontaneously combusted . . .

The little mews was bustling with people so that it was hard to remember that it used to be deserted on even the loveliest summer days like this one. People were sitting on the benches and there was a small queue outside the tearoom — Verity could not wait for the day that the council finally granted them permission to have a small number of tables and chairs outside.

But none of the people in the mews were Johnny. Verity stood motionless for a moment until she saw two people come out of one of the shops on the other side of the courtyard and she did a double take.

The shops on the other side of the courtyard were boarded up and empty and had been for

210

the entire five years that Verity had been working in the bookshop.

Once upon a time the near-derelict buildings had housed a florist, a tea and coffee merchant, a haberdashers and a stamp shop. The premises Johnny and Posy had just exited, brushing themselves down as they did so, had once been an apothecary that even Posy couldn't remember ever being open and she'd lived in the mews most of her life. Though it wasn't surprising it had gone out of business when it hadn't joined the twentieth century, never mind the twenty-first, and rebranded as a chemist.

'Very!' Posy called out and Verity walked over. Johnny smiled and kept brushing his hands over his suit and Posy was patting down her hair and an odd feeling yanked at Verity's gut. A feeling that felt very close to jealousy at the horrible, world-shattering suspicion that Posy and Johnny had been doing things in the old apothecary shop that had got them all rumpled and in need of straightening up.

Then as Verity got closer, she saw the streaks of dirt on Posy's pretty face. 'Ugh! It's so dusty and rank in there and I think a bat just flew into my hair.'

'I'm sure it was just cobwebs,' Johnny said, reaching up to pull some out of his own hair. 'Though I wouldn't rule out rats. Hello,' he added to Verity as she tried out a welcoming yet slightly confused smile.

'Hello. Apparently I'm meant to be distracting you from giving Posy ideas, not that I'm going to.' When it came to taking sides, Verity was

Team Posy every time. 'What kind of ideas are these?'

'Oh, Very! You should see inside! Except you can't really because there's no electricity and the windows are boarded up and we think that one of the ceiling joists might have woodworm,' Posy said excitedly. 'But . . . but . . . the shop still has lots of its original fixtures and fittings.'

'Beautiful cabinetry,' Johnny said with a soft, wistful look in his eyes. 'Exquisite. And so many glass bottles and jars, even old-fashioned scales and several different sizes of pestles and mortars.'

'Boring! If I left it to you two, you'd want to preserve it as is as some kind of museum to dusty old things and inefficient business practices,' said Sebastian, who could never stay away from Posy's side for too long, even when she was glaring ferociously at him.

'I don't want to do that,' Posy countered. 'I just said that rather than tearing the whole thing down like some kind of capitalist philistine, you . . . *we* should think about other options. You could restore the shops, rent them out, and then the flats above them . . . '

'There are *flats* above them?' Verity asked in astonishment. 'Why have they been empty for so long?'

'Lavinia used to let her impoverished artist friends live there but then her impoverished artist friends all got old and died,' Sebastian said. When he talked about his grandmother who'd left him everything in the mews that wasn't the bookshop, his voice became tender and his face

212

lost its usual haughty look. 'I suppose Morland expects me to let them out rent-free too.'

Verity squirmed a little at that because Posy wouldn't even discuss the possibility of she and Nina paying any rent on the flat above Happy Ever After. 'Lavinia let me and Sam live there for nothing so I'm just paying it forward,' she insisted each time they broached the subject.

'You could rent them out at a not stupidly exorbitant fee,' Posy said now. 'As live/work spaces for young artisans, for example.'

Sebastian pretended to yawn.

'It does seem a pity to ruin the integrity of the buildings,' Johnny said before Verity could tell him not to bother getting in between Posy and Sebastian when they were having an argument. In fact, it was best to stand well back and if possible pull on a hazmat suit. 'I'm not sure that they were originally a stable block, like you said. And they look early eighteenth century to me. Might be worth checking with the Land Registry.'

'Oh! I bet they really should be Grade 2 listed,' Posy exclaimed triumphantly.

'Over my dead body!' Sebastian huffed back.

'That could be arranged!'

Verity had the unwelcome feeling, not for the first time, that unlike herself who would do anything, even walk a mile out of her way, to avoid a confrontation, Posy and Sebastian enjoyed disagreeing with each other. It was a theory Nina shared.

'I don't think that is arguing, Very,' Nina had remarked a couple of weeks before when she and

Verity were cowering on the stairs as Posy and Sebastian had a furious row about the two carrier bags full of books that Posy intended on taking home with her. 'I think it's foreplay.'

As the newlyweds circled each other, Verity took Johnny by the sleeve of his suit jacket. 'It's really best not to get involved,' she said, as one of the benches became free so they could sit down. 'What brings you to this part of town?'

'I thought we should have a chat about all sorts of awkward things that it would be easier to leave unsaid.' Johnny made sure to look Verity straight in the eye and, though she didn't feel that she was personally responsible for much of this alleged awkwardness, it was still hard not to wriggle under his gaze. He'd really caught the sun over the last few weeks, his face tanned, which made his eyes seem impossibly blue. 'Like last Saturday, for instance. It all got rather intense. I wouldn't blame you if you were very cross with me.'

'I wasn't cross,' Verity said though she'd been pretty tight-lipped on the way home from the wedding reception. 'I wasn't expecting to meet Marissa . . .'

'I didn't know she and Harry were going to be there. Not for sure.'

'And I wasn't expecting you to abandon me,' Verity said in an aggrieved voice as she remembered all over again how Johnny and Marissa had sat there for ages, their heads together, as if the whole world, and especially Verity, didn't exist any more.

'I didn't abandon you. You left the table and

never came back,' he protested. 'So, what did you think of Marissa?'

Merry's pithy summing up of Marissa as a 'stealth bitch' after a Sunday debrief pretty much seemed to cover it, not that Verity would ever admit that to Johnny. She believed in what she called the solidarity of sisterhood and what Merry and Nina called hos before bros. Verity wouldn't want to be one of those women who ran other women down, that was never a good look. 'I didn't really get a chance to talk to her properly,' she said vaguely.

'Well, when I spoke to Marissa the next day, she said that she thought you were fascinating,' Johnny said, which Verity found hard to believe but props to Marissa for continuing to be able to do no wrong in Johnny's eyes.

'You talked to Marissa the next day?' *About me? Even after the argument you had with Harry?* Unlike Johnny, Verity was determined to leave the awkward things unsaid but she hoped her incredulous tone would say them for her.

'I talk to Marissa most days,' Johnny said evenly. 'Is that really so odd, now that you know what she means to me?'

'Well, no,' Verity admitted. Or rather, it wasn't a surprise but it was odd. The whole Johnny/Marissa/Harry thing was odd in ways that defied reason and logic.

'And my father thinks you're, and this is a direct quote, 'an absolute smasher'. He used the word 'wonderful' several times too, also 'intelligent, well-read, kind' and what was the other thing? That if he were thirty years younger, he'd

215

be head over heels in love with you himself.' Johnny shifted on the bench and moved his hand so it was almost but not quite touching Verity's hand, which she was resting on the seat between them. 'I am so sorry, I had no idea that he even knew about you, let alone that he'd come and bother you at work. Apparently, I have Harry and Wallis to thank for that.'

Just the thought of William made Verity smile. 'He didn't bother me.'

'He's also very disappointed with me for not reading *Pride and Prejudice*,' Johnny said with a reluctant smile of his own. 'Demanded that I rectify this at once.'

'Oh, you don't have to do that,' Verity assured him.

'He seemed to think that if I did, you and me were a done deal and that he could look forward to hordes of fat-cheeked grandchildren running amok.' Johnny shook his head as if nothing could be further from the truth, which was fine. Verity knew that anyway. 'He means well but . . . '

'He does mean well and all he wants is for you to be happy. That's not such a bad thing for a father to want for his son,' Verity said. 'It's just that you both disagree about what will make you happy.'

Johnny thought that Marissa was the answer to all his prayers and William thought that Verity was what was missing from Johnny's life. It was a bad case of crossed wires. Then there was William's own *affaire de coeur*. 'So, did he say anything else?' Verity asked casually though the words got a little stuck in her throat. 'Give any

216

other reasons about why he was hanging about in a romantic fiction bookshop?'

'He told me about Elspeth, if that's what you mean,' Johnny said. He leaned forward, elbows on his knees, chin resting on his hands, his gaze fixed on Posy and Sebastian who were still arguing so it was impossible for Verity to see anything other than his profile, which gave no indication as to how he might feel about his father's new girlfriend. Although she hadn't sounded new but rather as if she'd been in William's life for quite some time. 'Which I'm fine with. I was surprised, yes, and maybe even a little hurt that he thought I wouldn't be fine with it.'

'He was worried that you might think that it meant that he loved your mother less,' Verity ventured gently. 'That you had this romantic idea that everyone only had one true love, like penguins or swans.'

'He's not in love with the woman. Let's not get carried away. They're just friends,' Johnny said in a voice that dared Verity to disagree so she decided it was best not to. 'Though William did tell me your theory that people who've lost a love are better at finding it again. I had no idea you were such a hopeless romantic.'

'Well, not everyone who's lost a love,' Verity muttered because Johnny had lost Marissa to Harry years ago but was still pining. So if anyone was a hopeless romantic, it was Johnny. She racked her brains for something that would steer them to calmer waters.

'Anyway, for what it's worth, William has

taken rather a shine to you. He's going to email to invite you to dinner so we can both meet this Elspeth. He actually called it a double date.' Johnny laughed at the notion, though it sounded rather hollow to Verity's ears. 'Can you imagine it?'

'Not really,' Verity said although she would have liked to spend time with William in different circumstances and not in the circumstances where William was hoping that Johnny was going to welcome 'this Elspeth' with open arms, then drop to his knees and propose to Verity. 'Usually, it's my family who can't stop themselves from meddling — not that your father was meddling.'

'Actually that's the other reason why I'm here.' Johnny was looking at her now, his expression amused, eyes twinkling so she could see the resemblance between father and son again. 'I had an email from your mother. At least I think it was your mother. She did sign off as Our Vicar's Wife.'

Verity choked. 'Say what now?'

'You might want to brace yourself,' Johnny advised her.

'Oh God, what fresh hell is this?' Verity moaned. 'Why on earth would Muv be emailing you? How did she even get your address?'

'She got it from Merry, who I can only imagine got it from the company website,' Johnny said calmly enough, even though Verity could feel her heart hammering away like a woodpecker on steroids.

'I am going to kill my sister,' Verity promised

in a suitably murderous voice. 'Slowly and painfully.'

Johnny shook his head like he didn't want to be an accessory to these plans. 'Anyway, your mother has invited me down for the weekend. Apparently Our Vicar is keen to show me his beehives while you ladies are occupied with wedding planning. Is showing me his beehives some kind of religious euphemism?'

'No! He's very into beekeeping. He has hives in the back garden and two at the local primary school. Once he starts talking about his bees . . . ' Verity sighed. 'It's a toss-up which is worse, wedding planning with all four sisters and Our Vicar's Wife, or Our Vicar explaining how he plans to introduce a new queen to one of his colonies. It's just as well that you can duck out. I'll phone Muv, extend your apologies and all that.'

'Oh. You don't want me to meet your parents?' Johnny asked, his brow furrowing in a way that pinged in a small corner of Verity's heart until she reminded herself of one important fact.

'You don't need to meet them. We're just friends, as Merry knows only too well so I don't know why she's meddling too!'

'You've already met my family, so I don't see why I shouldn't meet yours,' Johnny argued, like there was some kind of *quid pro quo* thing going on when there really wasn't.

'I only met your father. We're talking about a full house here,' Verity sighed. 'Mum, Dad, all four sisters, maybe even a couple of cousins.' She was running out of fingers to count on.

'Probably a couple of stray parishioners, who've come to talk about the church flowers and ended up staying for a week because their boiler's on the blink.'

'William is my only family,' Johnny reminded her. 'He and my mother were both the only children of couples who married quite late in life. It's been just the two of us for as long as I can remember.'

He was using his hurt voice and his brow had furrowed again so Verity had a glimpse of the little boy he might once have been with elderly grandparents and no siblings or cousins to run riot with, invite on to his pirate ship . . .

'Look, it just feels like a lie if I introduce you to my family,' Verity tried to explain. 'If I bring you home, you don't know what they're like, they'll read into it.' Verity pulled a weary face because this was not her first time at the rodeo, no sir. 'They'll read an entire library worth of books into it.'

'But it's not a lie. Your sisters already know the truth and we've never told anyone that we're dating. We've always introduced ourselves as friends,' Johnny persisted though Verity didn't know why he was bothering. If he thought he was being invited to a pleasant weekend in a rambling vicarage with a charmingly eccentric family in the East Lincolnshire Wold, he should think again. He was being invited to an apocalypse.

'We've let people think that we're dating. We've lied by omission. There's a reason why lying is frowned upon heavily in the ten commandments,' Verity said in a manner that was far too close to Mary Bennet, her fictional nemesis, for her liking.

'Actually it isn't,' Johnny said with just enough smugness that Verity didn't feel that much sympathy for his lack of family any more. 'Thou shalt not lie is not one of the ten commandments.'

'Really? You really want to go there with me? A bona fide vicar's daughter?' Verity demanded. 'The commandment you're after is thou shalt not bear false witness against . . . '

'Oh God, you two, get a room!' snapped Sebastian as he strode over. 'Word of warning, don't start arguing with any of these bloody bookshop shrews. The next thing you know, you're married to one of them. Ow!'

Posy didn't look even a little bit sorry for slapping her husband upside his rude head. 'You *begged* me to marry you,' she hissed. 'I have witnesses.'

Verity hated arguing with anyone, unless that anyone happened to be one of her sisters and then arguing was not only necessary but about as useful as howling at the moon. She certainly didn't want to argue with Johnny, especially if it led to matrimony.

'Look, if you really want to come for the weekend you can,' she said and as soon as the words were out of her mouth, she wanted to pluck them from the air and stuff them back in.

Johnny beamed so hard that, sitting there in his suit, tie loosened, top button undone, he looked like he'd stepped out of a *GQ* fashion editorial, damn him.

'I'm looking forward to it,' he said. 'You're still quite a mystery to me, Verity. I can't wait to figure out a few more clues.'

Verity wished that she were more enigmatic and then she'd never have started down the road of fake boyfriends and ended up in this mess. 'Well, don't say you weren't warned. And you'd better pack earplugs and a stun gun, because you're going to need them.'

17

'One must speak a little, you know. It would look odd to be entirely silent for half an hour.'

The following Saturday Johnny picked up Verity, then Merry who immediately booted Verity out of the passenger seat ('You know I get sick if I sit in the back') then barely drew breath for the next hour. First, she filled Johnny in on the likes and dislikes of Our Vicar and Our Vicar's Wife whether he wanted filling in or not, then moved on to her sisters when Johnny asked if Immy was short for Imogen and Chatty short for Charlotte.

'God, no! Hasn't Very told you anything about us? How rude, when we're all so endlessly fascinating! We're all named after virtues, though Farv and Muv say that they needn't have bothered, because none of us are the least bit virtuous. Apart from Very, of course.'

'So, your name isn't Merry, then?' Johnny ventured as Merry did finally stop talking but only so she could shove another Percy Pig in her mouth. 'I did wonder.'

'It's Mercy,' the woman herself said witheringly as if Johnny was an utter imbecile for not being able to figure that out on his own. 'Con is really Constance, we call Patience Immy because she's totally *impatient* and Charity is Chatty because she never shuts up.'

Johnny caught Verity's pained look in the

223

rearview mirror. 'Talking of never shutting up, I'm going to dump you at Birchanger Green services if you don't zip it for at least fifteen minutes,' Johnny said but Merry just grinned then launched into a long story about the psychological warfare she was waging on a woman in her department at work who kept sending round-robin passive-aggressive emails about the state of the office fridge.

Actually three hours in a car with Merry was a good way to desensitise Johnny for the ordeal ahead.

As usual, his phone beeped constantly to compete with Merry's verbal diarrhoea and when they did reach Birchanger Green services, Johnny immediately seized the phone, thrust a ten-pound note at Verity and asked her to get him a coffee and a muffin. 'Darling,' she heard him say as he strode away. 'First chance I've had to call you.'

Verity wished that Costa Coffee did shots of love-repellent so she could slip a couple into Johnny's latte. She also wished she could get a shot of liquid Valium to add to Merry's cappuccino. As it was her sister only stopped talking when they left the A16 at Louth, which put the SatNav into such a panic that it tried to direct them back to the motorway, and Johnny finally snapped. 'Have some mercy, Merry! Can you please be quiet before I lose my mind?'

Merry couldn't even be quiet quietly but huffed and sighed as they drove up the hills and down the valleys of the Lincolnshire Wold and through tiny villages, each prettier than the last, until they came to Lambton. It had a village green with duckpond, a Post Office cum general store, a pub, the Lambton Inn, and a church, which had been rebuilt in utilitarian brick and stone with very few fancy flourishes in the mid eighteenth century though no one could say what had happened to the old church. Across the road from the church was the Old Rectory, built a hundred years later; a three-storey Gothic-style redbrick house, which had all the fancy flourishes that were missing from the church including mullioned windows and a hexagonal turret that overlooked the side lawn.

It was nearly twenty-six miles and a world away from the three-bedroom prefab on the edge of a sprawling council estate in Grimsby where they'd grown up. As the tyres crunched over the gravel drive, Verity wondered, not for the first time, if life would have been different if they'd had a bit of breathing space then. Room to roam and grow, instead of being heaped on top of one another, with nothing to do but bicker and gang up on each other. Perhaps she wouldn't have been the only quiet one.

'Oh my God! Am I allowed to talk now?' Merry dramatically gasped for air as if Johnny had told her to stop breathing too and Verity revised her opinion. It was possible that, if they'd had a bedroom each and a huge garden to play in, so there had been further distance between them and a genuine need to shout, her sisters would have been even louder than they were, which didn't even seem possible.

'I do like a good turret,' Johnny remarked, as

he turned off the engine and took a moment to give the Old Rectory the once-over. 'Looks like it may have been designed by S.S. Teulon. He was quite a famous Victorian architect.'

Merry had already scrambled from the car so it was just the two of them.

'It's not too late to turn round,' Verity said and she wasn't even joking. 'We could be back in London by ten.'

'We're not turning round,' Johnny said firmly with a reassuring smile. 'For one thing, I can't wait to explore the house.'

Verity gave Johnny one last chance to back out. 'Are you sure you're up to this?' she asked him as she unlocked the front door, because of course Merry didn't know where her keys were.

'It's twenty-four hours in the Lincolnshire Wold, what could be more pleasant?' he asked even though through the open windows Verity could already hear three separate sources of music, a dog barking, children shrieking and what sounded like a rugby team running up and down the stairs in hobnailed boots.

Then Verity got the door open and the noise became a veritable wall of sound that would have even Phil Spector begging for a pair of ear defenders. In the front room on their right, the TV was on and three small children, whom Verity had never seen before, were leaping from armchair to sofa and back again, screaming as they went.

'Mind the boxes,' Merry told Johnny as they inched down the hall past a stack of cardboard boxes and a teetering pile of laundry bags spilling out old clothes, battered toys, dog-eared paperbacks and assorted items to be filed under bric-a-brac. 'Must be for the jumble sale.'

Through the next doorway, the dining room, a girl of about nine or ten was pounding away at the piano.

'Hello! Hello! Who are *you*?' Merry asked and the girl swung round. She had a stubborn tilt to her chin, a turned-up nose and a ferocious glare.

'Madison,' she said. 'Who are *you*?'

'All right. Moving on,' Verity said and they proceeded to the big kitchen at the back of the vicarage, where Our Vicar and Our Vicar's Wife were standing, with their backs to them, at the sink happily peeling vegetables and singing 'I Like To Be In America' from *West Side Story*.

'Farv! Muv!' Merry cried and their parents turned round.

'Oh, hello,' Dora Love said vaguely as if she wasn't quite sure who they were or what they were doing in her kitchen. She was the sort of woman who drooped slightly at the edges. Even when they were freshly ironed, her clothes looked rumpled. Her messy bun, wisps of ash-blonde hair escaping, rivalled any messy bun that Posy had attempted, but she had the warmest brown eyes, which were never anything but kind.

'What visions of loveliness stand before me?' intoned Ken Love in a loud voice perfect for sermonising and leading the congregation in song. He was a head taller than his wife, equally crumpled, and with the wild hair of a mad professor. To a stranger, Mr Love might seem imposing but Mr Love also firmly believed that there was no such thing as a stranger, only a friend you hadn't met yet, so would usually end up inviting said stranger back to the vicarage for supper. 'Second daughter! Middle daughter! Come give your father a fortifying kiss! And who is this handsome chap? Has he come to ask for one of your hands in marriage?'

'Not my hand in marriage,' Merry said as she pushed Verity out of the way so she could be first in line for one of the vicar's exuberant hugs. 'Maybe Very's.'

'Ignore her,' Verity advised, as she offered her left cheek for her father to kiss, then her right cheek to her mother for the same treatment. 'This is Johnny, my friend. He's an architect. He knows who designed the vicarage.'

'Oh! Your friend! Johnny! Yes, so pleased you could come.' Dora Love took Johnny's hand. 'And so pleased you and Very are spending time together.'

Our Vicar looked Johnny up and down. Johnny suffered the attention with a patient smile until Ken nodded. 'I will execute great vengeance on them with wrathful rebukes. Then they will know that I am the Lord, when I lay my vengeance upon them,' he said by way of a greeting. 'Ezekiel 25:17. Be nice to our Verity. We're rather fond of her, you see.'

It was the first time that any of Verity's boyfriends had got a bible verse but then the only other boyfriend she'd ever had was Adam and before she'd brought him to meet the folks, she'd pre-warned her father that Adam didn't

228

have the inner reserves of strength to cope with a bible verse.

As it was, Verity had been terrified that the combined force of all the Loves would destroy Adam before he'd even taken his coat off. They hadn't but they'd certainly crushed his spirit. He'd barely spoken two complete sentences during the entire uncomfortable weekend that he'd spent at the vicarage.

Johnny was made of stronger stuff because he simply dipped his head in acknowledgement of Our Vicar's implied threat. 'I'm rather fond of Verity too,' he said and though he meant in a friendly way because they were friends, it made Verity's heart do a strange, skippy thing. Then Johnny held up a bag from the very posh Ottolenghi deli in Islington and a bottle of red wine that looked as if it had cost a lot more than six quid, which was the most that Verity had ever paid for a bottle of wine. 'Thank you for inviting me.'

'Is that chocolate brittle?' Merry asked, trying to make a grab for the Ottolenghi bag but was held back by her father. 'Did you get the salt caramel?'

'Desist, devil child!'

'Actually, talking of devil children, who are the rugrats wrecking the front room and the piano?' Merry asked, as Verity watched Johnny look around the kitchen, the late-afternoon sun streaming in through the large window by the sink.

With its Aga, Welsh dresser full of mismatched crockery, scrubbed pine table and sagging sofa covered in a threadbare collection of blankets where Picasso and Dali, their two Calico cats, snoozed, the kitchen was the heart of the vicarage.

There was always something simmering on the hob, a cake baking in the oven, the kettle whistling as parishioners were counselled and given a sympathetic ear, a shoulder to cry on and/or a piece of cake.

'The kiddies are from the next village. Mum's been rushed to hospital with an almost burst appendix and dad's working on an oil rig in the middle of the North Sea, though he should be with us later tonight.' Dora Love frowned. 'They're very nice children but I keep forgetting their names.'

'So, there's no room at the inn, then?' Verity asked hopefully. 'Because we could just go . . .'

'There's plenty of room. The children have made a den in my sewing room, you and Merry can have the blue room, Chatty and Immy are in their old room and when we emailed, Jimmy said he didn't mind sleeping on your grandfather's old camp bed,' Mrs Love said calmly. 'That reminds me, we still need to get it down from the attic.'

'Jimmy? It's Johnny,' Verity said. 'And really Johnny is a guest so he should have a proper bed. He can have the blue room and Merry can sleep on the sofa in the front room and I'll sleep on the camp bed.'

'Sleep on the sofa? With my bad back?' Merry complained.

'I don't mind the camp bed,' Johnny said just

as there was a commotion at the back door and two women burst in followed by a large golden retriever who tried to jump on the kitchen sofa but was kept at bay by the two cats who had woken up and transformed into hissing, spitting monsters.

'Poor Alan,' Verity said, because in the six years since Poor Alan had been the vicarage's resident dog, its resident cats had always treated him with disdain and, in the case of Picasso and Dali, outright hostility. Not that Poor Alan took it personally. Now, he caught sight of Merry and Verity and bounded over, tail wagging, only to be mown down by the twins.

'Chatty! Immy!' Merry yelled loud enough to burst eardrums before she was engulfed in a sisterly huddle. 'So good to see you! Where's Con?'

'She's at the farm. Some kind of cow emergency.' Immy scrunched up her face at the horror of what a cow emergency might be.

'As long as she doesn't have to put her hand up a cow she'll be all right,' Chatty added, her own face contorted in disgust.

Chatty and Immy were similar enough that most people thought they were identical until they stood still long enough so that it became obvious that Chatty was taller and Immy had a slight cleft to her chin and her hair was flaxen rather than just blonde. But now they turned to Verity with matching expressions of up-to-no-good. 'Hey Very, can we get some love?' Immy asked, advancing on her elder sister as Chatty brought up the rear and Verity didn't even have

231

time to shrink back before she was enveloped in a double hug, both her cheeks peppered with slobbery kisses. Not out of sisterly affection but solely to torment her.

Verity suffered the onslaught for a count of ten then pinched them both on an arm so they released her with indignant squeaks. 'Not cool, Very,' Chatty said.

'Not cool at all,' Immy echoed.

Verity assumed her most saintly smile, because she knew just how to torment her sisters too. 'But we must stem the tide of malice, and pour into each other's wounded bosoms the balm of sisterly consolation,' she said in her prissiest voice.

All three Love sisters groaned. Merry made a point of checking the clock on the microwave. 'We've only been here ten minutes and Very is already quoting *Pride and Prejudice*. I think that must be a personal best.'

Johnny had been watching all these sisterly shenanigans with an air of bemusement but when Verity caught his eye he smiled and she rolled her eyes in the direction of her sisters and smiled back.

'Who's this?' asked Chatty from behind her.

'Is this your young man, Very?' Immy had her back to their parents so she treated Johnny to a theatrical wink because Verity's sisters were nothing if not predictable.

'Less of the young I'm afraid,' Johnny said with a rueful grimace.

Chatty and Immy both grinned. 'We like him,' Immy announced. 'He can stay.'

232

'Of course he can stay but I need you all out of the house now,' Mrs Love announced. 'The children have to be fed and they'll only eat chicken nuggets and chips and your father still hasn't written his sermon for tomorrow. He was meant to be done with it by Thursday.'

'There was a fellow in Hull who was having trouble uniting two colonies of bees so I felt duty-bound to drive over and lend my assistance,' the good vicar protested. 'I wonder if I shouldn't just sermonise extempore. It might be quite freeing.'

'You what?' Merry grunted.

'He wants to wing it,' Verity replied as Mrs Love shook her head.

'Last time you winged it, your sermon lasted nearly two hours and all the Sunday roasts in the village were ruined.' She gave her husband an affectionate slap on his rump. 'Go to your study and no supper for you until you're done.' She made a shooing motion with her hands at her four daughters and Johnny. 'Go to the pub. Take Poor Alan with you,' she added as Poor Alan once again tried to get up on the kitchen sofa only to get swiped by a furious Picasso.

★　★　★

'Sorry,' Verity said to Johnny as they exited the vicarage a scant twenty minutes after arriving. 'So sorry that you haven't even been offered a cup of tea or a chance to sit down.'

'It's fine,' Johnny said. 'I could do with stretching my legs after all that driving.'

'There's not much scope for stretching,' Chatty told him. 'Pub's only a minute away.' Then she winked at him. 'Very, does he know that we know?'

Verity decided that she must have done something very bad in another life, or even something bad in this life — namely inventing fake boyfriends — to deserve all this misfortune. 'Well, if Johnny didn't know then he knows by now.'

'Knows what exactly?' Johnny asked and Verity was at a loss to explain how he managed to keep his voice calm and his face grimace-free.

'That you and Verity are just 'friends'.' Immy air-quoted and smirked. 'Though Farv and Muv aren't buying this friends malarkey at all. They're praying, literally praying, that you're in love.'

'We're not in love, but we are friends,' Johnny said with a sidelong look at Verity.

'Yup, just friends,' she confirmed.

'Don't worry, you can just be yourselves around us,' Chatty said kindly. 'You don't have to pretend to even like each other if you don't want to.'

'We do like each other!' Verity and Johnny said in unison and Immy smirked again and Chatty and Merry nudged each other and even Poor Alan looked as if he were laughing at them.

'Yeah, but you don't 'like' each other,' Merry said and now she was air-quoting too.

Verity rolled her eyes so hard it was a wonder she didn't strain something. 'Well, I certainly don't 'like' *you* very much right now,' she said tartly. Merry pouted as Chatty and Immy snorted like two gleeful little piggies.

'If you really want to stretch your legs, shall we go for a walk before we head to the pub?' Verity suggested to Johnny, who nodded gratefully. 'You're not invited,' she added to her three sisters. 'Only Poor Alan and that's because he can't talk.'

There was a gate set into the stone wall, which bordered the side lawn. Verity and Johnny headed for it, Poor Alan happily trotting ahead to lead the way.

'I'm so sorry,' Verity said again; she suspected it wouldn't be the last time she said it over the next twenty-four hours. Johnny hadn't even met Con yet.

'Not too many secrets between sisters?' Johnny guessed as they crossed over the lane to another wooden gate that led to a footpath that would take them for a gentle stroll on the outskirts of the Wolds.

'Not between my sisters,' Verity agreed. 'Even if I don't tell them everything, they can always tell when I'm withholding and manage to winkle the truth out of me through sheer persistence.'

'Sounds exhausting.'

'It really is.'

Verity risked a glance at Johnny to see how annoyed he was, but he didn't look the least bit cross. 'Well, I say we stick with the friend defence unless questioned under oath. Sound like a plan?'

'It does.'

'If you like we can walk in silence for a while,' Johnny suggested. Before Verity could ask him how he knew that she didn't want to hear another word from anyone for at least half an hour, he pressed the tip of one finger to her brow bone. 'I've noticed that when you're about to go all Greta Garbo, a little muscle starts banging away here.'

It was true. When modern life with all its noise and chaos started getting to Verity, a tic just above her right eyelid began to spasm in much the same way as it was doing now.

'Also, you're going monosyllabic on me,' Johnny pointed out. 'That's another sign, so I'm going to shut up now.'

If Verity truly was going 'all Greta Garbo' then she'd want to be alone, preferably in a dimly lit, soundproofed room, but as it was she was quite happy to be outside. The sticky heat was gone now they were further north and a delightful breeze rustled the leaves. The air was glorious and fresh and Verity took big lungfuls of it in as if she were a hardcore vaper.

Verity loved London. Loved how easy it was to be anonymous in a big city. Loved her friends and her little rent-free flat and the life she'd made there for herself, but she did wonder if really she was a country girl at heart.

As the long grass edging the path kissed her bare legs and Poor Alan happily gave chase to a lazy butterfly darting through the flowers, Verity could feel all the tension from three hours in a car with Merry incessantly yapping float away.

It would have been perfect but for one thing. Johnny. Or rather Johnny's phone, which beeped regularly with messages that Verity would bet at least five English pounds were from Marissa. Perhaps the beeping was a sign of a celestial kind and the good Lord had sent Johnny her way so that Verity could free him from the Marissa-shaped millstone that was dragging him down. After all, Verity was a Love woman, which meant, though it pained her to admit it, that she had the meddling gene hardwired into her DNA.

Then the beeping gave way to Johnny's ringtone. Nothing fancy, just the classic *brrrrrr brrrrrr* but it was as unwelcome as an outbreak of chicken pox in a primary school.

'I'm sorry,' Johnny said, as he'd said so many times before for exactly the same reason. 'I have to take this.'

He didn't *have* to take it. It wasn't as if there was some kind of Marissa-related emergency and only Johnny could save the day.

'Marissa? What's the matter? You sound upset. What? What's that? You're breaking up. I can hardly get a signal. Damn it!' Johnny veered left, his phone held out in front of him as if he were divining for water.

Maybe that was another reason why Verity loved the country. When she came to visit, mobile phone reception was terrible unless you took a chair out to the northernmost point of the vicarage garden and climbed on top of it.

Verity walked on until she came to a stone bridge and waited for Johnny, who eventually appeared, flushed and apologetic. 'So sor — '

'Your phone.' Verity didn't need any more apologies. 'Is it insured?'

'What?' Johnny looked at her as if she'd

237

started speaking in tongues. 'Um, yes. Why?'

Verity was undeterred. 'And do you back up regularly?'

'Yes and anyway, pretty much everything is uploaded to the Cloud,' Johnny replied, with a frown. 'Again, why?'

Verity folded her arms. 'Because I'm seriously considering taking your phone and throwing it down there. That's why.'

They both peered over the bridge where a little stream merrily flowed over pebbles.

'If you did that, I doubt it would work again even if I stuck it in a bag of rice for a week,' Johnny said gravely.

'I'm not going to do it but I've thought about destroying your phone a lot,' Verity admitted. 'Because, and I'm really not trying to pry, but you did mention that you and Marissa were meant to be giving each other some space this summer, but that . . . ' she gestured at Johnny's iPhone, his gateway to Marissa, ' . . . hardly counts as you and Marissa giving each other some space.'

It was Johnny's turn to fold his arms and treat Verity to a look that would have withered a lesser woman. As it was, it wilted her slightly. 'You don't understand,' he said crisply. 'It's complicated.'

'Doesn't seem that complicated to me,' Verity muttered. 'She's married, has been for the last umpteen years, and not to you.'

She didn't have the courage to say the words any louder or add that Johnny would still be single on his deathbed if he continued to hold out in the faint hope that Marissa would one day come to her senses.

'You seem quite the expert on love,' Johnny noted, with a touch of acid to his voice, as they began to retrace their steps.

'Not an expert, not by any means,' Verity said shortly.

'What about that guy you met at university? Alan?'

'Adam!' Just saying his name out loud, as ever, made Verity's hands clammy. 'What about him?'

'You said you were in love with him,' Johnny reminded her and Verity wished that he'd let the subject drop. She didn't want to even think about Adam, much less talk about him.

'I *was* in love with him and that's why, when it ended, I knew it was best to make a clean break. No regrets, no recriminations, absolutely no texting,' she said firmly. 'Anyway, we're talking about you, not me.'

'So, you've had one relationship that you were able to get over pretty quickly? Doesn't really sound like any kind of love that I know,' Johnny said as if Verity couldn't begin to understand any torrid affairs of the heart, which was absolutely untrue. She still bore the emotional scars of that one relationship and though she'd stayed resolutely single since then, she knew plenty about love. After all, she'd read *Pride and Prejudice* hundreds of times and Johnny hadn't read it once because if he had, he'd know, as Verity had on first meeting her, that Marissa was a Caroline Bingley through and through.

It wasn't just *Pride and Prejudice* or the

countless romance novels that Verity had read. She was also surrounded by love on all sides. Our Vicar and Our Vicar's Wife were devoted to each other. There was Con and Alex, Merry and Dougie, Sean and Emma, even Posy and Sebastian. So Verity might only have been in one relationship but she hadn't forgotten what love looked like and it didn't look like Marissa and Johnny riding off into the sunset together any time soon.

The gabled roof of the vicarage came into view just as Verity's own phone pinged.

We're about to get a second round in. Hurry up!
Merry x

Verity decided to let the matter of Johnny and Marissa drop for now. It was only her first foray into meddling and if her sisters were anything to go by, you had to keep meddling, wearing your meddlee down until they were so weakened that they'd agree to anything to get the meddling to stop. Besides, she hated fighting with people and it turned out that she particularly hated fighting with Johnny. Didn't care for the sharp tone to his words to match the sharp look on his face.

'Look, shall we just agree to disagree about love?' Verity said. 'It's hardly worth arguing about.'

Johnny looked at Verity incredulously. 'I think love is absolutely worth arguing about.'

Verity was saved by her phone pinging again. It was a text from Nina who'd sent a photo of Strumpet sitting on his bottom, back legs

240

splayed, like a tiny little drunk man, with a glass of red wine and the remains of a kebab in front of him.

Come home soon, Mama. Auntie Nina is corrupting me. Lots of love, Strumpet (Mr)

Verity snorted with mirth in a very unladylike fashion and dared to show her screen to Johnny, who was silent and scrunched of face. Verity almost sighed in relief when he grinned. 'Are we going to have to hotfoot it back to London to save your cat from a life of vice?'

It was a tempting thought, but so was the prospect of a gin and tonic at the Lambton Inn. 'I think Strumpet will be all right and if he's not, I'll check him into cat rehab on Monday. Talking of which, shall we head to the pub?'

★ ★ ★

As soon as Verity and Johnny appeared in the doorway that led to the beer garden of the Lambton Inn clutching a gin and tonic and a bag of salt-and-vinegar crisps apiece, they were greeted by an ear-splitting cry.

'Very! Come and give your big sis some love!'

'That would be Con,' Verity told Johnny as her eldest sister, all six glorious feet of her, stood up from the bench she was perched on and waved wildly.

'The bossy one?' Johnny queried out of the side of his mouth as they walked over, Verity smiling as various people turned to look at her and say hello. Everyone knew everyone in Lambton and being one of the vicar's five daughters, even one of them who lived in that London and didn't visit as often as she should, conferred celebrity status on Verity.

'The bossiest one,' Verity confirmed as they reached the table and benches where the Love sisters and Alex, Con's fiancé, were sitting with, shudder, George, her father's curate. George was wearing shorts with beige socks and black sandals and didn't look up because he was explaining to Immy, who had a frozen expression on her face, that being an art teacher was all well and good but it didn't give her real-world skills.

'I have a pretty mean right hook,' Verity heard Immy mutter under her breath to Chatty. 'Would that count as a real-world skill?'

And then Verity couldn't hear anything because Con had seized her and was hugging her so tightly that rib breakage seemed a distinct possibility.

'Very! It's been too long,' Con said and she didn't let go, testing the theory that the longer she squeezed her tight, the more Verity would squirm and wriggle.

Verity had long suspected that her sisters had a book running on how long she could be forced into an embrace and now she heard Merry say, 'Past the minute mark. Is that a new record?'

'Gerrooffffffff!' Verity fought her way to freedom then punched Con on the arm. 'You all set for wedding prep bootcamp? Are you in a decision-making frame of mind?'

'Plenty of time for that tomorrow,' Con

decided with a shake of her gorgeous strawberry-blonde curls. She had pointy features, which were softened by her riotous hair and the ready smile she always wore, which was much in evidence now as she ran her eyes up and down Johnny who'd been buttonholed by Immy so she could be rescued from George's mansplaining. 'Oh my word, Very! Is that Johnny? You never said how handsome he was!'

'Shhhh!' Verity flapped her hands at Con and by the time Johnny turned away from Immy, the eldest Love sister had a serene, innocent smile on her face.

'I'm Con,' she said. 'You must be Johnny. I've heard so much about you!'

Johnny didn't flinch. 'I've heard quite a few things about you too. Are you any nearer to picking your signature wedding colours?'

'Narrowed it down to a shortlist of about four. Maybe six. Possibly seven. It will all be fine,' Con said though with a wedding less than two months away, it wouldn't all be fine unless she started committing in the same way that she'd committed to Alex when he'd asked her if she fancied becoming a farmer's wife. 'Right, you sit down next to me, Johnny, so I can ask you loads of really personal questions. Go away, Very.' Con gave her a not-so-gentle shove.

'I told you she was the bossiest one,' Very said, as she shoved Con back. She didn't go away but sat on the other side of Johnny so she could talk to Chatty and eavesdrop on Con and Johnny's conversation, which wasn't as prying or inflammatory as Verity had feared.

Mostly Con wanted to pick Johnny's brains on the likelihood of it raining in late September — as if Johnny was a keen amateur meteorologist and familiar with the weather patterns of Lincolnshire.

'My sisters are being so doom and gloom about it and insisting it will rain but I looked up the weather for late September on the internet and it doesn't rain *that* much,' she said to Johnny who had to be regretting his eagerness to meet Verity's nearest and dearest.

'Maybe a rain contingency plan?' he suggested. 'A marquee in your parents' garden, though you have left it rather late to book one.'

'Shut up!' Con moaned like Johnny was family and not a guest. 'I suppose there's always a barn, but all of the barns on the farm have rats nesting in them or broken pieces of machinery that have been there since the First World War.'

Verity tuned Con out because this was nothing she hadn't heard a thousand times before and turned her attention back to Chatty who'd now been joined by Immy so they could whisper excitedly that 'Johnny's so dreamy-looking. Are you absolutely sure you're not even the tiniest bit in love with him?'

With a quick check to make sure that Johnny was still listening to Con and now Alex bang on about barns, Verity replied, 'Look, I can appreciate him on an aesthetic level, I have eyes, but I'm just . . . just . . . '

'An idiot who doesn't know a good thing when she's got one?' Immy suggested sweetly.

'I haven't got him. He's not mine,' Verity said

244

and in the pause between words she had to steel herself not to grind her back molars. 'His heart is otherwise engaged.'

'By that Marissa,' Chatty muttered darkly. 'Have you been on her Instagram?'

'You've been on her Instagram?'

'Only Kardashians take more selfies than her,' Immy said disparagingly, so she'd obviously been getting in on the Marissa Instagram action too. 'She was in Dubai . . .'

'I know she was in Dubai . . .'

'Twenty-seven bikini shots, all of them hashtagged thigh gap!' Chatty said. 'Isn't she in her thirties? I expect hashtag thigh gap from some of the teenagers I teach but not from a proper grown-up woman.'

'She's very intelligent,' Verity insisted though she didn't know why she was defending Marissa. 'She went to Cambridge.'

'Who went to Cambridge? Are you talking about me?' Johnny asked and as Verity had swivelled round on the bench to face Immy and Chatty, she had her back to him and so thankfully he couldn't see the rosy-red hue of shame that swept over her skin.

'No, we were talking about somebody else.' Chatty fixed Johnny with her most doe-eyed look. 'More importantly, has Very filled you in on all of the most embarrassing moments of her life up to date? We'd hate to think she was holding out on you.'

Because she still had her back to him Johnny wouldn't be able to see the pain-of-death glare that Verity levelled at her two younger sisters, but he must have been able to see how rigid her shoulders and spine were because he ever so carefully patted her arm. 'Well, she's told me that you'd pretend to be the Mitford sisters and how you'd also play at being the Bennet sisters but I haven't read *Pride and Prejudice* so . . . '

'Ugh! Just what kind of freak are you?' Immy demanded. She didn't wait for a reply. 'Did Very also tell you how we played at being Puritans who denounced each other as witches?'

'We didn't have a telly,' Verity said, swivelling back round so Johnny could see the agony in her eyes. 'We had to entertain ourselves somehow.'

'We also made up our own Puritan names,' Chatty remembered. 'Immy was Impatience Is A Loathsome Sin.'

'And Chatty was Charity Always Goes To The Least Deserving,' Merry shouted from across the table. 'I'm still quite proud of that one.'

Johnny looked around the five sisters with glee. 'Con's Puritan name was?'

'A Constant Source Of Sorrow,' Verity recited with her hands in the prayer position, as Merry hooted her delight.

'Shut up, Very Vexatious To All Who Know Her,' Con looked daggers at Merry. 'And as for you, God Is Merciless . . . '

'Actually I've always found God to be *merciful*,' Mr Love said as he sat down at the neighbouring table with a pint of bitter. 'I do hope this delightful trip down memory lane isn't going to end up with Immy and Chatty tied to the washing line while you other three chant 'Burn the witches! Burn the witches!' instead of

246

setting a good example.' He paused to take a refreshing sip of bitter. 'Sermon's done. I thought the return of the prodigal son was appropriate with all five of you home for the weekend.'

'Where's Muv?' Con asked. 'You haven't left her on her own to deal with all those children, have you?'

'Their father arrived just as I was finishing my sermon. Apparently he had to be airlifted off the oil rig. Anyway, your mother will be along shortly. She was hunting down an errant Barbie doll last I saw her . . . Oh! There she is!'

Mrs Love, looking even more flustered and rumpled than before, arrived in the beer garden with a glass of red wine so large it could have doubled as a small bucket. 'I asked Jean if she had something we might nibble on and she's going to rustle us up egg and chips,' she said. 'I've already cooked tea for the kiddies. I'm not cooking tea twice in one evening.'

'No one would expect you to, my dear,' Mr Love said. He shot his wife a fond look. 'And past experience has shown that I should never cook tea.'

'When we were little, Muv was in Newcastle visiting our gran and Dad was left in charge,' Merry explained to Johnny. 'He forgot that he'd put sausages under the grill and they were charred to cinders. Of course, we only realised that after we'd put out the fire in the chip pan.'

'One time my father decided to make a Thai curry and forgot that scotch bonnets were the hottest of all the chillis but I've managed to

247

repress the memory,' Johnny said. 'Though I'm still waiting for my sense of taste to come back.'

'Talking of all things Scotch, I have several beekeeping friends in Scotland,' Our Vicar said, because he could always find a way to make any conversation about beekeeping. 'As luck would have it they're based in Moray, which also has several rather fine whisky distilleries.'

'Dad's two greatest passions in life: bees and malt whisky,' Con exclaimed, as Jean the landlady and her teenage son, David, who liked to refer to himself as the only goth in the village, started to bring out their laden plates.

Verity was sure that it wasn't what Johnny was used to when he went to the country for the weekend; egg and chips and a raucous conversation, everyone shouting across each other, which touched on the division of church and state, *The Real Housewives of Beverly Hills*, which Con and Our Vicar's Wife were obsessed with, and the Head of Modern Languages having a tempestuous affair with the Head of Pastoral Care at the school where Immy and Chatty both taught. But if Johnny was dying a thousand deaths and would rather be anywhere but in the beer garden of the Lambton Inn, he was putting a very brave face on it.

In fact, his face was exceedingly smiley, which made him look even more handsome than usual so that all four of Verity's sisters managed to give her a surreptitious thumbs up at some point. Even Our Vicar's Wife caught Verity's eye and winked at her.

Which was embarrassing, and Verity would

have been mortified if Johnny had caught any of this, but mostly she felt at peace even though the noise levels around the two tables they'd commandeered were inching towards deafening. This was her family; her maddening, loud, eccentric family. Despite their teasing and the way their volume knobs were all stuck on eleven, Verity was pleased she'd come home: a place which had nothing to do with that long journey up the motorway but was being with the six people who she shared DNA and a long, long history with. Who'd seen the very best and the very worst of Verity and accepted and loved her no matter what. If she could find those same qualities in a man who also had the ability to make her heart skip a beat just by smiling at her, then maybe she'd rethink the whole forswearing romantic love thing, Verity thought to herself.

Not that this mythical man could ever be Johnny. Not when his heart was already taken and he'd told Verity very sternly, on a number of occasions, not to fall in love with him. But as Verity watched the way Johnny neatly folded into the fabric of her messy family — listening patiently to Our Vicar as he wittered on about his bees, standing up to her sisters, even laughing at one of George's laboured jokes — Verity couldn't remember for the life of her why she'd been so worried about letting him come home to meet her folks.

18

'Do not give way to useless alarm; though it is right to be prepared for the worst, there is no occasion to look on it as certain.'

Johnny was still in good spirits the next day even though he'd spent the night in Our Vicar's Wife's sewing room on the camp bed that had belonged to Our Vicar's father in his Scouting days and predated World War Two. It was made of canvas, through which various rusting metal poles were attached and was marginally less comfortable than calling it quits and sleeping on the floor. But all the sofas in the house had been far too small to accommodate Johnny's six-foot-and-two-inch frame and he wouldn't hear of switching places with Verity and sleeping in a proper bed.

He didn't mind either that breakfast was a makeshift affair of toast and gooseberry jam, because the children had ridded the house of anything more appetising.

'I really don't mind going to church,' he also told Verity when she explained to him yet again that he didn't have to just to be polite. 'I can't say I believe one hundred per cent, I'm more agnostic than atheist, but I'm interested to see your father in action.'

'Be warned: he does go on a bit,' Merry said, who was sitting across the big kitchen table from

250

them and munching toast. 'Ugh. This gooseberry jam is rank. No wonder there were so many jars of it left in the pantry.'

'If I get bored, which I'm sure I won't, I can study the architecture,' Johnny said and when Mr Love did bang on a bit too long about the prodigal son, Johnny's gaze became quite fixated on the sleek, graceful pillars of the nave, while the female portion of the congregation seemed fixated on Johnny's bone structure. When he lifted his hand to run his fingers through his hair, some of the more flighty members of the Women's Institute sighed.

Johnny's good-natured smile only dimmed after lunch when Mr Love presented him with a white boiler suit and a big white hat with a veil. 'I don't suppose you know if you're allergic to bee stings, do you?' he asked.

Johnny's smile dimmed even further. 'I don't know. I am allergic to mangoes. Do you think that might make me more susceptible to bee stings?'

Mr Love clapped Johnny on the back again in what he must have imagined was a comforting manner. 'It's highly unlikely you'll get stung but better safe than sorry' he said. 'Now, let's hasten to the hives, before the onslaught starts.'

'Onslaught?' Johnny asked over the two long peals on the vicarage doorbell as the vicar hurried him out of the back door.

Verity wished, how she wished! she could hurry after them but instead she took her place at the kitchen table as Con came in with Sue, Alex's mother, Jenny, Alex's sister, and 'This is

251

Marie, Jenny's best friend.'

They all knew Marie but she was an acquaintance, rather than a friend, so what she was doing at a family-only wedding prep bootcamp remained to be seen.

'What are you doing here, Marie?' Merry asked, because she never shied away from the difficult questions.

'I've seen every episode of *Say Yes To The Dress*,' Marie said, settling herself at the head of the kitchen table. 'I've even seen every episode of *Say Yes To The Dress: Bridesmaids* AND *I Found The Gown* — you need me. Also, my Kayleigh is going to be one of the flower girls. Jenny said.'

Jenny, who spoke only when she was spoken to and then in the softest of whispers, shrugged and shook her head as if she was no match for the iron will of her best friend. Verity could empathise.

'Con hasn't even decided if she's having flower girls,' Chatty hissed to Verity. 'She said she'd prefer to have Poor Alan as what she called 'Dog of Honour'.'

'Well, try telling that to Marie and Kayleigh,' Verity muttered back as Marie pulled something out of the carrier bag she'd brought with her.

'A corn dolly,' she announced with some satisfaction. 'As a centrepiece. Jenny said you were wanting to go rustic.'

The corn dolly looked as if it was possessed by a malevolent spirit. Mrs Love, coming into the kitchen with her sewing basket, reared back in alarm. 'What is that doing in the house?' she shrieked. 'Everyone knows they bring bad luck.'

'I'm a vicar's daughter, Marie,' Con pointed out. 'I can't have a pagan symbol as a centrepiece. No.'

The Love sisters and their mother all looked at each other, eyebrows raised. That was a decisive no from Con. Did it mean that she was going to be issuing lots of other firm and fast decisions? One could only hope.

There was a pause as Mrs Love took a jug out of the fridge. 'This is the first batch of my homemade elderflower cordial,' she announced. 'We did talk about using it in your signature wedding cocktail.'

Chatty and Immy sprang up from their chairs to gather glasses so they could all sample the golden elixir that Mrs Love made every year while Con frowned. 'I did?'

'You did,' Merry said, accepting a glass of watered-down cordial from Chatty. She took a tentative sip and sighed appreciatively. 'Think this might be your best batch ever, Muv. I say we mix this up with some Cava, or lemonade for the teetotallers, and job's done.'

'I second that,' Verity piped up, because if they could get one item ticked off in the first five minutes, it boded well. 'Dare I ask if you've made a drinks shopping list like you said you would so that Alex's brother can book tickets for the booze cruise?'

Alex's brother, conveniently, managed several orchards in Kent and had offered to do a booze run across the Channel as soon as Con and Alex told him exactly how many crates of Cava (which was much cheaper than Prosecco), lager, and red and white wine were needed. Judging from the beleaguered look on Con's face, she'd done no such thing.

'I haven't had time yet,' she said. She visibly brightened. 'Anyway, it's only the end of July. We've got loads of time. Months and months.'

'Two months,' Chatty warned.

'Not even two months,' Immy added. 'The only thing you've done is book the church and that's only because Our Vicar did it for you.'

'Sounds to me like you don't even want to get married,' said Sue, Alex's mother. She looked like the archetypal farmer's wife; as if Duncan, Alex's dad, had found her in central casting rather than at a Young Farmers' Ball. She was rosy of face, sturdy of limb and usually very smiley, except now as she all but hoisted her sizeable bosom and sniffed. 'You'll not do any better than our Alex, young lady, so if you're delaying the wedding arrangements in the hope that someone more to your fancy is going to appear, then best to stop stringing my poor boy along.'

'I'm not! I wouldn't. I love him!' Genuine anguish pulled Con's brows together until they almost met in the middle. 'I'd be quite happy to just love him without all this wedding nonsense, but apparently that's setting a bad example as the eldest daughter of the local vicar.'

'And a bad example to your four younger sisters, who look on you as their spiritual pathfinder,' Merry said and made the sign of the cross so that Con jabbed her with an elbow and

254

grinned and the tension was broken. 'Right, so Con, Rome wasn't built in a day and a wedding can't be planned in an afternoon, but will you please at least pick your sodding signature colours.'

Chatty reached for her bag and pulled out a fistful of paint charts from the local B&Q. 'Not green. You're getting married in the country, there'll be enough green as it is. Not yellow. Me and Immy look awful in yellow.' She threw away a few charts, which still left a hell of a lot for Con to wade through.

'Orange is quite cheery,' Mrs Love suggested but was shouted down by her daughters and Jenny's friend, Marie.

'Pink,' she said firmly. 'Our Kayleigh loves pink. It's her favourite colour.' As if that settled it, which it didn't.

'Pink?' Merry spat, her face squinched up in horror. 'We don't do pink. We've never done pink. We are, as a family, emphatically anti-pink.'

'Actually, Posy used a clover pink as an accent colour in the shop and it looks quite pretty,' Verity said, even as her four sisters collectively glared at her. 'I was only saying!'

'What about blue?' Immy suggested. 'A nice duck-egg blue.'

'Urgh, so basic!' Chatty rolled her eyes. 'What about a nice silvery grey?'

'Boring!'

'We can't have our little Kayleigh and the other bridesmaids in grey dresses. They'll look like nuns and your dad is C of E.'

'Are you even getting married in white, Con?'

'Yes! Or maybe ivory, though I did see a champagne satin dress in Monsoon that I quite liked except it was meant to be ankle-length but it hit me mid-calf.'

'But champagne just looks like a dirty white, doesn't it?'

This was going to take hours, Verity thought. It was half two now and she'd wanted to leave by four though it was obvious that by four nothing would have been decided. She glanced towards her mother in the vain hope that she might, as she did on very rare occasions, step in to kick some very mild arse but Mrs Love just smiled vaguely at Verity and carried on mending a tear in a pillowcase.

Verity's gaze drifted past her mother to the window behind her and the garden in all its glorious and slightly overgrown splendour. At the bottom of the garden were her father's hives. She could see him and Johnny clad in their white outfits and beekeeper hats and Poor Alan, in the custom-made canine beekeeping suit and adapted cone of shame her father had commissioned after Poor Alan had been involved in a multiple sting incident and had swelled up to look like a balloon animal. Everyone agreed that what really made his beekeeping outfit were the four booties that went on Poor Alan's paws and made him clomp around like a doggy zombie. He was clomping about now in the bushes as the two men peered into one of the hives. Verity hoped her father wasn't asking Johnny what his intentions were towards his middle daughter. Or worse, quizzing Johnny on

256

his favourite Rodgers and Hammerstein musical, which was another of Mr Love's favourite conversational gambits, mostly so he could break into a chorus of 'I'm Gonna Wash That Man Right Out of My Hair' from *South Pacific*.

Her father pulled one of the frames out of the hive, a cloud of bees hovering about it, and she could see Johnny pointing and nodding so perhaps he really was interested in bees and honey and all points in between. From what she knew of Johnny, even if the subject bored him rigid, he'd pretend to be interested because it was the polite thing to do. Because whatever else they were, he and Verity were friends, and Johnny wouldn't want to offend her family. Whereas someone like Sebastian would probably yawn in her father's face and proclaim 'Boring!' at the top of his voice.

As it was, her father was gesticulating wildly, which meant he was in full oratorical flow. One time, he'd got so animated during a sermon about the feeding of the five thousand that he'd knocked his hymn book straight into the font. Of course, Verity wouldn't swap her family for anything but sometimes she wished that they were just a bit less . . .

'And do you mean to say that we've spent a whole year buying up vintage tea cups in charity shops only for you to decide that you're going to do mason jars after all?'

'I said, I was seriously considering mason jars. I have to have options!'

While Verity's attention was elsewhere, World War Three appeared to have broken out.

'The time for options is bloody well over. Now is the time for decisions!'

'I wouldn't really go for anything breakable with our Kayleigh and the other little 'uns about. We should get some plastic champagne flutes from Costco.'

'Oh, shut up, Marie!' The last was shouted at great volume by the ever silent Jenny, now as cross as everyone else. 'Just shut up! No one even asked you!'

'I won't shut up . . .'

Meanwhile Con, Chatty and Immy were bickering over vintage tea cups versus mason jars, and Merry was telling Sue that no one 'likes rich fruit cake so I wouldn't bother making one if I were you,' while Sue was all but hoisting her bosom again and snorting like a furious dragon and . . .

'Enough! That's enough, people!' Verity exclaimed, jumping to her feet. 'This is not wedding planning or being respectful of other people's opinions.'

'I'm not being respectful of other people's opinions if their opinions are rubbish!' Con snapped with a ferocious scowl at her two youngest sisters and honestly? Verity had expected this.

Expected it and had prepared for it with the help of Pippa, Sebastian's director of project management, who had seen them through the shop relaunch with the minimum of meltdowns and a hell of a lot of aspirational quotes and holistic management techniques.

So, Verity reached across the table to snatch up

the evil-looking corn dolly. When Pippa had employed a similar technique, she'd used a beanbag, which had doubled up as a stress ball, but needs must. 'This . . . this is a symbol of communication and cooperation. You can only talk when you're holding the doll of truth!'

'My God, Very, have you taken a huge amount of drugs?'

Verity brandished the corn doll in front of her like it was locked and loaded. 'Are you holding the doll of truth, Merry? I don't think you are, so zip it!' she said in her scariest voice. It was the voice she had to employ when Nina broke the cardinal rule of their living together and tried to engage Verity in conversation as they left the shop for the flat upstairs, instead of waiting at least thirty minutes for Verity to recover from the rigours of the working day. It was also the voice she'd used on Posy when she'd caught her trying to order more tote bags.

Now it shocked all four of her sisters into slack-jawed silence. There was an actual bosom hoist from Sue, a thumbs up from Jenny and a mild look of bemusement from Mrs Love. Marie stood up.

'Well, I'm not staying here to be insulted,' she announced and departed with a toss of her head and a slamming of the front door.

'No one asked her to . . . ' Merry began until Verity shook the corn doll in her direction.

'Zip it!' Verity said again and, keeping tight hold of the doll, she got up from her own chair to walk to the pantry, where she'd stashed her secret weapon. Verity had hoped it wouldn't come to this but when she'd explained the situation to Pippa, Pippa had said it was best to expect a worst-case scenario.

'By failing to prepare, you are preparing to fail,' Pippa had warned Verity.

Except, with a wedding less than two months away, failure was not an option.

So, with the corn dolly clamped under her arm, Verity brought out the flip chart and stand that she'd borrowed from work.

'We have been Skyping and What's Upping about this wedding for months,' Verity told her sisters. 'Hours and hours of discussions about everything from signature colours to hog roasts and when I went back over our conversations, there were lots of good ideas, lots of times that we agreed about stuff. I've collated it all.'

'You did? That must have taken you hours and hours too,' Con said, in direct contravention of the rules that Verity had just laid down. 'But I don't remember much agreement.'

'That's because you shot down everything that anybody else agreed on,' Verity panted, as she wrestled with the flip chart stand. Posy had been right when she said that trying to make it stay upright was like trying to hold back the tide. 'And that . . . bloody hell! Why won't this thing behave? . . . is why, if you haven't made a decision in sixty seconds, it goes to a vote. Majority wins.'

'You can't do that!' Con clenched her fists. 'It's my wedding. I'm not having my feelings overrun. This isn't a dictatorship!'

'Con, I'm not being a dictator, this is coming

from a place of deep love,' Verity protested. 'And also a place of anxiety that it will be the day of the wedding and we'll have to do a trolley run in Tesco's to feed the guests while you're still dithering over your signature colours.'

Con wasn't having any of it. 'I would never have expected this from *you*, Very,' she said, and there was no one who could wound a girl like her own sister could. 'Merry definitely, the twins perhaps, but not you.'

Finally the flip chart stand was in position so Verity was able to turn round and brandish the corn doll pointedly in Con's direction. It was quickly snatched from her by Chatty. 'Don't pick on Very. None of this is her fault and actually, Con, you'll find that putting things to a vote is the foundation of democracy. So, where to begin, Very? Can we start with bridesmaid dresses, please?'

Verity nodded and flipped her flip chart to the page where she'd already stuck pictures of the three ASOS dresses that they'd all decided that they could live with. They'd been waiting for Con to choose between an empire line cut, a fifties silhouette and a floaty maxi dress.

The corn doll was yanked away from Chatty by Immy, who demanded: 'Start the clock, Very. Con, you have one minute to decide.'

'I hate you all!' Con groaned, her hair in her hands as she squinted at the dresses. 'The maxi dress, then! No! Very and Merry don't have the length of leg for a maxi dress. Perhaps the empire line? It's quite flattering or does it scream maternity dress? Hmmm.'

Having to witness Con try to reach a decision was up there with listening to people crunching ice cubes or running their nails down a blackboard. Verity gritted her teeth and, from the clenched jaws around the table, she could see that she wasn't the only one. Con was still hemming and hawing and fifty seconds had sped by. Fifty-five, fifty-six, fifty-seven, fifty-eight, fifty-nine . . .

'Give me that,' Merry said, taking custody of the corn doll. 'Ladies, the fifties dress with the defined waist like we talked about months ago. All those in favour, raise your right hands!'

Everyone's right hand shot up, except Con's because her hand was still in her hair and she was moaning like she was in pain. Verity sincerely hoped that she wasn't so ineffective on the farm when it came to calving season or ordering animal feed.

Merry ignored her eldest sister's inner torment. 'If we carry on like this, we'll be done in no time at all. Now we've eased ourselves in gently, let's get these signature colours locked down once and for all.'

Just over an hour later, though Verity could scarcely believe it, the wedding planning was all but done. From bouquets to menus, invitations to order of service, all over bar the shouting. Mostly Con's shouting. She'd got so into the spirit of quickfire decision making that she'd begun to shout out her preferences on everything from wedding cake ingredients to footwear for the bridesmaids before anyone else could venture an opinion.

The corn dolly was in shreds. It had been torn from limb to limb as the Love sisters wrestled it out of each other's hands and Verity felt as if she were in shreds too. She sat on the sofa, a cat on either side of her and a cold compress clutched to her head.

'Your eyes are glazed, Very,' Merry told her, putting her face so close to Verity's that their noses touched. 'Are you completely overloaded?'

She was overloaded. Overstimulated. Just generally over. 'No words,' she managed to whimper. 'No talking.'

The kitchen door opened and Our Vicar, Johnny and Poor Alan trooped in from the garden. 'I said we'd give young Johnny a couple of jars of our finest honey,' Mr Love said in what sounded to Verity like his most boomingest voice ever.

'We should start making tracks if we want to get back to London at a reasonable hour,' Johnny said and even his modulated tones were like a thousand violins screeching. His eyes narrowed as he took in the forlorn and droopy picture Verity made as she sat with eyes closed, finger and thumb pinching the bridge of her nose. 'Have you got a headache? Nosebleed?'

'Worse than that,' Merry said in a whisper. 'We've broken her.'

Mrs Love pulled Johnny to one side. 'She just needs quiet. Merry, dear, you're not capable of being quiet, are you? Why don't you go back to Manchester with the twins and catch the train from there tomorrow?'

'Don't do that,' Verity said, because doing that

263

was a major faff especially on a Sunday afternoon when it was more than likely that part of Merry's journey would involve a rail replacement bus. But even as she said it, she didn't know how she was going to deal with Merry talking all the way back to London. Just the thought of Merry reading out every motorway sign they passed had Verity's head hanging down so low that her chin was on her chest. Even the stereophonic purring of Picasso and Dali was making her nerves jangle. 'I'm fine. Honestly. I'm just being a wet blanket.'

'You wouldn't be you if you weren't a bit of a wet blanket,' Con said fondly as she departed with Sue and Jenny.

'Don't get me wrong, your Very's a lovely girl but she needs more iron in her diet,' Verity heard Sue say before Constance slammed the door behind them, because none of her sisters, or her parents for that matter, were physically capable of closing a door quietly.

Verity winced, then struggled to her feet. She felt as wobbly as a newborn foal. 'We should get going,' she said to Johnny, who was now laden down with tin foil parcels from Mrs Love.

'Just something for the journey,' she insisted and Merry, who was deep in conversation with Chatty and Immy, rolled her eyes.

'It's a three-hour drive, tops. There's enough food there to last them for days,' she said.

'Them?' Johnny queried, with a glance at Verity, who was slowly gathering the last of her belongings together in the manner of someone recovering from major surgery. 'You're not coming with?'

'I will go back to Manchester with Chats and Im. I'd booked tomorrow off before you kindly offered to give me a lift.' Merry fluttered her eyelashes.

'Oh, really? I offered, did I? That's not quite how I remember it,' Johnny said with a wry smile and at any other time Verity would have been impressed that he could stand up to one of her sisters. Lesser men had tried and failed. Adam had met Merry twice then begged off ever meeting her again, and Merry was a pussycat compared to Con or the dual onslaught of Chatty and Immy.

But right then, nothing could impress Verity. She said her goodbyes, apologised a few more times for bringing the weekend to such an abrupt halt and, finally, she was strapped into the passenger seat of Johnny's car and they were leaving the scene of Verity's shame behind.

19

'Till this moment I never knew myself.'

Thankfully, Johnny didn't ask her if she was all right. He did shoot her a couple of anxious glances but mostly he kept his eyes on the road and Verity tried to ignore the maddening hum of the air conditioning and the purr of the engine, which she could hear over the roaring in her head. It was as if all of her was itching inside and out and although Johnny hadn't said a word, being shut in a confined space with another person was as excruciating to her stripped nerves as standing in the middle of a noisy crowd of people.

Verity concentrated on breathing in and out for a count of five. She was so busy flexing her fingers and toes on the breath that it was some time before she realised that they weren't moving. That Johnny had pulled into a layby.

'We've got plenty of time to get back to London,' he said. 'So, if you wanted to be by yourself for a little while and go for a walk, there's a sign to a public footpath over there.'

'Yes.' Verity nodded her agreement to this unexpected but very welcome plan. 'Yes, please.'

Furnished with a bottle of water and one of Mrs Love's ham and pickle sandwiches, Verity was on her way with barely a backward glance. She followed the signs to the public footpath, which was more of a roughly hewn trail through dense woodland. At any other time she might have been worried about the dangers of her lone walk, but homicidal axe-wielding maniacs lurking in the undergrowth or being bitten by horseflies — none of that was important at this moment.

What was important was that soon Verity came to a stream and next to it was a plush, luxurious patch of grass padded with clover, just waiting for her to take the weight off her feet. She lay back, starfished her arms and legs, shut her eyes and reclaimed herself. Starting at the top of her head and imagining that there was a spiritual squeegee scraping away all the stresses and strains and the static noise still clinging to her.

Verity didn't stop until she reached her toes and it was only then that she felt clean, calm and back to her self. The counsellor she'd seen at university had always described it as something similar to recharging a phone with zero battery life. The quiet restored the calm and balance Verity needed to be a fully functioning member of society.

Verity had only started seeing a counsellor after being referred by her course tutor when she had managed to get through the first two terms of her first year without saying a single word in any of her lectures or seminars. She'd also been separately referred by the Residential Adviser on her floor of the halls of residence, a very annoying third-year Sports Science student that everyone called Banjo, except his mum and dad who called him Paul.

When Verity had arrived at Manchester University and seen her tiny cell-like room she had been overjoyed as, for the first time in her life, she had her own space. She was no longer sharing a room and every single one of her personal possessions with her sisters. She'd taken to the solitude the way most of the other students had taken to drinking their body weight in WKD in the student union bar. However, Banjo was a great one for fancy dress, communal drinking in the common room before 'going out and getting slaughtered' and everyone joining in. Three things that Verity had loathed with a passion and when Banjo and Professor Rose had both referred her to the student health centre — the word 'depression' had been bandied around — Verity had loathed that too.

Counselling meant she had to talk about herself, which was another thing Verity wasn't a big fan of, but she'd quickly become a big fan of her counsellor, a very gentle-mannered, softly spoken, liquid-eyed Spaniard called Manuel. Secretly, deep down, Verity had always wondered if there was something wrong with her that she wanted to be so quiet and alone. To shut down when the world, or more usually her sisters, were roaring at her. To always feel slightly wistful when Our Vicar talked about his very strict parents, who'd been big believers in children being seen and not heard and were adamant that after lunch on Sunday, silence was to reign supreme until Evensong.

Perhaps she really did have depression. Verity was used to being the odd one out of five already very odd sisters and perhaps that oddness had a clinical diagnosis.

'It sounds to me as if you're an introvert,' Manuel said during their third session when Verity had finally, haltingly, explained that after too much time with other people, she felt like an overwound wind-up toy that refused to start up again. 'Some people find life quite overwhelming, there's nothing wrong with that.'

Manuel was adamant that introversion wasn't a problem to be fixed but instead recommended that Verity look into ways of establishing boundaries with the noisy world. And slowly, once she realised she had somewhere to come back to that was quiet and calm, Verity left her little room. She found friends, though they tended to like going to the cinema or for long walks rather than downing three for £2 shots in the union bar. She started attending a yoga class and learned a whole arsenal of meditation techniques, which always restored Verity back to her factory settings — in much the same way as they had now.

Verity opened her eyes to see that Johnny was slowly walking towards her. He stopped and shrugged as if to ask whether his presence was unwelcome. Verity waved him nearer.

'Do we need to be getting on our way?' she asked him.

'We're OK for a little while,' he said, coming to sit down on the grass next to her. 'All good?'

'All good,' Verity confirmed and she didn't feel like saying any more than that, though she should probably apologise a few more times, but

Johnny stretched out so he was flat on his back and after a while Verity lay back down too.

Neither of them spoke, they certainly didn't touch though their hands were only centimetres apart. Instead, they watched the clouds roll by in an impossibly blue sky, listened to the happy chirp of birdsong and the bubbling brook and Verity couldn't remember the last time she'd been with someone whom she could be so comfortably quiet with.

A person like that was a rare breed. She'd thought that Adam was someone she could share companionable silences with but she'd never been more wrong about anything or anyone.

Verity tried not to think about Adam (there be dragons) but lately she was thinking about Adam a lot. After all, he was the reason Verity had taken a vow of singledom and it was only natural that, now that she had a fake boyfriend, her thoughts would turn, again and again, to her last real boyfriend.

So, later when they were back in the car and heading towards the motorway, Verity heard herself say, 'Now you've seen what I'm like at my very worst.'

Johnny shot her a lazy smile. 'Believe me, your worst is nothing compared to other people's worsts.'

His phone was in the well in front of the gear lever. He must have put it on silent, for which Verity was eternally grateful, but it flashed every minute or so with incoming text messages. It was safe to assume that some of them had to be from Marissa. What were Marissa's 'worsts' like?

Maybe Marissa at the wedding, wrongfooted by Johnny turning up with another woman, was the worst Marissa there was. Maybe she was absolutely splendid the rest of the time.

Still, Verity could only worry about her own worst. 'But you can see now why I've decided that relationships, boyfriends, they just aren't for me. When I was with Adam . . . it was a disaster. I ended up treating him really badly.'

'You? Verity Love?' Johnny scoffed at the very notion. 'I've known you a few weeks now and I can't imagine you treating anyone badly.'

'Well, I have. I did. The thing is, I thought he was like me. Quiet. Introverted. But it turned out that actually Adam was shy and once he was comfortable around me, he never stopped talking. Not like my sisters, who don't require any audience participation.'

'I had noticed that,' Johnny remarked. 'Merry's thirty-minute monologue on Coldplay — '

'And she doesn't even like Coldplay!'

' — on the way up here was proof of that.' Verity and Johnny shared an exasperated look in the windscreen mirror.

'But Adam wanted my opinion on everything. And because he was shy, he needed constant reassurance too. Hourly progress reports on the state of our relationship.' Verity shook her head to remember it. How Adam always wanted to know what she was thinking when a lot of the time she was thinking of very mundane things like what she was going to have for tea that night or if she had enough

271

dirty clothes to do a dark wash.

'We're all right, aren't we?' Adam would frequently ask. He'd always wanted to hold her hand too and pat bits of her and nuzzle. Always with the nuzzling and Verity had felt as if it would be churlish and rude to constantly remind Adam that she wasn't a toucher. He'd always take offence as if there was something deeply wrong with their relationship if they weren't in skin-to-skin contact at all times.

They'd met at university but hadn't got together until they both moved down to London and bumped into each other browsing the tables of the sprawling bookstalls outside the BFI cinema on the South Bank. Early on in the first fumbling months of their relationship, they'd considered themselves to be kindred spirits but as the months became a year, Verity realised that they'd been at cross-purposes. For just as Verity had mistaken Adam's shyness for a quiet soul, Adam mistook her quiet nature for shyness. Imagined that she'd spent a lifetime being lonely like he had and, no matter how many times Verity had tried to explain that wanting to be alone and being lonely were two very different things, Adam hadn't understood.

'As far as he was concerned, we were two people who never had to be lonely again because now we could spend every waking moment together,' she told Johnny. 'I had counselling when I was at university so I could learn to deal with the stresses of modern life better. But Adam's neediness was no match for the techniques I'd learnt to establish boundaries.'

'So, you were spectacularly incompatible. It happens,' Johnny said, as he changed lanes. 'It happens a hell of a lot. Can't let one bad relationship sour you for ever more.'

'No, you don't understand. I was horrible to him.' Verity shuddered to think about it. 'All he ever tried to do was make me happy. For my twenty-fifth birthday, he surprised me with a minibreak to Amsterdam. And when I saw the tickets tucked into my birthday card . . . well, any normal person would have been delighted.'

'If you weren't delighted then I'm sure it was only because you don't like surprises, that's hardly a crime,' Johnny said carefully, but Verity shook her head.

'No, it wasn't that,' Verity said, her heart plummeting in much the same way it had when she'd seen those plane tickets. 'I tried to pretend that I was pleased but actually I was horrified at the thought of spending forty-eight hours with Adam, with nowhere to be alone, apart from occasional loo breaks. Forty-eight hours with Adam was like spending two weeks with anyone else.'

Verity had tried her hardest to simply live in the moment for the first day of the minibreak. She did the hand-holding and answered, 'I'm great. This is great. Thank you so much,' every time Adam asked her how she was and if she was happy and if she liked her birthday present so far.

Verity lasted a whole twenty-six hours. Then the next morning Adam had insisted on nuzzling her as she brushed her teeth and holding her

273

hand as she tried to make her selection from the breakfast buffet but when he asked her three times in the space of twenty minutes, 'So, are you happy with your birthday present then?' something inside of Verity gave. Like she had a gigantic rubber band wrapped tight around the nagging, throbbing mess inside of her that was making her jaw lock and her head pound and her skin feel as if it were crawling with millions and millions of microscopic ants. Adam had pinged that elastic band so many times that it was no surprise when it finally snapped under the strain.

'No! I am not happy! You are absolutely doing my head in with your incessant questions and touching me all the bloody time,' she'd shrieked. 'I can't stand being touched and I don't ever want to hear a single word coming out of your mouth ever again because I HAVE HEARD ALL THE WORDS! THERE ARE NO MORE WORDS I EVER WANT TO HEAR! God, I can't *breathe* when you're around.'

'It didn't feel good to get it off my chest,' Verity explained to Johnny, who'd said nothing during her shameful confession but every now and again he'd caught her eye and given her a small, sympathetic smile. 'It felt awful. The words were wrenched out of me under extreme duress so they were very unkind words. And anyway my duress shouldn't have been that extreme. Adam wasn't doing anything awful. He'd taken me away for the weekend to celebrate my birthday.'

'I know you said that you were in love with him but you haven't mentioned the L word at all,' Johnny said idly. 'Was it a case that you loved him at the beginning and then it just faded away?'

'I don't know why you keep asking me if I've been in love. Of course, I was in love,' Verity said defensively. 'I wouldn't have tried so hard to make it work otherwise.' Adam had declared his love a few weeks in and Verity had declared it back — it would have been rude not to — and at the start of their relationship, she had been happy. She'd thought, in those heady, early days, that she might even have found her soulmate. But when doubt crept in, she refused to give it houseroom. If she couldn't love Adam who shared so many of the same interests as her and was as kind and gentle as Charles Bingley, then Verity feared that there was something very wrong with her.

After her outburst in that blighted hotel room in Amsterdam, Adam hadn't said anything at first — not one single word — which should have been a relief except it wasn't. Not when he had the look of a cartoon character a nanosecond before a cartoon anvil landed on his head. Then Adam had blinked and one solitary tear had trickled down his cheek before he could furiously scrub it away.

'I'm sorry,' Verity had gasped, but Adam had held up his hand to silence her.

All her life Verity had craved, yearned, hungered for silence but the silence between she and Adam in that hotel room was so loud it screamed and slashed the air with tooth and claw.

She'd stared at the floor, ashamed, heartsick after what she'd just said, and when Verity had found the courage to lift her head, Adam was staring at her as if all his love was gone. Worse, as if all that love had turned to hate.

'You don't deserve my love,' he'd said in a voice that was as quiet as Verity had ever wished it to be. But she hadn't been careful about what she wished for. 'I would have done anything for you but it's never good enough.'

'It's not that . . .'

'I have tried and tried but I've always known that you don't love me like I love you. You've never really let me in. You've always kept me at a distance.' Adam had frowned, his face screwed up in concentration as he tried to explain exactly what was wrong with Verity. And she was curious to find out herself, because despite the counselling and the meditation and the mindfulness techniques, she still suspected that the way she was simply wasn't right. 'You're just not capable of feeling emotions the way other people do.'

'I do feel things,' Verity had protested, though admittedly the things she felt tended to be quite low key. No rapturous delight, no towering rage or deep wells of sadness either. Verity was strictly middle of the road but that didn't make her . . .

'You are a cruel person, Very,' Adam had pronounced petulantly. 'I will never be able to trust another woman after this. You've ruined all my chances of ever being able to have a normal relationship.'

Then he'd walked out and, far from not

276

feeling anything, Verity had felt so many things. She'd cried and cried. Angry tears. Sad tears. Tears at the injustice of the things that Adam had accused her of.

But when the tears had dried and Verity was splashing her face with cold water, it was guilt and self-loathing that came calling. There *was* something wrong with her that she needed so much space that there simply wasn't room for anyone else.

Despite having Elizabeth Bennet as her role model and *Pride and Prejudice* as her bible, Verity had always had a horrible suspicion that she simply wasn't the type of person capable of great passion and now she knew it to be true.

Three years on and Verity was older and wiser and had made her peace with the sad truth that tempestuous love affairs were not her thing. They were the domain of women like Nina and Posy who wore their hearts on their sleeves, whereas Verity preferred to tuck her heart away, out of sight, where it was safe and couldn't get broken again. Because Adam had broken her heart in a hotel room in Amsterdam and it had never properly healed.

'He came back to the hotel eventually but he still wouldn't speak to me and when we got to the airport to fly home, we had to sit next to each other and it was terrible.' Verity gave another little shudder. 'He wasn't even angry any more, just utterly miserable and I was responsible for it and I decided then that I was done with relationships. I'd only ever make someone else unhappy or make myself unhappy trying to please them. Either way, there'd be unhappiness.'

'You don't think that it was simply that you and this Adam just weren't meant to be?' Verity didn't think she'd imagined the way Johnny's lip curled as he said the name of the man she'd wronged. 'He sounds spectacularly needy, if you ask me.'

'Well, perhaps he was,' Verity conceded — Merry's name for Adam had been The Drainer. 'Still, it's not unreasonable, is it, to want to hold hands and spoon and be both giving and receiving of affection?'

'Do you think your Elizabeth Bennet and what's his name . . . ?'

'Oh, come on! You must know his name or are you deliberately trying to wind me up?' Verity asked. Unbelievably she could feel a smile tugging the corners of her mouth upwards. 'It's Darcy. Fitzwilliam Darcy.'

'Who has a name like Fitzwilliam anyway? But from what I've gathered about that book, him and Elizabeth Bennet, they didn't moon about declaring their love every five minutes and indulging in public displays of affection.'

'Absolutely not!' Verity was aghast at the very notion. Neither Lizzie nor Darcy could ever be described as snugglers. 'Even when they danced together, they'd barely have touched.' Verity couldn't help but sigh a little. 'I really think I'd be much better suited to life in Regency England.'

'Apart from the likelihood of dying young of some illness that would easily be treated with modern medicine,' Johnny said dryly. 'There's a service station coming up. Do you want to stop and get tea? It seems to be the one thing that your mother didn't pack for the journey.'

'Yes please.'

Verity had shared her darkest secret with Johnny. She still wasn't sure why: she hadn't even told her sisters. She was so ashamed of what had happened and so used to carrying that shame around on her back like a hairshirt, that she didn't want anyone to try and make her feel better, which was what her sisters were contractually obliged to do.

But Johnny had listened and though he wasn't contractually obliged to, he'd stuck up for her. Hadn't judged her actions too harshly. Hadn't turned his face away from her in disgust. He'd even made a joke about *Pride and Prejudice*. And Verity's reward for opening up and trusting someone in a way that she'd never been able to do with Adam was to realise that the world hadn't ended just because she'd been genuine with her emotions. Also, that metaphorical hairshirt wasn't half as itchy as it had been. If Verity ever were to decide that she did want a relationship, she'd be lucky to find someone like Johnny. Not Johnny because . . .

Verity's eyes drifted down to Johnny's phone, which had been inactive for a good ten minutes. What a pity that Marissa had already claimed him, because Johnny's friends were right, he really was too lovely to be left adrift in a romantic limbo and Verity really should gently try to disentangle him from Marissa. Make a concerted effort to find him someone equally lovely. She knew lots of wonderful women. Perhaps Mattie or even Pippa.

'So . . . thank you for telling me about Adam,' Johnny said, as they flashed past a sign that promised that they were three miles from the nearest service station. 'If I thought I could persuade you that you can't judge all relationships on the basis of one bad one and that there is someone out there for you who would never, ever crowd you or hold your hand without your consent, then I'd give it my all.'

'Oh, please don't,' Verity begged. 'Not when we've been getting on so well.'

Their eyes met again and this time Johnny's smile was amused but maybe a little frustrated too. 'Still, you've made me realise that perhaps I need space too.'

For one horrible heart-slamdunking moment, Verity thought that Johnny was dumping her. That her fake boyfriend was breaking up with her because she was just as rubbish at fake relationships as she was at real ones. That he had actually been repulsed by her revelations. 'Oh, I didn't realise you needed space,' she croaked.

'Yes, because you were right when you said that all this texting and calling Marissa every few minutes isn't giving either of us the distance we said we wanted,' Johnny said and Verity's heart gave one last emphatic thump then settled back into its normal steady pattern. 'I have to at least see what life is like without her in it, don't you think?'

Verity didn't reply because it seemed as if

Johnny was searching his own soul for the answer rather than wanting Verity's opinion.

'So, my mind is made up,' Johnny decided. 'I'm going cold turkey on Marissa for a month. No phone calls, no text messages, no tweeting, no liking her photos on Instagram. There are a hundred ways not to give each other any space and I'm stopping them all.'

'Cold turkey seems a bit drastic,' the outer Verity noted, while the inner Verity punched the air. 'But they say, don't they, the best way to give up smoking is to not bother fannying around with patches and gum but to just stop?'

'Right,' Johnny agreed, turning onto the slip road for the service station. 'It's the twenty-third of July today and I'm going to have nothing to do with Marissa until the twenty-third of August.'

'And you might even find that by then, you won't want anything to do with her. Not that I'm saying she's horrible,' Verity quickly added. 'But you might realise she's not what you want any more. That you want to move on.'

'Maybe. But first I'm giving her up for a month and if I look like I'm about to fall off the wagon, you have my permission to throw my phone in the nearest pool of water.' Johnny pulled into a parking space and turned off the engine. 'Deal?'

'Deal.'

They shook on it. A firm handshake between friends. And if they locked eyes just long enough for it to start to get awkward, well that was because it had been a long day and Verity was still off her game from her emotional meltdown and Johnny . . . well, Johnny had obviously had too much sun.

20

*'There seemed a gulf impassable
between them.'*

After her heart-to-heart with Johnny in the car, it
had occurred to Verity that if one good thing had
happened as a result of the awful break-up with
Adam, it was the life lessons she'd learned. Not
just swearing off coupledom but that, if she set
very clear boundaries from the start, then people
would have very low expectations of her socially.

So, as the summer's giddy whirl of parties and
celebrations continued, on non-going-out nights,
she was in bed by nine. Even missing The
Midnight Bell pub quiz, much to Tom and
Nina's dismay because Verity could answer
questions on obscure saints and feast days and
was no slouch on geography, beekeeping and the
collected works of Enid Blyton (though admittedly those last two categories rarely came up).

'You can't expect me to be social all day *and*
every night of the week too,' Verity said with
absolutely no remorse. 'I'm having to spend a lot
of time making small talk with strangers and
eating things in pastry that I really don't want to
eat. I'm stretched too thin.'

It still didn't stop people expecting Verity to be
social. Especially Nina who'd refused to read the
memo (an actual literal memo that Verity had
emailed to her) and frequently tried to persuade

Verity that a quick drink in The Midnight Bell wouldn't kill her. Though a quick drink with Nina often turned into a four-hour session, as Verity knew only too well.

They were closing the shop on a Thursday afternoon nearly two weeks after the visit to the vicarage: two weeks during which Verity had attended a wedding, both a thirtieth and fortieth birthday party, and several unprecedented during-the-week dos. From the tearooms came the clink of china and cutlery as Mattie, Sophie and Paloma cleaned up. Tom was sweeping the floor and doing a very poor job of it, Verity was cashing up, Posy was shelving the many books that had become unshelved and Nina, who'd won tickets in a Twitter competition for an al fresco showing of *Grease* at Somerset House, was trying to raise a posse.

'It will be fun,' she insisted. 'We could dress up as Pink Ladies. I know it's short notice but everyone has something pink in their wardrobes, right?'

Verity was too busy doing sums on her calculator to reply at first but she could hear Posy say, 'Normally I'd love to but tonight is our ten-week anniversary and Sebastian will have something planned.'

'You have week anniversaries?' Tom and Nina asked in unison and disbelief.

'It's a thing,' Posy mumbled. Verity glanced up to confirm that yes, Posy's face was flaring red. 'Well, it's a thing with Sebastian. He really is a lot more romantic than anyone would give him credit for.'

'No disrespect, Posy, but I preferred Sebastian when he was being unspeakably rude,' Nina said with a sniff, because as far as Nina was concerned, romance didn't begin to compare to passion and heartache.

'He's still unspeakably rude too,' Posy said but Nina had already turned to Verity.

'You'll come, won't you, Very?' she asked fluttering both her real eyelashes and her fake eyelashes at Verity. 'If Posy would rather be boring and spend the evening with her husband, then we could ask Merry along instead. We'd make amazing Pink Ladies, especially if you let me pin-curl your hair.'

Verity winced. Not at the thought of dressing up as one of the Pink Ladies, though that was never ever going to happen, but at memories of her sisters singing along to a warped vinyl record of the *Grease* soundtrack. Con and Merry would always come to blows as to which one of them was Rizzo. Needless to say, Verity got stuck with Jan or Marty. Either way, it was a no.

'Sorry, but I can't. I have other plans for tonight,' she said apologetically.

'You and that Johnny are joined at the hip,' Nina muttered.

'You never saw this much of Peter Hardy, oceanographer,' Tom commented with the little grin he broke out whenever he mentioned Verity's former fake beau. Then he did a couple more flourishes with the broom but not much actual sweeping of dust. 'Where's your new boyfriend taking you? Engagement? House-warming? Maybe a little dinner à *deux*?'

'FYI, Peter Hardy was away a lot oceanographing,' Verity said grandly though she wasn't sure oceanographing was a proper word. 'I'm not seeing Johnny tonight: I've been out for three successive evenings and I need alone time. I need to potter and not do anything and especially not talk to anyone. And, by the way sweeping the floor doesn't mean spreading the dust from one side of the room to the other.'

The three of them left eventually. Posy back to her newly wedded bliss and Nina, with a reluctant Tom in tow, had managed to persuade Mattie and Paloma to take the other two tickets.

Verity couldn't wait to climb the rickety stairs to the flat where Strumpet was waiting for her. Just as Verity was starved of the solitude she craved, Strumpet had been starved of company and of food. Since the tearooms had opened, Verity had taken to locking the flat door after an incident when Strumpet had burst into the tearoom and managed to get his podgy self airborne enough to land in a woman's lap so he could help himself to her cream tea. The woman had taken it in very bad humour and threatened to phone the council. Since then Strumpet had been confined to quarters.

Now he howled his outrage, weaving in and out of Verity's legs then stalking off in a huff when he remembered that he was furious with her. As ever, Strumpet's fury lasted the time it took for Verity to open a tin of catfood and while her feline dictator was occupied, Verity took the opportunity to rid herself of the workday kinks with a little light yoga until Strumpet came to lie

286

on his back on her yoga mat while she tried to do sun salutes.

It was odd that neediness in a pet, be it Strumpet or Poor Alan, was much easier to deal with, even charming, than it was in a human being, Verity reflected as she showered while Strumpet, scared of water as he was, meowed plaintively at the bathroom door.

They shared a light supper of grilled halloumi cheese and salad, then Verity read her current book, a modern retelling of *Pride and Prejudice*, which wasn't half as good as the half a dozen other modern retellings of *Pride and Prejudice* she'd previously read.

It was a boring evening, even by Verity's standards. She did some laundry. Painted her toenails. Tided up her bedroom. Ate a second supper of salt-and-vinegar Pringles and a bag of Percy Pigs and it was exactly what she needed after two action-packed weekends and lots of mid-week parties.

By nine o'clock, she felt zen and chilled enough to log on to WhatsUpp to check in with Con but before Verity could, she heard a sound downstairs. She surreptitiously peered out of the window to see if the neighbourhood hoodies had scaled the electronic gate that had been installed last week but there was no one congregated on the seating outside.

She heard another noise, as if the gate were being rattled but she couldn't see that far out of the window and as she was wondering, with mild panic, what the best course of action was, her phone buzzed.

It was a text from Johnny.

Sorry to call around so late. I'm at the gate but I can go away if you'd rather be alone?

Verity took a moment: would she rather be alone? It turned out that she wouldn't. She texted back.

The code for the gate is 2811813.

It was the date that *Pride and Prejudice* had first been published. Not a date that everyone would remember but a date that they could look up if they forgot the code.

It was just as well that Verity had had three hours of alone time so the flat was vaguely presentable for visitors. Now, she stuffed the half-eaten Pringles and Percy Pigs in a kitchen cupboard and removed her damp bras and pants that were hanging up in the bathroom to dry.

Too soon, there was a knock at the shop door. Verity ran down the stairs.

Johnny waved through the glass as Verity hurried over to the door and unlocked it. 'What's up?' she asked, because there had to be something up for Johnny to visit. They might be friends but they weren't the kind of friends who simply dropped by unannounced. Verity didn't have friends like that — they all knew better.

'I was just in the area,' Johnny said smoothly. Although it was a hot, humid night, he was wearing a suit, tie loosened, top button of shirt unbuttoned. Maybe he'd had a meeting that had run late. Even so, he looked delightfully dishevelled; all he needed was someone to ruffle his hair to complete the picture of slightly louche abandon. Verity mentally shook herself. That was what came from reading one of Posy's beloved Regency romances. 'Actually that's a lie. I wasn't in the area at all until I walked here from Clerkenwell.'

'OK. You'd better come in,' Verity decided then realised how ungracious and unwelcoming she sounded. 'I have gin upstairs and a bottle of my mother's elderflower cordial, so we can have cocktails. Or red wine if you prefer it. Also, salt-and-vinegar Pring — Jesus! Strumpet! Catch that cat!'

Strumpet had followed Verity downstairs and was attempting a lumbering streak across the yard so he could reach the earthly delights of No Plaice Like Home. Verity doubted whether he'd be able to squeeze through the railings of their new gate, but she didn't want to put her theory to the test. Or call the fire brigade if Strumpet got stuck.

Disaster was averted by Johnny easily overtaking Strumpet then gingerly scooping the cat up as if he were handling molten lava. 'Your famous cat. Is it friendly?'

'It's a he and he's ridiculously friendly,' Verity said as she followed Johnny back into the shop. 'Strumpet doesn't believe he's a cat, he thinks he's a lapdog.'

'Why is he called Strumpet?' Johnny asked as the cat in question squirmed ecstatically in his arms.

'Because he's an absolute tart and I thought he was a she,' Verity explained as Strumpet wriggled and wiggled until he was lying on his back, cradled in Johnny's arms, front paws waggling frantically. 'He wants you to rub his belly.'

'I'm not really a cat person,' Johnny said, as they climbed the stairs. 'You know where you are with a dog. Apart from Chihuahuas. I'd never trust a Chihuahua.'

'When we used to live in Grimsby, the local park was ruled by two Chihuahuas called Lola and Tinkerbell. Our old Labrador John Bunyan was terrified of them.' Verity paused at the door to the lounge, quickly scanned the room for any incriminating evidence, and decided it was safe for visitors. 'Take a seat. Have you had anything to eat?'

'Oh, you don't need to go to any trouble,' Johnny said, which wasn't yes so Verity decided the answer was probably no.

'Won't be a tick.' She was back four minutes later with a motley assortment of left-over grilled halloumi and salad in some pitta bread, a selection of day-old cakes and pastries courtesy of Mattie and a bottle of red wine, which was a step up and a couple of pounds more expensive than the red wine she and Nina used for cooking.

Johnny was sitting on the sofa with Strumpet sprawled in gay abandon on his lap, legs akimbo, back arched as Johnny rubbed his belly. Strumpet didn't even stir when Verity put her laden tray down on the coffee table. There was only one thing in the world that Strumpet loved more than food: the attentions of a man and he currently had all of Johnny's attention.

Johnny smiled lazily at Verity and nodded as she held the bottle up, then, turned back to Strumpet. His long fingers rubbed circles on the cat's furry tummy as Strumpet purred so loudly Verity feared he was about to detonate.

'Oh, you like that, don't you?' Johnny said to Strumpet who purred his agreement. 'What about when I do that?'

He tickled Strumpet under his chin for a while then went back to belly rubbing. 'You really do love it. Maybe a bit too much. Should I stop?' Johnny's fingers stilled for a moment until Strumpet head-butted his stroking hand so that Johnny would resume his ministrations. 'You're insatiable, you little hussy.'

Verity's limbs turned alarmingly jelly-like so she sloshed the wine she was pouring over the coffee table instead of into a glass. 'That's quite enough,' she said desperately, because parts of her were coming to life that had been lying dormant for years. 'Any more of that and Strumpet will demand to come home with you.'

'Oh, we can't have that,' Johnny drawled at Strumpet who was gazing up at him with a blissed-out look in his green eyes. 'Next door's ginger tom would eat you for breakfast. Oh, is that food for me? You're setting a dangerous precedent here, Very. I could get used to this kind of treatment.'

'It's a bit makeshift, I'm afraid,' Verity said, as Johnny, encumbered as he was by a cat who refused to leave his lap, reached forward for the plate that Verity handed him. 'Sorry about the mess, by the way.' She glanced up and winced. 'And the holes in the ceiling. We've just had the flat rewired. They're coming back to do the plastering at some point but we're not sure when.'

Verity, looking around the room, saw it through the eyes of a critically acclaimed architect, who probably didn't care that Verity and Nina had gone to great lengths to choose the books displayed on the shelves inset on either side of the fireplace. Or that the fifties minibar shaped like the prow of a ship was Nina's most prized possession, even though it clashed with the sofa and chairs, formerly belonging to Lavinia, covered in a flowery William Morris print.

It wasn't chic but it was definitely shabby.

'Beautiful fireplace,' Johnny said enthusiastically. 'Art nouveau influence on the tiles. I'd say late Edwardian, though the building is older, isn't it?'

'I have no idea,' Verity admitted, but as Johnny ate supper she told him about Lady Agatha Drysdale, Sebastian's great grandmother, who was gifted the bookshop by her parents in the hope it would distract her from her work with the Suffragettes. 'She chained herself to the railings outside Buckingham Palace and got sent to Holloway Prison for public disorder offences. I suppose that must be where Sebastian gets it from.'

After he'd eaten, Johnny asked for a tour and

Verity could hardly refuse, though she made him wait in the living room for several panic-stricken moments as she charged around the flat to check that she really had removed anything incriminatory first time around.

Unlike other people, say Merry, Johnny didn't pass comment on Verity and Nina's soft furnishings or knick-knacks but ummed and ahh-ed at the cornicing and architraves. Sucked in a breath when he saw the ancient geyser in the kitchen and clasped his hands together in quiet joy when he caught sight of the old butler-style bell pull installed so Lady Agatha could summon people from the shop. The whole time that he peered into corners and ran his hands over their mouldings, Verity was free to peer at him.

There was a man in her house. Johnny was in her home and as soon as Verity realised the enormity of this — having a man who wasn't her father or an electrician or Tom (though Tom hardly counted as a man) in her home — she didn't know what to do with herself. Or her mouth and hands, both of which twisted nervously.

What was Johnny doing here?

'There are so many charming quirks to this building. I think it originally dates from the eighteenth century with a lot of renovating done when it became a bookshop,' he was saying as he poked at the window casement in the kitchen. 'Not very skilled renovations, I'm afraid. I've already counted at least ten serious health and safety issues. Do you want me to have a word with — '

'Why did you walk all the way here from Clerkenwell?' Verity interrupted because she already suspected the flat was a deathtrap but it was a rent-free deathtrap and Posy and Sebastian were going to do something with the antiquated hot-water system next. Verity wasn't entirely sure what, but that wasn't important right now. 'Because we're friends who go to social engagements together but I didn't think we were friends who dropped in on each other.'

'You're more than welcome to drop in on me,' Johnny said casually, even though they'd already established the boundaries of their friendship/ fake relationship. He held Verity's gaze with his cool stare but Verity was a past master, a grand champion, in staring competitions with her sisters so it was Johnny who blinked and looked away first.

'So, really, why are you here?' Verity asked gently.

Johnny sighed, long and low. 'I'm wavering,' he said. 'Marissa.'

If his sigh spoke several volumes, then the three-syllable word that was his beloved's name contained the entire collected works of Shakespeare with particular reference to the Bard's tragedies. 'Oh.' It was Verity's turn to sigh. This wasn't entirely unexpected. There'd been a restlessness to Johnny over the past two weeks, similar to the restlessness she'd witnessed when Dougie had stopped smoking earlier in the year. Same fidgeting, same drumming of the fingers, same faraway look in Johnny's eyes, though he was probably imagining Marissa standing in front of him and not a packet of Marlboro. 'But you haven't actually wavered?'

'I've thought about it. She's been calling. Texting. Using a variety of social media platforms to try and make contact.' He dug his phone out of his back pocket.

Verity folded her arms. 'Have you replied to her at all?' It was quite an effort to keep her voice calm and neutral when she didn't feel at all calm and neutral.

'No. I told her that Sunday that we travelled back from your parents that I was going radio silent so we could give each other space like we agreed. She hardly seemed bothered about it. Whereas I've been very bothered by it.' Johnny wasn't even trying to be calm and neutral. As soon as he started talking about Marissa, his shoulders fell, his voice grew hoarse; as if he'd already admitted defeat. 'It's been hard. I've been twitchy. Thought time and time again that one little text wouldn't hurt, but I stayed strong.'

'You've been very strong,' Verity said encouragingly, because after all she'd witnessed the twitchiness first hand and had fretted that Johnny would cave in long before the month was up. 'It's only another fortnight or so. It'll be over before you know it.'

'It's been almost two weeks and not a phone call, text, she never even liked a single one of my tweets, which was a little hurtful,' said Johnny as if he hadn't heard Verity's pep talk. 'I made a really funny joke about Donald Trump, even if I do say so myself. Then last night, the onslaught started.'

Johnny switched on his phone, which beeped frantically like there was a fire close by, then handed it to Verity so she could see that he had fifteen missed calls, twenty-seven text messages, all from Marissa, and who knew how many emails, tweets and WhatsUpp alerts?

'Do you think there might be an emergency? That she *needs* to talk to me?' he asked Verity a little desperately.

'Well, if there was a genuine emergency, then she has Harry,' Verity reminded Johnny. Normally Johnny was quite suave and smooth. Not in the horrible smarmy way of men who wore snakeskin loafers with no socks and thought they were charming because they called every woman 'sweetheart', irrespective of whether they wanted to sleep with them or not.

No, Johnny was the kind of man who could meet your parents, even your four sisters, and do nothing to embarrass you. More than that, he would be accepted and welcomed by your flesh and blood without once having to ingratiate himself. And fifteen minutes earlier, when Verity had been lamenting the dripping tap in the bathroom that Posy swore had leaked for the entire twenty-five years she'd lived there, Johnny had stated with quiet assurance that if Verity had a wrench, he could fix it. You could even argue that in some ways, on paper, Johnny was too perfect.

When Con and Alex had got engaged and Merry had asked Con how she'd known that Alex was the one, Con had said simply, 'He brings out the best in me.' But Marissa did not

296

bring out the best in Johnny. She brought out the insecure, sad bits of Johnny and held them up to the light so everyone could have a good look then say in pitying tones, 'Poor Johnny.'

'You understand why I'm here, don't you?' Johnny asked. He loosened his already loosened tie then shoved his hands in his pockets. 'It was either come here or ring Marissa and lose myself all over again or worse.'

'What would be worse than losing yourself?' Verity asked, because she liked to know where she was at all times.

Johnny shook his head. 'I could go out and get very drunk and pick up someone so I can forget about her for a night.'

'Does that even work?'

'Not really.'

It must have been much easier to forget someone, cut them out of your life completely, in the days before people were expected to be contactable twenty-four/seven. Verity looked at the phone again. For a man about town and a busy architect, it seemed odd that the only person that ever contacted Johnny was Marissa.

'This isn't your only phone, is it?' she said slowly.

'It's my Marissa phone,' Johnny said then quite rightly cringed at how that sounded.

'Well, that makes things simpler.' Verity walked down the hall to her bedroom. Johnny followed her as far as the doorway and watched as Verity dropped the cursed phone in the top drawer of her old-fashioned desk and locked it. 'Is that all right? If you prefer I could flush it down the loo?'

Johnny stared at the closed drawer and then wriggled his shoulders like someone shrugging off a heavy weight. 'I've never had anyone I could confide in until you came into my life. You seem to understand me in ways that I don't even understand myself.'

Verity swore she could see his troubles leaving him. He stretched his arms above his head; his shirt riding up so Verity could see a sliver of taut skin. She quickly averted her eyes then wished she hadn't when she saw the pile of damp pants and bras on her bed that she'd dumped there after she'd removed them from the bathroom.

'I can do this. I can be Marissa-free for a month and then . . . and then . . . '

'And then . . . ?' Verity prompted.

'And then we'll see,' Johnny said. 'Maybe we'll realise that being apart is too painful and that we're meant to be together. Properly. Just the two of us.'

All the worry that had left Johnny flew across the room and landed squarely on Verity's shoulders so she buckled under the weight. That was not the plan! The plan was that Johnny would see that he could manage perfectly well without Marissa. He'd be free to find someone who appreciated that he was perfect but with an edge . . .

'We will see,' Verity muttered, suddenly as exhausted as if she'd been on one of Nina's quick-drinks-that-had-turned-into-an-almighty-bender. She shifted towards Johnny to begin to gently chivvy him out but he moved towards her. Taking the two steps that meant he was standing in her bedroom, next to her, so he could take her hand.

She stared up at Johnny, her eyes wide as he raised her hand to his mouth and pressed a kiss to the back of it, long enough that her skin tingled underneath his lips. 'Very, thank you,' he murmured. 'You're a real friend in need.'

'That's what friends are for.' It felt like the right thing to say but Johnny hadn't let go of her hand and he was gazing deep into her eyes as if he could —

THUD!

CRASH!

BANG!

'Wella . . . wella . . . wella! Uh!'

They both sprang apart when the shop door opened with great force and was then slammed shut with even greater force and Nina could be heard singing with a lot of enthusiasm and not much tune.

Then clomp clomp clomp up the stairs. 'Very! You should have come! Tom tried to deny it but he knew the words to every song. We must tease him about it tomorrow. Oh!' Nina rounded the corner and caught sight of Verity and Johnny now standing awkwardly outside Verity's bedroom. 'I had no idea that you were planning a night in. Just the two of you. Cosy.'

One of Nina's greatest talents was for making even the most innocuous words and phrases sound like the rudest double entendres.

'Johnny was just going.' Verity gestured at the stairs. 'Weren't you?'

'I was? Apparently, I was,' Johnny confirmed. He turned to Verity, reached for her hand again but she put her hands behind her back and yet hated herself for it. 'So, I'll see you tomorrow then.'

'You two! How many nights a week is that? Sounds like it's getting serious,' Nina decided, brushing past them. 'I'm gasping for a brew. Do you want a cuppa, Very?'

Verity led Johnny out. They walked through the darkened shop, past the books full of starcrossed lovers battling all manner of obstacles to get their happy ever after. That's all you want for Johnny, Verity told herself, a happy ever after with someone who isn't Marissa, because he really deserves it.

Verity would settle for a different kind of happy ever after. One that involved opening a cat sanctuary on the other side of the mews and seeing out her days surrounded by romance novels and moggies. There were worse ways to live.

'Are you all right?' Johnny asked as Verity unlocked the shop door. 'You've gone all quiet on me.'

'Oh, I'm fine.' Verity summoned up a bright smile from somewhere deep in her vaults. 'Just wondering what I'm going to wear tomorrow evening. It's a restaurant opening, isn't it?'

'Yes. A friend is opening a month-long Hawaiian-themed pop-up in a car park in Dalston. I'm not entirely sure why.'

Johnny and Verity shared a look of mutual confusion over the concept of pop-ups and serving food in Hackney car parks. 'Well, I'm not going to wear anything fancy then.'

'Good plan.' Johnny stepped through the door, paused then turned back to place a hand on Verity's arm and lean down to kiss her cheek, though until this evening they'd marked their hellos and goodbyes with a brief waggle of their fingers. 'Until tomorrow. I'll pick you up at seven.'

Another shared look, which lasted long enough that it probably counted as having a moment. 'Um, you have to press the button on the right to open the gate,' Verity said, because she'd been killing moments since 1989.

'Will do.' Johnny was already gone, striding across the mews, as Verity stayed frozen to the spot, her hand on the tingling spot on her cheek that Johnny had kissed.

21

*'Heaven and earth, are the shades of
Pemberley to be thus polluted?'*

It was a pity that Con's wedding planning was all but done — there was still a question mark over mason jars versus vintage tea cups — because over the following weeks Verity had become a world expert on weddings. She could go on *Mastermind* with weddings as her specialist subject.

In fact, her newfound knowledge didn't just extend to weddings, but all manner of parties. Every weekend throughout August, quite a few weeknights too, Verity and Johnny had attended weddings and birthday parties and garden parties and we're-jacking-in-our-jobs-and-the-exhorbitant-rent-on-our-poky-flat-and-backpacking-around-the-world parties.

They'd eaten beef en croute. Chicken en croute. Salmon en croute. And a weird mushroomy thing en croute. Verity's friends didn't do things en croute but preferred to provide sausage rolls for their guests. Or vegetarian sausage rolls and, once, even vegan, gluten-free, dairy-free sausage rolls that tasted of cardboard, glue and despair.

They'd drunk champagne occasionally, but mostly Prosecco. Prosecco with orange juice. Prosecco with peach juice. Prosecco with

302

pomegranate juice. But no Prosecco with elderflower cordial, Verity was happy to report to Con, so that her elder sister could sleep soundly at night knowing that no fancy London folk had ripped off her signature wedding cocktail.

Verity and Johnny had danced (well, more of a self-conscious shuffle in Verity's case) to the music of Abba, Burt Bacharach and Dougie's little brother's best friend's ska punk band.

They'd posed for pictures with selfie sticks, in photo booths with silly hats and joke props, and even for a proper 'prom'-style portrait when the photographer had urged them closer and closer together. 'Give her a kiss then, mate!' he'd exhorted Johnny. Johnny's arms had closed around Verity's waist and she'd had to put her arms round him too so it wouldn't look like Johnny was hugging a plank of wood in a party frock.

'You don't have to kiss me,' she'd hissed just as the photographer bellowed, 'Come on, don't be shy!'

Johnny had lifted her chin with his hand and frowned. 'I probably should kiss you for appearance's sake and we are holding up the queue,' he pointed out rather reasonably. 'Don't worry, I'm minty fresh.'

'Oh, well, go on then,' she'd muttered awkwardly even as her heart had started thrumming so loudly, Verity was sure that it could be heard over the sound of 'Blame It on the Boogie' coming from the dancefloor. Johnny had lowered his head and Verity held her breath and just as his lips were about to make contact with her trembling mouth, there was a flash and a triumphant 'Got it!' from the photographer and they'd broken apart.

It was more socialising in one month than Verity had done in a lifetime and she'd managed not to have a single meltdown, though a couple of times she'd had to go to the ladies' cloakroom for a five-minute power charge. (And after that almost-kiss, to run her wrists under the cold tap and give herself a stern talking to about unavailable yet charming and handsome men.)

But if Johnny was out with Verity, nibbling on canapés and catching up with his friends, he wasn't obsessing over Marissa, though sometimes Verity would glance over at Johnny and see a haunted, lost expression on his face. Then he'd become aware of Verity's gaze on him and he'd catch her eye and smile, say something funny to make her smile too.

Verity was in no doubt that these last few weeks had been far from easy for Johnny but his Marissa-free month had been over for three days and he still hadn't asked for his phone back. Verity had been worrying about the weekend just gone, in which she hadn't seen Johnny at all because Con, Chatty and Immy and assorted friends and relatives descended on London for Con's hen do. She knew only too well that the devil found work for idle hands or for a man with a spare weekend and an all-inclusive mobile phone tariff. But, happily, one of his father's godsons and family were visiting and Johnny had promised to escort them from one tourist attraction to the other, which left him no time to dwell on Marissa.

Indeed, Johnny had sent Verity a series of anguished selfies from the London Eye, Buckingham Palace, Hyde Park, Madame Tussauds and M&M World. In most of them he was being set upon by small children.

Not that Verity's weekend plans had been that sedate either. The hen celebrations had started decorously enough. Even though they were taking away tables from paying customers, Posy had insisted that they use the tearooms for a fancy High Tea late on the Saturday afternoon, once everyone had assembled. Mattie had agreed. 'You'll need to line your stomachs with some heavy-duty carbs.'

Of course, when the Love sisters heard that there'd been no time for Posy to have her own hen do, they invited her to join Con's, as an honorary guest, along with Nina, Mattie and Paloma, the new barista. It had then gone downhill quite rapidly after the carb-loading. There had been cocktails, so many cocktails, dancing, more cocktails, an ill-advised kebab with chilli sauce, and at three o'clock on Sunday morning Verity found herself with twenty other women playing a raucous game of football in Coram Fields until a passing police car stopped and told them all to go home.

Those twenty other women had come back to the flat above the shop for a few scant hours' sleep and then it was out for brunch, which, as it always did, involved fried food and more alcohol. There was barely an avocado in sight.

At six on Sunday evening, after she and Merry

had made sure that everyone was on a train back to the East Midlands, Verity felt as if she'd been run over by a truck. Even Merry was quite subdued. 'Jesus,' she said in a dazed voice. 'I have nothing left in the tank. Is this how you feel after a couple of hours in the tender but noisy embrace of your family?'

'Yes,' Verity said, resting her head on Merry's shoulder as they sat on the 73 bus. 'Please stop talking now.'

Even an early night hadn't quite rebooted Verity. On Monday she hid in the back office shunning all attempts at conversation until she got a text message from lovely Stefan from the Swedish deli. They always went to the bank together so that Stefan, who was six foot two of rippling muscle and Viking genes, could protect Verity from any would-be muggers.

Now, as she wended her very weary way back to Happy Ever After, Verity hoped that the last two hours of the day would be quiet ones. She planned to skulk in the office performing tasks of gentle admin.

The shop was full, which was a sight that gladdened Verity's heart but also had her head sinking down as she walked through the door. Despite the branded grey-and-pink Happy Ever After T-shirt, which Posy was still insisting they all wore, Verity found that if she walked through the shop in a hurried fashion, like she was late for an important meeting, and didn't make eye contact with anyone, the customers generally avoided her.

She charged across the main room, dodging

book browsers, and was within touching distance of the counter when she felt a hand on her arm.

'Leave me alone!' Verity shrieked but it was a silent, internal shriek, and she was forced to turn around with a wan smile on her face, which she dropped instantly when she saw it was only Tom waylaying her.

'Not now, Tom,' she begged. 'If there's any ordering to be done, it can wait until tomorrow.'

'No orders,' Tom said. Unlike the rest of the staff, he wasn't wearing a Happy Ever After T-shirt, but his usual shirt, bow tie and cardigan. As befitted someone who'd been toiling away on a PhD for years, Tom preferred to dress like an elderly, absent-minded academic. Posy's entreaties about her precious staff T-shirts had been firmly ignored in a way that Verity didn't dare. 'Friend of yours is on the sofa. She's been waiting for ages.'

Verity frowned, which made her headache, the last legacy of her hangover, pound at the inside of her skull. She'd partied with every friend she had in the world on Saturday night so what any of them were doing on one of the Happy Ever After sofas was beyond her. She peered around Tom and saw a small blonde figure draped on the sagging brown leather Chesterfield as if it were a sumptuous chaise longue, and thought she might throw up the smoked salmon bagel she'd had for lunch.

Verity cowered behind Tom. Perhaps if she used him as a human shield to provide cover until she reached the safety of the office . . .

'Yoo hoo! Valerie! There you are!'

307

If the smile she'd given Tom was wan, then the grimace on Verity's face as she locked eyes with Marissa was so lifeless it should have been declared dead on arrival.

'Oh, hi,' Verity said, shuffling a little closer.

'Why don't you sit down next to Marissa and I'll organise a pot of tea and some scones with clotted cream?' The crowds parted to reveal Posy sitting on the sofa opposite. 'We've been having a good old natter while we waited for you. Gosh, I feel like we've known each other for years.'

'Me too,' Marissa said with an enthusiasm that was hard for Verity to take in, considering Marissa had been less than enthusiastic when they'd first met. 'Can I just get a green tea, no cream scones? It's not my cheat day.'

'Oh, I know what you mean,' Posy said as she got up, even though she'd often been heard to proclaim, usually when Mattie brought through a plate of cakes, 'Every day is my cheat day.'

'Come. Sit next to me,' Marissa said to Verity, patting the space next to her on the couch. It sounded more like a demand than a suggestion and Verity didn't see how she could refuse. 'So, tell me, how have you been?'

'All right,' Verity muttered as she sat down. Marissa was wearing white jeans with a pretty pin-tucked top in an *eau de nil* green and strappy flats. Her clothes were crisp, her skin sun-kissed and glowing, her streaked blonde hair silky and radiant like something out of a shampoo commercial. Next to Marissa, Verity felt like a huge galumphing beast. Though admittedly, that was Verity's own issue and

308

nothing to do with Marissa. 'I'd be better if you actually remembered my name. It's Verity.'

Marissa had the grace to look away and flush delicately. 'I'm sorry,' she said. Up close, she even smelt amazing; of peonies and something a little sharper to cut through the sweetness. 'I'm so bad with names. Sometimes I even call Harry, Gerry. It makes him very cross. I probably wouldn't forget your name if I'd seen more of you over the summer. I was hoping we could get to know each other, become friends. Everyone I know has fallen in love with you.'

She was? They had? 'I've been around,' Verity said. Johnny had probably selected parties for them to attend where he knew Marissa and Harry would be a no-show. Then Verity thought of Johnny's Marissa phone stashed in a locked drawer upstairs and there was absolutely nothing delicate about the flush that stained her face. 'Johnny's friends have all been very welcoming.' Even saying his name in Marissa's hearing felt like she was committing a crime.

'That's because everyone is so pleased to see Johnny in a relationship,' Marissa said as Little Sophie arrived with her green tea, a mug of builder's for Verity and some cream scones that Verity didn't dare put anywhere near her mouth. Marissa rewarded Sophie with a dazzling smile that seemed to come with its own flawless Instagram filter. 'Thank you, darling. Love your little pinny. It's adorable.'

Mattie was even more of a martinet than Posy and insisted that Paloma and Sophie wore black dresses and little white aprons in the style of the

309

Nippies, who used to wait tables at the Lyons' Corner Houses. Sophie had been very sulky about it but now she beamed at Marissa before returning to the tearoom.

Marissa turned back to Verity. 'Now where were we?'

'Urgent orders. Last post,' Verity muttered desperately, but Marissa patted her arm with one immaculately manicured hand.

'Never mind that,' she said breezily in the manner of someone who'd never had to fulfil an urgent work order in time to make the last post. 'So, you and Johnny. It seems to be going well. You're taking up so much of his time.'

Marissa finished on a little wistful sigh that automatically made Verity feel guilty until she reminded herself that Marissa was a married woman and that Johnny was free to have his time taken up with anyone he pleased. There was nothing else Verity could do but channel Elizabeth Bennet in a way that she hadn't needed to do for weeks. Not Elizabeth Bennet employing the smackdown on Lady Catherine de Bourgh, but certainly Elizabeth Bennet refusing to let Caroline Bingley walk all over her. 'Johnny's great,' Verity said and actually there was no need to lie when she could just tell the truth. 'He's so easy to get on with; kind and funny. We've been to a lot of weddings, a lot of parties, and he's absolutely the person you want to be sitting next to when you're listening to yet another best man's speech.'

Verity had to bite her lip so that she didn't start waxing lyrical about how the corners of

Johnny's eyes crinkled up when he smiled at Verity as they shared a pained look over having to eat anything else en croute. How she could walk into a church or marquee or East London pub with Johnny's arm in hers and never feel out of place. Also, it gave her an opportunity to feel the muscles in his forearms — he had really good forearms — and it must be the lingering traces of her hangover and being so near to clotted cream scones and not being able to eat them, which were causing this mild delirium.

'Yeah, Johnny and I, we're good,' she summed up and Marissa took her hand again.

'All I want is for Johnny to be happy,' she breathed, her brilliant blue eyes, the colour of gentians, because having normal blue eyes wouldn't be good enough for Marissa, suddenly tearing up. 'And really, I couldn't be more pleased for the two of you.'

'Oh, it's still early days,' Verity said and she couldn't tear her gaze away from Marissa, whose bottom lip was now trembling.

'You know that Johnny and I have a history. A very long history. Harry said he'd told you about how he and I fell in love and got married behind Johnny's back,' Marissa confessed, dropping her voice down to a conspiratorial whisper. 'There will always be a part of me that feels absolutely rotten about that.'

Verity nodded. She could understand that, and she had to give Marissa major points for confiding in her like this, even though it had to be difficult to dredge up such a painful moment from the past. 'But we can't help who we fall in

311

love with,' Verity said soothingly. 'You couldn't help falling in love with Harry, could you?'

'I really couldn't,' Marissa said. 'And I love Harry even more now than I did then. But when you're married, you can't help but take each other for granted and what Johnny and I had was always so intense and so I suppose it's always been rather nice, validating even, to have Johnny still in love with me a little. Is that very wrong?' Marissa asked Verity, her sparkling blue eyes wide, her expression troubled.

Verity was starting to get what the deal was with Marissa. Why Harry had chosen her over his best friend. Why Johnny was still so doggedly in love with her. Why Posy and Little Sophie had been instantly smitten.

It was because when Marissa looked at you, let you drift into her glorious orbit, confided in you, it was easy to believe that you were the most important person in Marissa's world. It was heady stuff. Verity could feel herself succumbing — Marissa did smell amazing too — but she would be strong, God damn it and sorry, Lord, for taking your name in vain, Verity sent up a silent prayer, but extenuating circumstances and all that.

'Are you telling me that you're not in love with Johnny?' Verity demanded and Marissa smiled as if Verity had just cracked a joke. And not a very funny one at that. 'That you don't return his feelings?'

'Oh, that really is the sweetest thing I've ever heard.' Marissa forced out a tinkling laugh. 'Johnny and I are loving friends, nothing more.

312

Well, certainly not on my part. But I think I know what's really going on here.' She jiggled Verity's limp hand.

'What is going on here?' Verity asked because she was so confused. She'd never had a 'loving friend' herself so she didn't know what the correct etiquette was but surely it didn't involve bombarding your 'loving friend' with as many text messages and phone calls as Marissa did. Especially when, as far as Marissa knew, Johnny had found himself a girlfriend.

Marissa tilted her lovely head and gave Verity a smile that oozed sympathy. 'I suppose you think that you are in love with Johnny. And you tell yourself that because he's so special, so smart, so handsome, that everyone else must be in love with him too. But no, Vera, I'm not in love with Johnny. Not in that way. I think Harry would have something to say about it if I were.'

'But at the wedding in Kensington, Harry said that . . . '

'Harry says a lot of things.' Marissa pulled a pretty face like those things were no concern of hers. 'I couldn't be happier that Johnny's finally found a lovely girl to spend time with. I mean, there was that Karen, a few years ago . . . '

'You mean Katie?' Verity didn't know whether to be relieved or offended that Marissa also couldn't remember the name of the only other woman Johnny had been seen with in the last ten years.

'Karen. Katie. Whatever. She wasn't right for Johnny. Not at all.' A dismissive wave of her fingers, as if that was all poor Katie deserved.

'Honestly, suspicion isn't an attractive quality in a woman, Velma. Really, if I were in love with Johnny, why would I be here?'

'Actually, why are you here? Just to have a chat? Or did you want to buy some books?'

'Don't get me wrong, it's a lovely shop, really quite charming as I was saying to Posy, but I only read literary fiction,' Marissa said. 'I always think there's something quite sad and unfulfilled about women who read romance novels . . . '

Nothing was more guaranteed to break the spell that Marissa had cast over Verity. There was nothing wrong with reading romantic fiction. It wasn't there only to fill the gaps in the lives of lonely people. You could be in a romantic relationship and still read romantic fiction. It wasn't as if there was a romance quota and Marissa had exceeded hers. 'Actually,' Verity began with a little spurt of temper that would have had all four of her sisters exchanging looks. 'Actually, I think you'll find that most of the classics could be classed as romantic fiction. From Ovid's love poems to *Romeo and Juliet*, *Pride and Prejudice* of course and even so-called literary writers like Ian McEwan and Sebastian Faulks who we also stock, FYI.'

'No, I'm afraid you're wrong and I should know. I have a first in English Literature from Cambridge,' Marissa said crushingly as if that settled it, which it didn't but as Verity opened her mouth to argue the point a little more strenuously and then to inevitably start quoting from *Pride and Prejudice*, Marissa grabbed Verity's arm and applied enough pressure that

Verity reflexively shut her mouth. 'We're getting off-message. I didn't come here to discuss books but to issue an invite in person. Johnny hasn't RSVP-ed but I can only imagine how busy you're keeping him.'

It was as if Marissa's powers of attraction only had a shelf life of twenty minutes maximum. No longer charmed and taken in by her seductive sway, Verity reverted to her former position. Marissa was poison. A very dangerous, insidious poison and keeping far away from her was the only effective antidote.

'I'm sure you can remember what it's like at the start of a relationship; Johnny and I just want to spend as much time alone together as possible,' Verity said so sweetly that it made her back teeth ache. 'So, an invite to what?'

'Our tenth anniversary celebrations,' Marissa said. 'Harry and I are making a weekend of it. We've booked a huge house on a small island in Cornwall and we've invited all our dearest friends. Of course, we invited Johnny months ago and I've been trying to contact him to confirm but, like you've just said, he doesn't have a moment to himself, the poor lamb.'

'He still has quite a lot of moments to call his own,' Verity said crossly because, despite what she'd just said, she would never be a clingy girlfriend. Never. 'Maybe he just hasn't got around to getting back to you.'

'I find that hard to believe,' Marissa said just as crossly and for a split second, so afterwards Verity would wonder if she'd imagined it, she glared malevolently at Verity as if she were nothing but a blight on Johnny's life that had to be removed ASAP. Then Verity blinked and Marissa was back to looking wide-eyed and winsome. 'You're invited too, obviously. It's this weekend . . . '

'What a shame. I think we're already booked this weekend,' Verity said, though if they were, she couldn't think what the occasion was. It was August bank holiday weekend. The summer season was almost over, the invitations dwindling and soon there'd be no need for her and Johnny to carry on this charade. The thought made Verity panic though outwardly she didn't so much as twitch an eyelash. 'I'll talk to Johnny tonight. See what he wants to do.'

It was a very girlfriendly statement. Marissa's eyes flashed again and she embarked on a long speech about the private chef who'd be catering the weekend, how he'd worked for all sorts of celebrities, and that he needed final numbers and it was very rude to leave it so late to confirm.

' . . . he's cooked for the Duke and Duchess of Cambridge and even they managed to produce a final guest list a month in advance . . . '

'We're closing now. If you're not waiting to have your purchases rung up, I'm afraid I'm going to have to ask you to leave,' said a voice behind them and Verity swivelled around to see Nina standing there with her hands on her hips. 'Also, Very, the cashing up isn't going to do itself.'

Marissa gave a little shudder at the words 'cashing up' as if this glimpse into the working

316

day had made her skin crawl. 'Look, I really have to go now,' she said as if Verity was the one who'd been keeping her there against her will. She stood in one fluid movement. 'Please let me know about this weekend. Johnny knows where to find me.'

Then she was walking out of the shop as if the scarred wooden floor was a Milan catwalk.

'My spider sense was tingling,' Nina explained as Verity hauled herself up from the sofa depths with a lot less grace than Marissa. 'I never trust anyone whose hair is that shiny. It's not natural. I mean, who *is* she?'

'One of Johnny's university friends.' Verity tried to keep her tone noncommittal but that telltale muscle was twitching away in her eyelid. 'Apparently she has a first from Cambridge in English Literature and I really do not like her.'

'Very!' Tom popped up from behind the counter. 'You know it unsettles me when you express an uncharitable thought.'

'And you a vicar's daughter too.' Nina supplied the punchline with a throaty gurgle of laughter.

As was so often the case, Jane Austen could sum up Verity's thoughts on the matter far better than Verity could. 'She is one of those young ladies who seek to recommend themselves to the other sex by undervaluing their own, and with many men, I dare say, it succeeds,' she said with a sniff. 'But, in my opinion, it is a paltry device, a very mean art.'

Nina and Tom slowly backed away. 'Well, we'll just leave you in peace to do the cashing up,'

Tom said, making sure to keep his voice low.

'You just take your time,' Nina cooed. 'And I'm going out tonight. With a guy I met on HookUpp who says he's in the Marines so you can have the flat all to yourself. You'd like that, wouldn't you?'

'More than you could ever know,' Verity said feelingly.

22

*'I believe I must date it from my first seeing
his beautiful grounds at Pemberley.'*

There was nothing Verity wanted more than to
lie down in a dark room with a damp cloth over
her head, but first she had to talk to Johnny.

Much as it pained her to admit it, it wasn't the
kind of talk they could have via the medium of
email or text message. It wasn't even a phone
call kind of chat.

When you had to break it to your fake
boyfriend that the love of his life required his
presence at the celebration of her tenth wedding
anniversary to her actual husband, only a
face-to-face would do.

Still, it didn't hurt to test the water with a text
message, Verity reasoned and perhaps Johnny
would be unavoidably busy for the next few days
and by that time the weekend would be upon
them and it would be too late to attend, much
less give details of any food allergies to Marissa's
celebrity chef.

Are you around this evening? We need to talk.

She texted as soon as she locked the door behind
Nina who was quite giddy about her date with
the Marine.

'An actual Marine, Very,' she'd sighed in a very

unNina-like way. 'He says that he could easily pick me up and throw me onto the bed in a fit of passion and you know how I've always wanted a man who could do that.'

Unfortunately Johnny texted back before Verity had even finished climbing the stairs to her blissfully empty flat.

Have you forgotten that you were meant to be coming round for dinner tonight? Our 'double date' with my father and that Elspeth. Please hurry! (Though your message sounds ominous.)

She had completely forgotten about it. William had sent a charming email with an invitation to dinner after he'd dropped by and though Verity had confirmed, she'd then repressed all memory of it, as she often did with things that she knew were going to be awkward.

And now, as Johnny would have it, there was a whole other level of ominous added on to the ordeal. You don't know the half of it, Verity thought to herself glumly. Johnny had attached a location pin with his message and, after feeding Strumpet and retrieving Johnny's Marissa phone from her drawer, Verity set off for Canonbury with dread in her heart. No one liked to be the bearer of bad news and everyone knew what happened to the messengers of said bad news.

Verity had planned to walk the two miles or so, weaving her way through the back streets of Clerkenwell and Islington, but it was just prolonging the agony so she squeezed onto a bus packed tight with hot, fractious people on their way home from work and became increasingly hot and fractious herself.

Though the bus crawled through traffic-clogged streets, it arrived at Highbury Corner far too soon for Verity's liking and it was only another five-minute walk along pretty, tree-lined streets of solid Victorian houses before she was trudging unhappily up the path and ringing Johnny's door-bell. She'd read all about its four-storeyed glory in the *Guardian*, but still she wasn't prepared for how huge his house was, how immaculate everything from plasterwork to pointing was; even his front door was the perfect shade of pale grey.

Verity felt like a grubby urchin who should go round to the tradesmen's entrance, especially when she glanced down and saw to her dismay that she was still wearing her Happy Ever After T-shirt. Hadn't even thought to run a brush through her hair or dab on a little perfume. Oh goodness, she hadn't even stopped en route to pick up a bottle of wine or a bunch of mixed blooms.

It was too late for regrets. The door opened and there was Johnny, who had clearly had time for a shower and change since he'd got home from work. He was wearing jeans and a black shirt, the sleeves rolled up, and looked pleased to see Verity, judging from his relieved smile.

'Thank God you're here,' he said, yanking her forward for a kiss on the cheek that seemed to surprise them both, then ushering Verity through the door and into a wide hall with what looked like the original black and white tiles on the floor, a wooden bench built into the back of the staircase and delicate fretwork framing the top of the stairs, all of it painted white. 'We're having Pimm's in the garden.'

It didn't sound as if it was going that well; Johnny meeting 'that Elspeth' for the first time. With even heavier heart, Verity followed him down the hall, glimpsing through an open door an open-plan living room flooded with light, walls painted a soft smudgy off-white, sofa and rugs and cushions and a collection of glassware on the shelves inset on either side of a grand fireplace, in different shades of blue.

Then through to the kitchen, as featured in the *Guardian*. The units that Johnny had built himself and the gigantic burnished-steel kitchen table, the white walls this time relieved with cheerful green accents and a big Swedish-style dresser full of brightly coloured china.

One wall of the kitchen was entirely taken up by glass doors, which were open onto a large garden, mostly given over to lawn. 'I can't say that it's going terribly well,' Johnny said to Verity out of the side of his mouth as they stepped out onto the decking. Just round the corner, sitting on a bench, were William and a woman in a pretty flowery dress, with delicate features that age could not wither.

Their heads were close together as they whispered, then the woman giggled and William nuzzled her neck and, to the untrained eye, it looked a lot like they were canoodling.

'I can't leave you two alone for a minute, can I?' Johnny asked with a touch of exasperation so that the woman laughed again, but very nervously. Johnny tugged Verity forward with a tight, desperate grip of her fingers. 'We have company. Very, you've met this old reprobate before, haven't you? When he was interfering.'

'I wouldn't call it interfering so much as taking a keen interest in my only child's emotional well-being,' William said grandly. He put his arm around the woman. 'And this is Elspeth, my friend. Elspeth, this is Verity, Johnny's friend, who advised me to get you that beautiful cloth-bound edition of *Pride and Prejudice*.'

'Oh, such an inspired choice!' Elspeth said and she beamed at Verity, who smiled back and made 'no, don't get up' gestures at the older woman.

Then Verity looked down at her T-shirt again. 'So sorry, I didn't have time to change after work.' She put a hand to her hair, which was feeling quite bedraggled.

'True beauty needs no gilding,' William said gallantly, then raised his eyebrows at Johnny. 'This lovely girl needs a drink.'

Soon Verity was clutching a glass of Pimm's crammed full of strawberries and cucumber and as Johnny fired up the barbecue to grill some tuna steaks, she talked to Elspeth, who had been an English teacher until she'd retired a couple of years before, about books. Unlike say, Marissa, Elspeth had no problem with a lot of the greatest works of literature being classed as romantic fiction. 'And who cares anyway?' Elspeth asked. 'Some of my happiest moments in life have involved a packet of dark-chocolate stem-ginger cookies and the latest Diana Gabaldon.'

'Lucinda, my late wife, did love a romantic novel,' William remembered and Elspeth smiled warmly and squeezed his hand while Johnny watched with narrowed eyes. 'I'm sure she would have loved talking about books with you, Verity.'

Verity mumbled something about how that would have been nice and lapsed into silence, like Johnny, who apart from asking how rare people wanted their tuna steaks, had been monosyllabic and boot-faced. Still, William and Elspeth attempted to keep the conversation going with Verity contributing where she could. Over dinner, Elspeth explained how she'd retired and been unexpectedly widowed all in the space of two months and to get herself out of her 'dreadful funk' she'd adopted a dog, a poodle cross called Peggy, and signed up for a yoga class, where she'd met William.

Johnny scoffed very quietly though Verity wasn't sure if it was because he was anti-poodles or anti-yoga, or more likely it was the thought of William and Elspeth locking eyes while doing the Downward Dog. His scoff was still loud enough that Elspeth faltered mid-sentence and William, no trace of twinkle, sent his son a hurt, angry look.

'I think . . . Will you excuse me?' Elspeth stood up. 'I need to powder my nose.'

'I'll show you where to go,' William said, standing up too, and shooting his son another baleful look before he took Elspeth's arm and guided her across the decking.

'I'm not sure this was a good idea,' Verity heard Elspeth say, which meant that Johnny could hear her too, but he didn't even have the grace to look ashamed of himself.

'I never imagined that you could behave like such a dick,' Verity blurted out, because she was too cross to choose her words with care or have to work herself up before she could say something. 'You're being so rude to poor Elspeth. She's your guest.'

Johnny had given a start at Verity's opening salvo but now he was back to looking as if he were chewing rocks. 'She's my father's guest,' he corrected Verity.

'She's in *your* house and you're making her feel unwelcome. That's the very definition of bad manners,' Verity persisted. 'Come on, you are better than this. Or I thought you were.'

For a second, Verity thought she'd overstepped her remit as fake girlfriend because Johnny narrowed his eyes all the better to glare at her. She glared right back, holding his gaze until he sighed. 'I thought I was better than this too but it's hard . . . seeing my father with another woman.' He shook his head. 'All the kissing and touching. They could take it down a notch.'

'It's not like they're full-on snogging!'

Johnny pinched the bridge of his nose. 'Very, please, don't say things like that.'

Somebody had to say something though and that somebody was Verity. 'Elspeth is your father's girlfriend whether you like it or not so I suggest that you *do* like it and you *do* get used to it because you're hurting Elspeth and William's feelings. Worse than that, you're making your father feel guilty when he has nothing to feel guilty about. He's allowed to find love again and that doesn't diminish any of the love he had for your mother.'

'But he did really love my mother,' Johnny said, not in an argumentative way but as a wistful observation.

'And how lonely it must be to keep loving someone for so many years when you can't be with them,' Verity said with heavy emphasis and she took Johnny's hand, both thrilled and appalled at her own daring, so she could thread her fingers through his.

Verity could see Johnny's struggle in the furrowing of his brow, the tenseness in his fingers as he clutched hers. Then he shook his head, not in disbelief, but as if he were clearing out all the bad vibes. 'Oh, Very . . . ' he murmured, then turned his head as his father and Elspeth emerged from the house.

'Elspeth,' he said and swallowed hard. Verity squeezed his fingers again. 'I've just had it pointed out to me that I really have been behaving quite appallingly. I hope you'll forgive me.' Johnny smiled at Elspeth. One of his lovely, warm, kind smiles and Elspeth visibly relaxed and smiled back as she sat down, while William managed to look both tender and exasperated with his son.

'You're still grounded,' William muttered and any remaining tension evaporated as if everyone had been holding their breaths and now that they could exhale, they were quite light-headed from the lack of oxygen.

Perhaps that's why none of them could stop

laughing after Johnny described Strumpet as a 'cat of very easy virtue' and Verity was forced to defend Strumpet's extreme sluttishness then show Elspeth and William the pictures she had on her phone of Poor Alan's beekeeping outfit because words didn't really do it justice.

They made a very fine couple, finishing each other's sentences, giggling at each other's jokes, always with the little touches — Elspeth's hand resting on William's knee, him tucking a lock of her hair behind her ear — so that it was hard to believe that they'd only been courting for 'not even a year. Gosh, though it seems longer, doesn't it?'

Now that he'd wrestled with his demons and won the battle, Johnny no longer seemed the slightest bit put out by his father suddenly acquiring a girlfriend after ten years of being a widower. On the contrary, Verity couldn't help but notice that he made sure to smile every time he spoke to Elspeth.

'I really liked Elspeth,' Verity said later as she and Johnny were clearing up and William was putting Elspeth in an Uber that would take her back to Crouch End. 'You do like her, don't you?'

'I do.' It was a sigh. 'Very much and once I got over myself, I could see how happy she makes my father so that made me even more inclined to like her,' Johnny said as he rinsed plates, then handed them to Verity to put in the dishwasher. 'Thank you for that.'

'Thank me for what?' Verity asked. 'I didn't really do anything.'

'You gave me a stern talking to when I sorely needed one,' Johnny said. 'It made me see how rude I was being, how childish. That if my father likes Elspeth, even loves her, then it doesn't take away any of the love he had for my mother.'

'Of course it doesn't,' William said from the doorway. 'I was devoted to your mother and I've been so lonely without her, which was the one thing she didn't want me to be.'

Verity fluttered the tea towel she was holding like a matador's cape. 'I'll go out into the garden, so you can talk,' she said quickly, but William shook his head and Johnny gently captured her wrist.

'You don't have to go,' he said with a rueful smile. 'You already know just how much of a bloody idiot I am. You're right, of course Mum wouldn't have wanted you to be alone,' he added to his father.

'She did make me promise that I wouldn't become one of those sad old men who lived on baked beans and let their personal hygiene slip.' William perched nimbly on one of Johnny's burnished-steel stools. 'There was even talk of me taking up swing dancing or painting with watercolours so I could meet women. 'You've loved me so well, that it would be a terrible waste if you never loved again,' Lucinda told me just before she died but it was because I loved her so well that I wasn't ready to meet anyone else for quite a while.'

'And now?' Johnny prompted, his fingers still curled around Verity's wrist so he had to feel how fast her pulse was racing as she was forced

328

to bear witness to a conversation that was nothing to do with her, even if she did have a vested interest in anything that might influence Johnny's own views of love.

'Now I realise that if you spend too much time living in the past then you miss what's right in front of you,' William said, with what seemed to Verity a pointed look at his only son. 'Now . . . I'm going down to my basement hovel . . .'

'Hardly a hovel,' Johnny protested but he sounded slightly distracted, as if his heart wasn't in it.

'Why don't you show Verity round?' William suggested and Verity, though she pretended she could take or leave a guided tour, was eager to have a good snoop.

Johnny was mostly silent as he showed Verity the ground-floor rooms, only muttering something about the engineered wooden floors. It wasn't until he showed Verity the guest bathroom on the first floor, which had a freestanding clawfoot bath that would be absolutely perfect to read in, that he spoke. 'Why on earth did I expect him to pine after my mother for the rest of his days? That was so unreasonable of me.'

Pot, meet kettle, thought Verity as she took a deep breath and plonked herself down on the window seat in the bathroom. Despite its sense of uncluttered space, there were lots of spots, cosy nooks, in the house where someone could curl up for an hour or so with a book, or just be alone with their thoughts.

There was no easy way to say this, Verity thought, as Johnny looked quizzically down at her. 'Come and sit next to me?' Unlike Marissa, Verity made it a heartfelt plea rather than a peremptory demand and when Johnny sat down so they were squeezed in tight together, she took his hand. It felt like the right thing to do.

'Suddenly I'm very worried,' Johnny said in a voice that sounded a lot more amused than it had done a minute before. 'You're either breaking up with me or about to tell me you've only got three months to live.'

'Neither, except, well, I had a visitor at the shop today.' Verity patted Johnny's hand. 'And that visitor was . . . Marissa.'

Verity was a little surprised that there was no 'dun dun dur!' spooky music after she uttered the dreaded name. Instead, Johnny stiffened slightly. 'Oh, really? How is she?'

'Well. She looked well.'

'Good. That's . . . good.'

Johnny's reaction, while not exactly exuberant, wasn't at all what Verity had been expecting. Secretly she'd been hoping for a callous indifference because a month of space had finally cured Johnny of his Marissa habit. Or a worstcase scenario, which would be Johnny rushing off into the night to pledge his undying love to his lady fair.

'Anyway it's been a month. Actually longer than a month so I should give you the phone back as Marissa says that she's been trying to contact you because — and you're not to freak out or get upset about this — it's her and Harry's tenth wedding anniversary bash this weekend . . . '

330

'Oh, it's this weekend, isn't it?' Johnny remarked casually as if he really were over Marissa and had barely given her a moment's thought over the last few weeks. 'I saved the date ages ago but never confirmed.' He smiled the kind of smile you might give to an acquaintance or neighbour you passed in the street — a smile that was impossible for Verity to read. 'Was she furious?'

'Quite furious.' Verity couldn't say any more than that because if she did, she'd be cast as the kind of woman who badmouthed other women in the presence of men. 'Needs final numbers and dietary requirements for the private chef.'

Johnny nodded. 'Marissa. Oh, Marissa.' He let out a long breath. 'The very last time I saw my mother smile was when Marissa and I told her that we were engaged. She asked me if I was happy and when I said I was, she said, 'Well, all I ever want is for you to be happy. Then I'm happy too.' '

Verity rested the flat of her hand on Johnny's back as he hunched over, elbows on his knees. For someone who wasn't very tactile, she was making great strides in her personal development this evening. 'You must miss her so much.' She decided it needed further clarification. 'Your mother, I mean.'

'So many of my last memories of her are tied up with memories of when Marissa and I were at our best,' Johnny said, as he leaned in to Verity's touch. 'It's easy to sugarcoat what Marissa and I had, because in reality, we always seemed to be either in a fight or making up from a fight or

331

spoiling for a fight but then when my mother became ill all that stopped.' Johnny straightened up so he could look at Verity with a troubled expression. 'Marissa was my rock. Every evening when she'd finished work, she'd come and sit with my mother and give Dad and I a break. She'd wash her hair or paint her nails, little things that made Mum feel in some small way like herself when she hadn't felt like herself in weeks.'

It was a side of Marissa that Verity hadn't seen but then she'd only met the woman twice. But however unpleasant Marissa had been to her, when it really mattered, she'd been there for Johnny, for his mother, and now Verity could understand just how tight were the ties that bound him and Marissa together. 'No wonder you still love her,' she said softly, though she wanted to groan and gnash her teeth in frustration.

'I am painfully aware that it seems to most people that I moon after her like a lovesick schoolboy without any encouragement from her but just when I'm at my lowest, when I believe that this whole sorry business should be done, she always manages to pull me back in.'

Johnny was a hopeless case. Verity wasn't sure what more she could do for him, but by God, she was still going to try.

'I can't stand to talk about this any longer,' Johnny said and he stood and held out his hand to Verity. 'Come on, I haven't shown you the second floor, or where the magic happens as I never call it because that would be cheesy.'

Johnny was right. There was nothing else to say on the sad subject that was he and Marissa and it was time to drop it and lighten the mood. Verity let Johnny pull her to her feet. 'You're really not the cheesy type.'

'Though I do love a nice runny Stilton,' Johnny said, as they climbed up yet another flight of stairs — living here must be quite the aerobic workout — and passed another window seat set into the stairwell.

There was a guest room, a bathroom, Johnny's dressing room and then he opened another door onto the master bedroom and en suite. 'Absolutely no magic goes on in here, just sleeping mostly. You can come in, I promise I won't seduce you.' Johnny cocked his head and gave Verity, who was hovering in the doorway, a weary look as if seduction was the very last thing on his mind, which it probably was, considering he loved Marissa and he always would. Then the weary look became more wolfish. 'Unless you really want me to, that is?'

Verity could only answer the question in the same spirit in which it had been delivered. It would be madness to do anything else. 'Not on a full stomach,' she decided then stepped past a now grinning Johnny and into his room.

Unlike the light, bright, sunny feel of the rest of the house, his bedroom was cosy despite its enormous size, rich, maybe even a little bit sexy. The walls were covered in an opulent dark grey and silver wallpaper that featured densely coloured trailing vines with insects and flowers dotted carelessly about. It should have been overpowering but the room's dimensions were large enough for it to work.

There were a couple of plush, outsized grey velvet armchairs by the window but mostly the room was dominated by a huge bed, heaped with crisp white pillows, a duvet that billowed like a cloud and a grey waffle-knit blanket draped neatly at the foot. It was far too big for one person, especially if that person didn't have someone to share it with, not even a pet. Johnny sat down on the bed and patted the space next to him so Verity had no choice but to sit down too.

The mattress was very firm but with just enough give to it and it was hard not to resist the temptation to bounce.

'I like your house,' Verity said nervously. 'I didn't count a single health and safety violation.'

'I should think not.' Johnny leaned back on his elbows. 'So, are you up for it then?'

'I beg your pardon!' Verity achieved an indignant top note that any Austen heroine would be proud of, even as other feelings overwhelmed her. They made her stomach clench and her mouth suddenly Sahara dry in a way that wasn't entirely unpleasant even as she tried to squash those inconvenient feelings down. 'You just promised not to seduce me!'

'I was talking about this weekend,' Johnny drawled, not even bothering to hide his smirk. 'The anniversary party.'

Verity's stomach unclenched, her ardour doused as surely as if Johnny had thrown a glass of cold water in her face. 'You want to go to the anniversary party? Even though you've just said that you still love her? How is going to her anniversary party, seeing Marissa and Harry together, going to be an enjoyable experience for you?' Her voice was so squeaky she was sure that it was only audible to bats.

'I can't avoid her for ever, can I? And what better way of reminding myself that she'll never really be mine than by celebrating her wedding anniversary to her husband of ten years? If I can do that, then maybe there's hope for me after all.' Johnny gazed up at the ceiling, his expression thoughtful. 'Life after Marissa. And you'll be there, won't you, to stop me falling off the wagon? I wouldn't have got through this summer without you.'

'I can't see that I did that much. Just took custody of your phone and, to be honest with you, that wasn't really any great sacrifice,' Verity admitted. She thought a bit harder. 'And the whole fake girlfriend thing, but even that wasn't as bad as I thought it would be. Apart from that time you made me dance with you to 'Hi Ho Silver Lining'. That was bloody awful.'

Johnny laughed. 'It was, wasn't it? But we have had some fun, haven't we?'

This was starting to sound like a post-mortem on their fake relationship. In fact, it was starting to sound a lot like goodbye and though Verity had complained about all the food en croute and public displays of dancing and being expected to be social, in a strange way she'd miss it.

But not half as much as she'd miss Johnny. In some ways, he was so strong, so sure of himself in a way that Verity never was. Then in other ways, she was pretty sure he'd slide back into his old, bad, Marissa-shaped habits as soon as they'd said their goodbyes. Suddenly she was keen to prolong their experiment. 'You really want to go to their anniversary party?' she asked Johnny. 'Even though it lasts the whole bank holiday weekend, which is longer than a normal weekend?'

Johnny gave her a sideways look, like he'd been caught with his hand in the biscuit tin. 'I haven't been a hundred per cent honest with you. I do actually have an ulterior motive,' he said hesitantly, then caught sight of Verity's stricken face. 'Oh God, it's nothing bad!'

Verity had shut her eyes and braced herself as if she'd been expecting a body blow or for Johnny to confess that he was only going so he could persuade Marissa to run off with him. 'What is it then?' she asked.

'The house Marissa and Harry have booked. It's generally considered to be one of the finest examples of a privately owned art deco house in England,' Johnny said a little wistfully. 'Ten years ago it was all but derelict until the current owners painstakingly restored it. I'd love to see it.'

'Well, Cornwall is lovely.' Verity was wavering. The last thing, the very last thing, she wanted to do was spend any more time in Marissa's company, but . . . 'If you're sure this weekend won't be too much of an ordeal?'

'There's only one way to find out, isn't there?' Johnny sounded quite jaunty about the prospect of being over the woman who'd been the beat of his heart for over half his life. 'And you'll be there to keep me on the straight and narrow.'

And then he wouldn't need her any more. The thought made Verity feel unbearably sad, though she'd known perfectly well what she'd been getting into. In fact, she hadn't wanted to get into it in the first place, but now she had, she suspected that losing a real fake boyfriend might hurt almost as much as losing a real boyfriend.

'One last hurrah, then?' she asked in a voice which was pretty steady, all things considered.

Johnny reached across to give Verity a gentle push that almost toppled her off the bed. 'Hardly! We still have Con's wedding in a few weeks and who knows what else?' He looped an arm around Verity's shoulders to tug her close enough that her face was tucked into a comfortable space between Johnny's neck and shoulder where the smell of him, all crisp cotton and that zingy aftershave and something else that was all Johnny, was at its most intoxicating. She could feel his breath stir her hair. 'Look at me, Very,' he said in a tone that she couldn't refuse.

Verity raised her head. Johnny was looking at her with . . . well, in the softening light, shadows creeping in, it looked like tenderness, but it was more probably fondness . . . or likingness . . . Something ending in ness anyway.

'I should probably go home quite soon,' Verity mumbled though she could have quite happily stayed where she was for a good few hours.

'Not yet,' Johnny insisted and then he was cradling Verity's face in his hands, his fingers tracing along her cheekbones so she suddenly forgot how to breathe. 'Very, I don't know what I'd do without you,' he said huskily and he leaned in closer so that Verity's eyes widened and she still couldn't remember how to breathe and . . . he was definitely going to kiss . . . oh, just the top of her head. Then Johnny pulled back so that Verity could see the soft look in his eyes. 'One last hurrah indeed! You're not getting rid of me that easily.'

23

*'I was uncomfortable enough. I was very
uncomfortable, I may say unhappy.'*

Verity and Johnny left London at lunchtime on
Friday for the drive down to almost the very tip
of Cornwall.

It was a drizzly day with ninety per cent
humidity, which did terrible things to Verity's
hair, but the further west they drove, the clearer
the skies became until there was nothing but
blue above them and green fields around them.
Though Verity had a hard painful knot in her
stomach at the thought of seeing Marissa again
— and seeing Johnny with Marissa again — the
rhythms of their usual road-trip routine soothed
her.

They listened to 6 Music, or 'indie hits of
yesteryear' as Johnny called it, and she filled him
in on all the latest developments of the
#lovesimpsonwedding because Con and Alex
now had an official wedding hashtag — apparently all the best weddings had their own official
hashtag.

Then they came off the motorway not long
after Taunton so they could have lunch at a
pretty little pub that Johnny knew. It wasn't until
they left Devon to be greeted by a 'Welcome to
Cornwall' sign that the knot returned and Verity
grew quieter and quieter.

The knot had upgraded to a boulder lodged deep in her solar plexus as they came off the dual carriageway again to drive along narrow lanes liberally splattered with roadkill. Verity knew exactly how those woodland animals must have felt when they realised death was imminent.

All too soon, they were driving through Lower Meryton, a pretty seaside village, then pulling into the car park of the local pub. They'd decided that Verity would liaise with Marissa over the final details and Verity was under strict instructions to text an unfamiliar mobile number from the pub car park to let them know of their arrival.

They could see their destination about two hundred and fifty metres in the distance. A low hill, more of a mound really, with a white house perched atop it, glittering sea all around. Visitors were able to walk to the island at low tide, but it very obviously wasn't low tide, which was why they were waiting for something that an incoming text message referred to as a 'sea tractor'.

'I have no idea what that is,' Verity said to Johnny as he took their cases out of the car.

He straightened and stretched, then looked out to sea. 'That's what it is.'

'Dear Lord,' Verity said faintly.

A strange contraption was lumbering towards them. It looked like the chassis of an open-top lorry, a row of seats along either side, floating on the water, but as it got closer to shore the vehicle's lower half — four wheels and a series of supporting metal cantilevered poles — came into view and Verity realised that the water couldn't be that deep. In fact, she'd rather take her chances and swim to the island if it was all the same.

'It's perfectly safe,' Johnny said, picking up their cases. 'Sea tractors were quite popular in the thirties for scenic tours of waterfront attractions, but I suppose most people use boats nowadays.'

A set of metal steps had now descended and a man waved at them as they hurried down the slope that led to the beach.

'Jeremy,' he shouted when they were within shouting distance. 'You must be Johnny and Victoria.'

'Verity,' Johnny and Verity said in unison.

Jeremy, it turned out, owned Wimsey House, their destination, and was a City acquaintance of Harry. Verity clung to her seat, eyes shut, praying to God to deliver her safely over the sea, which had seemed quite calm but now to her delicate sensibilities seemed decidedly choppy, as Jeremy and Johnny happily chatted away about Wimsey House and the renovations that had taken over five years and the best part of two million pounds.

It's really not *that* deep, Verity told herself. And you're not on a boat; you're on a really high-up, motor vehicle. But still her guts heaved as the sea tractor carried her to an uncertain fate or at least a weekend-long party hosted by a woman that Verity disliked more than any other person that she'd ever met since secondary school, when her games mistress, Miss Harriss,

341

had taken violently and instantly against her. The feeling had been entirely mutual.

Still, the injustice of all those push-ups Miss Harriss had made Verity do at the slightest provocation took her mind off the nausea and the feeling that she might die at any moment. Not that Johnny noticed her discomfort. He was listening, rapt, as Jeremy waxed lyrical about his four different sun terraces.

They reached the island, not a moment too soon. The sea tractor left the water and came to a juddering halt that had the inevitable effect on Verity's shuddering stomach. She leaned over the side of the vehicle so she could throw up the ploughman's she'd had for lunch.

'Oh God,' she moaned. God had featured quite heavily over the last hour and yet he seemed to have forsaken Verity in her hour of need.

'Poor Very.' She felt a hand on her shoulder and then Johnny was rubbing soothing circles on her back though it was very much a case of shutting the stable door after the horse had well and truly bolted.

He helped her down the steps and even when her feet were firmly on solid ground, her legs were as unsteady as blancmange and she felt shaky and emotional the way she always did after she'd been sick. For once Verity didn't mind when Johnny put his arm around her as they walked up the path to the house. Like any couple would.

'We'll go straight to the lower terrace,' Jeremy decided, unlatching a side gate to a gravel path, bordered by lush succulent plants, which wound round the building. Even before they turned the corner, Verity could hear from the chink of glasses and ice, the chatter and laughter of a drinks party in full flow.

Or it was in full flow until the three of them came into view and then everyone stopped talking and turned to look at them. Perhaps it was because the people clutching martini glasses were dressed all in white and Johnny and Verity weren't. Also, Verity was pretty sure, from sense of smell alone and without even daring to put a hand up to check, that she had vomit in her hair.

'Darling! I'm so glad you're here, Johnny.' Marissa detached herself from a throng of people at the end of the terrace. She was wearing a simple draped dress that made her look like a Greek goddess just popped down from Mount Olympus. She glided towards them so she could detach Johnny from Verity's limp grip, slink her hand up his chest and kiss him on the cheek. 'Now the party can really get started.'

'Looks like the party's already well under way,' Johnny said and he gently but firmly pushed Marissa away; a gesture that warmed the cockles of Verity's tired little heart. 'Happy Anniversary to you and Harry. Where is he?'

'Around somewhere,' Marissa said, eyeing Johnny up and down as if she were planning to have him served up medium rare. 'Why don't you go and get changed. I'll make sure there's a cocktail waiting for you when you get back. Martini, isn't it?'

Johnny shook his head, smiled regretfully. 'We

both know martinis were always more your thing. I'd love a G&T if there's one going.'

Verity had rarely been more proud of anyone. Then Marissa turned to her with a cold-eyed gaze. 'Valerie. You made it,' she said flatly as if she'd been hoping that Jeremy would have pushed Verity off the infernal sea tractor halfway through the crossing. 'Goodness, you're looking rather . . . forlorn.' Marissa sniffed the air delicately, then took a hasty step back, not that Verity could blame her for that. 'Luckily you've got time to freshen up and change into your LWD before dinner. It's at seven thirty, sharp. Chef is very particular about these things.'

Half an hour to shower, wash her hair like it had never been washed before and change into a . . . 'LWD? What's that?' Verity asked nervously because Marissa seemed to think she should already know what a LWD was.

'Oh, Valentine! Everyone knows what a LWD is,' Marissa said loudly, then finished up with a tinkling laugh.

Johnny wasn't laughing though. Despite the possible vomit-hair, he put his arm round Verity again, pulling her in close so she could lean against something solid and steady. 'You know perfectly well that her name is Verity,' he said quietly so only Marissa could hear because it wasn't Johnny's style to publicly humiliate someone. 'And I don't know what a LWD is either so maybe you can enlighten us both.'

Marissa didn't flush or turn away or apologise, because that wasn't her style. She stood her ground and tilted her head upwards so the sun

344

caught the beautiful planes of her face like the heavens were backlighting her. 'It stands for little white dress,' she explained slowly as if she was talking to a pair of idiots. 'It's an all-white themed weekend. Traditionally, the tenth wedding anniversary is tin but what would I want with anything made of tin? This was all in the email I sent you, Verity.'

'I didn't get an email about little white dresses or little white anything,' Verity said, because she absolutely hadn't. Just one very brusque email acknowledging that she and Johnny had now RSVP-ed and details of who to text once they'd reached Lower Meryton. 'I don't have any white dresses with me. I'm really sorry. I hope that won't ruin your weekend too much.'

Verity was sincere enough but she did half hope that Marissa would send them packing, even if it meant a return trip on the infernal sea tractor.

'I know for a fact that I sent you an email about the dress code,' Marissa insisted so vociferously that even though Verity knew for a fact that she hadn't, maybe, just maybe, Marissa had sent her another email and for some strange reason it had ended up in Verity's spam folder. 'Oh well, it can't be helped. At least tell me that you brought evening-wear? We're dressing up for dinner tomorrow night. White tie and formal gowns.'

'No evening wear,' Johnny said calmly as Verity was contemplating flinging herself off the sun terrace. Yes, she might get dashed to death on the rocks below but at least no one would expect her to wear a formal gown for dinner tomorrow. 'We don't mind eating in our rooms though if . . . '

'Don't be silly,' Marissa said quickly with a tight smile. She looked around the assembled guests who had gone back to talking and laughing and clinking their glasses. 'We could probably rustle up a spare dinner jacket and perhaps someone could lend you a gown, Verity . . . ' Marissa tailed off, her eyes locked on Verity's body like she'd never been confronted by a size-ten woman in the flesh before.

'It's just as well Very is one of those women who could wear a bin bag and still look beautiful,' Johnny said smoothly, which was such an outrageous lie that Verity was amazed he wasn't struck by a lightning bolt where he stood. Still, she was glad of the outrageous lie and his unfailing, good-humoured support.

She said as much to him after Marissa relinquished them to the care of the housekeeper who would take them to their rooms. 'Thank you for having my back,' she whispered as they climbed up a gracefully curved staircase and marvelled at the sleek white interior of the house. 'But, honestly, I'm ninety-nine per cent certain I never got an email about a dress code.'

'Oh, I'd put money on it,' Johnny said cheerfully. He shot Verity a sideways glance. 'Don't look so glum, Very. If nothing else, Marissa being so vile is great aversion therapy. Funny how you only remember a person's better qualities when you haven't seen them for a while.'

If Marissa had any better qualities she kept

346

them hidden well, Verity decided as they were shown to their room. One room. Singular. A beautiful room with huge picture windows that looked out onto an impossibly blue sea and an impossibly blue sky now tinged pink and orange as the day gave way to evening. And in this beautiful room was a bed. One bed. Because Verity hadn't thought to inform Marissa that she and Johnny would be sleeping in separate beds, preferably in separate rooms. She could imagine, all too clearly, the look of malicious glee on the other woman's face if she had.

'Look, this is fine,' Johnny said before Verity could say that it wasn't. 'We've shared a room before. We might not have shared a bed but we're both adults. I'm sure we can rise above any lustful urges we might have.' He laughed, awkwardly.

'And if we can't, we could always sleep with a pillow between us,' Verity joked, even though there was nothing funny about this. Then she thought about the events of the last hour and how she'd make her sisters, not to mention Posy, Nina and Tom, hoot with laughter when she told them about rocking up to the welcome cocktail party with bits of regurgitated cheese and pickle in her hair. It was one of those situations where if you didn't laugh about it, the only other course of action was to collapse on the huge super-kingsize bed and weep until your tear ducts ran dry. 'If nothing else, I'll keep my family entertained for years telling them stories about this weekend.'

'And it could be worse. For instance, we could

347

be doing hard labour in a salt mine in Siberia,' Johnny pointed out.

'I once spent a summer holiday working on the fish jerky line of a pet food factory in Grimsby,' Verity said, entering into the spirit of things. 'This is definitely not as bad as that. I don't even smell as bad as that. Talking of which, I'll let you freshen up first as long as you're really quick in the bathroom because I need to shower as a matter of some urgency.'

24

'I should infinitely prefer a book ...'

It very quickly became apparent that they were not among friends. The guest list was exclusively made up of men that Harry knew from the City and their wives, who were all groomed and glamorous and worked as fashion or media consultants and got up at six every morning to do yoga in a very hot room, then have a blow-out before their first breakfast meeting.

They were civil but utterly disinterested. Their collective gaze faintly pitying, their smiles condescending every time Verity appeared in their midst in another non-white ensemble.

At dinner that first night, while Johnny was far down the other end of the table and deep in conversation with Jeremy, Marissa had been quick to inform her other guests that Verity was a vicar's daughter who worked in a shop. 'And she has to wear a uniform,' Marissa helpfully pointed out. 'And the shop only sells romance novels. I had to check that I was still in the twenty-first century.' She'd then gone on to explain that Verity was a product of a state school education and hadn't been to either Oxford or Cambridge.

'I've never met anyone quite like you before,' Trudie, a holistic interior design consultant, told Verity at breakfast the next morning when Verity timidly asked how bircher muesli differed from ordinary muesli.

Johnny was faring no better. He'd been all but ostracised because he hadn't made obscene amounts of money betting against the pound or shorting on the dollar or whatever it was the other men had done to make their fortunes. Also he didn't live in West London, play squash or pay alimony to his first wife and complain bitterly about it.

The only way to get through the weekend was for the pair of them to bond over not being good enough and attempt to keep each other's spirits up.

'At least we're not breaking rocks in a chain gang in the American Deep South,' Johnny had said to Verity before dinner on the Friday night when everyone else was dressed in white and had a three-drink lead on them.

'At least we're not trapped in a malfunctioning space pod endlessly orbiting the earth with dwindling rations and fuel supply,' Verity said to Johnny as they lay in bed that night, window open to let in the breeze and the sound of the sea, a pillow down the middle of the bed only because Johnny had admitted to being a fidgety sleeper and Verity quite liked to sleep without a stray elbow or knee banging into her.

'At least we're not crossing the Appalachian mountain trail on foot, carrying all our worldly goods on our backs, because our mule has gone lame,' Johnny said the next morning after breakfast when they were meant to play mixed doubles but were banished to the net to serve as

350

ball boys because they hadn't brought any tennis gear with them.

'At least we haven't gone back in time to London in 1666 and if the bubonic plague hasn't got us, then the Great Fire of London probably will,' Verity said later that afternoon. Everyone else was lounging round the swimming pool on the Upper Terrace — only Johnny and Verity were brave enough to take to the water. Even wearing a sensible one-piece swimsuit and not a tiny white bikini, Verity felt a lot more comfortable with her body submerged. They lazily swam lengths, until Harry said that it was time to get dressed for dinner and they'd be serving cocktails on the Crescent Terrace (so many terraces) at seven.

The only vaguely white clothing Verity had packed was one of Lavinia's old dresses; another fifties frock adorned with jaunty yellow, pink and blue sailboats on white lawn cotton. She'd even attempted a jaunty ponytail to match the sailboats but as she arrived at the Crescent Terrace and saw Jocasta, Rainbow and Solange draped elegantly on the art-deco-inspired lounge chairs in their white art-deco-inspired bias-cut dresses, Verity felt as out of place as a dominatrix at a vicarage tea party.

Though if a dominatrix in a latex catsuit had turned up at one of her mother's tea parties, then Our Vicar's Wife would never have made them feel out of place. Unlike Jocasta, Rainbow and Solange who gave Verity a cursory once-over, raised their eyebrows at each other, and then went back to discussing Jocasta's

Spanish au pair and how she'd better buck her ideas up.

Their husbands were clustered around the bar and had already made it clear that as Verity wasn't a friend of their wives or attractive enough to flirt with, they had no use for her.

Verity stood in a corner with a glass of champagne (no Prosecco here, no sir). It was a lot like the school discos Merry and Con had always dragged her to. They'd immediately disappear with their friends and Verity would be left to her own devices, which usually meant holing up in the girls' cloakroom with the book she'd brought with her expressly for that purpose.

Now, she thought longingly of the new Santa Montefiore novel she had upstairs: would anyone notice if she slipped away? But before she could put her plan into action, Johnny was at her side.

'You look lovely,' he said, tugging the end of her ponytail. 'You also look like you're about to bolt. Please don't leave me on my own with them.'

Verity looked up at him. The closest he could come to full dinner dress was a white shirt that he'd begged the housekeeper to iron for him and a pair of cream-coloured chinos that really could have done with a press too. But Johnny was so comfortable in his own, tanned skin that he looked perfectly at ease and not like he wanted to melt into the walls as Verity did. 'I'm pretty sure I have a protein bar and a packet of Strepsils in my handbag. I'm happy to split them with you if we sneak back to our room.'

'It's a tempting offer,' Johnny agreed. 'Perhaps one of us could fake a headache and — '

'Darlings! Sorry to keep you waiting,' Marissa cooed at the assembled company from somewhere behind them. 'Harry distracted me, the naughty man.'

He hid it very well, but Verity just caught the flicker of something that looked a lot like anguish on Johnny's face before he masked it with a bland smile as he turned to face Marissa and Harry.

'Well, you deserved it,' Harry said to Marissa with a wolfish grin and Verity was thinking it was a bit much to talk about their pre-dinner quickie in front of their guests when she caught the flash of something sparkly on the third finger of Marissa's left hand.

It was hard not to miss it as Marissa was waggling her fingers at her friends who were moving in closer to admire and fuss over the ring.

'An eternity band,' Marissa explained. 'Because Harry says that's how long our love will last.'

'Platinum band with a cobblestone setting often rose-cut and round diamonds,' Harry announced. 'One diamond for every year we've been married and none of them less than a carat.'

'You are too good for me,' Marissa said and for once she didn't coo or trill or say the words with an edge but as if she really meant them. Next to Verity, Johnny's whole body was rigid and she instinctively reached out to comfort him, to place her hand on his arm. He hesitated then wrapped his arm around her waist, which was unexpected. As was the way he pulled her flush against him, her back to his chest, so she could feel the heat coming off him, which made Verity shiver though she wasn't cold, far from it.

'Dear, sweet Very,' Johnny said in a throaty voice and when Verity looked up at him, he lowered his head and brushed his lips against her cheek because they were friends, very good friends, and everyone thought they were a couple and what better way to show that he was moving on with his life. Anyway, it was no big deal, just an innocent kiss on the cheek.

She looked up to see that while everyone was looking at Marissa and Harry, Marissa and Harry were staring at Verity and Johnny like they'd never seen two people, dear friends, exchange an affectionate gesture.

Then Johnny raised his glass. 'To Marissa and Harry!' he said and the other guests joined in with the toast as Johnny let Verity go, so she felt suddenly chilled from the loss of him. Not as chilled as she was when she caught sight of the expression on his face, which was positively frozen.

He still had the same deathly look on his face as they went into dinner and though Verity had thought this weekend would be a good idea — that Johnny would see, once and for all, that there really wasn't room for three people in Harry and Marissa's marriage — she ached for him. Wished that she could shoulder some of his pain herself, but at least Johnny knew that she was there for him. Always.

The dinner was delicious. Exquisite champagne and locally sourced food: from asparagus soup, Cornish crab and poached lobster to the chicken breasts, which not even a week ago had been plucking and clucking in a farmyard a mile away. The rhubarb in its light-as-clouds soufflé had been grown on the patch of land behind the house and was a testament to the skills of the private chef who had cooked for the Duke and Duchess of Cambridge, as Marissa kept reminding them.

Verity barely tasted any of the mouthfuls that she mechanically chewed and swallowed. There was Johnny across the table, sitting next to Marissa because she'd obviously forgiven him for going AWOL for a month. They were deep, deep, *deep* in conversation but every now and then, Johnny would catch Verity's eye and smile at her, mouth 'Are you all right?' in a very boyfriendly way. Every time he did, Marissa put her hand on his arm to draw Johnny's attention away. And every time it hurt Verity to see how quickly, how eagerly, Johnny turned back to Marissa, and not just because Johnny's occasional glances were Verity's only respite.

On her left she had Miles, an oil trader, who would turn to her every couple of minutes or so to bark out a comment on the food and then turn back to Solange, who was much more scintillating company. On Verity's right was Yuri, a Russian bond trader, who was quite happy to talk to Verity though his conversation consisted of long, meandering rants about the stock exchange.

355

Johnny had got her through the weekend. He'd been her partner in crime, her back-up plan, her exit strategy, always sensing when she was flagging and whisking her off to a place of quiet. Now Verity realised that she hadn't once had to message one of her sisters for sympathy or a pep talk, as she so desperately needed to do now.

The effort of sitting there with an animated expression on her face, shoulders straight, all ready to smile and nod and say, 'Oh, yes, the brown butter sauce is lovely' or 'US Treasury bonds sound like very tricky things,' was exhausting. Verity could feel her battery charge running down so that it got harder and harder to maintain her smile and mutter inanities at her neighbours.

What must it be like to be Marissa at the head of the table, whose sparkle and glitter outshone even the ten rose-cut stones on her new eternity ring? Verity couldn't begin to imagine how easy life must be when you were so certain of your place in the world, were sure that you were absolutely deserving of all your good fortune.

As the pudding plates were cleared away, Marissa tapped her glass with a knife to get the room's attention. 'Ladies? Shall we retire to the Sun Room for coffee?'

Verity didn't need to be told twice. She was already out of her chair and halfway out of the door before anyone else had stood up. 'Just going to get something from my room,' she called over her shoulder, not that she expected anyone to care.

In her panic, Verity got turned around so that the blessed sanctuary of her room remained elusive. The house had two internal staircases and three floors but after minutes of stumbling about and peering round doors, Verity found something even better than the room she shared with Johnny.

The library.

Verity stepped inside, shut the door, and took a moment to calm herself. Breathed in. Breathed out. The sight and smell of books all around her was an instant comfort, almost as good as being back at Happy Ever After.

Now, if only she could get a signal, Verity was free to phone Merry or any one of her sisters who would commiserate with her on the sheer hideousness of the weekend. Whatever they were doing, they'd immediately stop doing it, to pour on some of that balm of sisterly consolation.

But it was Saturday night and Verity was sure that all four of her sisters had more fun things to do than talk her down from the ledge and, as if she had a sixth sense about these things (which she was pretty sure she did), Verity found herself homing in on a set of shelves to her right. She ran her fingers along the spines of the old, leather-bound books and stopped when she came to the words that her hands, her heart, her soul, knew so well.

Pride and Prejudice.

Verity smiled. She was with friends after all.

She took refuge in a huge wing-backed chair that looked out through an open set of doors to a balcony. It was a hot night but she welcomed the faint breeze that came in from the sea, even briefly admired the view, the twinkling lights of the mainland, before she opened the book at the very first page.

'It is a truth universally acknowledged, that a single man in possession of a good fortune, must be in want of a wife.'

It was impossible to know just how many times Verity had read that first sentence so that she wasn't even reading it, but reciting it from memory. And because she'd read *Pride and Prejudice* countless times, and because she was in need of comfort, she skipped quickly through the chapters to get to her favourite part.

Darcy's declaration to Elizabeth Bennet.

'In vain I have struggled. It will not do. My feelings will not be repressed. You must allow me to tell you how ardently I admire and love you.'

Verity settled back with a happy sigh, even though Darcy was about to blow it by telling Lizzy that her family were an embarrassment, she was entirely beneath him in status, and that he loved her against his better judgement. But it was all right. It would sort itself out in the end.

That was the thing with a favourite book; it never let you down, she thought, then froze as she heard the door behind her open gently.

Verity was about to make her presence known when she heard a familiar voice hiss quietly and furiously, 'There's nothing you can say to me that I want to hear, Marissa. Why don't you save it for your husband?'

'Don't be like that, darling. If anyone should be furious, it's me,' Marissa hissed back to Johnny.

Johnny.

Marissa.

And Verity, cowering where she sat, and in an agony of indecision. Should she reveal herself or would that make the situation even worse? Though she feared it was already worse. It was at least a full one thousand on the worse scale.

She quietly closed her book and tried to will her mouth to open, her legs to move to the standing position.

'Oh, what's the matter, Rissa? Does it hurt to see me with another woman?' Johnny taunted in a hateful way that Verity wouldn't have believed was possible from the Johnny she thought she knew so well. 'Well, now you know what it feels like.'

'That insipid creature?' Marissa made a noise in the back of her throat like she was about to hack up a hairball. 'She's even more dull than that Katie you were so taken with a few years back.'

'Well, you got rid of her quick enough, didn't you?' Johnny snapped back. 'One girly lunch with you and I didn't see her for dust.'

'Honestly, Johnny, we've been through this a hundred times,' Marissa said in a more soothing tone. 'She wasn't good enough for you. Nothing would make me happier than you finding a woman who deserved you but it wasn't Katie and it certainly isn't the vicar's daughter. She's so basic. Just a boring little shop girl. You can do so much better than that.'

Well, there was no way Verity could expose herself now. She'd hate to interrupt Marissa's pithy character assassination. All Verity could do now was wait for Johnny to rush in and defend her, though he was taking his own sweet time about it.

'This has nothing to do with her, she was just a means to an end,' Johnny said and Verity put a hand on her heart, which felt as if it had suddenly caved in. 'A little experiment, shall we say. How ironic that you're jealous of someone I've known only five minutes when I've had to watch you with him for the last bloody ten years. I have tried to stay away from you, God knows I've tried, but we both know you get a sadistic kick in rubbing your supposedly happy marriage in my face. Well, I can't, Rissa. Not any more.'

'Don't say that. Sssh. No, not another word.' It sounded as if Marissa had her hand to Johnny's mouth. 'I love Harry, I've never pretended otherwise, but I still love you too. Not in the same way, but I've loved you for so long that I don't know how to not love you, Johnny. Not loving you would be torture.'

Really? Really? Verity risked a sigh and rolled her eyes. She'd read a few torrid, overblown romances in her time, her grandmother had had a huge stack of them, and all this forbidden love crap that Marissa and Johnny were spouting

360

could have been lifted straight from the pages of one of them.

'I don't know how to not love you either,' Johnny said and Verity shut her eyes because she could hear the hitch in his voice and then the sound of material rubbing together as if they were embracing while she had to sit there hidden and hurting. 'I wish I could stop loving you.'

Verity heard a step in front of her and she opened her eyes, shut them, then opened them again so wide it was a wonder they didn't spring from their sockets because standing at the open French doors was Harry with a face like thunder and lightning, gales and torrential rain.

He walked towards Verity and she wasn't sure if he'd even seen her but then he nodded as he passed her. 'You want to stop loving each other? Well, here's a tip. Try harder,' he said loudly.

Verity risked peering round the edge of the chair to see Johnny and Marissa standing a whisper apart from each other. Johnny looked sickened and ashamed (as well he might) and Marissa . . . Marissa looked kind of smug, as far as Verity could see.

Then she pulled a pretty face, lowered her lashes as she gazed at her husband. 'Darling, it's not at all what it looks like.'

'Yeah, it is. It's exactly what it looks like,' Harry said flatly.

'I was just telling Johnny that he deserves someone much better than that Verity,' Marissa explained earnestly.

'What you really mean, my love, is that no other woman could ever measure up to you,'

361

Harry drawled. 'But you shouldn't be so sure of that. I might put it to the test myself.'

Marissa was at his side in an instant, Johnny forgotten. 'You wouldn't! Don't even joke about it. Johnny and I . . . we have history, you know that.'

Harry ran the back of his hand along his wife's cheek. 'Oh God, do I know it. But enough is enough. Just . . . leave him be, give him a chance to be happy with someone else. This has gone on long enough and I am not going to put up with it any longer.'

'But — '

'But nothing.'

'Harry, you know I love you,' Marissa said, her voice trembling with the weight of her words. 'You can't be in any doubt of that.'

'Ten years ago you promised to love me *and* forsake all others, Rissa. It's about time you kept up your end of the deal. It can be your anniversary present to me: your undivided attention. We are going to have a serious talk about this. But now isn't the time or place.' He took a step away. 'You should get back to our guests.'

'Of course,' Marissa husked. Verity risked another peek. Marissa was fluffing up her hair, then without a backward look at Johnny she picked up the train of her white liquid satin gown and hurried out of the room.

And then there were three. 'I'm sorry, Harry,' Johnny said. 'Really I am. But I just can't give her up.'

'Doesn't matter, you've already lost her,'

Harry replied without any heat, as if his anger was spent. 'I was smoking out on the balcony. Marissa hates me smoking so she insists I do it outside. We both have our little habits that irritate each other. You're Marissa's version of a packet of Marlboro Lights, but I'm going to be forty in a few years so it's high time I gave up the smokes and it's about bloody time Marissa gave up you.'

Johnny made an indeterminate noise (disagreement, despair, it was hard for Verity to tell). 'Isn't that up to Marissa?' he asked finally. 'Anyway, I loved her first. I loved her long before you and you knew that and yet still, as soon as my back was turned, you — '

'Enough!' Harry's deadly quiet command was worse than if he were shouting. 'I don't feel guilty, Johnny. Haven't done for quite a while. Marissa and I have been married for ten years and you need to get over it, because I won't be the bad guy any more. Ten years! You're the bad guy now. So stay the hell out of my marriage.'

'But she loves — ' Johnny insisted.

'God, you poor bastard, you just don't get it. She. Is. Using. You. She loves me, she married me. If Rissa still loved you as much as you seem to think she does, she would have left me a long time ago. She keeps you around because it feeds her ego, my friend.' Harry laughed mirthlessly. 'What's the point in trying to get through to you? Maybe Verity can talk some sense into you where everybody else has failed.'

'Leave Very out of it,' Johnny all but snarled and Verity heard her cue and this time her legs obeyed her and stood up when she wanted them to.

'Bit late for that, isn't it?' Her voice was in full working order too though Verity hardly recognised the cold, bitter tone to her words.

'So, you were eavesdropping, listening to my private conversation?' Johnny had the nerve to spit out.

'Listening to you and *that* woman rip me to shreds, you mean? Next time the pair of you are sneaking about behind her husband's back, maybe you should check that you really are alone.'

'Well, I'll just leave you lovebirds to thrash things out,' Harry said cheerfully, his work done, as he slipped out of the door.

And then there were two.

25

'Angry people are not always wise.'

Verity had come into the library to escape because she was overloaded, overstimulated, on the verge of shutting down, but now she was ready to go another round.

In fact, she was furious. Itching with anger, it made her toes and fingers tingle, and she really wanted to start throwing things, preferably at Johnny's incredibly dense head. The only thing stopping her was that they were in a library and it went against everything Verity believed in to start chucking books about.

'I have never lied to you,' Johnny said, folding his arms, face cold, his expression haughty as if he were entirely unrepentant. 'You knew I was in love with Marissa. I was just fooling myself when I thought I wasn't.'

'Oh God, I am so over you being in love with Marissa,' Verity snapped. 'Marissa is not worthy of your love. Yes, she came through for you all those years ago but it seems to have escaped your notice that these days, Marissa is a spiteful, selfish, raging narcissist so if you're in love with Marissa then it really doesn't reflect well on you!'

Woah! Verity had to steady herself on a conveniently placed side table because all this emotion . . . All of a sudden she was back in that hotel room in Amsterdam destroying someone by giving a voice to all the feelings she'd tamped down for so long.

'You're being ridiculous. You barely even know Marissa,' Johnny said coolly because he was made of much stronger stuff than Adam. 'She's actually really lovely when you — '

'She called me insipid,' Verity interrupted, because that description would be etched into her cerebral cortex until the day she died. 'A boring little shop girl. Basic.'

Verity liked to think she had hidden depths. Everybody did. That though she liked her quiet life and routine, she still had imagination and potential. Well, Marissa had blown that notion away in two sentences.

'You're not basic,' Johnny said impatiently. 'It's only natural for Marissa to feel a little threatened by you but that doesn't mean that — '

'And *you* said I'm a means to an end.' Verity cut through the rest of his bluster. 'This whole time I've been such a fool! You never wanted a pretend girlfriend to get your friends off your back; you wanted to make Marissa jealous.' It was all so obvious now. This fake relationship of theirs, what Verity had thought of as a real friendship, was nothing more than a plot to make Marissa jealous and conquer the hard piece of carbon where her heart should be. 'Oh my God, you couldn't *wait* to introduce us at that wedding and even tonight, when you kissed me, kept looking at me, it was all for her benefit, wasn't it?'

It was dark outside now and the only light came from the lamps dotted about but Verity could clearly see the taut, tight set of Johnny's mouth; the insistent muscle that pounded away in his neck, and also the hot red blush that had turned his face dusky.

'That was never my intention, not at the beginning, you have to believe that, Very.' Johnny took a step forward. He really was beautiful and yet so damned. Condemned to love the wrong woman for an eternity. 'But Marissa was jealous. You heard what she said; that she still loves me. She doesn't know how not to love me.'

Incredible. Johnny was an intelligent man. He had a Cambridge degree, for God's sakes, and yet he was one of the most stupid people Verity had ever come across. Her limbs twitched, heat rising up from her toes so her whole body felt as if it were on fire; she clenched her fists and pressed her lips together but couldn't do anything to contain it.

'SHE IS NEVER GOING TO LEAVE HARRY!' It was a howl of rage and frustration that had Johnny clamping his hands over his ears so Verity made sure to shout even louder so he'd be able to hear the next part. 'SHE'S BEEN MARRIED TO HARRY FOR TEN YEARS! WHAT PART OF THAT ISN'T REGISTERING WITH YOU? BRRRINNNGGG! BRRR-IIINNGGG! EARTH TO JOHNNY! SHE IS NEVER GOING TO BE WITH YOU! IT'S NEVER GOING TO HAPPEN!'

'Shut up! You don't know what you're talking about.' Johnny took another step towards Verity, who tossed her head back to glare up at him.

'Marissa doesn't love you. If she did, she'd let you go. That's just good manners. To think that I used to feel sorry for you. Not any more! Ten years, Johnny! This is entirely your own fault now.'

'I said, shut up!' Johnny was at Verity's side now. He was close enough that Verity could smell the brandy he must have drunk after dinner. Could see the flush still dotting his cheekbones. Then his fingers were around Verity's wrists. Not hard enough to hurt, not even close, but enough that she couldn't get away. 'And what about you? You're not perfect either!'

'I didn't say I was perfect — '

'At least I have the guts to love someone,' Johnny said, lowering his head so they were practically nose to nose. 'I haven't locked myself away because of one mediocre relationship. All your 'I'm an island' bullshit is pathetic!'

'It was a metaphor,' Verity protested but it was weak because although she'd dished it in large quantities, it wasn't much fun having it dished right back at you.

'My mistake. You're an 'introvert'.' Johnny took his hands away from her wrists so he could make air-quotes like introvert wasn't even a real word. 'Even though you have a huge family, friends, pets, can walk away from loneliness any time you want, apparently all that love and affection is too much effort.'

Everything Verity had told Johnny, all the secrets she'd trusted him with, he was twisting out of shape so they didn't even resemble the truth any more. 'I hate you,' she flung at him.

'And *I* hate *you*,' he snarled back at her. Verity raised her hand. Maybe it was to hit him, maybe to push him away, but instead her hand was at the back of his neck, fingers sliding into his hair, and Johnny's hands were around Verity's waist to haul her closer and they seemed to be . . . it couldn't be . . . but they were . . .

Kissing.

Kissing like it was the end of the world.

Kissing like they couldn't get enough of each other.

Kissing like two people who hadn't kissed anyone in months, years.

Mouths locked together, hands clutching, bodies straining towards each other.

It turned out that Verity had desires that couldn't be satisfied with a bar of chocolate and a good book. All that longing and need that she'd pointedly ignored now rose up and clamoured for release. But it wasn't a case that any man would do; this was all for Johnny.

Though Verity hated Johnny in this moment, it was as if Verity's body already knew Johnny's touch and curved obediently under his hands. The feel of his mouth on hers was shockingly new but also comfortingly familiar.

'Oh, Verity,' Johnny whispered against her skin because somehow during all the kissing and clutching, his shirt had come unbuttoned and her dress with its jaunty sailboats had been pulled over her head and tossed into a far corner of the library 'What you do to me.'

'I'm very angry with you,' Verity whispered back, because she didn't want Johnny to think he

369

could kiss her into the middle of next week and all was forgiven. 'But I will die if you don't kiss me again.'

There was more kissing. Then cannoning off side tables and reading chairs until the safest thing to do was to collapse onto a red velvet sofa and that way all of Johnny was pressed against all of Verity and it was much easier to wriggle even closer and her last coherent thought before she wrapped her legs tight around him was, 'I can't believe we're going to do it in front of all the books.'

★　★　★

There was no time to bask in the afterglow. To whisper sweet words like lovers did because they weren't lovers but two people who'd been fuelled by anger and betrayal and had just made the mother of almighty mistakes.

They'd come to their senses, or so Verity had thought, backs to each other as they hunted for items of clothing that had been so hastily discarded.

Then Verity had remembered their argument all over again. 'Was that insipid enough for you?' she hurled at Johnny who was hunting for his left shoe.

'And was that your idea of a pity shag? Because you feel sorry for me?'

They argued in whispers all the way back to their room. Then argued in much louder voices once they'd closed the door, until it happened all over again.

The kissing.

The hands.

The frantic removal of their clothes.

The sex.

Then they dozed, still wrapped round each other, only stirring to begin all over again without another argument as foreplay, but just for the sheer hell of it because what they'd done twice before had felt so good.

Now it was four in the morning and Verity was sitting up in bed, hugging her legs, chin resting on her knees as she watched Johnny sleep.

Not in a creepy way but so she could memorise all the details; the long sweep of his spine, the freckles that dotted his shoulders, the disarray of his fair hair rumpled by her own hands. She even catalogued each gentle snore.

Then Verity got off the bed and, bathed in the glow of the moonlight, she quietly packed her case.

She couldn't stay any longer, not when she hated Johnny. But also, though she could hardly say when it had come about, she loved him too. Wanted to save him from Marissa's evil clutches not so he could love another woman more deserving of him, but because Verity had wanted him to love her. Only her.

She'd thought that Johnny was being unbelievably arrogant when he kept telling her not to fall in love with him. She hadn't realised that he was giving her fair warning and now it was too late.

Loving Johnny was an exercise in futility. It could lead to nothing, no happy ever after, just heartache and despair.

Johnny hated her. He'd said so. And even if he didn't, he was in love with Marissa. Had been for the last seventeen years and having sex three times with Verity wasn't going to be the magic cure to that. Not even close!

To stay and have to suffer through the awkward morning after then come face to face with Marissa and Harry at some point before they left — it didn't even bear thinking about.

So, it was better not to think at all but simply leave.

Verity tiptoed her way through the silent house, hoping that there weren't any motion sensor alarms or locked doors to impede her progress. But they were on an island; someone would have to be really determined to want to break in . . . or break out.

As she tripped down the stone steps that led to the beach, Verity realised that there *was* something stopping her speedy getaway; two hundred and fifty metres of sea.

Short of either waking up Jeremy, the owner, or the housekeeper's husband who was the island's general factotum, there was no way back to the mainland unless Verity hotwired the sea tractor. And there was no way that Verity could do that; she couldn't even get enough of a phone signal to google the instructions.

She gazed out on the water, the moon reflected back at her on each ripple of each wave. Then she sank to her knees. Verity had quite a cordial relationship with God, both of them free to do their own thing, but now she wondered if praying, really praying, might help, even though

372

she'd just had sex three times out of wedlock. And it wasn't even as if she were a virgin before that.

Also she lied. It had been her pretend boyfriend that she'd just had sex three times with after all. And she coveted that pretend boyfriend though his heart belonged to another and she'd pretty much broken every commandment there was, although she hadn't murdered anyone as yet. Though that could all change if she was forced to spend any more time in close proximity with Marissa.

Oh God . . .

The ripples of the sea seemed especially ripply, given the stillness of the early morning. The sky was yet to lighten from a deep navy blue, hardly a breeze to stir the water and yet it was stirring; the waves small but insistent. Verity watched for long agonising minutes, hardly able to believe her eyes until the water parted to reveal the sandy seabed beneath.

Just like God had parted the Red Sea for the Israelites, so he was parting a much smaller expanse of water for Verity so she could grab her case and run across the causeway back to the mainland like she was Usain Bolt determined to smash his own world record.

26

'She was humbled, she was grieved; she repented, though she hardly knew of what.'

When Verity had broken up with Adam and they'd flown back from Amsterdam in their allocated seats, side by side, every time Verity had caught his eye, he'd looked at her like she was a monster who'd killed his entire family, pets, friends.

They'd formally parted company at Customs. 'Have a nice life,' Adam had tried to say with icy dignity but it had come out as a choked cry and, as Verity travelled back into London on the tube, her mind was made up. It was very clear what she needed to do to make sure that she'd never have to feel this horrible shaming combination of guilt and relief, to never again be responsible for making a man cry. In future, she would shun all romantic attachments.

Although she was sure that she had loved Adam, had declared that love to him and her sceptical sisters repeatedly, Verity had hardly mourned the end of it. There hadn't been any need to drink too much wine, eat a lot of ice cream and have her friends say, 'He was a bastard and I never liked him anyway!' Those were the rituals, which her sisters all observed when they were dumped, but Verity managed without them. Compared to how much she'd

374

missed the quiet pleasure of her own company in the three years that she and Adam had been dating, she hardly missed him at all.

But this time? It felt as if Johnny had taken out her heart, kicked it about, rubbed salt into its many open wounds then stuffed it back into her chest cavity. Because carelessly, without even realising it, Verity had given him that heart, even though she'd known Johnny would never return the favour. But then, his heart wasn't his to give — Marissa had it under lock and key.

'Along with his balls,' Merry had said savagely, when she arrived at Exeter St Davids station to pick Verity up the Sunday morning of her escape from Wimsey House.

After crossing the miraculously parted sea, Verity had walked through Lower Meryton, until she'd arrived at Upper Meryton just as the local vicar and his wife, early risers, were doing a spot of t'ai chi on the vicarage lawn. Verity had begged for their assistance and it turned out that the Reverend Michaels had met her father several times. He also knew of a parishioner who was driving to Exeter that morning to pick up their in-laws for Sunday lunch because most of the South West rail network was down that weekend, necessitating a seven a.m. phone call to Merry while the vicar and his wife made Verity breakfast.

Merry hadn't even changed out of her pyjamas. She'd borrowed Dougie's mother's car and had leadfooted it all the way to Exeter so she was there to pick up Verity by eleven.

Verity had sworn to be economical with the

truth, not go into too much detail, no oversharing, but as soon as she'd opened the passenger door of Dougie's mum's Nissan Micra and seen Merry's familiar face and its put-upon expression, she had burst into tears.

Then it had all come spilling out. Everything. Merry had managed to keep silent, only gasping in indignation as Verity had given her a play-by-play of Marissa's evil words and deeds. Then she yelled, 'Three times? Three times? Three times! Oh my God!' and missed the turn-off for the motorway.

It seemed to Verity that she spent the whole journey back to London crying, hiccupping or blowing her nose. That had been three weeks ago and she was still crying, hiccupping and dealing with a permanently runny nose.

There had even been instances of crying at work, which went against Verity's whole brand ethos. All it took to get her tear ducts going into a frantic production drive was for Posy to relay the plot of a particularly angst-ridden romance she was reading or Mattie to run out of clotted cream scones before the afternoon tea break or Nina to state firmly that Verity needed to go out on the pull because 'there were plenty more fish in the sea'. And that 'The only way to get over someone is to get under someone else,' or 'You have to get back on the horse as soon as possible after it's thrown you to the ground, even if you feel like you've broken every bone in your body.'

Nina had a frightening amount of advice for the newly dumped, though Verity couldn't say if she was the dumped or the dumpee. Or if she had any right to have turned into a sniffing, snivelling shadow of her former self, when it hadn't even been a proper relationship.

She'd thought, at least, that it had been a proper friendship until those horrible moments in the library having to listen to what Johnny really thought about her. He hadn't leapt to Verity's defence when Marissa had said that she was insipid, boring and basic, so he must have agreed with his spiteful inamorata. Worse! He'd described Verity as a means to an end, which meant that all the weeks they'd spent together, every secret Verity had shared with Johnny, even taking him home to meet her family, had been a lie. Simply a way to make the relationship look convincing enough that Marissa would become jealous, realise what she was missing, leave Harry and declare her undying love for Johnny.

Well, it had all been for nothing, because Marissa would never leave Harry and Johnny was a lost cause.

Verity even offered up a prayer to St Jude, the patron saint of lost causes, that perhaps Johnny wasn't as far gone as she'd thought. She'd settle simply for being friends again if he got in touch and was suitably contrite. Except Verity really had no interest in being friends with Johnny; she wanted all of him, even though she'd sworn off that sort of thing. And no wonder; even in her wildest imaginings, she'd never have dreamed that this sort of thing could hurt so much.

As it was, Verity hardly recognised the teary, snotty girl she'd become who now answered the phone on the first ring, just in case it was Johnny. Who got the flutters every time she heard the ping alerting her to a new email or text, though they were never from Johnny but usually from one of her sisters phoning to commiserate and tell her again that Johnny was a bastard. Much to Posy's consternation, because she said Verity looked like she worked for a company called Unhappy Ever After, Verity even found herself haunting the shop floor, ever hopeful that each customer that set foot through the door might be him, but Johnny remained a no-show.

After work was even harder, because for the first time since records began, Verity was sick of her own company. Nina had given Gervaise, the sexually fluid performance artist, another chance so she was out every evening. Posy, unreasonably, wanted to spend time with her new husband. Tom was very close to finishing his mysterious PhD dissertation so couldn't be persuaded to The Midnight Bell much, which left only Merry, who to her credit was a frequent visitor to the flat above the shop.

Not just because it was part of the sister job description but because Con had charged them with making industrial quantities of wedding bunting. 'It's more personal if you make it,' she'd said, when they'd begged her to just buy bunting off the internet like any normal person. Verity was glad not to be alone though she had to ban Merry from listing the many tortures she'd inflict on Johnny if their paths ever crossed, because even Johnny didn't deserve to have his toenails slowly detached from his nail beds. So

Verity and Merry would sit on Verity's sofa, and sometimes in the pub, cutting, pinning, sewing and bitching about Con until, inevitably, Verity would look up to see Merry staring at her in disbelief. Then Merry would shake her head, 'Three times? Three times! And since then no emails, no phone calls, no texts to make sure that you didn't actually drown making your escape. What a bastard. Oooh! I'd love to get my hands on him. Shall I tell you what I'm going to do to him?'

'Please don't.'

'First I'll flay him alive with a blunt potato peeler from the pound shop . . . '

Still, it was better than evenings spent with a box of tissues and her own maudlin thoughts for company. Even *Pride and Prejudice* was no longer the comfort that it usually was, for when Verity asked herself what would Elizabeth Bennet do, the answer wasn't at all helpful.

'She was humbled, she was grieved; she repented, though she hardly knew of what. She became jealous of his esteem, when she could no longer hope to be benefited by it. She wanted to hear of him, when there seemed the least chance of gaining intelligence. She was convinced that she could have been happy with him, when it was no longer likely they should meet.'

No, there was no solace to be found among the pages of her favourite book and Verity took little pleasure in knowing that she wasn't alone in feeling just like the soggy, wadded-up tissues piled around her. That despair and heartache transcended space and time. Were universal. Far from being a special suffering snowflake, Verity was just like any other sucker who had been bruised by a love affair gone wrong.

Why hadn't it hurt like this after Adam? Verity was beginning to suspect that, despite all the times she'd read *Pride and Prejudice*, she hadn't really known what love was like. Hadn't experienced it until now. And it was only now that Verity could truly appreciate how much she'd hurt Adam. If she'd made him feel even half as wretched as she had felt ever since her moonlit flit from Cornwall, then she owed him one hell of an apology. So, one evening when she was sick of thinking about Johnny and crying and particularly sick of making bunting, she logged on to FaceUpp, Sebastian Thorndyke's social media network that the whole world and his wife was signed up to.

It was easy enough to find Adam through mutual university friends. He was still living in London and working at Goldsmiths College though he didn't have any relationship information listed. Probably because Verity and her stand-offish, emotionally stunted ways had scarred Adam for life. Still, there was only one way to find out for sure.

Verity hoped her message would read as a heartfelt apology, something she'd agonised over for months, and not something she'd written while under the influence of a bottle of Chenin Blanc.

Hey Adam

It's been a long time. I hope life is treating you kindly.

I'm good. Still working at that bookshop, still in possession of four sisters, still a bit odd.

Talking of being a bit odd, I've been doing a lot of soul-searching of late and I really must apologise for how I behaved towards you when we were dating. If I ever came across as being quite detached . . . Actually, I was very detached. I needed so much space that I constantly pushed you away. The more I think about it, the more I realise that I was a terrible girlfriend. I still go clammy when I think about how vile I was when you took me to Amsterdam for my birthday because you never deserved that. You didn't deserve any of it.

I have thought about you and that morning in Amsterdam quite a lot over the years and I'd hate to think that what you said came true. That I'd ruined you and that you were never going to be able to love another woman. That hasn't happened, has it? Oh God, please say it hasn't.

Anyway, better go now.

All best, Verity.

PS: Do you still keep in touch with Banjo (Paul), my old Residential Adviser from university? My sister Merry now works in medical research at UCH and legend has it that Banjo came into the A&E at St George's with a satsuma stuck under his foreskin after he lost a bet.

In the dim light of eleven thirty p.m., the message hadn't seemed so bad but in the glaring light of early morning and with a hangover, the message seemed absolutely appalling. As clingy and needy as Verity had once accused Adam of being, and what had she been thinking when she decided to add in a postscript about Banjo's foreskin?

It was something else to agonise over as Verity was wedged into the back seat of Dougie's mum's Nissan Micra next to three boxes of bunting, two bridesmaid dresses and sundry other items that wouldn't fit into the boot. It was D-Day minus one. The Friday before the Saturday when Con and Alex would plight their troth, then celebrate with a hog roast and booze cruise Cava in the vicarage grounds. Unfortunately they'd left it far too late to book a marquee and the weather forecast was for rain.

In fact, when her phone pinged, Verity thought that it might be Con with one of her half-hourly weather updates. Then her heart fluttered and she thought it might be from Johnny, just maybe checking that she wasn't lying in a watery grave. Then the heart fluttering upgraded to a full-on thudding, when she saw she had a WhatsUpp message from Adam.

Verity groaned like she was in pain, though Dougie and Merry couldn't hear her because they were singing along to *Hamilton*. Although she was always a slow peeler of plasters, Verity decided that it was best to get Adam's reply out of the way as quickly as possible. She sent out a quick heartfelt prayer that he hadn't become a monk or one of those women-hating men's rights activists, though it would be her own fault if he had.

Hello stranger!
I'm not going to lie. It was a bit of a surprise to see I had a message from you, not altogether a pleasant surprise either because I've gone quite clammy too when I've thought about you over the last few years.
Not because of anything you did but because I cringe about what a total cling-on I was when we were dating. If anyone is owed an apology it's you for the guilt trip I tried to lay on you about ruining me, and how I was never ever going to love another woman again. So many times I wanted to get in touch to say sorry, but I was too ashamed. I really am sorry, Very.
The way I look at it is that it was a first relationship for both of us and we were both a bit crap at being boyfriend and girlfriend. I don't think either of us had a clue what love really was. So, yeah, maybe you were a bit odd but I was too and my next girlfriend after you had never eaten a vegetable in her life and could only sleep with all the lights on and the radio tuned to Talk FM, so I guess being a bit odd is relative.
So, no, you didn't put me off relationships. Not bloody likely! (Though I have no wish to ever go back to Amsterdam.)
Anyway I'm seeing someone really special at the moment and hoping that you are too because I'd hate to think that I put you off men

for life. Would be great to catch up properly over a drink sometime.

Adam x

(I don't see Banjo anymore but I heard it wasn't a satsuma, but a grapefruit. How? Why?)

The breezy tone of Adam's message was a sudden and welcome reminder that their relationship hadn't been all about Adam clinging and Verity withdrawing. When he wasn't asking her what she was thinking about and if she loved him, Adam had been really good company. He'd been funny haha, rather than funny peculiar, they'd laughed a lot. He was a great cook too and they'd shared a love of classic old Hollywood movies and would often spend weekends watching Katharine Hepburn being sassy or Cary Grant being suave.

And oh! There was also the sheer sweet relief that Verity hadn't ruined Adam's life and left him with deep psychological scars! She was absolved from the guilt that she'd always carried with her like a cumbersome backpack that had been surgically attached. Adam had, in fact, been mature and philosophical about the whole sorry episode. He'd treated that weekend in Amsterdam as a teachable moment then jumped right back into the dating pool.

Was it possible that Verity had read more into that weekend in Amsterdam than she should have? That perhaps it had been nothing more than the end of a so-so relationship between two inexperienced, impressionable people? Certainly not anything so serious it was worth swearing off dating and the possibility of love forever more? Could it be that everyone from her mother, to her sisters, to her friends and colleagues, were right when they insisted that once Verity met the right man everything would magically slot into place?

No. Verity refused to entertain the possibility that she'd overreacted and set her life post-Amsterdam, her entire future, down a path that it wasn't meant to go down; that she'd wasted three prime years of her life clinging to singledom like a life raft. She couldn't juggle relationships and all the other demands on her time and still manage to find the space and quiet she needed to be her best self.

Or could she? What did it even matter when the only man she wanted didn't want her? He loved someone else and, even if he didn't, he'd told Verity that he hated her. So, she was destined to have all the space and quiet she needed, which was great. Except it didn't feel great; it felt like the end of the world.

Her phone pinged yet again as the singing and rapping from the front seats reached a crescendo. Verity definitely wasn't going to have any space or quiet this weekend either, but she'd made her peace with that. It was Con's wedding and Verity wouldn't do anything to spoil one minute of the next forty-eight hours — she'd even gone to the doctor and begged a prescription for two Valium to ward off any potential meltdowns.

'Is that Con *again?*' Merry swivelled round.

Verity looked down at her phone. 'Yes. She's

checked the Met Office, BBC, Google and Yahoo weather apps and is devastated that they all predict a thirty to fifty per cent chance of rain tomorrow and she wants to know if we think that means just a light shower?'

'I am so sick of talking about the weather!' Dougie chimed in.

'I hear you,' Verity said as her phone pinged again. Her heart didn't even have time to flutter at the vain hope that it might be Johnny. 'It's Con again *again*. Apparently we're not using her wedding hashtag enough on social media for it to ever start trending. She expects us to tweet at least once every half hour with fun wedding content.' Verity nudged the back of Merry's seat with her knee. 'How come she's not texting you?'

'Blocked her number, didn't I?'

Verity didn't even have it in her to be angry. 'I wish I'd thought of that!'

It was too late to block Con now and so for the rest of the journey as Dougie and Merry lustily sang along to *Hamilton* several more times from start to finish, Verity's phone continued to ping with weather forecasts, hashtag demands and panicked updates about everything from the cake to the flowers to whether Con could lose five pounds in the next twelve hours or did she have time to go to Lincoln and buy some gutbuster knickers and a minimiser bra in M&S?

Verity remained surprisingly calm throughout. She'd coasted so many big emotional waves over the last few weeks she had no emotion left to give. She was an empty vessel.

Finally, they were driving through the Wold, through all the little villages and hamlets they knew so well until they could see the spire of their father's church in the distance. Then the village sign with said church painted on it:

Welcome to Lambton

'Home,' Merry said with some satisfaction. Then. 'Oh God, do you think Con bullied them into it?'

Every gatepost of every house in the village had a cornflower blue (Con's signature wedding colour) ribbon tied around it; the bows fluttering in the breeze.

'Probably,' Verity sniffed, blinking her eyes rapidly to try and ward off the threat of tears. 'But it's still lovely.'

'Very, are you crying? Don't cry!' Merry snapped, her own voice breaking. 'You know that it makes me cry if you're crying. These last few weeks, I've been a wreck!'

'I can't help it!' Verity sobbed as Dougie drove up the vicarage drive.

The front door of the house opened before Dougie had even switched off the engine. A gaggle of people spilled out headed by Con, dressed only in pants, the official wedding T-shirt emblazoned with #lovesimpsonwedding, and Our Vicar's Wife's old wedding veil, which was yellow with age and should really have been soaking in OxiClean by now, according to the detailed timesheet Con had emailed everyone earlier in the week.

'Once more unto the breach, dear friends, once more,' Dougie quoted as Con strode over.

The driver's door was wrenched open and Con stuck her face into the car. 'You were meant to be here seventeen minutes ago,' she said by way of a greeting. 'You'd better have remembered the bloody bunting!'

27

*'I shall end an old maid, and teach your ten
children to embroider cushions and play their
instruments very ill.'*

Despite the dire warning of the weather apps,
Saturday dawned bright and sunny. Natural light
flooded the vicarage for the 'before' photographs
of Con getting ready, ably assisted by her sisters,
with her face and hair done by Chatty because
she was the most artistically minded of her
brethren and had spent the last two weeks
watching YouTube make-up tutorials.

After most of the wedding prep had been
done, there'd been a raucous kitchen supper in
the vicarage the night before with huge
quantities of cheese toasties and red wine
consumed so everyone was quite fragile and the
noise levels were manageable. Besides, Con had
surrendered timesheet and to-do list to Verity,
who had to keep running across the road to the
church then back to the vicarage to check on so
many last-minute things that she couldn't care
less whether people were using their indoor
voices or not.

After greeting the hog roast guys and showing
them where to set up in the garden, Verity was
running out of time to get changed and have her
own hair and make-up done. As she hurried up
the drive, she was overtaken by a van from the

389

very fancy wine merchants in Lincoln, even though Verity knew for a fact that no very fancy wine had been ordered.

'Well, I have a delivery note right here,' the driver insisted, waving a handheld device at Verity.

'It's my sister's wedding. She's in full Bridezilla mode but on a very small budget. She was meant to clear all purchases with her fiancé, her fiancé's mum and my parents first,' Verity said in a panicked voice. 'There's no money left. The kitty is empty.'

'Already been paid for, love.'

Two boxes of champagne were unloaded and Verity was handed an envelope addressed to Con and Alex. She gave it to Con as soon as she walked into their parents' bedroom, which had been repurposed as a hair and beauty salon.

'Very! Sit down and let me beautify you,' Chatty snapped. 'The bishop will be here in ten minutes.'

Con and Alex were to be married by the bishop of the diocese because Mr Love had said that, for today, he simply wanted to be a proud father walking his daughter down the aisle. Then Con, who'd been banging on for weeks about how she refused to be given away like she was an unwanted pet or a second-hand car, had cried and said that actually she didn't mind being given away after all.

'We must all remember not to swear in front of the bishop,' she said now as she lounged on the bed in a cat onesie and tore open the envelope that Verity had given her. 'Not too much smoky eye, Chatty. We're going to church not a nightclub . . . Bloody hell! Did you say it was two boxes of champagne, Very?'

'Yeah. Perrier-Jouët,' Verity mumbled because Chatty was smothering her face in foundation. 'Who's it from?'

'I'll read it out,' Con said, holding it up so that Verity could see a block print of two hearts on brown card. ' 'Dear Con and Alex, Congratulations on this most special of days. May the years you spend together be full of happiness and love. Best wishes, Johnny True.' '

'Johnny!' Merry, Immy and Chatty screeched in unison.

'That bastard! We hate him!' Immy said. 'For all the wrongs he's done to our Very.'

It was impossible to cry because Chatty was now attacking Verity's eyelids with grey powder. 'I have been thinking about that,' she said, because she'd done little else. Taking responsibility for the rest of Con's to-do list had been a welcome break from thinking about Johnny. 'About the wrongs. How maybe they weren't so wrong when we were only pretending to be in a relationship. I mean, I always knew he was in love with Marissa.'

'What do you mean by pretending to be in a relationship, dear?' Mrs Love asked mildly from the corner where she'd been keeping out of the way and sewing a button back on Mr Love's best shirt. 'And are you saying he was in love with another woman the entire time?'

Verity pushed down Chatty's hand, which was

391

brandishing a mascara wand. 'It's very complicated. Very, very complicated.'

'Never mind that,' Con snapped, waving the card at Verity. 'Johnny True! His surname is True?'

'It is,' Verity confirmed. 'Though I don't see what that has to do with anything.'

'Johnny True! How funny!' Chatty hooted and now Verity thought maybe she should pop a Valium because she'd forgotten that when Chatty and Immy started to shriek, they reached a top note that could shatter all the glasses washed and polished and lined up on the kitchen table, all ready for the toasts.

'Just as well he did do you wrong,' Immy said rather callously, all things considered. 'Imagine if you'd got married and double-barrelled your surnames. Then you'd be the True-Loves. Hilarious!'

'So funny,' Con agreed with a snort of mirth. 'The True-Loves! Can't you get back with him just so you *can* get married?'

'I'm not getting back with him,' Verity said crossly. 'I was never *with* him. Like I said, it was very, very, very complicated.'

'And he's still a bastard, no matter what his surname is,' Merry said loyally. Then she looked pensive for a nanosecond. 'But it's all right to drink his champagne even if he is a bastard, isn't it?'

★ ★ ★

It was a picture-perfect wedding full of #nofilter moments.

392

Verity and her sisters walking slowly down the aisle clutching bouquets of meadowsweet and Japanese anemones picked that morning from the neighbouring fields. They wore cornflower-blue fifties-style dresses bought in the ASOS summer sale for twenty-five quid a pop and Converse sneakers in different colours; a Con-approved nod to individuality.

Con coming down the aisle in a simple ivory chiffon maxi dress with flutter sleeves and a petal applique, also from ASOS, her hair loose and flowing with flowers entwined in it, Our Vicar at her side, both of them beaming. She'd never looked more beautiful, her sisters had assured her as they waited in the church vestibule for Mrs Reynolds, the church organist, to sound out the first bars of 'I Could Have Danced All Night' from *My Fair Lady*.

The bishop asking if there was anyone who knew of any lawful impediment as to why Con and Alex shouldn't be wed and God answering with a massive peal of thunder that made the entire congregation shriek.

Poor Alan absolutely stealing the show as Dog of Honour cum ringbearer as he gleefully tore down the aisle, towards the cocktail sausage that Our Vicar was waving.

Con and Alex wiping away each other's tears as they promised to love each other for richer or poorer, for better or worse, in sickness and in health.

Then, Con and Alex leaving the church under a canopy of umbrellas to protect them from the torrential downpour as the stalwart ladies of the

Lambton and Area Women's Institute descended on the church hall to set up trestle tables and chairs and hang bunting while Mr and Mrs Love and daughters began the arduous task of transferring the buffet from the vicarage to the new venue. Verity, meanwhile, supervised the hog roast guys who were setting up under canvas in the churchyard. The bishop had decreed that, given the circumstances, God wouldn't mind them roasting pork on hallowed ground.

The laughter and tears during the Father of the Bride's speech as the Vicar described how 'No other man has been as blessed as I am to have five daughters, though none of the other four are allowed to get married now. Not because we can't bear to part with them but because this wedding has already taken years off Barbara and I.'

The cutting of the cake made with honey from the vicarage bees and toasts drunk with proper champagne, Cava or homemade elderflower cordial. The first dance to Etta James's 'At Last' and some time after that all five Love sisters taking to the floor in a group hug to dance to 'We Are Family', all of them shout-singing and sing-crying.

It was the best of days. The most special of days. The happiest of days. And to the casual and even the most keen-eyed observer, the middle Love daughter looked uncharacteristically cheerful, apart from one fretful moment when the church hall was still in chaos and the guests were threatening to break free of the holding area in the Scout hut.

Verity *was* happy for Con. There was nowhere else that she'd rather be than watching her oldest sister marry the man she loved but ever since the two boxes of champagne had arrived with the note, she'd been in torment. Now, Verity realised that hope, even the faintest glimmer of hope, was much worse than the despair she'd known ever since she'd left Johnny sleeping in a bed wrecked from their lovemaking.

Every time there'd been a ring on the vicarage doorbell, or a tall male guest walked into the church, or she heard her name being called, her heart would lift then sink back down because it was never him. It was never Johnny.

Worse, being at a wedding made Verity miss Johnny even more, because they'd been to so many weddings together that summer. When her mind should have been only on Con, she was distracted by memories of sitting next to Johnny on church pews and in registry offices or at the fun couples' table in marquees and fancy restaurants.

Countless times throughout the day, Verity would turn to Johnny to share a smile or a muttered aside or even an eye roll when Marie turned up with little Kayleigh in a pink princess outfit and ordered the child to walk down the aisle scattering petals. But each time Verity turned, Johnny wasn't there, even though she was sure that the champagne, the card, had been A SIGN.

As the day wore on, Verity found herself muttering under her breath, '*If he does not come to me, then I shall give him up for ever.*' It was a side of Elizabeth Bennet that Verity had never wanted to channel.

At last it was time for Con and Alex to spend their first night as a married couple in the executive suite of the only five-star hotel in Lincoln. They were being driven there by Alex's teetotal uncle in his Ford Mondeo, with the obligatory 'Just Married' sign and tin cans tied to the back bumper.

Verity waved them off as exuberantly as the other guests, but when everyone else trooped back into the church hall to continue the celebrations, Verity headed for the vicarage. She fed the cats and Poor Alan but, opening the fridge to see a couple of bottles of champagne chilling in there, ordered by Johnny because he'd remembered the date, which meant in some small way that he was thinking of Verity, unleashed the tears that had been threatening all day. If only he'd followed up the champagne with a call, even a text message, something to let Verity know that he wasn't just thinking of her but thinking of her *kindly*.

Curling up on the kitchen sofa, even though it was covered in a liberal coating of animal hair, with Poor Alan anxiously resting his head on her knee, Verity cried. Some of the tears were for Johnny because she loved him and he was going to waste his life, his *whole* life, loving a woman who didn't want to be with him. But the majority of her tears were for herself because there'd been a moment during the reception when she'd had an epiphany. A whole wattage of lightbulbs suddenly pinging over her head.

Her sisters had been dancing with their respective boyfriends. Our Vicar and Our Vicar's Wife were sailing across the floor in a stately tango, even George, her father's annoying curate, was slow-dancing with the equally annoying Marie, while little Kayleigh stuffed cocktail sausages into her mouth like they were Smarties.

Verity had been sitting by herself. Alone. And now, alone felt a lot like being lonely. For so long, Verity had been sure she couldn't inflict her quirks, her quiet, on someone else, but now she realised it was the worst idea she'd ever had.

Her sisters would be the first to admit that they were aggravating and talked too much, but they'd never decided that that was an obstacle to finding true love. And what were the odds that Our Vicar and Our Vicar's Wife with their love of musicals, whist drives and adding Tabasco sauce to *everything* would ever find each other? Yet they had.

Once, as a joke, Nina had pinned a postcard on their fridge, which showed at least a dozen cats peering through an open door with the caption, 'Hello, we hear you are forty and not married.' It was no longer an amusing gag about being a mad cat lady, but a frightening look into her future.

Verity cried a bit harder as she imagined being forty and a spinster of the parish. How her sisters would all be married to men who adored them and they'd have children and when Verity came to stay at Christmas and Easter and special occasions because she didn't have a family of her own, her sisters would all say in uncharacteristically hushed tones, 'Now remember to leave Auntie Very alone. She leads a very sheltered life and you know how crabby she gets when you don't use your indoor voices.'

Johnny had been right when he accused Verity of being a coward. Love had seemed too hard, so she'd just given up at the first hurdle, whereas Adam, always so insecure and helpless, had sailed over that same hurdle with ease. He'd learned huge lessons from that life-changing morning in Amsterdam, had gone out into the world determined to be different, to be happy, to try again at love. And Verity? Verity had done none of those admirable things, but had withdrawn completely and pretended that being fairly content was the same thing as being happy. Well, it wasn't.

It was a half life and not the one that Verity wanted to be living. The life she now wanted so desperately had a man in it who understood that she needed space but yet when she spent time with him, she never felt crowded. A man who was good with his hands, whether he was building houses from scratch or building a fire in Verity that still smouldered weeks later. A man who was just as lonely as her, but not of his own free will.

'She hardly knew how to suppose that she could be an object of admiration to so great a man.'

'Oh God, Elizabeth Bennet, will you just shut

up?' Verity said out loud, because lately, rather than having Miss Eliza Bennet as her go-to guru on all matters, that lady had become the doubting voice in Verity's head.

Instead of asking herself 'What Would Elizabeth Bennet Do?' it was time for a different way of looking at the world. A different question.

What Would Verity Love Do? And would she do it soon?

28

*'Nothing remains for me but to assure you in
the most animated language of the violence
of my affection.'*

It was late Sunday afternoon when Merry and
Dougie dropped Verity off at the corner of
Rochester Street.

An hour later, after yet another attempt to
wash the smell of hog roast out of her hair, Verity
was ready. Well, not ready. She didn't feel as if
she'd ever be ready, but she was going to do this.
She *had* to do this.

'Look, Gervaise, if you need to explore your
sexuality then that's fine, but I don't see why I
have to have a three-some with you and your
German friend, Helga,' Nina was hissing down
the phone as Verity left. She waved and rolled her
eyes. 'Now, if it were your German friend, Hans,
then that might be a different story.'

Verity rolled her own eyes and shook her head
as she walked through the shop, ran her hand
along the spines of the books on one of the
Classics shelves for good luck.

It wasn't even seven thirty but already the sky
was dusky. A bite to the air that foretold of
autumn; crisp leaves being crunched underfoot,
the smell of bonfires, hurrying home to draw the
curtains and snuggle on the sofa. Not that Verity
was the snuggling sort, but then there were lots

of things that Verity hadn't thought she was the sort for and it had turned out that she was wrong about them. Who knew what else she was wrong about?

The central London streets were quiet at this time on a Sunday evening and it was easy enough for Verity to see the city's secrets: the ornate keystones and datestones, mouldings and carvings, the plaques and nameplates on the buildings, because Johnny had taught her how to look up, to see beauty lurking everywhere.

When Verity reached Canonbury, she was back to looking down again. Staring at her feet as they carried her towards the reckoning, though they really didn't want to finish the job and climb the five steps that led to the front door. Then her hands really didn't want anything to do with ringing the bell but Verity was the boss of them and then there was nothing to do but wait, ears straining for the sound of footsteps.

Perhaps he'd gone out. He'd once told Verity that he hated Sunday evenings, how they always gave him 'a back to school feeling'. So maybe he was in the pub, or out with friends, or, God help him, with Marissa.

But he wasn't because the door opened and there he was. Johnny. He didn't look especially pleased to see Verity and gave her a suspicious, wary glance as if she were about to try and sell him double glazing.

'Hello,' he said tiredly, because each time Verity steeled herself to brave a look at him from under her lashes she was struck by his air of exhaustion.

He was still beautiful, but now it was a terrible kind of beauty. Standing there in jeans and a faded grey shirt, Verity could tell that he'd lost weight. The angles of his face, his cheekbones, stood out in stark relief. Even his eyes seemed to have lost their lustre.

Johnny looked like Verity felt. As if, though the world continued to turn, it had stopped turning for him. The days stretching on and on, with nothing to look forward to.

Harry must have stayed true to his word when he issued Marissa with that ultimatum; him or Johnny, and she'd made her choice and that was why Johnny looked so utterly wretched.

'Are you just going to stand there and gawp?' Johnny asked sharply and Verity realised that she'd been doing just that; staring at him with her mouth hanging open. Though his expression and his tone weren't welcoming, she'd come too far to lose her nerve and turn back now.

'Hello,' she said shyly and she waited for Johnny to ask her in but he folded his arms. 'I came to thank you for the champagne though Con's going to write you a note, though knowing Con, you'll probably get it some time just after Christmas. I actually brought you a couple of bottles because it's very nice champagne but there was no way we could drink it all when we already had crates of Cava chilling in ice in the bathtub. I also brought you some wedding cake.' Verity heaved up the heavy tote bag she'd been lugging around, but Johnny was motionless and didn't take the bag from her. 'It's a honey cake,' she persisted, even as her heart gave up the

402

ghost. 'Muv got the recipe from her best friend Sylvia, who's a rabbi's wife. Con got married on Rosh Hashanah you see, the Jewish New Year, and it's Jewish tradition to have honey cake to symbolise a sweet new year and what with Our Vicar's bees, well, a honey cake was the way to go.'

Even her sisters at their most rambliest had never rambled this much. This wasn't why Verity had come — to talk about Judeo-Christian customs and any other random thing that came to mind.

She raised timid eyes to Johnny's face. She was sure that she saw something in his eyes, something that looked a little like hope, before he blinked and was back to standing there as cold and remote as if he were carved from granite. How could she chip away the wall that he'd built around himself? Each brick cemented into place by Marissa because if she couldn't have him, then no other woman was going to have him either.

'I appreciate the gesture, but I don't need either champagne or cake,' Johnny said brusquely. 'Was that all you wanted to say?'

Verity knew what she wanted to say, if she could ever find the courage to say it when all the odds were stacked against her, but the words remained just out of reach.

What would Elizabeth Bennet do?

She didn't feel like Elizabeth Bennet any more. In fact, Verity felt more kinship with Darcy at this moment. He knew what it meant to open his heart, to speak his truth, even though he was sure that it was a hiding to nothing.

What would Darcy do then?

And as soon as she asked herself that question, those elusive words found her.

'Johnny,' Verity said haltingly. 'Johnny, in vain have I struggled. It will not do. My feelings will not be repressed . . . '

Even though she now knew what to say, Verity swallowed hard, unsure how she could finish her speech because, even though she'd read these words so many times, speaking them, giving voice to their true meaning, was a task so enormous, so life or death, that she faltered.

She met his eyes, which were now fixed unwaveringly on her face, but still it was impossible to know what he was thinking. Was he prepared to give her a fair hearing or was he about to banish her from his sight forever more, leaving her to wander the world alone, unloved?

If these were her last moments with him then she had to make them count. 'My . . . my feelings will not be repressed,' Verity said again, her voice squeakier with each word until she couldn't even form sounds any more.

She gazed up at Johnny imploringly. His eyes had never looked so blue, so soft, so . . . tender? Did she dare to hope?

'Johnny . . . my feelings . . . ' Oh God, she'd already done that bit twice. 'I . . . you . . . you . . . '

'Verity you must allow me to tell you how ardently I admire and love you,' Johnny said as he took the words right out of Verity's mouth and took her hands in his.

'You've read *Pride and Prejudice?*' she asked incredulously as Johnny pulled her, unprotesting, into the house, into his arms.

'I asked Dad to dig out my mother's old copy and then I read it from cover to cover,' Johnny said, as he relieved Verity of her very heavy tote bag so that he could wrap his arms around her unhindered and bury his face in her hair so that his next words were muffled. 'It was the only thing I had left of you. You do remember that you were the one who left?'

'How could I have stayed? You said you hated me!' Verity reminded him and the memory of it made it hurt with a hot piercing ache all over again. She struggled in his arms, until Johnny calmed her by smoothing the hair back from her face so he could press kisses to her forehead, her eyelids, which fluttered closed, her cheeks. If Johnny hadn't been holding her up, Verity's knees would have crumpled. Then he drew back.

'I've wanted to come to you so many times, even walked halfway to Bloomsbury once, but then I'd remember *you* telling me you hated *me*, the contempt on your face as you said it, and all hope was gone,' Johnny said softly. He brushed Verity's cheek with the back of his hand. 'But now I'm suddenly full of hope, even though I've had so many years of rejection, Very, and I'm not strong enough to take even five minutes more of it.'

And just like that, Marissa was coming between them, as she always did.

'Marissa.' Even saying her name made Verity

shiver and start to move away from him. 'It, this, us, is impossible.'

'It's not. We're not,' Johnny insisted, his hands on her again — pulling her close, stroking her hair, her face, as if he couldn't bear not to be touching her. He ran his hands down her arms to link his fingers with hers, and she allowed him to lead her into the front room. The shutters were closed, it was lit softly by lamps, though she hardly took in her surroundings when she only had eyes for Johnny as he gently pulled her down next to him on the sofa, their fingers still entwined.

'Marissa?' Verity said again, a little desperately because Marissa made it all wrong.

'She never made me happy. My happiness was not her endgame,' Johnny admitted wearily as if he'd spent long sleepless nights puzzling this out. 'And yet I was unhappy without her. Then I met you and you did make me happy and without you these last few weeks, I haven't been just unhappy. I've been miserable. Desperate. Utterly bereft. You get the general idea?'

'I think so,' Verity said but she daren't believe that Johnny meant what he said. He might believe it at this moment but the spell Marissa had cast on Johnny was unbreakable. 'But you love Marissa. You've loved her half your life.'

'I loved the fantasy of what I thought Marissa and I were. What I thought we could be. And then you came along and I began to suspect that I didn't want a woman that I'd put on a pedestal but someone who would stand by my side, someone who I could laugh with . . . '

'You never laughed with Marissa?' Verity asked sceptically.

Johnny shook his head. 'There weren't that many laughs with Marissa. There wasn't any laughing either when I asked her and Harry to meet me for dinner last week so I could apologise to Harry for all the grief I've put him through, and tell Marissa that she'd married a man who brought out the best in her, while we only brought out the worst in each other. I'm not going to be the third person in their marriage any more.'

'Goodness,' Verity breathed, barely able to process what Johnny was saying. 'That must have been hard.'

'Actually, weirdly, it wasn't that hard. In fact, once it was done, it was a relief but it still counts as one of the most hideous experiences of my life. And when I thought about it, what Marissa and I had was nothing more than tortured longing and a lot of drama.' He sighed. 'You can't build a real relationship with someone based on nothing but drama. It would burn itself out in no time.'

'So what should you build a relationship on?' Verity wanted to know in a raspy voice that sounded as if she'd just had her tonsils removed.

Johnny lifted Verity's hand to his mouth so he could press a kiss to her tense, white knuckles and she was in a torment to know what his answer would be.

'You build a relationship on laughing together, discovering new things you never even imagined you might like, *Pride and Prejudice* for example, and being welcomed into the heart of each other's families. And, say, you find a prickly sort of woman who likes quiet and won't hold your hand and doesn't believe in love . . . well, when she finally lets you hold her hand, you'll do anything, *anything*, to persuade her that love can actually be rather wonderful.'

Verity could have sworn she was all cried out, but now she was blinking back tears again. 'Oh. Oh my,' she said weakly, and as well as tears her nose was running because she wasn't a pretty crier. She fished for a tissue and blew her nose. 'I've got through three boxes of tissues since that weekend in Cornwall.'

Johnny brightened anew. 'You cried over me?'

'I did, though there was just as much snot as there were tears. It turns out that when I'm racked with grief, my nose just won't stop running,' Verity confessed, though Johnny didn't look too repulsed. Instead he leaned over to kiss the tip of the nose in question. 'The thing is, I'm terrible at relationships. I don't have the first idea about them.'

'I was about to say exactly the same thing.' Johnny shrugged. 'We can figure it out together. Look at Elizabeth Bennet and Darcy if those two crazy kids can make it work, then I'm sure we can too.'

'It was only meant to be for one summer,' Verity said and Johnny smiled. His mouth. Lips. Now Verity was remembering what they felt like on hers.

'I was so busy warning you not to fall in love with me — '

'Yes, I did notice,' Verity said very dryly for someone who still had tears running down her cheeks.

'But I forgot to tell myself not to fall in love with you. But now that I have I'm afraid you're stuck with me. I don't love in a half-hearted fashion. It's all or nothing with me,' Johnny said, and Verity felt a thrill run through her at his words.

'I haven't actually said that I'm in love with you,' she pointed out, croakily. 'Although I am very pleased that you love me. Ardently.'

'It felt appropriate to quote from the source text.' He sighed. 'But there is one thing that's been tormenting me,' Johnny admitted and now he looked rather tortured again so that Verity's heart hurt a little on his behalf too. 'It's been keeping me up at night.'

'What has?' Verity asked with some trepidation because if he mentioned that woman's name again, or how he couldn't give her up completely, then she'd have to find it in herself to leave, to walk away and keep on walking because Verity wanted all of him, not just a part share.

'If we can do it, have sex, wonderful, amazing, remember-it-on-my-deathbed sex, three times in one night after we've both said we hate each other, then can you even imagine how much more wonderful and amazing it will be now that we've said that we love each other?' Johnny asked a little dreamily.

'Still haven't actually said I love you,' Verity said in her primmest voice. Then she relented

409

because God, she really did want Johnny's mouth back on hers and all the other parts of him too. 'But perhaps I should say it so we can see how much better the sex is. We might even manage four times, though it is a school night.'

'We could call in sick tomorrow?' Johnny suggested and he was sitting so close to Verity now that she was more or less on his lap and she couldn't think of anywhere else she'd rather be. 'If you did want to say it.'

'I do, I really do.' Verity shut her eyes, summoned up all her nerve, and took a big leap into the unknown. She could do this. It wasn't so hard. She had nothing to lose and everything to gain. 'I realised that I've never been in love before. I never felt about anyone the way I feel about you.' She opened her eyes to see Johnny gazing at her expectantly, lovingly. 'So, yes, I do love you. I love you so much.' Verity let out a shaky breath. 'OK, that's quite enough talking for now. You know how I'm not a big fan of too much talking. I'd much rather be kissing you.'

Then his lips were on hers, his arms around her, and Verity was kissing Johnny back so passionately and yes, so ardently that she couldn't even remember her own name, much less why she'd ever thought it a good idea to shun all romantic entanglements.

In fact, she couldn't wait to get romantically entangled with Johnny again. And again. And again.

Epilogue

'I am the happiest creature in the world.'

Later, much later, weeks, months, even years later, when people asked them how they'd met, Johnny and Verity said that they owed their warmest gratitude towards an oceanographer called Peter Hardy who had been the means of uniting them.

Acknowledgements

Thank you to my agent Rebecca Ritchie for impeccable agenting and cheerleading, Melissa Pimental and all at Curtis Brown.

A huge debt of gratitude is owed to Martha Ashby for such incisive, good-humoured editing and chats about Georgette Heyer, as well as Kimberley Young, Charlotte Brabbin and the team at HarperCollins.

Thanks also to all the readers, bloggers, reviewers and lovers of romance novels who have taken the trip to Happy Ever After with me.

We do hope that you have enjoyed reading
this large print book.

Did you know that all of our titles
are available for purchase?

We publish a wide range of high quality
large print books including:
Romances, Mysteries, Classics
General Fiction
Non Fiction and Westerns

Special interest titles available in
large print are:
The Little Oxford Dictionary
Music Book
Song Book
Hymn Book
Service Book

Also available from us courtesy of
Oxford University Press:
Young Readers' Dictionary
(large print edition)
Young Readers' Thesaurus
(large print edition)

For further information or a free
brochure, please contact us at:
Ulverscroft Large Print Books Ltd.,
The Green, Bradgate Road, Anstey,
Leicester, LE7 7FU, England.
Tel: (00 44) 0116 236 4325
Fax: (00 44) 0116 234 0205

Other titles published by Ulverscroft:

THE LITTLE BOOKSHOP OF LONELY HEARTS

Annie Darling

Once upon a time in a crumbling London bookshop, Posy Morland spent her life lost in the pages of her favourite romantic novels. So when Bookends' eccentric owner, Lavinia, dies and leaves the shop to Posy, she must put down her books and join the real world. Because Posy hasn't just inherited an ailing business, but also the unwelcome attentions of Lavinia's grandson, Sebastian, AKA The Rudest Man In London. Posy has a cunning plan to transform Bookends into the bookshop of her dreams, if only Sebastian would leave her alone to get on with it. As Posy and her friends fight to save their beloved bookshop, Posy's drawn into a battle of wills with Sebastian, about whom she's started to have some rather feverish fantasies . . .

CONFETTI AT THE CORNISH CAFE

Phillipa Ashley

Cal and Demi are preparing to launch their beloved Kilhallon resort as a wedding venue. Cakes are baking, Cornish flowers are blooming, and fairy lights are twinkling. It's the perfect place for a magical marriage ceremony. But their first clients are no ordinary couple. The bride and groom are internationally famous actors Lily Craig and Ben Trevone. Kilhallon is about to host a celebrity wedding . . . With the pressure on, Demi and Cal are doing all they can to keep their guests happy and avoid any wedding disasters. But is the unpredictable weather the only thing standing in the way of the Big Day? As secrets surface and truths are told, can Demi and Cal ensure that Kilhallon's first wedding is a success? One thing's for sure — this will be a Cornish celebration to remember . . .

MY HUSBAND THE STRANGER

Rebecca Done

When Molly married Alex Frazer, she knew it was for ever. Theirs would be the perfect future. However, after a night out with his twin brother, Graeme, a terrible injury leaves Alex with permanent brain damage. In a single moment, the man she married is transformed into someone new. Someone who has forgotten how to love her. And someone Molly isn't sure she can ever love again. The Alex she married no longer exists. Even with Graeme willing to help, Molly isn't sure that she can go on. How can she stay married to a man she doesn't know? Should she let the future she dreamed of slip through her fingers? And what really happened on the night that turned her husband into a stranger?